An Orphan's Christmas

Katie Flynn

An Orphan's Christmas

CENTURY

1 3 5 7 9 10 8 6 4 2

Century
20 Vauxhall Bridge Road
London SW1V 2SA

Century is part of the Penguin Random House group of companies
whose addresses can be found at global.penguinrandomhouse.com

Penguin
Random House
UK

First published in the UK by Century in 2016

www.randomhouse.co.uk

A CIP catalogue record for this book is available from the British Library.

ISBN 9781780892320

Typeset in India by Thomson Digital Pvt Ltd, Noida, Delhi
Printed and bound in Great Britain by Clays Ltd, St Ives plc

Penguin Random House is committed to a sustainable future
for our business, our readers and our planet. This book is made
from Forest Stewardship Council® certified paper.

MIX
Paper from
responsible sources
FSC
www.fsc.org   FSC® C018179

For Shirley Snowden – Keep on dancing!

Acknowledgements

Thanks to Pip Beck, the author of *A WAAF in Bomber Command*, a book which I used constantly as a work of reference as well as a pleasurable read.

Letter to the Reader

Dear Reader,

Christmas always comes as a surprise to me, despite the fact that the date is always the same! There is my current book to be finished, presents to buy, decorations to be put in place and cards to be written, and somehow it is always pandemonium.

This year, however, there was an additional event. My son-in-law, Simon, a keen biker, joined a motorcycle group – 45 to 50 strong – who go round every year on their motorbikes, all dressed as Father Christmas, to the care homes and children's wards in the local hospitals, where they distribute gifts and chat to those incarcerated over the Christmas season; it is all very organised and impressive.

Simon went out and bought an outfit, complete with foaming white beard. Trying it on before the mirror he was pleased with the result and turning to his lurcher, Snoopy, he asked him what he thought. Not surprisingly the dog stared in some perplexity at this peculiar getup, but when Simon said: 'Ho, ho, ho', Snoopy, deciding that this was a grand game, leapt forward, hitting Simon amidships and knocking him on to his back. Then he seized him by his Santa beard, and pulled and pulled until the elasticated band on the beard snapped, zinging back into Simon's face, nearly chopping his nose off.

Despite this shaky start, and the terrible weather, all went well with the Bikers' Santa trip, which was a great success, but, needless to say, Simon did not again ask what Snoopy thought of his 'new look', and we are now all forbidden to utter the phrase: 'Ho, ho, ho' . . . just in case!

Hope you had a wonderful Christmas as we did.

All best wishes

Katie Flynn

Chapter One

December 1936

It was a bitterly cold night and the sky above the city of Liverpool was dark as ink, save where it was illumined by the hard silver light of the moon. In dormitory four of the Haisborough Orphanage, Molly Penelope Hardwick lay in her narrow little bed and longed for morning. As usual, Matron had insisted that the children undressed and got into their skimpy cotton nighties regardless of the cold, but as soon as she had departed, bound no doubt for her own warm bed, thcy had tumbled from beneath their thin blankets and put on every article of clothing they could find. Then they had climbed back into bed and despite the cold had apparently fallen asleep – or at any rate, when Molly looked around her, no one else seemed to be stirring. Even as she craned her neck to be sure, she heard the sound of the church clock striking midnight. Had she been in her own dormitory she would have climbed into bed with her friend Beth so that at least they could share what warmth there was, but because of what Matron termed 'disruptive behaviour', which meant talking after lights out, she had been moved from dormitory two to dormitory four, where the girls were older and mostly unknown to her. Furthermore, she had been given the bed directly under the window, a position popular in summer but shunned by one and all in winter on account of the draught that whistled through the ill-fitting window frame, denying the occupier any chance of getting warm and thus to sleep.

Molly sighed; it was useless to beg Matron to let her return to her own dormitory, for the woman was a strict disciplinarian, and would never go back on her decisions. However, Miss Hornby, Molly's best friend on the staff, might put in a word for her and in the meantime Molly decided to wriggle as far down the bed as she could, tuck her frozen feet up inside her nightie and make up stories in her head, a pastime which might make life a little more endurable until the getting-up bell rang. At least for breakfast there would be hot porridge and maybe even a slice of toast, since when she awoke it would be Christmas Day.

But when the chiming of the church clock informed her that a further hour had passed she decided she might as well look outside and see if anyone else was stirring on Princes Park Row. No people would be around at this hour, for it was a quiet and respectable neighbourhood, and no dogs either Molly hoped, for she was frightened of dogs. She liked cats but thought them mysterious creatures, melting into shadows and disappearing as though they had never been. So, flinchingly, she sat up, drew back the curtain and pressed her palm against Jack Frost's latest artwork. After a second or two she withdrew her hand, leaving a palm-shaped hole in the delicate pattern on the glass, and peered through. The scene that met her eyes was beautiful, in its way. There were three fir trees opposite the orphanage entrance, now silvered by frost and gilded by moonlight, and Molly was reminded of a pantomime rehearsal they had been invited to watch the previous year. It had been wonderful! Miss Hornby had been pleased by her reaction and had offered to lend her a book of fairy stories, one of which was about Dick Whittington, the very pantomime she and the other children had seen. She had taken the greatest care of the storybook and returned it in good condition, and since then Miss Hornby had provided her with many such. Molly had taught herself to read when she was about four, she supposed, and now reading was her chief pleasure, taking her to lands so magical and adventurous that returning to the real world was sometimes both difficult and painful. There was a man called Robert Louis Stevenson whose book *Treasure Island* had been so exciting that she was sure her hair must have stood on end, and *At the Back of the North Wind* by George MacDonald had filled her mind with such strange and exciting thoughts that she had begged Miss Hornby to track down as many others by the same author as she could find.

But right now she was turning into a little icicle, and not even the thought of the wonderful book which Miss Hornby had promised she should have to read over Christmas was enough to take her mind from her frozen extremities. If only she could get warm! She visualised Matron's room, which she had seen once when Matron had ordered her to bring in an extra chair for a visitor. It had cheery red curtains the same colour as the carpet and beautiful shiny furniture which the older girls took it in turn to dust and polish. There had been a bright fire burning in the grate, sending out a great deal of heat, and a gleaming brass coal scuttle; and the fire irons included a grand poker made to look like a sword, which impressed other girls as well as Molly.

One day I'll have all sorts of nice things, Molly told herself, remembering her last conversation with Miss Hornby. They had been discussing a storybook which had captured Molly's attention to such an extent that she had actually read straight through it twice, and when returning it to its owner and accepting its replacement with a happy sigh she had made up her mind to tell Miss Hornby her great decision.

'I didn't think there could be a book in the world as good as this one,' she had said, handing the volume over. 'It made up my mind that when I'm really old, as old as you, Miss Hornby, I shall become a writer. And my very first book will be about how orphans should be treated.'

She thought Miss Hornby looked a little upset and went on quickly: 'Or perhaps I'll do a fairy story first, and save the one about orphans until you aren't here any more, because if all the staff were like you . . .'

Miss Hornby had made a little choking sound but had then smiled brightly and patted Molly's skinny shoulder.

'I'm not that old,' she had said. 'In fact, dear, I'm the youngest person on the staff.'

'Younger than Miss Annabelle?' Molly had said, unable to keep the incredulity out of her voice, and that had made Miss Hornby laugh out loud.

'Well, not quite as young as Miss Annabelle,' she had admitted. 'She's a pupil nurse and barely sixteen years old! And now run along to your dormitory and put my book somewhere safe. I value every volume I possess, and I wouldn't lend them to you if I didn't know you valued them too.'

All the time she had been thinking, Molly had been breathing on the little porthole she had made in the frost and her breath had sent little rivulets of melted water down the pane, so that each time she looked a little more of the outside world appeared within her range of vision. But it was too cold to sit up any longer and she was about to shrink back under the cover of her thin blanket when an indignant voice spoke.

'Oi, whatsyername. There's folk here wantin' to go to sleep, so you just draw the curtain back across that window else I'll gerrout of me bed and give you a good clack.' It was the head of the dormitory, a large bony girl who was often left in charge of the younger ones when no member of staff was available. Molly had been hit with a cane or a ruler often enough, but the beefy Jane didn't know her own strength and could inflict more pain than any teacher bent on corporal punishment.

'Sorry, Jane,' Molly said in a tiny voice. 'I'm so cold I can't sleep so I thought I'd take a look outside. But I'll draw the curtain back again . . . I'm sorry.'

''S all right,' Jane said. 'You ain't a bad kid. Just you think about tomorrow; that should send you to sleep happy. There'll be meat in the stew at dinner time, and a real Christmas pudding, and a silver threepenny bit for every orphan from one of the board of governers. Dunno which one. And unless it's actually snowin' Matron will send the whole lot of us out to have larks in Princes Park. I happen to know there's an old lady at the top of the road here what loves knittin', and she's made scarves for every single one of us kids in the home, so we'll be able to have a good frolic between dinner and tea. Does the thought of that warm you up?'

'Yes, Jane,' Molly said obediently, staring regretfully at the curtain she had just pulled across to meet its fellow. Both were thin and much patched but she told herself firmly that they must stop the worst of the cold getting into the room, and anyway, the moon was waning now, no longer lighting up the scene outside with its cold brilliance. Suddenly feeling sleepy, Molly turned her face into the pillow, and within moments had fallen fast asleep.

Despite remembering past Christmases, which had seldom, if ever, lived up to her expectations, Molly accompanied the rest of her dormitory down to the dining hall with a pleasant feeling that today *was* special, even for orphans.

The dining hall was a long and chilly room equipped with narrow deal tables and chairs. At the head of each table stood a big girl doling porridge on to tin plates whilst the children formed a queue. The porridge was gone in a trice, for today it was topped with a sprinkling of the coarse brown sugar which had become traditional, as had the shining threepenny joe handed round to each child. And as soon as everyone had finished they were told to put on their winter coats and line up to be taken to morning service.

'Don't it look grand?' Beth whispered to Molly as they filed in to the little grey church, which today was not grey at all, for every available space was decked with wreaths of ivy and bunches of red-berried holly. Molly cast an approving eye round the pews which she herself had helped to decorate with greenery earlier in the week.

'It does look nice,' she admitted. 'Did I tell you what Jane said about them scarves the old lady up the road has made for us? I thought we'd get them before we came out but it seems I were wrong. Ah, here comes the Reverend, beaming away like Santa Claus. I hope he's chosen good carols; I do love "Away in a Manger."'

'Hush,' Beth whispered as the choirboys in their cassocks and surplices moved slowly up the aisle towards the choir stalls. 'Did you know some churches have girls in the choir? Wouldn't it be grand to be a choir girl!'

When the service was over the children returned to the orphanage, and presently repaired to the dining hall for a Christmas dinner of stew and mashed potatoes, followed by Christmas pudding and custard. It was a very plain Christmas pudding, but welcome nevertheless. Then old Mrs Ashby's scarves were handed round amidst much hilarity, for they had clearly been made from any scraps of wool the old lady could find and were a strange mixture indeed.

Matron, obviously hearing the giggles, frowned warningly. 'Mrs Ashby has worked long and hard to make sure every child has a warm scarf to call her own,' she said reprovingly. 'Naturally, she could not buy balls of brand new wool or the scarves would have cost her a small fortune, but I think we owe it to her to send a deputation round to her house at tea time to thank her sincerely for all her hard work. Now, you may all play out in the park until, let us say, three o'clock, and then I shall choose two neat, tidy girls to visit Mrs Ashby after we've all enjoyed our Christmas tea.' Matron looked round at her audience. 'Who's been especially good this year?' she asked, with an attempt at a roguish twinkle. 'I think I shall send Ann and little Bridget.' She smiled at the chosen girls. 'I'm sure you will do us credit.'

As soon as Matron had dismissed them the children wound their new acquisitions briskly round their throats and set off for the park. They often went there for organised games, supervised by a member of staff or one of the older girls, but today was different. Matron had made it clear that they might for once play anything with anybody they chose, and might even join the boys if they so wished. Given a free hand, Molly and Beth decided to walk over to the little lake. They strolled around the perimeter, disappointing the ducks who thought that everyone who approached them did so in order to throw them bits of stale bread, and then decided to watch what appeared to be a cricket match going on between some of their schoolfellows and the choirboys, almost unrecognisable without their vestments. There was a bench conveniently close and Molly was just pointing out that the reason for this oddly unseasonable game was undoubtedly the bright red cricket ball, a Christmas gift if ever she saw one, when there was a warning shout from the players. Molly glanced towards them even as something hit her hard on the chest, knocking her flat on her back in the somewhat soggy grass.

'Molly! Are you all right?' Beth asked anxiously, for one minute her friend had been talking in a rational manner and the next she was flat on her back, gasping for air and trying in vain to regain her feet. She was just struggling into a sitting position when a couple of boys arrived and bent over their victim. One was tall, fair-haired and blue-eyed whilst the other was dark, squat and clearly not about to apologise.

'Gerrup, you stupid girl, and gimme the ball back,' he said in a hectoring tone. 'You ain't hurt, just winded. Aw, don't lie there like a stranded fish, pretendin' you're at death's door. Here, Dick, you grab a holt of one arm and I'll grab the other and she'll soon be on her perishin' feet.'

Molly knew who the shorter of the two boys was but not the taller one, though she recognised him from school. The squat dark one was Lenny Smith, a notorious troublemaker a couple of years older than her and Beth, and she glared up at him from her position on the grass.

'Leave off,' she said crossly, then sat up straight and addressed the older boy. 'I've seen you in the playground. I reckon the ball must be yours, 'cos no one would give a brand new cricket ball to a twerp like Lenny.'

The boy raised a brow. 'I'm Dick,' he said. 'And the ball *is* mine. My uncle Fred give it to me, and a bat, but it was Lenny what hit you for six. So hand it over, young 'un, so's we can gerron with our game. Choirboys versus the rest.'

Molly looked around and then realised she was sitting on the ball. She shifted her position to hook it out from under her skimpy – and now mud-splattered – skirt, then changed her mind. She stared straight up into Lenny Smith's dark and scowling countenance.

'Say please,' she commanded. 'And say sorry, as well. That bleedin' ball nigh on cut me in half. I reckon I'll be achin' till the New Year.'

Lenny sniffed scornfully. ''Tweren't but a tap,' he said contemptuously. 'And why should I say please? It's our ball and we want it back. Where's you hid it?'

'M.y.o.b.,' Molly said promptly. 'If you want it back you can bloody well ask nicely, else the next time you see it it'll be as I hurl it into the lake and watch the ducks divin' for it.' As she finished speaking she heard Beth and Dick gasp simultaneously, and remembered belatedly that Lenny Smith had a reputation for being the sort of boy who would object strongly to being blackmailed and was quite capable of simply snatching the ball and walking off without even dreaming of 'asking nicely', or indeed asking at all.

'Molly, I do think perhaps you ought to give it back,' Beth hissed, sounding worried. 'It's Dick's Christmas present, after all.'

Molly saw the reasoning behind her friend's remark and was about to comply when she remembered the ball's situation. She was still sitting on the damn thing, and if she pushed her hand beneath the skirt of her shabby old coat and produced it she could just imagine the rude remarks which would follow. *Are you hopin' to hatch little cricket balls of your own?* was probably the most polite thing

Lenny would say. Other comments could be a lot worse and she did not fancy giving Lenny Smith the chance to crow over her. On the other hand, though, it was his pal's ball, and Lenny would be a bad enemy. Molly sighed.

'All right, then, I'll let you off sayin' please, but you must turn your back. 'Beth, you make sure they ain't lookin' at me whiles I fish their ball out from where it got put.'

Lenny gave a jeering laugh. 'Stuffed it up your knicker leg, did you?' he asked nastily, but then, perhaps reading reprisals in her scowl, he backed down, to Molly's surprise. 'All right, all right, I'm sorry,' he said, and actually sounded almost contrite.

He turned his back with studied care and Molly got to her feet, rescued the ball from beneath her and said loudly: 'You can look now.'

Both boys turned, Lenny with one hand held out, and Molly, true to her word, dropped the prize into his outstretched palm.

'There you are; now you can start your game again,' she said graciously, but Lenny shook his head.

'Too late. I've been invited to a party at Dick's parents', it being Christmas, and they said to get back to their place before dusk or all the nicest cakes and pies will be gone. Where's you two havin' your tea?'

Molly was still weighing up some snappy retort like 'Where d'you think? Buckingham Palace, of course!' when Dick spoke.

'I'd ask you to our place, 'cept I've already asked Lenny,' he explained. 'Because of this here Depression food's kind of scarce, you see, and even though our mam's a grand cook and can make sixpence do the work of two bob, given the chance, she can't make something out of nothing.'

Molly nodded. 'Thanks for the thought, but we's havin' Christmas cake at the home,' she told them. 'The food's not bad, it's just borin'.' By now the four of them were strolling back towards the park gates and Molly looked curiously across at Lenny. 'I saw you when they took us to the pantomime last year, which means you must be at the home, same as me and Beth, only in the boys' half, of course. Am I right?'

Lenny answered readily enough. 'Yes, but I'm not an orphan. My dad's a seaman and used to hire a room for us quite near the dock so's he could spend time with me when he were ashore. Only somethin' happened, dunno what, and I'm bettin' he were thrown into prison in South America or somewhere, because he never came home. As soon as I get free from this place I shall go over there and search him out, clear his name and bring him back to England. When the money stopped comin' for the room I were too young to be left on me own, so there weren't much I could do about it when the scuffers came and told Mrs Prothero – that's the landlady – she should put me in the orphanage until such time as Dad came back and claimed me.' He grinned at Molly; it was meant to be a cheerful grin but Molly thought she could read the desolation in his eyes, and knew it mirrored her own. Whether his father was dead or alive she could not say, but whichever it was the truth was clearly painful. Hastily, she burst into speech.

'That's like me,' she exclaimed, 'only the other way round! My mam went off to get better-paid work than what she could get here. She wrote lovely long letters to me aunt's, sendin' money for me keep and promisin' to make a home for us both as soon as she could, only then the letters stopped, and of course the money stopped comin' too . . . I reckon me mam must've been ill or summat, or perhaps in prison like your dad. Mebbe that's the likeliest . . . anyway, Aunt Clara said she couldn't afford to keep me no more, so I'd have go in a home till me mam came back. I'm eleven now – nearly twelve – and I were only three or four at the time, Matron said, so that were eight years ago. Matron thinks she's dead – me mam, I mean – but I'm sure she's wrong, and she'll come back just as soon as she can afford to make us a home again.'

Both boys nodded their comprehension, then looked at Beth, who answered the unasked question.

'I'm one of thirteen children and my dad is a docker. He'd been in the army during the war and when he came out there was almost no work for him down on the docks. He and my mam did their very best to keep us, honest to God they did, and it were all right until my eldest brother Freddie got the little brown envelope at Cammell Laird's, but then they had to put us young 'uns into the home, just until better times came along, you know.'

The boys nodded. 'We'll have to see who's gettin' out of the home first,' Lenny said jokingly. He grinned at the two girls. 'And now we'd best get a move on, or it'll be dark before we get to Dick's.'

Molly and Beth waved a cheery goodbye as they reached the gates and joined the trickle of girls returning from the park. Back indoors, they shed their coats and scarves in the hall and went straight to the dining room, where the Christmas tea awaited.

When the last girls had taken their places at the table Matron informed everyone that she would cut the cake as soon as the last sandwich had disappeared. Rather reluctantly, Molly and Beth reached for the sandwiches, but to Molly's surprise and delight they were filled not with marrow jam but with plum. It was a considerable improvement, and, munching happily, Molly nudged the girl sitting on her other side.

'What's goin' on?' she enquired thickly. 'These sandwiches are real nice; I hates marrow jam, I does.'

Nora Bates grinned. 'Me too.' She swallowed a mouthful of sandwich. 'Apparently a member of the board's wife had a baby last week, and to celebrate she's paid for a real nice tea for all us girls and boys at the home. Not that I care whether the boys have marrow jam or not, 'cos I reckon they allus do better than us. One of the teachers at school once said boys needs more grub 'cos they helps with the heavy work whereas we just do cleanin' an' dustin' an' such . . .' She snorted. 'You name it, we does it, and I reckon we ought to be fed the same as the fellers. Norras I know any of 'em, of course.'

Molly reached for another sandwich and noted with satisfaction that the pile was dwindling fast. 'We met two of 'em this afternoon, me and Beth,' she remarked. 'They was playin' cricket, choirboys against the rest, and I got hit with a ball. D'you know a feller called Lenny Smith?'

Nora, cheeks bulging, shook her head wordlessly and Molly could tell by her expression that she had no desire to know any of the boys at the home. She waited until Nora had disposed of her mouthful and was reaching for another sandwich, leaving only two on the plate, before going on. 'He was all right, honest to God he was. He was short and thickset, very dark. His friend was called

Dick – he was tall with fair hair – and it was his cricket ball what whacked the wind out of me.' She chuckled at the memory.

Beth leaned forward and spoke to Nora across her friend. 'That Dick was real nice,' she said. 'He's not in the home like the rest of us, and he'd invited Lenny to a party at his parents' house . . .'

At this point, however, Matron rose to her feet and all conversations were suspended. She cut the large square cake into exactly the right number of slices, the plates were handed round, and when the cake was finished to its last crumb the girls were dismissed to go to the playroom, where they might remain until the bell which announced bedtime was enthusiastically rung by an assistant for whom the special day had meant more work than usual.

Molly and Beth sat on the draughty window seat so that they could talk in comparative privacy, and presently were able to inform anyone interested that it had started snowing.

Watching the slow descent of the flakes Beth remarked, 'Tomorrow's Boxing Day, so no school. I wish someone would pay for us to go to the pantomime like they did last year,' she added wistfully. 'And if it goes on snowin' Matron won't let us play out. I do hope it stops. Last year we made the biggest snowman of them all, didn't we, Molly?'

Molly nodded, but picked up a pack of cards which someone had laid down and began to spread them out, face downwards, on the window seat between herself and Beth. 'It'll stop,' she said confidently. 'I challenge you, Beth Patterson, to a game of Pelmanism, or Pairs as them what don't know any better call it.'

Beth groaned. 'You know very well you'll win because you always does,' she said bitterly.

Molly chuckled. 'How about I start off by giving you three pairs of cards? But even so I shall still beat you,' she said mockingly. 'Not that it matters who wins, because there's no prize involved . . . oh, Matron . . .'

The matron's large figure loomed over the couple on the window seat. 'Playing Pelmanism, I see,' she said approvingly. 'I like to know my girls are stretching their minds, and it seems that Elizabeth has already made a good start, which I'm afraid I'm going to interrupt. Doubtless you heard me say this morning that two of you girls should go and thank Mrs Ashby for her kindness in providing you all with a warm, hand-knitted scarves. Unfortunately, however, little Bridget has thrown out a rash which I fear will prove to be measles, and it is only too likely that Ann will have caught it too. I looked up the sanatorium records and found that you have both had them, so I have decided that you two should take on the task.' She glanced sideways as the wind threw a flurry of snow at the long, cold pane. 'I'm sorry the weather has turned to snow but doubtless that will not daunt you. It does not appear to me that the snow is likely to lie, so if you hurry you may complete your errand and be back here in the warm in a mere ten minutes. Doubtless Mrs Ashby will offer you some little treat, but you may refuse politely and say you must hurry home before the snow begins in earnest.'

Molly and Beth got reluctantly to their feet, murmuring, 'Thank you, Matron,' as they crossed the playroom, and went out to the hall to put on their coats and scarves. Matron had followed them and now she swung open the heavy front door and ushered them out into the whirling flakes.

'Off you go, girls,' she boomed. 'Top of the road on the left. The house is called *Rows Lodge*, and speak loudly, because Mrs Ashby is a trifle deaf. I'll tell one of the big girls to listen for your return.'

Beth and Molly linked arms, exchanged rueful grins and set off. Despite Matron's words the snow was growing heavier and by the time they reached the house with the name *Rows Lodge* written in curly script above the number they were well coated with white. Molly and Beth both dived for the tiger's-head knocker and banged it imperiously; neither of them wanted to be out in the snow one moment longer than necessary, for they knew all too well that once you got cold you were unlikely to warm up in the playroom at the home. The big girls always surrounded the fire whilst the little ones went early to bed, and since Molly and Beth were neither young enough for a seven o'clock bedtime nor old enough to claim a place by the hearth they were almost always cold.

The sound of their frantic knocking died away and Molly had just seen a large white bell with the word *Push* written across it when they heard footsteps approaching. The door opened a crack and was then thrown wide by a tall, sturdy woman who was clearly well aware of their errand.

'Come in, come in,' she shouted above the noise of the storm, for it really was a blizzard now and no mistake. 'Fancy Matron sending you out in a snowstorm.' She tutted disapprovingly, ushering them in and slamming the door against the elements. 'Mrs Ashby told me to expect you – I'm the housekeeper – but doubted that you would arrive once the snow had begun in earnest. She's in the library . . . oh, but you won't know where the library is! Follow me.'

She stopped before a large mahogany door, turned to the girls and spoke in a conspiratorial whisper. 'Mrs Ashby is a little deaf; well, if I'm honest she's very deaf, so you must speak up. Don't shout, just speak loud and clear.'

She turned away from them to open the library door and Molly took the opportunity to hiss into Beth's ear, 'What's the difference between shouting and speaking loud? Why don't she use an ear trumpet like other people do, or one of them new-fangled hearing aids what you stick in your ear?'

Beth had drawn in a breath to whisper that she had no idea when the housekeeper cleared her throat noisily and ushered them into the room. Somehow, perhaps because at first Molly had thought the housekeeper to be Mrs Ashby herself, she had expected their benefactor to be tall and heavily built. Instead, Mrs Ashby proved to be a tiny white-haired old lady, dwarfed by the big leather chair before the warm fire and dressed in a woollen gown with long tight sleeves and a little collar. But what interested the girls most was the small table drawn up to the fire, upon which stood a platter of what looked like mince pies. Molly's and Beth's mouths watered as the delicious smell of fruity mincemeat assailed their nostrils.

'Good evening, young ladies,' Mrs Ashby said with a twinkle. 'Once the storm started I assumed Matron would put off a visit of thanks, but clearly she has not done so.' She had been sitting down, but now she stood up and hobbled towards them, the plate of mince pies in her hand. 'Help yourselves.'

Both girls took a mince pie and then, at her gesture, seated themselves upon a green and gold upholstered sofa and bit into their treats. Despite having had a slice of Christmas cake that very afternoon they thought they had never tasted anything as delicious as the mince pies, for the cake had been plain, though good, and the pastries were infinitely better. Molly said so, adding hastily: 'But how rude you must think us, Mrs Ashby! We've come to thank you for the beautiful warm scarves; which, as you can see, are much appreciated!'

The old lady smiled at them. 'Yes, but take them off now, and your coats, and I'll ask my house-keeper to dry them out before the kitchen fire, so when you go out again at least you won't start off wet.' She rang a little bell and very soon the door to the library opened to reveal the housekeeper stand-ing in the aperture. 'Mrs Williams, these young ladies have got very wet coming all the way here just to thank me for their scarves,' she said gently. 'Can you dry their things out before the kitchen fire, please?' She turned to the girls. 'I dare say you wonder why I don't hang them over the fender in this room, but I have a weak chest and steam is not a good idea. Besides, I have no doubt that Mrs Williams's fire will be considerably warmer than the one in here.'

Beth had already handed over her coat and scarf and Molly was about to do the same when the housekeeper took it gently from her and spoke in ringing tones.

'Yes, I can do that, Mrs Ashby. Fortunately the girls had brushed the loose snow off their cloth-ing before they entered the hall; so thoughtful, Matron's young ladies. Give me five minutes and they'll be dry and warm as toast, and in the mean-time a small glass of ginger wine will warm your visitors' little insides.'

Molly and Beth exchanged delighted looks and sipped the ginger wine with enthusiasm, for it did indeed warm them nicely. They thanked Mrs Ashby effusively, both for the scarves and for what Beth termed 'the refreshments', and told their kind hostess how Molly had been struck down by a cricket ball earlier in the day. They had to repeat themselves several times when the old lady cupped her hand round her ear and asked them to speak up, but she laughed delightedly over the tale. Presently the housekeeper returned with their coats and scarves ready to wear.

'Take a mince pie each to eat as you go home,' Mrs Ashby instructed them. She held out a tiny claw of a hand, each finger bearing a weight of gold and jewels. 'It's been very nice to meet you, girls, and you must pop in again when you're pass-ing. Mrs Williams will see you out.'

Outside the wind still roared and the snow still whirled, but Molly and Beth felt they were able to cope with anything. They were warm and dry, the mince pies they had been given were delicious and they had actually been invited to 'pop in again' should they happen to be passing *Rows Lodge*.

'Wasn't she a lovely lady?' Molly bawled above the howling of the wind. 'I'm going to wear my scarf in bed tonight – I'm sure it will smell of ginger wine and mince pies for weeks. Weren't we lucky, Beth? I think this is the best Christmas Day I've ever had, and I do feel rather guilty that poor old Ann and little Bridget missed out on it. I bet they didn't even have any appetite for that Christmas cake. Come to think of it, they were neither of them in the dining hall, so far as I can remember. Did you notice them?'

Beth shook her head. 'Can't say I did,' she admitted. 'Oh, Molly, do gerra move on; I'm sure there's an icicle formin' on me nose, and I've ate me mince pie. With a bit of luck we'll be back indoors before our coats get soaked again, because it's downhill all the way now. I reckon we'll have half an hour in the playroom before the bell rings.'

As they hurried down the hill, still glowing, Molly glanced sideways at the lighted window of a private house whose owners had not bothered to draw the curtains to shut out the whirling snow. Through its flakes she could see a woman fastening the top button of a child's cosy cardigan. The room was beautifully decorated with wonderful paper chains, Chinese lanterns and whole branches of holly and ivy. There was a Christmas tree decorated with glass birds and small golden trumpets, and every face in the room – and there were at least half a dozen – wore an ecstatic smile.

In the brief glimpse which Molly got before they were past she suddenly knew she would have swapped every present she had ever received for one smiling glance from that woman, clearly the mother of the small children playing within the lighted room. Christmas wasn't just about presents or nice food, it was about family and love and all the things that even the best of orphans do not have. When I grow up I mean to have a lovely home like that one, and a husband of my own, Molly thought. I wouldn't mind marrying Lenny, because he'd understand about not having a family. Dick's better-looking, of course, but Lenny's the one I feel I really know.

'Molly, do get a move on,' Beth called over her shoulder.

'Sorry. Was I lagging behind?' Molly shouted above the howl of the wind. She caught her friend up and was about to link arms when she noticed a figure coming towards them. 'There's someone else out in this horrible weather,' she announced as they reached the gates of the orphanage. 'What d'you bet me it's that boy, that Lenny, coming back from his party?'

Beth shrugged. 'I don't care if it's Santa Claus himself,' she said. 'I'm going in, even if you aren't.' She made for the front door and Molly was about to follow when the figure drew level with her, and even through the whirling flakes she could see that it was indeed Lenny Smith. His cap was crowned with a small mound of white and even in the dim light she could see his nose was pink with cold, but she grinned at him and was pleased when he grinned back.

'Did you have a good party?' she asked. 'Me and Beth were sent up to old Mrs Ashby's to thank her for the scarves, which is why we're out in this awful weather. But it's pretty late – I suppose your party went on longer than expected, am I right?'

Lenny grinned. 'Spot on,' he said cheerfully. 'Your name's Molly, ain't it? I hoped we'd meet again. I thought we might combine forces to try and find out what happened to your mam and my dad. What d'you say? I don't mean right here and now, but when we leave the home.' He chuckled. 'Two heads are better than one, they say. D'you have any clue that might give us a start? Was your aunt's surname the same as your mother's, for instance?'

Molly was about to reply when they both heard Beth banging imperiously on the black-painted door. Lenny, who had no intention of announcing his tardy return by marching in through the main entrance, and had his own ways of gaining admittance to less populated regions of the orphanage, bade Molly a hasty farewell, and she hurried to join her friend just as the door shot open and Beth led the way in to the comparative warmth of the hall. Faintly on the wind they heard Lenny's voice.

'We'll have to get together when school re-opens,' he shouted. 'See you then.'

Molly hung her dripping coat back on its peg and smiled at Beth. 'Wharra day!' she exclaimed joyously. 'It's the nicest day I've had since I came to the home, and it's made me think. I were very young when I were dumped here so I don't know much about the outside world . . .'

'The real world, you mean,' Beth commented, tugging at her friend's arm. 'Do stop mooning and come along. The hall felt quite warm when we first came in but already I'm feeling colder. I'm chilly and want to get near the fire for a quick warm-up.'

Molly seized her friend's arm. 'All right, all right, only shouldn't we report to Matron first? She doesn't know we're back . . .' She giggled. 'On the other hand, if she smells ginger wine on our breath she'll think we're drunk as lords and send us straight to bed.'

The girls were still chuckling as they entered the playroom, where they were immediately beckoned over to the fire by the big girl who had opened the door for them.

'So you've shed your wet things. Save my place – you can have a warm-up whilst I just nip along to Matron's room and tell her you're in. Shan't be a tick,' she said. 'I'll want it back, though, so make the most of it!'

Chapter Two

Lenny lay in bed and relived his day with a glow
of pleasure. It had started with a proper hot breakfast, and progressed from there. The midday meal
had been stew and plum pudding and in the afternoon he and Dick had organised a cricket match
at Princes Park between the choirboys and anyone
else interested in having a game. Then of course
there had been the incident of the cricket ball
which had laid that Molly low – Lenny gave a subdued snigger at the thought – and the conversation about their lives, which rather to his surprise
he had really enjoyed. Then the girls had gone
back to the home and he and Dick had made their
way to Dick's cosy house on Daisy Street where
the Fletchers were holding a party for relatives
and friends and with their customary generosity
had included Lenny. They had enjoyed the most
delicious tea, made memorable by Mrs Fletcher's
homemade cakes and mince pies, and then settled
down to play games, some of which Lenny knew

and others which he soon learned. In fact he had been so happily engaged with Dick's large family that he had been downright astonished when his hostess came in from the scullery and addressed him.

'I dunno if you realise it, young man, but there's a rare nasty old snowstorm out there, already well into its stride,' Mrs Fletcher had said. 'We must get you back to Princes Row before we have to dig our way out. Besides, you told us you had permission to be out until eight o'clock, and it's past that already.' She lifted the cheery red curtain to allow him a glimpse of the whirling snow and with reluctance Lenny hooked his coat from its place by the back door and began to struggle into it.

'Thanks, Mrs Fletcher. That were a grand tea,' he had said breathlessly. 'And I've had a wonderful time playing games. In fact, it were the best day I've ever had in me whole life.'

Mrs Fletcher was a plump and pretty woman in her forties with curling blonde hair and twinkling blue eyes, and she smiled very kindly at her young guest. 'It's been a pleasure, Lenny; you must come again,' she had said cordially. 'Now, how are we going to get you home? It's norras if Dick's dad could take you up on the front of his bicycle, 'cos there won't be no cycling done until the traffic has cleared the snow. I'd suggest Dick went with you, but he's promised to escort his cousin Susan back to Bootle. Will you be all right to walk home alone?'

'Course I will. And thanks again for a wonderful party,' Lenny had said. He had grinned at the thought of wanting to be accompanied over the distance between the flower streets and the home. He enjoyed the freedom of being alone, and opportunities for solitary wanderings were few and far between. So he turned up his coat collar, pulled his cap as far as he could get it over his eyes and set off into the storm.

Had he been with Dick they would have discussed the party, but as it was Lenny relished being on his own and given time to think. He was beginning to wish, now, that he had been a little more truthful when telling the story of his past to Molly and . . . Beth, was it? Not that it really mattered. It hadn't been a huge lie or anything like that, just a slight exaggeration so that the girls would see him as the son of a loving father who would, one day, be reunited with his parent to their mutual delight. His brief meeting with Molly outside the home might've been an opportunity to put his story straight, but the weather had prevented any sort of prolonged conversation. I'll tell her next time we meet that I exaggerated a little, he told himself.

'There's a fire in the playroom, a real good 'un' the door opener informed him as Lenny was divesting himself of his wet outer clothing.

'Someone came round earlier with a basket of logs and Father O'Leary said we might have one – a log, not the basketful – and stay up half an hour longer. So all in all it's been a pretty good Christmas.'

Lenny looked forward to taking Mrs Fletcher up on her kind invitation to visit again, but on the very first day of the new term his hopes received a crushing blow. Dick's father was a corporal in the army, and Dick had explained long ago, when he first sat next to Lenny in class, that his father had previously been posted somewhere in the highlands of Scotland. The walk to school in the winter had been impossible, so whilst his father was based there Dick had regularly missed his lessons, and he had been put in Lenny's year until he caught up with his proper age group.

And now he was approaching his friend with a troubled face, which was not lost on Lenny. 'Mornin', Dick,' he said cheerfully. 'Lost a guinea and found a sixpence? Don't tell me old Tomkins has been handin' out order marks so early.'

'Wouldn't care if he gave me a dozen,' Dick said gloomily. 'It's worse than that; and just when I were beginnin' to catch up, too.'

Lenny's heart immediately slumped into his boots. 'Your dad's been posted,' he said. 'Will you be going far?'

Dick blinked. 'How did you guess?' he said sadly. 'Oh, Lenny, this is the longest posting we've ever had; over two years, we've been in Liverpool. And I'm afraid it's back to the Highlands. Dad's already spoken to his commanding officer about it, but no joy. Mam's fed up too, but of course when she married Dad she knew how it would be. It's different for me . . . oh, what's the use of talkin'? We've got two weeks to pack our bags and then it's off up to Scotland. If it wasn't for you and me bein' bezzies I wouldn't mind so much, but who will you go around with once I'm gone, our Lenny?'

As he spoke they had been hanging their outdoor things in the cloakroom and now Lenny looked bleakly around the room with its wooden benches and rows of pegs.

'Don't worry about me,' he said huskily. 'I gorron all right before you come and I reckon I'll gerron all right when you're gone. But I shan't half miss you, old feller! Does they tell you how long a postin's goin' to last?'

'No. I don't think they know themselves,' Dick admitted. 'But I'll write to you, tell you what goes on, and you can write back with all the news.' He heaved a sigh. 'Well, as they say, worse things happen at sea, but if I can't have you as my bezzie then I don't know as I want anyone else.'

So for the first two weeks of the term Lenny and Dick spent as much of their time as possible together. And when at the end of that time Dick departed, Lenny had grown accustomed to the fact that he was losing his friend, and was able to put a brave face on it. He even went to the station to see the Fletchers off on their long journey north, and on his return was given two order marks and forbidden to play football with the rest of his class that day, being told instead to write out two hundred times *I must not evade my teachers* in his very best handwriting, though this deteriorated sadly as he neared the end of his task.

One or two of the other boys tried to include him in their amusements, for he was good at all sports and generally well liked, but no one could compensate for losing Dick. He had tried to make good his promise to meet Molly to discuss how they would search for their parents, but what had seemed a simple thing at the time had proved to be anything but easy. Although in theory the inhabitants of the home might mingle when they broke for lunch or elevenses, both boys and girls tended to remain in their own half of the playground and any boy who deliberately sought out a girl would be jeered at accordingly. What was more, the chance of a private conversation turned out to be practically nil, for when they did meet and tried to talk, curious friends soon gathered wanting to know what was so interesting. And on top of everything else, the weather had been against them. Lenny had heard the month of February referred to as 'February Fill-dyke', and so indeed it had proved. Looking back at it Lenny thought that it must have rained at break time virtually every day so that by the time April put in an appearance, bringing spring-like weather in its train, he had all but forgotten about Molly.

'Pssst!'

Lenny heard the urgent hiss, but did not immediately connect it with himself. He looked round wildly at the patterns of moonlight but could see no one, and was just about to put it down to his overactive imagination when it came again.

He was in the jigger which ran along behind the orphanage, intending to walk down to the docks to see if the air was cooler as he neared the Mersey, but the strange sound had unsettled him. If he was caught . . . but it didn't bear thinking about. It was one of the strictest of Father O'Leary's many rules that no boy ever went anywhere unaccompanied. Lenny shrank back into the thick shadow of the nearest wall, but as far as he could see there was no one else around. Besides, the teachers and other staff members never used the jigger but went to and fro by the front or the side door. He must be alone. Yet he still remained in the shadow of the wall. It was a clear June night and it followed a burning hot day, which was why Lenny had thrown caution to the wind and taken to the streets. He had waited until everyone in his attic dormitory was fast asleep and then descended the stairs with the utmost caution, padded across the hall and slipped through the baize doors into the kitchen quarters. He had traversed this way so often that he could have done it blindfold, and soon he was in the pantry and sliding back the little window through which he had so often escaped from the stifling rules and regulations of the Haisborough Orphanage. Then he had crossed the back yard on silent feet and had let himself out into the jigger, only to be startled into stillness by that commanding hiss. If Dick had been here they would have tracked the noise down, laughed at each other's fears and continued on their way, but Dick had been gone for the best part of half a year and no one else had come close to providing the companionship which the two boys had once shared.

And here am I, jumping at shadows like a silly girl, Lenny told himself, and was about to set off for the docks when two things happened at once. A large black cat materialised almost at his feet, purring like a motorbike and staring up at him with gleaming golden eyes. Lenny had seen the cat before on his night-time excursions, and even as he bent to reprimand it for scaring him so a figure detached itself from a patch of shadow and spoke reprovingly, causing Lenny's heart to leap into his throat.

'What are you up to, Lenny Smith?' a mocking voice enquired. 'I s'pose you'll try to tell me that it's only girls who're not allowed out at night. I 'spect you'll tell me you've got special permish to do as you like, 'cos you're a feller and the rules Matron beats into our heads don't apply to fellers. Yeah?'

Lenny had not realised that he had been holding his breath, but now he released it in a long low whistle. He knew that voice, though he had not heard it for months. It was the girl whom he had laid out with Dick's cricket ball.

'I'm not up to anything,' he said, with as much dignity as he could manage. 'It's a hot night and the fellers in my dorm will keep the window shut 'cos they say the traffic noise drifts upward and stops 'em sleepin'. Not that it's any of your business,' he added belatedly. 'And I'm not going to tell you anything of the sort: if I were caught out here they'd call it truanting and I'd be in deep trouble even if I am a boy. Anyway, you shouldn't be out here either. So what's your excuse? And how did you get out?'

Molly shrugged. 'Remember what I told you last Christmas? About my mam, I mean? Well, whenever I get the chance to sneak out I snoop around the docks or go up to where we used to live, just to make sure she's not come back looking for me. You might say I was preparing myself for when I'm old enough to leave the home and have a proper search. 'Cos no one else will bother.' She smiled at Lenny. 'And I get out by the pantry window 'cos the catch don't work, same as you, I bet.'

As she spoke the moon came out from behind a cloud and Lenny saw her properly: light brown hair, big eyes, a skinny figure in ill-fitting clothes. She was staring at him as though daring him to challenge her explanation, but he simply nodded.

'You're right. And I'm doing the same as you – seeing if me dad's ship has come into port, I mean,' he said. 'Father O'Leary thinks he'll never come back but he's wrong, I know he is, so I check the docks, like, for any sign of him.'

Molly was looking at him hard, her eyes positively blazing with excitement. 'What was the name of his ship?' she asked eagerly. 'We could find him a lot easier if we knew that.'

Lenny beamed. She had said 'we' which must mean that she hadn't forgotten their old plan, so the smile he gave her was friendly and grateful. 'Yes, I know, but my dad changed ships so often that I never bothered to take any particular note which one he were on,' he told her. 'I sometimes think he must have changed port for some reason and come into Plymouth or Southampton instead of sticking to Liverpool, but somehow I can't see my dad abandoning me just in order to get a better-paid berth.' He looked questioningly at his companion. 'Shall we go on down to the docks now and take a look around? Since we're both out of the home we might as well enjoy ourselves for a bit. Even down by the docks you can hear the church clock strike, so if we say we'll be home by midnight . . .'

'I'm game,' Molly said instantly, and with one accord they started to walk down towards the river. 'Ain't it funny what a difference it makes if there's two of you? When Beth were still around we'd have a laugh over dodgin' a watchman or a scuffer, or seein' a great big rat helpin' himself from a pile of fish heads. But when you're alone . . . oh, I dunno, things seem more serious. You hear strange sounds, you see funny shadows, and before you know it you're scrambling back through the pantry window and feeling quite glad to get into bed.'

Lenny stared at her with unassumed pleasure. 'That's exactly how I feel, now that Dick has gone,' he said. 'Which reminds me, why ain't you with that other girl, the tall one; was that Beth?'

Molly sighed. 'Her parents called for her a few weeks ago and took her off home,' she explained. 'I miss her, more'n I ever guessed I would . . . well, she were my bezzie, my only real friend. Our beds were next to one another in the dorm – at least

39

they were until Matron moved me for talking – so if it were too hot to go to sleep we'd sneak off via the pantry window and have a bit of a wander. It was grand with the two of us but a bit frightenin' now I'm alone.' She sighed again. 'I never knew how miserable it was not to have a bezzie. Some of the other girls are real nice, but none of 'em can fill Beth's place.'

'Same here, so far as being alone is concerned,' Lenny agreed. 'Tell you what, Molly, s'pose you and me make arrangements to do this again?' He glanced up into the clear blackness of the sky above them. 'We'll have a signal. My window's the third attic one along from the main block. If one of the curtains is half drawn across that means we'll meet in the jigger at, say, half past ten. Everyone will be in bed by then and there'll be no one about but that black cat and a few other scavengers. How about it, eh?'

Molly looked puzzled. The orphanage was a bit like a capital E only with the middle stroke missing, and the top and bottom wings, if you could call them that, faced one another across the length of the playground. She could look straight across to his attic room from her own dormitory, but the windows were small and set deeply into the tiled roof. 'Wouldn't it be simpler just to come up to me at break time and whisper "Tonight, eleven thirty" or whatever?' she asked.

Lenny shook his head. 'Whispering's all very well but watching for a signal is more fun,' he explained. 'And it will work in reverse; if you are the one who's able to get away you can signal from your window, if you tell me which one it is.'

'Oddly enough, it's the same as yours, third attic room along from the main block,' Molly said. 'If we had electric torches we could do a sort of Morse code. They give you the letters and blinks, or what-ever you call 'em, in the latest copy of the *Girl's Own Paper*, only as it happens I don't know anyone with a torch. Do you?'

'Actually, I do know someone with a torch and he's in our dorm,' Lenny said triumphantly. 'But he's a real thicko and if he ever discovered that we arranged to meet each other at night and go off the premises, so to speak, he'd tell. He wouldn't mean to – he's no tale-clat – but he's one of them as tongues are hung in the middle. He'd blurt it out by accident, telling someone that he'd lent me his torch so that I could signal to you . . .' Lenny chuckled. 'You can imagine the fuss! Poor old Bumble – that's what we call him, short for Bumble Bee; his real name's Mark Humble – would be real sorry to have give our secret away, but sorry or not that would be the end of what Father O'Leary would call our "moonlight wanderings".'

He chuckled again, and Molly laughed too, but perfunctorily. He glanced at her. 'What's up?'

'That reminds me. We can't leave the premises when the moon's behind the clouds, or really
new, or in other words when there's no light, or
the weather isn't right. So don't you go signallin'
unless you can be sure it's a clear night.'

By now they had reached the floating road, and
they hung over the water for a moment, before
turning reluctantly back.

'The more we explore the area the better we
shall be equipped to deal with running away, when
we're older,' Lenny said wisely. 'Isn't it a lucky
thing that we're both in the attic dorms?'

They reached the jigger and turned in to it, for-
getting caution and chatting freely, though still
keeping their voices down. 'The moon's at the full,'
Lenny said. 'Which means we're okay for the next
few days, so we might as well arrange when to meet
here and now and not wait for signals. Though I do
think watching for a sign that we mean to go out is
more interesting than just promising to meet.'

Molly grimaced. 'Well, not tomorrer night
because I'm really tired, and p'rhaps not the night
after either. But I heard someone say the fine
weather was likely to last all week, so shall we say
Friday or Saturday? Next time we can walk up to
Harebell Street and take a look at number twenty,
because that's where Mam and I used to live.'

'Hang on a minute,' Lenny said. He was frowning. 'You said you were only three or so when you

was took to the home, so how come you remember the address?'

It was the first time that Lenny had questioned her word and Molly flushed angrily. *Had* she said that? She was usually careful not to give anyone too much information; it was so easy to forget a casual remark and then have to get out of it when it was queried by someone with a better memory than her own. Hastily, Molly rearranged her story. 'Well, that was what Matron said, but the thing is, you see, my mam had made me repeat my name and address until I knew it by heart, in case I ever got lost.' She looked at him in the tricky moonlight, which showed him clearly one minute and obscured him utterly the next. 'Didn't your dad do the same? I thought all mams and dads did it.'

'Oh, I 'spect normal mams and dads make their kids learn all that stuff,' Lenny said easily, 'but I s'pose I were different. You see, sometimes Dad could afford Mrs Prothero's place, and sometimes he couldn't. If he had spent most of his money – usually on presents for me – then we moved into cheaper lodgings. So you see we never did have the same address for long.'

'Oh, I see,' Molly said. 'It would be interesting to have a look at Mrs Prothero's place, if that's where you lived most of the time. Was she kind to you?'

Lenny breathed an inward sigh of relief; the subject had been changed without his having to complicate matters with any more stories. 'Kind? Well, yes, she was very kind,' he admitted. 'She was kinder, though, when there was money coming in for my keep. When that stopped she said she couldn't cope any longer.'

Molly nodded wisely. 'Just like my Aunt Clara,' she said, allowing a tinge of regret to enter her voice. 'She's a very nice sort of woman – well, she would be, because she's my mam's sister – but of course times are hard and in the end she just had no choice; someone had to go so Aunt Clara could make ends meet and it had to be me.'

'Oh aye, it would,' Lenny said, dropping his voice to a whisper because they had reached the orphanage yard.

'So we're agreed?' Molly whispered back. 'We'll meet again Friday or Saturday at half past ten, if the weather's right, whichever day the curtain in your room is half pulled across. It'll give us something to look forward to.'

'D'you want me to give you a leg up through the pantry window?' Lenny suggested. 'I'm taller'n you.'

Molly shook her head. 'Thanks, but no thanks,' she said briefly. 'I put my foot on that there bit of fallen masonry and get in easy; watch!'

Lenny watched as his companion climbed on to a couple of bricks, squiggled through the pantry window and could be heard crossing the paved kitchen floor. Then he followed, telling himself that he must be careful to remember what he told Molly; he himself had just demonstrated how easy it was to pick holes in someone's story, and surely hers couldn't be anything like as far from the truth as his own. It had not mattered at first so he supposed he had rather let himself go, but from now on he really should watch what he said. If he did have to mention Mrs Prothero again he would just say sadly that she had died.

As he approached the bottom of the boys' staircase he glanced down the long corridor towards the stairs which led to the girls' dormitories and saw Molly disappearing round the bend. As he went up the staircase that led to the boys' dormitories it struck him that if Molly's Aunt Clara was as kind and generous as she had made out she must surely be visiting Molly regularly; most of the children had a relative of some description who visited whenever they were able. Perhaps he could even persuade Molly to ask her if he could go with them when they next went out. It would be such fun to see the inside of someone else's house and perhaps to be given a grand tea like the one he had enjoyed with Dick's parents all those months ago. Lenny grinned to himself; life was definitely looking up.

As she slid into her bed in number four dormitory Molly was full of the same anticipatory thrill.

Wouldn't it be grand to have a friend who could legitimately take one about, and with whom one could share a proper family life when his dad eventually came home? As she pulled the sheet up round her cheek she thought again about her mother, whom she could scarcely remember. So far as she could recall, Edith Hardwick had had a great deal of bright yellow hair, a pair of large blue eyes and soft, pink lips. But was this a true memory or had she simply superimposed the face of a film star upon her mother's less memorable features? Not that it mattered. If she ever did escape from the orphanage and begin to search for the elusive Mrs Hardwick, she would obviously look very different from the mother who had handed her over, without a second thought, to her Aunt Clara . . . oh, hang it, she had told the story so often she was beginning to believe it herself. Aunt Clara was a sheer figment of her imagination. Some man, and a man she disliked furthermore, had taken her for what seemed an extraordinarily long walk, which had ended at the gates of the Haisborough Orphanage. She had been pushed into a room full of other children, all girls, who had taken no notice of her whatsoever, and when the man had emerged from the office again, accompanied by Matron, he had simply bidden her to do as she was told until he returned to take her back home.

46

For many months Molly had waited expectantly for him to collect her and take her back to her
mother, but of course now that she was older she
realised it was never going to happen. Parents who
voluntarily abandoned their children – and there
were many – simply walked away, leaving a false
name if they left one at all, because they had no
intention whatsoever of being burdened by their
young. Molly knew of several girls in her position,
but always told herself that her own mother would
be back sometime and so held herself aloof from
them all. What was the point of making friends
when you knew you would soon be parted? Only
Beth had succeeded in breaking down her reserve,
and now, as she had foreseen, Beth and she had
been separated, although not quite in the way
she had envisaged. It was Beth who had gone,
leaving her alone once more, but she realised now
that she had found another bezzie in the dark-
haired boy she had just left. She had no doubt that
Lenny would help her to find her mother if he
possibly could. And by the same token she would
help in the search for his dad; she would persuade
him to take her, too, the next time he went to visit
Mrs Prothero. Molly saw a whole new life open
in front of her. Contentedly she snuggled into her
pillow and presently, despite – or perhaps because
of – her night-time activities, she slept.

*

The summer passed quickly, with Molly and Lenny meeting frequently in Princes Park. Rules were relaxed during the long school break, provided the children only went out in groups supervised by a member of staff, but even so the pair of them twice managed to slip away from an uproarious game of French cricket, sneaking into the Palm House at Sefton Park and discussing how they might discover the whereabouts of their elusive parents.

For elusive they certainly were, and as the autumn term began it was tempting to concentrate on exciting if unrealistic plans to rescue both Mrs Hardwick and Mr Smith from whatever was stopping them from returning to Liverpool. However, Molly was a little dismayed when, sitting on the wall at the corner of the jigger on their first moonlit meeting since the summer holidays, Lenny began to ask why his new friend's aunt Clara never seemed to take her home on a visit.

'It's different for me, 'cos Mrs Prothero ain't a relative, and besides, she's dead. I heard she went to visit her daughter who lives in Fleetwood, not knowing the woman had contracted a bad case of measles. Of course when kids get measles it ain't often fatal, but with an older woman . . .' he sighed dramatically, 'there ain't no resistance. She were dead as a herrin' and new tenants in the house before you could say knife.'

'Who told you?' Molly said, so quickly that Lenny very nearly forgot himself and blurted out the truth. Just in time he remembered the morass into which a complicated explanation might drag him, and a second later his reply startled even himself, it came so pat. 'The milkman told me, the one with the dapple-grey horse,' he said glibly. 'She were a good customer of his, was Mrs Prothero.'

'Oh,' Molly said rather blankly. There was something not quite right about Lenny's voice, but she could not put her finger on what it was. 'Oh well, in that case . . .'

In a bid to bring the subject back to Aunt Clara Lenny spoke quickly. 'So, when did she – your aunt, I mean – call for you last?' He pulled a face. 'She's not been to the home all summer, has she?'

Molly sighed deeply. The time had come to kill Aunt Clara off, send her away to some distant part of the country, or admit that she herself had not been strictly truthful. Inwardly, she cursed Aunt Clara; a more annoying figment of her too vivid imagination could not have lodged itself in Lenny's memory. On their second midnight wander they had gone to Harebell Street, and so convinced had she been of the truth of her own story that Molly had actually shed a tear when explaining to Lenny that No. 20 was still dear to her despite the many years that had passed since she had been through the front door.

49

Now, poor Molly wrestled with her conscience. Lenny had, all unknowing, ruined her chances of killing Aunt Clara off by doing the same to Mrs Prothero. So it would have to be the truth or a distance too great to allow visiting. She took a deep breath.

'Didn't I say I was called out of class to go to Matron's office?' she said, and was quite proud of the little tremble which she heard in her voice. 'She wanted to tell me that my uncle Doug – that's Aunt Clara's husband – has joined the army. He's an engineer, you know. Matron told me he might be away for years, so of course he's taken Aunt Clara and my cousins with him.'

'Oh!' Lenny said equally blankly. For a moment he looked so downcast that Molly was almost sorry to have banished her family for so long, but if she brought them back she would have to find some other excuse for Aunt Clara's non-appearance at the home, so she sighed and slipped off her perch on the wall.

'I'm sorry about Mrs Prothero,' she said politely, as they turned towards the street which led down to the docks. 'But we might as well check things out whilst we can, because once winter really sets in we shan't see so much of one another.' She eyed her companion narrowly. 'You did say Mrs Prothero was dead, and someone else was living in her house?'

'That's right,' Lenny said shortly. He glanced up at the moon, now peeping coyly out from a bank of cloud. 'We'll have to arrange some other meeting place once the weather turns really cold. The Palm House is locked at nights but we can talk anywhere and that's chiefly why we meet, ain't it?'

Molly agreed that this was so, but Lenny thought he could hear in her voice a thread of doubt, and redoubled his efforts to convince her that Mrs Prothero had once existed but was now no more. He described in some detail the room his father had rented from the old woman, and by the time they were outside the pantry window once more was pretty sure he had reinstated both Mrs Prothero herself – now dead as a herring – and Mr Ned Smith, Lenny's father, possibly still languishing in a South American jail.

Molly climbed nimbly through the window first. 'See you tomorrer,' she whispered. 'Night, Lenny; sweet dreams.'

She ascended the stairs and slipped into dormitory four, where she still slept despite having pointed out to Matron that she could scarcely be guilty of chattering to Beth after lights out now that that young person had been reclaimed by her family. Matron had refused to listen. 'You'll do very well where you are,' she had said in her don't-argue-with-me voice.

So now Molly stole across the floor as carefully as she could, for Jane had become increasingly bad-tempered over the last six months and now ruled her small kingdom of six beds with a rod of iron, apparently liking nothing better than to get someone into trouble. For some reason she seemed to have it in for Molly, who unfortunately on this occasion had not been careful enough, it seemed. Even as she paused by her bed to listen a large hand clamped down on her shoulder and a voice spoke in her ear.

'Just what do you think you're doing, you nasty little sneak? Thievin' from the pantry, no doubt, or takin' what ain't yours as usual, even if it's only a clean blouse or a pair of socks wi'out holes in 'em! Well, when I tells Matron you won't get no time off for a hundred years and serves you bleedin' well right.'

Before she could stop herself, Molly had given a squeak of fright and tried to wiggle out from under the other's tight grip. 'What's the matter, Jane? Why won't you leggo of me shoulder?' She was grateful that fear of Jane had made her prepare what she would say if challenged. 'I've only been to the lavvy. You know we's allowed, if we've gorra belly ache and need to go real bad.'

Jane sniffed scornfully. 'I've been waitin' for you to come back since the church clock chimed midnight. It don't take an hour for you to make your way down the stairs to the bogs,' she said nastily. 'Come on, where's you been? And who's you meetin'? No use to lie 'cos I heared voices . . . why, I do believe it's worse than I thought. You've been up to somethin'; I know it in me water. Tell me who you was with and what you was up to and mebbe I won't say owt.'

'I weren't up to nothin',' Molly said sullenly. 'As for voices, I were talkin' to that black cat, the one that hangs about the yard. Miss Hornby says we ought to encourage it 'cos it keeps the place clear of mice and rats. Honest, Jane, I weren't up to any sort of mischief.' She held out her hands to show that she carried nothing. 'It's just that it's so hot, and my belly aches so bad . . . please let me off.'

'But you was gone an *hour*,' Jane said, and now her voice was menacing rather than angry. 'And you weren't talkin' to no animal . . .' her voice strengthened suddenly, 'unless it were a fairy-tale cat, 'cos there weren't just one voice talkin', but two, and don't try to tell me that it were anyone from *my* dormitory, 'cos no one else is awake, and besides it sounded like a feller's voice to me. Why, I do believe you've been meetin' one of the boys!'

'I don't *know* any boys worth talkin' to,' Molly said quickly. 'You're barkin' up the wrong tree, Jane, honest to God you are, and though of course I can't stop you tellin' Matron I dunno quite what you're goin' to tell her. It's no sin to visit the bogs even if

53

you spend a long time there.' She was struck by a brainwave. 'I s'pose I could say you were away from the dorm yerself, and you *are* old enough to be meetin' some feller.'

Jane gasped. 'Why you nasty little beast!' she said angrily. 'If you go tellin' lies to Matron I'll make you sorry. If you can make up tales then so can I. Just you tell me what you've been up to and stop inventin' stories.'

All this while the pair had been standing alongside Molly's bed, but now Molly looked into the older girl's face in what little light there was and realised that Jane was tired of the whole affair and simply wanted to back down without appearing to do so. After all, it would take some courage to march into Matron's office and complain that one of the girls in her dormitory had spent an hour in the bogs after suffering from stomach ache. Molly could just imagine Matron's bushy grey eyebrows shooting up towards her hairline and her voice, icy and calm, enquiring sarcastically just what was wrong with a member of Jane's dormitory visiting the lavatories after being struck down with stomach ache.

'Better than leaving it too late,' she would say frostily. 'I can see no reason for your visit, Jane. Kindly don't bother me with trivialities.'

Even as the thought crossed Molly's mind she saw it reflected in the older girl's face, and knew that unless she had positive proof Jane would not bother anyone in authority with such a lame tale. As she slipped back into her bed she decided that perhaps a little tact was needed, so she smiled up at the dark shape above her.

'It's all right, Jane, you know it is really,' she said sweetly. 'And I give you my word of honour that I weren't up to anythin'.'

Jane stared at her for a long moment, then shrugged. 'I dunno what a word of honour from a kid like you means,' she said grudgingly. 'But I reckon you're too young to be up to much. Nevertheless, just you remember I'll be keepin' an eye on you; wherever you are, or wharrever you're doin', I'll be watchin', so you'd best be good. Is that clear?'

Molly muttered that she understood and pulled the thin sheet up over her shoulders, her eyes following Jane's tall hefty figure as the older girl climbed back into her own bed. The incident had passed off much more lightly than had seemed possible at first. Jane had her suspicions, but since she did not know about the pantry window, let alone Lenny, Molly thought that she herself had come out of the encounter rather well. In fact she was drifting off to sleep when another thought so horrid that it caused the little hairs on the back of her neck to stand up straight struck her with stunning force. Lenny! She had been so busy covering her own tracks that she had not thought of an obvious danger. For the next few days Jane would be watching her like a hawk, she had no doubt of that, and of course the moment Lenny approached her Jane would suspect him of being the reason for her leaving the dormitory at night, and begin to put two and two together. And once she put two and two together she would examine the premises and might actually realise that their escape route was through the pantry window.

Molly heard the church clock strike two before she gave up and slid into slumber, but just before she did so she made a decision. She would approach one of the other boys whom Lenny had casually mentioned and ask him to pass a message to Lenny explaining that they must not be seen together. She would include in this message the words *Jane caught me*, which should be enough to alert her pal to the danger and make him realise that for a while at least they would have to play their cards very close to their chests.

On the very edge of sleep, Molly tried to remember the name of one of Lenny's pals, but it was no use; she was too tired. In moments, sleep overcame her.

Chapter Three

Despite every effort, Molly had found it difficult to elude Jane's eagle eye, and her plan to pass a message to Lenny via one of his friends when the older girl was not watching had proved tricky to say the least. Fortunately Lenny had guessed immediately that something was up when Molly turned quickly away from him when he tried to approach her and had not come near her again, but it was nearly a week before Jane was called to Miss Carruthers's room to explain why she had not handed in an essay and Molly was able to rush across the playground and yank the sleeve of the boy they called Bumble.

'Tell Lenny Jane caught me the other night,' she said, and went on to explain that she would be unable to get away whilst Jane was still watching her like a hawk.

The boy, Bumble Bee, gazed down at her, eyes rounding.

'Why can't you tell him yourself?' he asked. 'I don't want no trouble. I didn't know Lenny was up to anything, and I don't want to get involved, so you can pass on your own messages, kiddo.'

Molly was still trying to impress upon this large boy that her name must never be linked with Lenny's or the pair of them would be in deep trouble when Jane came back into the playground and started towards them, clearly determined to catch Molly in some misdemeanour. But when Jane reached out a meaty hand and grabbed Bumble's shoulder he shook her off indignantly.

'Who d'you think you're grabbin'?' he asked. 'Just you stick to your own side of the playground and I'll stick to mine.'

And with that he went and re-joined his friends.

Molly was pretty sure that the false trail which she and the unsuspecting Bumble had laid would put Jane on entirely the wrong track, but of course it would not mean the other girl would stop watching her. Molly sighed to herself and was quite glad when the bell rang for the end of the lunch break and the children formed into lines and made their way back to their classrooms. But later that day, as she and the rest of her dorm prepared for bed, she realised how much she was missing both Lenny and their adventures in the streets of Liverpool. It was all very well for Lenny; he was older than her and would be free from the orphanage very soon now, whilst she was probably stuck here for another two years. The thought of losing Lenny's friendship and his company on her nocturnal wanderings was not a happy one. Jane or no Jane, Molly decided to give it just one more week and then to half draw the curtain in her dorm and go down into the town.

And then something happened which changed everything. Matron called classes five and six to her office, saying she had something important to tell them.

'Normally I give this talk to the young ladies who will be leaving us in the coming year, but today, because of the unrest in Europe and the possibility, however remote, that we might eventually be dragged into war, I am including you younger girls as well. You too must learn the value of money and how to obtain the best goods available as economically as possible.'

She went on to explain that a fund was to be made available so that the girls might learn how to get the most out of what they would earn when they had left the orphanage behind them. The dormitory prefects would distribute the money and keep the accounts, and the girls would take it in turns to make each purchase. Upon their return to the orphanage they would be closely questioned as to why they had favoured one shop or stall against another, and their answer recorded by the prefects.

When Matron had dismissed them Molly and a girl called Ellen sat in the corner of the wall which separated the playground from the jigger to discuss what they had been told.

'Well, I'm bleedin' well blessed,' Ellen said. 'I'm surprised Matron's willing to lerrus lay our hands on more than the few coppers what she give us sometimes to do her marketing for her. Of course, some of the prefects are quite decent; just our luck that it's Jane who'll be running round in circles blamin' us if anythin' goes wrong. But it can't be worse than sittin' in a classroom while Miss Carruthers drones on.'

'I think it might be fun,' Molly said decidedly. 'Fancy bein' treated like a human being instead of some sort of prisoner! I wonder how this rationing she talked about will work.' She giggled and put on a good imitation of Matron's voice. 'Here is an egg, young ladies; because of rationing youse is only entitled to a fifth of this 'ere egg. How does you mean to divvy it up so everyone gets a share? How would you deal with that, Ellen?'

Ellen was a skinny girl of about Molly's own age, though much smaller. She'd only been at the Haisborough a few weeks but was beginning to grow accustomed to the change in her circumstances. Her bed was next to Molly's and once or twice, Molly had heard muffled sobs coming from her neighbour. At last she had put out a cautious hand to give the other girl's shoulder a consoling squeeze.

'Don't cry, Ellen,' she had whispered. 'It ain't so bad here, once you get used to it. Keep on the right side of Jane and be polite to the staff, and when your mam and dad come to see you you can tell 'em how much you want to go home.'

Ellen had not replied but a small hand had crept up and given Molly's fingers a squeeze, and after that Ellen did not cry again, or at least not loudly enough to risk being overheard by anyone other than Molly. In fact she now seemed to have settled in well and proved to have a dry sense of humour similar to Molly's own.

'If it were a sausage it would be easier; but sausages don't come our way at the Haisborough,' she said now. 'In fact I've yet to see an egg put in an appearance.' She giggled. 'Perhaps we'd all be allowed a sniff; do eggs have a smell?'

'Bad ones do,' Molly assured her friend. 'Well, you and me'll stick together and do our best to see Jane gets value for money. Judgin' by what Matron was sayin' that's the object of the exercise, right?'

Before Ellen could reply Lenny strolled casually past, looking all round, and then doubled back to join them.

'Perishin' Jane's gone to ask Matron something or other,' he informed them. 'I say, what a turn-up for the books! We's goin' to be give some money to go marketin' with, so if war comes we'll be able to buy grub for ourselves. Good, ain't it? I feels like a prisoner walkin' out through them grim gates. I never thought I'd be grateful for them goose-steppin' horrors – them Nazis – but I bet I will be.'

'So're we – being given money, I mean, not grateful to the Nazis,' Molly told him. 'Tell you what though, once Matron's give permission for us to go out and run our own messages, she'll find it dead difficult to take it back again. Even girls like Jane who lick Matron's boots would be cross.'

Lenny looked at Ellen, raising one black eyebrow. 'Can you keep your mouth shut, little 'un? If not you can buzz off now.' He turned up his coat collar and gave an exaggerated shiver. 'If you asks me, Molly, we shan't have nothin' to hide pretty soon; it'll be too cold.'

Molly grinned at him. 'Ellen won't tell nobody nothin',' she assured him. 'Anything she hears she'll keep to herself, ain't that so, Ellen?'

Ellen nodded vigorously. 'Cut me throat and hope to die, if I should ever tell a lie,' she said cheerfully. 'Spit it out, Lenny; only I bet it ain't nothin' excitin', just some old rumour about the war. Judgin' by what I've heard from my family it ain't goin' to happen, or not any time soon, at any rate. Do you two hear the same from your relatives?'

Molly took a deep breath. Now was the time to fess up, she told herself, but when she spoke she averted her eyes from Lenny's. 'My mam dumped me. I don't think she had any intention of taking me back. I tell people she only left me at the home whilst she searched for work down south, but that's what Matron calls wishful thinking. Lenny's different; his father is a seaman, and Lenny thinks . . .'

'I know what you're goin' to say . . . Lenny thinks his father will come back for him one day,' Lenny interrupted. 'But that ain't true, it's just what I told you when we first met and I didn't know you very well. Father O'Leary, what's in charge of us boys, thinks my dad were killed in a drunken brawl, Ellen; I heard him tellin' one of the teachers. So you see I'm just as much of an orphan as Molly here. And – and although most folk would call it lying, I go along with the wishful thinking bit. So the only one of us liable to get to know what's really happening in the outside world is you.'

Ellen looked from face to face, her expression puzzled. 'Well, where's the secret in that, I'd like to know?' she asked plaintively. 'I bet the staff and Matron and that Father O'Leary of yours, Lenny, all know the exact truth. In fact you're the only ones who don't. So if that's all . . .'

'Oh, but it's not,' Molly said eagerly. 'Lenny and I have a secret sign: when either of us half draws our curtain across the window, especially when the moon's at the full, it tells the other one that we're goin' to get out of the home and start exploring the streets. We told each other we were searching for our parents, which was't true for either of us, as it turns out, but it helped us not to feel so . . . so abandoned, I s'pose. That's our secret, Ellen. All through the summer we've been meeting outside and getting to know the area. When winter comes it's going to be difficult, but perhaps we'll still manage a meeting maybe once every few weeks.'

'Gosh, that's a secret worth havin',' Ellen said enviously. 'Next time you go, can I come? How do you get out without anyone seeing you?'

Lenny ran his eyes over Ellen's skinny form. Then he grinned a trifle ruefully. 'To tell you the truth, I were comin' over to tell Molly that there was a bit of a problem. You see, Ellen, we gets out through the pantry window in the kitchen. We stick to the shadows until we're in the jigger and then we just slide along the wall and peep into Gulliver Street to make sure there's no one about. But it's an awful squeeze for me now because my shoulders seem to have got broader, and I tell you: by next summer there'll be no way I can get out of the place . . . well, not by the pantry window at any rate.'

Molly and Ellen looked at each other. 'How about usin' the front door?' Ellen said, after a moment's thought. 'I shouldn't have thought it'd be noisy when it's opened because the staff and visitors and that are goin' in and out that way all day, just about. And we could grease the bolts and the hinges just in case – not in the daytime, o' course, but we could do it tonight.'

Molly was about to agree enthusiastically when Lenny shook his head. 'We can't do that, because we'd have to leave the door unlocked so's we could get back in,' he said rather reprovingly. 'Remember the Christmas before last, Molly? When one of the staff forgot to bolt the door when she came in from visiting her parents up in Crosby, and a drunk got in? Apparently he'd been here when he was a kid himself and hated the place, so he started to smash it up, and when Father O'Leary woke and came downstairs the drunk chap swung a punch at him and the scuffers had to be called.' He patted Ellen consolingly. 'It's a grand idea, little 'un, but it's just norron. S'pose a mad axeman just happened to try the door?'

Molly sighed. It looked as though their midnight wanderings were doomed, but at least they would have the consolation of Matron's and Father O'Leary's marketing trips. She was about to point this out when Ellen gave a little crow of triumph and addressed Lenny.

'You're daft, you are,' she said. 'You've got *me*! I'll stay on the lookout by the pantry window, and when you give me the signal that you want to come in I'll go and unlock the door for you. How about that for a plan, eh? And whilst I'm waitin' I'll cut a slice off the loaf or get an apple from the fruit bin and have a bite to eat. Is there a comfy chair in the kitchen? If so I'll bring my blanket down from the dormitory and snuggle up in it, only don't be too long, will you, else I might fall asleep by accident.'

All this sounded a bit hit and miss to Molly but she agreed they would give it a go that very night. 'You and me can take turns,' she assured Ellen. 'It wouldn't be fair otherwise. How well do you know this part of Liverpool?'

'Not at all . . .' Ellen was beginning when the bell for school sounded and the trio had to scurry off to their classes. But when they met at midnight, all three excited at the thought of the adventure before them, Lenny had one piece of information which he apparently wanted to share only with Molly, for he did not disclose it until they were alone.

'I didn't say nothin' earlier, but Father O'Leary asked if any of us boys aged fourteen or over could ride a bicycle. I can't, of course, but I weren't goin' to say that. And anyway, ridin' a bike's easy as fallin' off a log. Apparently if the war happens lots of lads will be give bikes and take messages across the city. Then he asked who could swim, and of course

I said I could do that too. What's swimmin', after all? I seen a dog what fell in the dock once and all he did was run through the water, so I reckon that's all there is to swimmin'. And that means I can join the Navy when I'm old enough.'

Molly stared at him, thoroughly bewildered. 'But how can you swim on a bicycle? And why is it so secret that you couldn't let Ellen hear?' she asked. 'I think you've got moon madness. It's like sunstroke, only a night-time thing . . .'

They reached the docks and a black cat, tail erect and ears pricked, emerged from a pile of fish boxes. Molly bent and stroked it. She had always liked cats but was terrified of dogs. Matron thought she must have been attacked by a dog before she came to the home – she had a V-shaped scar on her arm to prove it – and if she knew where a dog lived she would cross the road rather than risk an encounter. She stopped stroking the cat and straightened, staring accusingly at Lenny. 'Come on, why the secrecy?'

'Because Father O'Leary only told those who put their hands up about ridin' bicycles about bein' messengers,' Lenny said. 'I imagine if war really does come there'll be a heap of fellers eager to join up as messengers, and I don't want my chances of actually bein' give me own bike spoiled. So I don't want no one knowin' I can't actually ride a bike.'

Molly understood; probably messenger boys would have a uniform and be regarded with awe by other lads. After having spent pretty well his whole life in an institution, Lenny would no doubt enjoy the sort of responsibility and respect that went with a uniform and the delivery of important messages. As they walked back to the Haisborough she put these thoughts into words, and by the time they were standing in the deep shadows by the pantry window she was pretty fully informed about the adventures likely to befall an intrepid cycle messenger in time of war. Experience had now proved to them that Lenny could not enter or leave the building by this route but even the soft sound of their approaching footsteps had been enough to rouse little Ellen, whose small face and untidy mop of dusky curls soon appeared in the aperture.

'Are you ready?' she whispered. 'I'll go and unlock the front door. No one's stirring in our dorm, Molly, though I can't answer for Lenny's, of course.'

Presently, when newly greased bolts and locks had been slotted not quite soundlessly back into place again, the three of them made their way through the silent house to the big kitchen which was common to all at the home. Here Lenny said his goodbyes and made for the boys' staircase, but at the foot of the girls' stair Molly grabbed Ellen's arm. 'Give it a minute before we go up,' she whispered. 'Listen with all your might, little

Ellen, just in case someone besides ourselves is on the prowl. Are you sure the front door is properly locked?'

'Course I am,' Ellen said rather shortly. 'Oh, do let's go back to bed now, Molly. I'm that tired I could sleep on a clothes line.'

Molly chuckled softly. 'You aren't the only one,' she assured her friend. 'Come on then, up we go, and remember, if you're challenged you've been to the lavvy.'

Ellen was watching her feet, making sure not to tread on the creaking board, but Molly, who knew the stairs like the palm of her own hand, was able to glance up at the head of the stairs. What she saw made her gasp and clutch Ellen's arm tightly.

'Did you see that?' she breathed. 'Somebody just come out of one of the dorms – I couldn't see which one. Oh lor', if it were ours and she's woken Jane we'll be in big trouble. Don't forget what I said: we've been to the lavvy.'

Moving with mouse-like care the girls reached the upper landing without incident. They peered round the door of dormitory four and Molly's first action was to stare at every bed in turn. To her relief, each one was occupied. *Had* she seen somebody, or was it just her overactive imagination? She knew Jane disliked her and would have been happy to get the pair of them into trouble, and if she had been awake when Ellen had opened the big front door they would be in worse trouble than any she could imagine.

However, although they waited for at least a minute before venturing to move, no one in the dorm was stirring, and Jane actually began to snore as they watched. Ellen would have hurried straight for her bed then, but Molly knew how devious Jane could be and made her friend wait for a minute more before entering the room. 'It must have been a shadow or something; everyone looks fast asleep to me,' she breathed rather uneasily at last. 'I think the coast's clear; into bed with you now. We'll find out how Lenny got on at break time tomorrow.'

Jane lay in her bed with one eye open, giving convincing little snores when she moved, and watched the two people she most disliked re-enter the dormitory. She knew that Molly would say they had been visiting the bogs and there was no way of proving that the girl was telling enormous lies, even had she not already threatened to tell Matron that it was she, Jane, who had been sneaking about with a boy in the middle of the night. No, in order to really get Molly into the sort of trouble she deserved, she would actually have to catch her away from the building, and Jane, who liked her creature comforts, did not intend to hang around outside as the weather grew steadily colder and the wind more bitter.

But there must be something she could do to discredit Molly and Ellen in the eyes of authority. There simply must be!

December 1938

Breakfast at Haisborough Orphanage was usually a subdued affair, with some girls still rubbing sleep out of their eyes and others thinking anxiously about the school day ahead, but one morning shortly before Christmas a ripple of interest ran through the dining room as Matron came in and rapped on the nearest table for attention.

'Girls, I think the time has come when I must tell you that this may well be our last peacetime Christmas,' she began. She waited for the murmur of dismay to die away before continuing, 'Mr Chamberlain has promised peace in our time, but there are those who think he is mistaken. Factories in this very city are making parts for aircraft, munitions, and even uniforms. You may think there is little young persons like yourselves can do to help their country but you would be wrong. As many of you know, I was matron of a large hospital for wounded soldiers in the last war and there were a multitude of tasks, performed then by VADs, which could have been done by some of our senior girls: rolling bandages and pushing tea trolleys, for instance, and later, when you are old enough, joining the Land Army or even one of the armed services.' Someone murmured that the boys had all the fun and Matron frowned. 'The boys have already taken over a large area of farmland which they intend to divide into allotments where they will grow all the food necessary to keep Haisborough Orphanage afloat.' She sniffed. 'Now, hands up who knows what "evacuation" means.'

Only two hands shot up, both belonging to dormitory prefects, and the one in charge of dormitory two said in a rather uncertain voice: 'Don't it mean movin' people around the country, Matron? Or somethin' like that, anyway.'

Matron nodded approvingly. 'That's right. Moving children from big cities into the country, because everyone who's ever seen a newsreel knows that the Germans have been bombing Madrid until there's scarcely a building standing. If the Spanish had had the opportunity to take their children into the country I'm sure they would have done so, but the war in Spain is what we call a civil war . . .' She frowned irritably. 'Never mind that. It may not be necessary for us to move into the country. And anyway, the war may never happen. The Duke of Windsor – he was the king for a short period two years ago, you may recall – is on friendly terms with Herr Hitler, which may save us from the threat of invasion. We shall see. On a happier note, the board of governors, to mark the occasion, is giving each of you a whole shilling to spend as a Christmas gift.' She flapped a hand as an excited 'hooray' went up from the ranks of girls before her. 'And I shall see that every one of you gets a good Christmas dinner,' she concluded. She looked round at them, a broad smile on her face. 'That's all!' she boomed. 'Go about your work.'

Christmas came and went and with it came trickling down the news of what the Germans were calling 'Crystal Night'. Molly's stomach turned over at the very mention of the words, for hundreds of Jewish people had been dragged out of their houses and business premises and viciously beaten in the streets, then left bleeding among the shards of glass from their broken windows that gave the night its horrible name.

'I wish someone would stick a knife in Adolf Hitler's back, as they say he did to his opponents years ago,' Molly told Lenny, 'although of course if someone did there'd be no nice jobs in the factories on Love Lane. One of the older girls said that the jam factory is making bullets now, and bombs and things, and the girls that work there get twice the money they used to for makin' jam and biscuits.'

A passing prefect sniffed. 'I'd rather have jam and biscuits thrown at me than bombs and bullets,' she said sagely. 'But it's all rumours, what they call propaganda, so don't you worry your head about it. It'll be nothin' to do wi' us; we're at the bottom of the pile and have to pick up what news we can when we can. But,' she repeated, 'none of it will affect us.'

Molly and Lenny had suspended their night-time wanderings. For one thing Lenny had discovered that riding a bicycle was neither like falling off a log nor a piece of cake. He spent many gruelling hours practising on an old and rusty machine, the property of Father O'Leary's gardener, and was far too tired to even think about a midnight sortie. He had examined all three services and decided that, as soon as he was old enough, he would join the Royal Air Force, and when one of the teachers explained that pilots needed a college certificate as well as an excellent grasp of mathematics, he became even less keen to 'waste his time' wandering the streets at night.

And as the new year gathered pace Molly, too, had other preoccupations. She had just turned fourteen and had been offered a job in one of the factories on Love Lane, where she and Ellen were due to start in ten days' time. She was a little sad when she realised that she and Lenny were drifting apart, but when she commented on this to Ellen, her friend gave her hand a consoling squeeze.

'You're daft, you are,' she said affectionately. 'You and Lenny will drift together again, 'cos that's the way it happens. Boys and girls grow up at different rates, or so I'm told, but in the end it works out for the best. Won't you be proud if Lenny gets into the air force? Course you will! And when the war's over you'll meet him as a grownup and find out whether you want him as a boyfriend or just a friend. That's how it happened with my mam and dad. I've heard Mam tell many a time how when they were kids she thought our dad the handsomest feller in the world and she were all set for the "happy ever after" bit. Then he went away and she met another feller – Jim something or other – and thought he was the one, until one day she suddenly realised it were our dad who mattered more to her than anyone else in the world, so she told Jim she'd made a mistake and three months later she and our dad was wed.' She grinned brightly at Molly. 'See wharr I mean?'

'Not really,' Molly said honestly. 'And I don't want to marry anyone, not until I'm old, at any rate.' She smiled affectionately at the other girl. 'But won't it be grand to have money of our own? We'll have to save real hard for the first year, whilst we're still living here and not having to pay much towards our keep, so that when we have to move out we can find a room together and have ourselves a high old time.'

So when Matron called a meeting of the entire home on a wild and windy February morning, with the snow whipping past outside and their fingers and toes freezing, Molly and Ellen were surprised when, instead of the expected homily on financial management, Matron began to address them on another subject entirely.

'Miss Whitmore and I have called this meeting in the hope that when I have explained what has happened the wrong-doer will repent of his or her action and no further steps need be taken,' she said. 'First, Miss Whitmore will explain to you boys what the girls already know, which is the story of how I came to be given my precious gold watch.' She turned to the teacher, who was looking most uncomfortable. 'Please begin.'

Miss Whitmore cleared her throat and began to describe how Matron, with great bravery, had gone out to the trenches in France in 1918 to take the place of a stretcher bearer who had been killed whilst bringing back the wounded. By so doing she had saved the life of a young soldier, whose grateful parents had presented her with the gold fob watch which she had worn on special occasions ever since.

When Miss Whitmore had finished she stepped back. 'You'd best take over now, Matron,' she said.

Molly and Ellen exchanged puzzled looks, but before either could whisper anything Matron took up the tale again. 'As most of you know . . .' she gave Miss Whitmore a quelling look, 'I *always* wear that watch when I am working, from the moment I get up in the morning until the moment I go to my bed at night. When I am off duty the watch and its chain live in a little green velvet presentation box in my quarters. Yesterday I was off duty so I did not wear the watch all day. This morning, since I was on duty once more, I went to fetch it, and that was when I discovered it was gone. Someone had stolen it. Several members of staff wanted me to report the theft to the police straight away, but since I believe it to be an "inside job" I have put off the moment of revelation until after this meeting to give the guilty person the opportunity to return my property. After all, what possible use could any of you have for a presentation watch with my name engraved upon the back? So I want you all to file slowly past Miss Whitmore and myself and to place your hand in the black velvet bag which is on the table between us. When everyone has done so, if the watch is in the bag I do not intend to inform the police or seek to punish the wrong-doer; his or her conscience will be punishment enough, and I would hesitate to ruin a child's name for what must surely have been a foolish prank. We'll start with the youngest children and work up through the ranks until everyone has had a chance to redeem themselves.'

Once more Molly's eyes met Ellen's, both expressions incredulous. 'I can't believe anyone but her would want that silly old watch,' Molly hissed. 'She didn't say if the thief took the box as well. What if the pin got loose and the watch just fell off somewhere? Matron wouldn't want to admit it was lost, because that sounds like carelessness. Tell you what, Ellen, the likeliest place to look for her watch is either on the ground – if it did fall off – or the pawnbroker's window on the corner, if it really was stolen. Why are you grinning?'

Ellen smothered a giggle. 'It's the expressions on the little ones' faces,' she said. 'Some of them didn't really understand what Matron was talking about, so when they put their hands into the bag they expect to find something exciting like a chocolate bar or a thruppenny piece. What use would kids like them have for Matron's fob watch?'

Molly laughed as well, but quietly. The staff were shepherding them into the queue, so when Miss Hornby got near enough Molly whispered quickly, 'Miss Hornby, don't you think it's possible that the watch simply fell off and wasn't noticed? Even the pawnbroker at the end of the road wouldn't take a watch with writing on it, would he?'

Miss Hornby shook her head. 'I'm sure we would all be very glad if there was the slightest chance of its having fallen off,' she said, 'but remember, Matron went to pick it up and then discovered that it was gone. There could be no possibility of accidental loss in those circumstances.'

'Well I don't believe anyone would have been so foolish as to steal it,' Molly began, but then the line of children moved on and it was her turn to put her hand in the black velvet bag.

When the last child had passed it the bag was still empty, so Matron ordered every child to stand by to turn out their bedside drawers in order that a member of staff might make a thorough search. 'We shall deal with the girls' dormitories first, since the theft occurred in their part of the house,' she announced. 'Boys, you may sit quietly with your books until you are called.'

In Molly's drawer was the letter from the manager at the munitions factory, offering her one of the jobs for which she and most of the other girls had applied, and she was reluctant to leave it in the jumble of possessions on her bed. She had seen the envy in Jane's eyes when the letter had arrived and knew the other girl was quite capable of tearing it to shreds and then taking her place when the job started. Manoeuvring herself between Jane and the heap of her belongings, she picked the letter up and jammed it into her skirt pocket, and was congratulating herself upon having taken the wind from Jane's sails when the other girl rushed forward and plunged her hand into the pile of Molly's underwear.

'What were that? That sort of sparkle?' Molly heard her exclaim. 'Miss, Miss! Young Molly here's took somethin' out of her clothes and she's tryin' to hide it from the rest of us! Make her turn out her pockets, Miss, so's we can all see what she's got. I bet she took it on one of her moonlight expeditions with that boy! I've seen 'em before, but didn't like to tale-clat, 'cos she fed me a string of lies about goin' to the lavvy.' She snorted. 'Goin' to the lavvy don't take a couple of hours, so I knew she were lyin', but I could never prove it.'

Molly gasped. She began to say that the only thing she was hiding was the letter offering her a job when she happened to glance at Ellen's face. It was rigid with horror, and when she followed her friend's eyes she saw that, indeed, there was something sparkling amongst her worn and ragged socks. She reached out a hand to see for herself, but Jane was too quick for her. She grabbed at the fob watch and held it tantalisingly aloft.

'Why, you dirty little thief,' she shouted gloatingly. 'Thought you'd got away with it, didn't you? First you cheat me out of a good job – and believe me, they won't want you when they realise that you're nothing but a common criminal – and then you steal Matron's presentation watch. Ho, you thought you'd got away with it, but I'm up to all your tricks, Miss oh-so-clever Molly Hardwick.'

Molly gave a derisive laugh. 'As if anyone would believe I was such an idiot as to steal somethin' which I could never wear nor use,' she said.

'You took that watch in order to plant it amongst my clothin'. Well, I know Matron is a silly old fool, but she won't believe a tissue of lies like that.'

Even as she spoke the words she glanced towards the doorway, in which was framed Matron's large and imposing figure. Instead of telling Jane to pipe down and stop making a fool of herself, Matron was glowering straight at Molly, her expression one of indignation and outrage.

'So I'm a silly old fool, am I?' she said grimly. 'Thank you, Jane, for restoring my property. And now I shall see what the police have to suggest for a thankless orphan who would steal her matron's most prized possession. Jane, you will apprehend her now and keep her in charge.'

'Matron, you can't possibly believe that tissue of lies,' Molly gasped. 'I'm sorry I was so rude, but Jane was accusin' me of theft, which is no light matter, and everyone in the dorm saw what she was up to. She thought if I was caught with the watch in my possession . . .'

'We'll let the police decide,' Matron said grimly. 'Jane is a good girl and I trust her to look after my interests.' She reached out a hand to grasp Molly's elbow, but Molly had had enough. She kicked Jane sharply in the shins and shot out of the dormitory and down the stairs, running too fast even to grab her overcoat as she passed through the cloakroom. Outside, snow whirled and the wind was bitter, but indignation warmed Molly's icy fingers and toes. She tore across the playground, into the jigger and out into Princes Row, at this stage merely wanting to put as much distance as possible between herself and the home, for even above the noise of the storm she could hear Matron and Jane shouting that the miscreant must be caught so that justice could be seen to be done.

Miss Hornby knows I wouldn't steal, she told herself, and of course Ellen saw what happened and will stand up for me. But Jane was right about one thing: when they hear I'm suspected of theft the factory will withdraw the job offer and all the lovely plans Ellen and I were making will be ruined. Oh dear, if only I'd not antagonised Jane and been rude to Matron! I'll hide up until the storm blows over and then go back and explain to Lenny the mess I'm in. He won't let his old pal down. And in the meantime I must find myself somewhere out of this fearful weather. Somewhere warm if possible . . . maybe there'll be something down at the docks.

Molly was in luck. The docks were deserted, for the ferocity of the storm was almost frightening, and she soon found a lorry whose tarpaulin hid the very sort of cargo she was searching for – sheep fleeces. The fleeces were a bit smelly but very warm, and Molly climbed into the back of the lorry and curled up in the most comfortable bed she had ever known, pulling the tarpaulin over her knees and tucking it in as securely as she could so that she would be invisible to anyone passing by. She wished she had managed to have a word with Ellen, but told herself the omission could not be helped. She would lie here in comfort until the storm eased, and then she would make her way to the Haisborough, somehow contact Ellen and Lenny and discuss her position. Either one or both of them would have some idea of what to do and neither, of course, would consider even for a moment that Jane had been telling the truth, or that Molly herself was the thief.

Satisfied on this score she snuggled down amongst the fleeces, keeping an eye on a slit in the canvas cover so that she would know what was going on outside her cosy nest. And presently, despite her determination to stay awake, she fell deeply and comfortably asleep.

Chapter Four

When the call had come for all the children at Haisborough Orphanage to assemble in the dining hall Lenny was up in his dormitory, sitting on the end of his bed – a practice regarded with disfavour by Father O'Leary and other members of staff – revising a maths paper he had been given by the astonished maths teacher, Mr Hebron. The teacher was not used to having pupils request extra work, but once he got used to the idea he had been, Lenny thought, almost helpful. At any rate, he had dug out past examination papers and given them to Lenny, offering to check the boy's answers and explain if there was something he could not understand. So when the rumpus made by children of various ages being herded into the dining hall came to Lenny's ears, not even curiosity persuaded him to join them. It was true that he got to his feet to look out of the window, but he could see nothing but the driving snow and, shrugging, he had returned to the end of his bed, pulled his work towards him and was soon oblivious of anything but the problems on the page in front of him.

So Lenny had no idea of the drama which was being enacted in the dormitory opposite. He did not hear Jane's accusation or Matron's response. He knew nothing of Molly's flight. All Lenny cared about was that the rumpus did not affect himself, and he could settle to his mathematical problems once more.

If one train leaves Piccadilly station travelling at 30 mph and another train leaves a half hour later travelling at 50 mph, when will the second catch up with the first?

Bumble was ambling along the corridor, wishing that the weather had made it possible for Matron to let them go outside instead of ordering them to stay quietly indoors, when Molly rushed past him and shot out of the door, straight into the raging storm. Several excited girls were hot on her heels, and amongst them Bumble recognised the one who had grabbed his shoulder in the playground. Incredibly, as she passed him she was shouting 'Stop, Molly, you nasty little thief!' at the top of her loud and very ugly voice.

Bumble was outraged and looked round for Lenny, but his friend did not seem to have put in an appearance, so Bumble, in a burst of energy that was not at all typical, rushed out into the blizzard himself. He was sure that Molly was no thief, and he felt that he had no choice but to follow. He knew Lenny would expect him to take her side, and was certain that any accusation of theft must be a false one, so he stumbled after her dimly seen figure, his progress somewhat impeded by the crowd of girls who had also emerged from the building until they were stopped in their tracks by a shout from Matron.

'Get back inside, girls,' she shouted. 'This is a matter for the police. You are behaving like hounds after a fox, not like civilised human beings. Molly will return as soon as she realises she has nowhere to go.' And with these words she began to herd the girls back into the building, her large red face shining with sweat and her bosom heaving.

Bumble hesitated; should he go after Molly or should he leave her to hide away somewhere until she felt it was safe to return? The thought of Lenny's concern made up his mind for him and he followed her doggedly into the jigger, where she proceeded to run like a hare until she emerged at the far end of Princes Row and disappeared from Bumble's view.

He reckoned she was making for the river, but when he got there the docks were deserted and Molly was nowhere to be seen. Searching for one small girl when you had no idea where she might be and there was no one around to ask was useless. But I'll come back later, Bumble told himself. I'll go

back to the home now, find where Lenny has hidden himself and discuss with him how we can best
help Molly. He'll know where she's likely to be.
And with these comforting thoughts he returned
to the orphanage, where already the drama seemed
to have calmed down as the prefects lined their
charges up for the walk to school.

By the time Bumble had a chance to speak to Lenny
in private his friend had already heard the story
from half a dozen lads, so when Bumble began
'Lenny, your little pal's in trouble. I didn't know
where you was . . .' Lenny gave an impatient
exclamation and punched his friend lightly on the
shoulder.

'If you think I've not been told by half the maths
class how that awful Jane person accused Molly
of theft, Bumble, you must be even thicker than a
tram driver's glove! Has she turned up again yet?
Molly I mean?'

Bumble shook his head. 'No, I don't think
so. I asked her pal, that wispy little thing what
looks about ten – her name's Ellen, ain't it? – to
let me know as soon as Molly reappears and she
said she would.' Despite his worries he grinned
at Lenny. 'I followed her as far as the docks but
the weather were awful wild and I couldn't see
a thing what with the snow blowin' into me face,
so I decided to come back and ask you where

you thought she'd gone. If anyone knows it'll be you, me old pal.'

Bumble looked hopefully at his friend and was surprised as well as disappointed when Lenny shook his head, replying impatiently: 'How the devil should I know where a girl would hide up after making such a fool of herself? Honestly, Bumble, the worst possible thing she could have done was run away. An honest person stays to face whatever charge there is; it's the guilty party what runs.'

Bumble's eyebrows shot up towards his hair-line. 'Are you sayin' you believe she took the wretched watch?' he asked incredulously. 'Lenny, she's your pal, mate! Next you'll be tellin' me you really think she did it and that the scuffers have already appre— appre— found her and she's in a cell at the police station.'

Lenny reddened. 'Course I don't,' he said abruptly. 'But I've got no idea where she might run and I don't intend to get a black mark 'cos Father O'Leary thinks I'm tryin' to help a thief. It'd be different if I did know where she was, but I don't. And anyway, what makes you think things will be any better when she does come back? She wouldn't have run unless she knew the cards were stacked against her . . . no, no, I don't mean she did it, you fool, but she'll have to work out how to prove her innocence before she comes back. Just you leave well alone, old feller, because there ain't a darned thing you can do to help her. Lots of the staff must know what a nasty piece of work that Jane is, and they'll persuade Matron that she's got the wrong sow by the ear.'

Bumble stared at his friend. 'So you won't help me to find her?' he said incredulously. 'Lenny, you're her pal, not me! According to Ellen it was plain as a pikestaff that Jane had set her up and intended her to be disgraced. So I'm afraid she may not come back but just keep running. Only I can't help thinking she'd try to get a message to you somehow.'

Lenny shrugged. 'If she does, what can I do? If I'd followed her at the time . . . but Bumble, old feller, she could be anywhere. If she jumped a leccy she could be in Seaforth or Crosby or even further, and I dare not get involved in a wild goose chase because I'm due to sit another exam in a few days and I dare say Father O'Leary would take me out of the special maths classes if he thought I was involved with a thief. But of course when Molly comes back . . .'

'But I don't think she *will* come back,' Bumble almost shouted. 'Why should she? I reckon she'll wait a while for us – you, I mean – to find her, and then she'll give up and go far away and get herself a job and we'll never see her again.'

'She's been offered a job in one of the factories. She was really thrilled about it . . . in fact she might have gone straight there. Now how's that for an idea? She could explain what happened to the man who interviewed her and if he's a nice bloke he'll take her side and all will be well. I bet that's what she'll do.'

Bumble's brow cleared. He had hated to think ill of his old friend Lenny and nodded enthusiastically. 'You're probably right,' he said generously. 'Though it would take some courage to walk into a factory and ask to see one of the bigwigs. Still, if you and I dig her out from wherever she's hidin' and go with her, it might clear the whole matter up.'

Bumble expected Lenny to agree but his friend shook his head. 'Don't think badly of me, but I can't simply walk away from the home and start searching for Molly,' he said earnestly. 'My whole future will depend on my maths results. You may not realise how much it means to me, but I'm sure Molly does. So I'm afraid searching for her is out. We'll just have to wait for her to come to me for help.'

The pair had been sitting on the window ledge in the boys' playroom and now Bumble stood up. 'Right. You keep telling everyone Molly's innocent and I'll start searching. It seems to me that the obvious place to start might be Ogdens – the flower streets – because wasn't that where her family came from?' He twisted round to look out of the window behind him. 'It isn't snowing any more and the wind has dropped, so perhaps now is the time to take a closer look at the docks.' He tried to grin at Lenny, but it was a poor effort. 'See you later, old chap.' He was turning to leave the room when a thought struck him. 'What am I to say if I do find her?' he said urgently. 'Do I tell her to come back with me and we'll sort the whole matter out, or do I advise her to stay hidden until you and I have discussed the matter again?'

Lenny hesitated. 'Best tell her to come back and face the music,' he said finally. 'Tell her we know it wasn't her . . . oh, I know! When you find her we'll talk to that Miss Hornby of hers and get her to put in a good word for Molly, which she will do, I'm sure. Yes, that's the best idea of the lot; knowing a member of staff is on Molly's side will make Matron think again.'

Bumble searched diligently despite the cold and the fact that he was missing his tea. He walked this way and that along the dock road but saw no elfin features set below a cap of straight hair. He ferreted amongst fish boxes and examined a great many sodden tarpaulins, but though he disturbed a large black cat he found no humans hiding away and of Molly there was no sign. At one stage he sat down on a bollard and checked that he had looked everywhere. He had been hopeful when the cat had approached him, purring loudly, and had wound its way around his legs, but the cat, though friendly, had not seemed more interested in one pile of boxes than another. It trotted beside him as he skirted a large lorry laden with fleeces, and as he put up a hand to push a protruding hank of wool back amongst its fellows he addressed it in a friendly voice. 'You could make a fine nest in there, puss, if you could worm your way under this 'ere tarpaulin,' he said. 'Come to think of it, it would have made a comfortable bed for Lenny's pal Moll, too, if she'd seen it.' The black cat leapt lightly on to the oiled canvas and stared down at him with wide yellow eyes, and Bumble chuckled. 'Are you tryin' to tell me somethin', old chap? Is she in there? Oh, but I'm sure I heard someone say in the playground that Molly was frightened of cats, so she wouldn't just lie there with you walking all over her, would she? So I'd better get up to Ogdens now and make sure she's not there either. Then I'll go and ask Lenny what he thinks.'

By the time Bumble had searched Ogdens and returned to the home everyone was in bed, but he knew that Lenny would have played the old pillow trick so that he, Bumble, would not be missed. He ascended the stairs as silently as possible and slid into the dormitory, and was pleased to see that

Lenny was still awake. He began to whisper where he had been, but Lenny cut him short.

'We can't talk here,' he murmured. 'Come down to the playroom.'

Once they were ensconced in a couple of chairs pulled up to the dying fire, Lenny raised his eyebrows. 'You won't have heard, but Molly's in the clear. Apparently they found the fastening clip for Matron's blessed watch hidden in Jane's drawer – I suppose she thought they wouldn't look there if she could plant the watch on Molly first – so Molly can come back and get on with her life. Only first we've got to find her and tell her that Jane's the one in big trouble. How did your search go?'

Bumble shook his head. 'She weren't on the docks, norras I could see,' he said unhappily. 'I tried calling her name, soft like, whenever I passed some spot where I thought she might be hid up, but no joy. Then I went up to Ogdens, which were a bit more difficult, but I went down the jiggers and looked in privvies and woodsheds, anything like that. It did cross my mind that she might have explained to one of the householders and got took in, but I don't think it's very likely. So what'll we do now, old feller?'

'I dunno,' Lenny admitted. 'Give up, I reckon; if she don't want to be found then she won't be. But sooner or later she'll gerrin touch. Remember when I first met Molly I was with a pal of mine called

Dick? His pa was in the army and got sent up to Scotland two years ago, but Dick and meself have stayed pals. We write to each other quite often, so Father O'Leary wouldn't be suspicious if I received one or two extra letters. Give her a chance to get settled somewhere and an envelope addressed to me will be pinned to the board, you wait and see. So no need to fret; cats allus land on their feet, they say, and I've often thought Molly was just like a little cat, purrin' like a Norton when things went right, but put a foot wrong and those sharp old claws would have you.'

Bumble chuckled. 'There was a cat down on the docks,' he observed. 'Ever so friendly it was, wound its way round my legs and purred like any-thin'. It even jumped up on to one of the lorries, which saved me searchin' there 'cos I remember somebody sayin' Molly was scared stiff of cats. If one had landed on her hiding place she'd have squeaked with fright.'

Lenny turned astonished eyes on his friend. 'Wherever did you hear that? Molly ain't afraid of cats, she loves 'em. It's dogs what scare her.'

Bumble stared. 'Then that cat *was* tryin' to tell me somethin', I reckon,' he said. 'Oh, Lenny, what a fool I've been! What better hidin' place could a slip of a girl find than a cargo of fleeces, all soft and warm. That's where's she's hid! I've got to get back to the docks right away and you'd better come with

94

me. Once she knows she's in the clear and it's us she'll pop out like a mouse out of a cheese. And we're in luck; you said that Father O'Leary and Matron said we were to keep our eyes open for her, so we're doin' just what the authorities want us to do. Come on!'

Down at the docks Bumble grinned at his companion. 'I knew you wouldn't let our Molly down,' he said. 'It's not far now. I remember the lorry had a big green tarpaulin over it and it was parked close to a large pile of fish boxes; in fact it was . . . oh, no!'

The lorry with the fleeces had gone.

For a moment, Bumble was almost struck dumb. He stared at the spot where the lorry had stood as though he expected it to materialise under the heat of his gaze. Then he turned imploring eyes on Lenny.

'It were there, I swear to God that's the exact spot, and now it's gone like mist in sunshine,' he gasped. 'Oh, Lenny, wherever it's gone our Molly will have gone with it. *Now* what do we do?'

Lenny stared at the gap in the line of vehicles and then back to his friend. 'Are you absolutely positive, old feller?' he asked at length. 'After all, you only saw the lorry for a few minutes, and anyway Molly might have woken when the engine started and climbed down on to the roadway. If so – and if she's got a grain of sense – she might easily have gone back to the home. I know I was having difficulty getting through the pantry window but Molly's half my size. Yes, she'll have woke when the lorry driver started his engine and gone straight back to Haisborough to find me, thinking no one else would be awake at this hour of night.'

Chapter Five

Molly was dreaming. First her dream took her back to the home, where she was being chased by Matron and all the staff, who were accusing her of every villainy under the sun. Only Lenny stuck up for her, vowing she would never take what was not hers, and then the boy she knew as Bumble came to her aid. He grabbed her hand and opened the gate which led into the jigger.

'Run, Molly!' he exclaimed. 'You don't want to get thrown into prison, do you?'

Before Molly could answer him the scene changed. She and Bumble were in what must be a police cell, with barred windows and a hard little bench against the wall, and before her very eyes Bumble was getting bigger and bigger until Molly was squeezed hard up against the bench. She had recently read *Alice's Adventures in Wonderland* and remembered the part of the book in which Alice takes a bite of cake and begins to grow enormous. So now she jerked at the huge Bumble's sleeve.

'If you get any bigger you'll squeeze me to death, Bumble,' she said. 'And if the jailer tries to come in there won't be room. Oh, I'm so frightened. I didn't take Matron's horrid watch and she won't stop the scuffers from thinking I did. Can't you *do* something?'

'*Do* somethin'?' the enormous Bumble echoed. 'Course I can, you silly girl. If you don't like the way I am now I can change in a trice.'

Molly had begun to ask him to do so immediately when the pressure on her suddenly disappeared, and where a large boy had stood seconds earlier she saw a perfectly ordinary bumblebee. She was about to ask if the boy could transform her into a bumblebee too when once more the scene changed. She was at the seaside, at the very spot where the pupils in her class had gone on a Sunday school treat the previous year. There was no sign of Bumble, but to her enormous relief, when she dug her spade into the sand, someone came up and stood beside her, and it was Lenny. 'Hello, queen,' he said cheerfully. 'Well, you served your sentence in prison and now they're going to let you fly an aeroplane, like what I do. Ain't we the lucky ones?'

Molly stared at him, eyes rounding with horror. 'I couldn't possibly fly an aeroplane,' she said wildly. 'Nor I don't want to. I'm gonna stay here, on this lovely golden beach, and get a nice safe job on the ground. You're the one what wants to fly, so just you carry on . . .'

Click! And she was sitting in the cockpit of an aeroplane with Lenny beside her, and instead of feeling terror she felt quite ordinary and was able to look out over the side of the plane and see the land far below.

'There's the beach, and the pleasure gardens and all the lovely things we saw last year,' she shouted. There was no engine noise but the wind was strong and presently Lenny got out of his seat and began to strap on a parachute.

'Have a good journey,' he said cheerfully. 'I'm off to join the Royal Air Force,' and he pushed back the cockpit cover and stepped out on to the wing as if it was the most natural thing in the world.

All Molly's fears came rushing back. 'Don't leave me!' she squeaked. 'If you're goin' to get out I'm gettin' out too.' And with that she grabbed hold of Lenny's shoulders and the pair of them plunged earthwards, whilst above them the parachute bloomed like a huge exotic flower, stopping their abrupt descent and turning it into a gentle floating experience. 'We're goin' to land in trees,' Molly said dreamily. 'Or no, there's a clearing directly below us. Oh, Lenny, this is the most loveliest thing that's ever happened to me. I wish it could go on for ever.'

'It's a dream, goose,' Lenny said with a chuckle. 'You've got to wake up, wake up, WAKE UP!'

In the dream Molly had been quite warm and comfortable, but now she was aware of a cold draught coming from somewhere, and a snow-flake – or perhaps it was a teardrop – touching her cheek. Someone was talking, a man with a rough voice and an unfamiliar accent. He seemed to be grumbling about something and suddenly Molly was wide awake. In the blink of an eye she remembered everything: Matron's fob watch, Jane's accusation and her own flight. She remembered climbing into the lorry and hiding amongst the fleeces. Gingerly she untucked the tarpaulin and sat up, and as she did so she realised that the lorry was moving, not fast, not at first; it felt as though it was going round a very sharp corner. Molly told herself afterwards that had she abandoned ship at once and jumped from the lorry as soon as she woke things might have been very different. As it was she scrambled to her knees just as the lorry picked up speed. Peering out through the slit in the canvas, still fogged with sleep, she realized that darkness had fallen since she had climbed aboard. All she could see in the glow of the headlights was trees and snow, and the only sounds were the clatter of the engine and the howling of the wind.

Molly sat back on the pile of fleeces whilst she thought what to do next. The main thing was to get herself off the lorry before the driver realised there was a stowaway on board, but jumping out of the vehicle whilst it careered along what appeared to be a very winding and narrow country lane would be complete madness. Staying quiet but alert, ready to bale out – shades of her dream – at the first opportunity would be the sensible thing to do. We're bound to come to a town or a village soon, so perhaps it would be better if I waited, she was thinking, when the driver suddenly jammed on his brakes and his passenger, caught unawares, shot across the lorry and crashed head first into a hitherto hidden obstacle. There was a moment of pain, and then darkness descended and she knew no more.

When Molly came to herself she was lying in the hollow of the roots of a great tree, and when she sat up there was no sign of the lorry. But there was something wet and sticky running down the side of her face and when she felt it cautiously she realised that it was blood. Somehow or other she had collided with something in the lorry and received a blow on the head which had rendered her unconscious. Molly looked around and saw only trees and snow and, above her head, a gleam of moonlight. Cautiously, for movement hurt her head, she got to her knees and then to her feet. Slowly and carefully she scanned her surroundings and then gave a little squeak. When the driver had accelerated after jamming on his brakes he had clearly not noticed his unconscious passenger sliding off the lorry behind him, and now she saw that she had brought with her, quite involuntarily, one of the fleeces. Perhaps he might come back for it, she thought hopefully, and then shook her head at her own foolishness. There must have been forty or fifty fleeces aboard that lorry. The driver would hardly notice had he lost half a dozen; the fact that one was missing would make no impression on him whatsoever.

Reluctantly, Molly climbed out of her hollow and took a really good look about her. There was the road, little more than a track, the snow on it silvered by the moonlight, and had she not been so afraid she might have thought it beautiful. As it was, however, it was simply frightening, for she knew nothing of the country, had no idea where she was, and feared that wild beasts might attack her at any moment. The obvious thing to do was to wrap herself in the fleece and walk along the road until she came to a human habitation of some description, where she might ask for help. If only she knew which way the lorry had been travelling! If she went back the way they had come she supposed she would eventually find herself within striking distance of the bright city lights of Liverpool, but if she chose the wrong direction she might walk for a day and a night and not see a soul who could help her. She was feeling very shaky from the bang on the head, and after a moment she began to whimper. It was just her luck to jump from the frying pan into the fire; if she had remained in Liverpool Matron would have handed her over to the scuffers for theft and now it looked as though she would probably die of cold and hunger. The whimpers became small dry sobs; why hadn't she thought before running away from the home? If only she had gone to Lenny, or even Miss Hornby, and shown them how wrong the accusation of theft had been. Come to that, if only she hadn't climbed aboard the lorry; what on earth had possessed her to do such a foolish thing? There had been other hiding places down on the docks where she would have been safe until morning. And now here she was, certainly miles from anywhere she knew, and probably miles from anyone who might help her. She was very tired, very afraid, and anxious not to make her position worse by setting out in the wrong direction. The road obviously went somewhere, so if she waited long enough surely another vehicle would pass by? The sensible thing was to return to the hollow, wrap as much of herself as she could in the fleece and, if she was lucky, sleep until morning. If a wild animal came across her she would arm herself with one of the broken branches which would be well within her reach, and defend herself as best she might against any attack.

Molly returned to the hollow and made herself as comfortable as she could. She felt safer here than anywhere else, as though someone had deliberately settled her in the shelter of the great tree before going on their way. The rational part of her mind knew that this was rubbish; no one, no matter how hard-hearted, would leave a girl with a head wound in the middle of an empty forest. No, she must have rolled into the hollow when she fell from the lorry. Presently, to her own surprise, Molly slept. She did not dream.

Morning brought little comfort; indeed quite the opposite. For she was awoken by the sound of running water and, looking around her, she realised that a thaw had set in. She was cold, and damp, and hungry, and she had no idea in which direction civilisation lay. Reluctantly, she clambered out of her hollow and slung the fleece around her shoulders, and then she hesitated, for it was quite wet and would not offer much protection and anyway the sun was coming up, red and glowing. She would do better to travel light and as fast as she could; the fleece would only impede her progress.

Molly knew very little about the country but she remembered books she had read where the young heroes and heroines had lived off the land. Only not in February, she reminded herself. When they got lost or abandoned by cruel step-parents the trees were laden with all sorts of useful things, like fruit and nuts and berries, and leaves to hide amongst, whereas the only things these trees were laden with was snow. Even mushrooms did not grow in February, apparently. Clearly, her best hope of finding succour came with finding habitation.

She turned left and marched off, and by the time the sun was beginning to sink in the west she had had to make yet another decision: forward or back? The road from the hollow had divided in several places and with each trackway leading off Molly had had to make a choice. Now the approach of dusk terrified her and she began to retrace her steps; better the hollow you know than the hollow you don't, she found herself saying, over and over. But she might have passed that same hollow without a second glance had it not been for the fleece. It hung over a low branch and poor Molly greeted it with a cry of joy, for at least it was something familiar in the strange world in which found herself.

She clutched the fleece to her bosom as though it had been an old friend and carried it back into the hollow, thinking that next morning she would turn to the right instead of the left and before she did anything else she would go down on her knees and pray to God for someone – anyone – to come by. She was so tired that she fell asleep immediately despite her hunger, but it was an uneasy and twitchy slumber and before many hours had passed she was woken by two things. The first was the moon, shining directly on to her face, and the second was something warm and wet being drawn across her cheek. Molly's eyes shot open and she drew in her breath in a gasp of pure terror. There was a huge animal, as big as a bear – bigger – looming over her, no doubt with the intention of tearing her limb from limb. Fairly sobbing with fright she flailed at it, imploring it to go away, not to hurt her. The creature, far from being put off by this reception, lowered its head to her face again, then jumped back as Molly's shrill scream echoed round the hollow. It was a wolf! Wolves, to Molly, were as bad as bears, if not worse. Her heart was leaping about in a terrified fashion and though she had tried not to move she must have done so, for she could feel the blood trickling down the side of her face once more. Blood! It was that which had attracted the animal, as much as her plight. She must not move, yet she must wipe away the blood. Feebly she tried to turn her head and almost immediately a sharp pain arrowed through her temples and she lost consciousness once more.

Molly opened her eyes. The scene had changed: gone was the tricky silver and black of the moonlight, gone the stark outline of trees against the night sky which had been paling into dawn. Instead she realised she was lying on some sort of bed in a small wooden room, and daylight was streaming through the windows. With returning consciousness came returning fear, but when she looked cautiously around her she could see no sign of the wolf. Emboldened, she was about to move when she heard voices. It was a man and a woman and they were talking in low tones. Carefully, Molly pulled herself into a sitting position and tried to take in her surroundings. The voices had ceased as soon as she moved and she wondered whether they had been a figment of her imagination. Yet someone had driven the wolf away and brought her here, and that someone was her friend, the answer to the fervent prayer which she had been intending to utter before she left the hollow.

Without moving her head any more than was necessary, she looked around and realised she was in what she would have described as a log cabin. It was roughly made and, she imagined, not permanently lived in, but just a building where one might take shelter when night had fallen and one was still far from home. Further examination of her surroundings told her that she lay on a bed of hay and that the fleece, which she was beginning to think of as an old friend, had been rolled up and placed beneath her head. Beside the fleece was a log with a flat surface and on that makeshift table was a tin mug. With great caution Molly picked it up and saw that it contained the remnants of what looked like milk. She smiled to herself. Now that she had seen the mug she realised that it had been she who had drunk the milk. She remembered a warm soft arm, plump as a pillow, curling round her shoulders as a gentle voice had encouraged her to drink up from the tin mug its owner was holding against her still half-unconscious lips.

So she had not been imagining the voices. A man and a woman had driven away the wolf, brought her to this rough shelter and fed her milk. They had undoubtedly saved her life and, galvanised by the thought, she sat up straighter and opened her mouth.

'I'm awake,' she called, and was shocked by the croak which emerged from her dry throat. It was scarcely human, but she wanted to thank her preservers as soon as possible and so tried to speak once more. 'I'm awake,' she repeated and this time the words, though emitted in a hoarse whisper, were intelligible and brought a response. Footsteps! Someone appeared at the edge of Molly's vision. A small, plump woman, her grey hair twisted into a bun and a smile on her full, rosy mouth, appeared as if by magic. Picking up the tin mug, she proceeded to fill it from a large jug and held it out to her uninvited guest.

'I dare say you can drink this without help, now you've come properly back to us,' she said.

Her voice was soft and gentle and Molly took the mug with a murmur of thanks. The milk was warm and delicious and she took several sips before lifting her eyes again to the smiling face above her. 'You're very kind, but you must be wondering—' She stopped abruptly, jumping so violently that she spilt the milk. The wolf had reappeared by the woman's side and was looking at Molly with an intensity which roused all her former terror. She clutched the woman's hand.

'The wolf!' she quavered. 'Don't let it get me! Wolves is dangerous beasts – they kill more people than bears!'

She was annoyed rather than reassured to see that her new acquaintance was trying to hide her amusement. The woman actually seemed to find Molly's fear funny, but when Molly turned incredulous eyes upon her the amusement vanished and the woman's glance was sympathetic.

'Sinbad was the one what found you,' she said rather reproachfully. 'Ain't you even the tiniest bit grateful? You was hid up so well under that fleece that if he'd not kept whinin' and runnin' back to the hollow we might not have found you for days, by which time you'd have been dead as a herrin'.'

'Dead as a herrin',' Molly said beneath her breath. Where had she heard that phrase before? Somewhere far away from woods, dripping fleeces and log cabins. But she could not call it to mind and anyway the woman was looking at her, expecting a reply to what she had just said. 'Did you . . . did you say it was the wolf who found me?', she said shakily. 'But I've always thought wolves was wild creatures, what run in packs and pull down any living thing they fancy . . .'

The woman gave an impatient snort. 'You've been listenin' to fairy tales,' she said. 'Sinbad is what they call an Alsatian, not a wolf. I admit Alsatians ain't like St Bernards what goes around wi' a barrel of brandy on their collars and searches for injured climbers in them there Swiss Alps, but old Sinbad is just as useful in his way. All you have to say is "search" and point him in the direction you want him to go and he'll sniff out anyone on that trail, anyone at all. As for wolf packs, there ain't no wolves in this country; haven't been for many a year.'

'Oh,' Molly said weakly. She took another drink of her milk. 'The thing is I'm scared of all dogs, even little ones. I think I must have been attacked by a dog when I were only two or three and it's left me scared I'll be attacked again.' She looked hopefully up into her companion's round and rosy face. 'You won't let him come near me, will you? Only I near on died of fright when I saw his face hangin' over me and his big teeth, just like Red Riding Hood's grandma.'

The old woman laughed. 'Seeing as how you've managed to drink the milk, and you seem not to have eaten for a considerable while, I'll crumble a round of bread into the next lot and I dare say you'll manage to finish it. But first you can get off my bed, sit on the stool by the fire, and tell me how you come to be wanderin' all alone in the pine forest.'

Molly heaved a sigh, but the thought of eating real food buoyed her up. The milk had been good but now her stomach yearned for something solid. Food at the orphanage was boring and often insufficient, but she had never before known real hunger and did not like it at all, so the suggestion of bread and milk was a welcome one. Accordingly she got up out of the cosy bed of hay, lurched across the room and sat herself down on the little three-legged stool which the old woman had indicated.

'It's a long story,' she began. 'In fact, before I tell you what happened I'd better explain that I'm an orphan and I live at the Haisborough home in Liverpool. I'd just got a job in one of the factories on Love Lane, and one of the older girls was jealous . . .'

She told the story to the best of her ability and was pleased when she realised that the old woman was hanging on every word. Indeed, when she finished with the driver of the lorry jamming his brakes on, her hostess began to ask questions which Molly thought both searching and strange. She wanted to know how long it would be before the staff at the home realised that Molly had gone; would the police be searching for her? Did she have any close friends amongst the other orphans who might try to trace her? Had she been happy at Haisborough? And working in a factory was hard and dirty; did she not think she would be better off working in the open countryside, even if the money was not particularly good? In many jobs in the country, the old woman explained, workers were paid in kind, which meant that they were given eggs or turnips or foodstuff of that nature instead of cash. Molly was tempted to say that this did not sound at all attractive to her. For one thing, she was frightened of the country. The prospect of meeting wolves and bears might have receded a little but there were still foxes and badgers, and who knew whether dangerous birds of prey still flew in country skies? But she realised it would be tactless to say so.

'I'm sure Matron will tell the scuffers that I've gone missin',' she said. 'But girls and boys do take off from the home sometimes and go their own way. Some of them of course have relatives to take them in, but I'm not like that. I were dumped, so though me name's me own no relative has ever come searchin' for me and I don't s'pose they ever will.'

Briefly, because she felt that she owed the old woman the truth, she told her about that long-ago walk which had ended at the Haisborough Orphanage, and her companion nodded understandingly.

'Aye, you're what they call a foundling, more or less. Do you want to go back?' She was looking straight at Molly as she spoke and Molly hesitated. She did want to go back, but she also realised that to say so would be both rude and ungrateful. And besides, she hadn't tried out country living any more than she had tried out factory life. Either one might be just what she was looking for, but she should give them both a chance, so she hesitated for several long minutes before admitting that whilst she might miss the warmth and companionship she had known in Liverpool she most certainly did not miss the Haisborough home.

'It's all rules and regulations, and when you gets up from the dining table you're always still hungry,' she said. 'I thought I'd be in clover when I got the factory job, but no chance of that now, with Matron backing up Jane's lies and the scuffers always believing a grownup against a kid. So I s'pose I'll be best off in the country, for a while at any rate.'

The old woman had been sitting in a creaking basket chair on the opposite side of the little fire, and now she nodded several times as though Molly had said something clever.

'Well, well, well. Can I take it you'll stay with me, then, and see how country life suits you? I'm Mrs Mathias, and you are . . .?'

'I'm Molly Penelope Hardwick,' Molly said at once, though she had an uneasy feeling that it might not have been the best idea to give the old lady her real name. She wondered if they had wireless sets in this wild country; if so, they might hear if the orphanage put out a message asking anyone who saw Molly to contact them. They would pretend it was so they knew she was safe but really it would be so that they could set the scuffers on her, haul her into court and possibly even throw her in prison for a crime she had never committed.

'Molly Penelope Hardwick. Molly Penelope Hardwick,' Mrs Mathias was saying as though committing the name to memory. 'I don't think they'll come after you. After all, from what you've told me the fob watch wasn't actually stolen by anyone; you could say it was taken for a sort of silly prank. The police aren't going to be interested in what amounts to a mean trick played by one girl on another, so unless you were a favourite with the matron . . .' She laughed. 'I can see from your expression that you weren't. No, I don't think any-one will be searching for you.'

Molly opened her mouth to say that Lenny Smith was very much her friend and would most certainly search for her, then closed it again. What could Lenny do, after all? He was working towards examinations and intended to enter the Royal Air Force just as soon as he could. There were boy entrants in the navy so it was quite possible that there were boy entrants in the air force too. She remembered that he had not been there to help her when she had run away from the Haisborough. In fact no one had helped her, not even Ellen. She realised of course that everything had happened so suddenly that no one could have done much, and for all she knew Ellen might have deliberately got in the way of the pursuit, but the main thing was that because of her foolishness in climbing aboard the lorry she had ended up in a place that might be absolutely anywhere. It was a rather nasty feeling. Orphans know they are alone and must make their own way in the world, but they try not to think about it. Now she was being forced to acknowledge her aloneness and she did not like it. Indeed, she made up her mind that as soon as she reached civilisation she would write to Lenny and give him her new address. She would ask him to tell her whether she was still wanted by Matron and the police and also whether the offer of the job still stood.

Mrs Mathias was staring at the small flickering fire as though reading her fortune in the flames, and now she looked startled and indeed none too pleased to find herself abruptly addressed.

'Mrs Mathias, where are we? You were talking about farm work, but this isn't a farm, is it? Only I think I really should send a postcard to the home saying that I'm safe and well.'

Mrs Mathias looked puzzled. 'But why would you do such a thing?' she enquired. 'You don't want them scuffers on your tail, do you?'

'No-oo,' Molly said doubtfully. 'But there's no harm in simply letting them know I'm safe. However, if you think it unwise I won't include my address.'

Mrs Mathias smiled grimly and got creakingly out of the basket chair. 'You don't have an address,' she pointed out. 'We travel the length and breadth of the country and don't stay nowhere permanent. The folk that matter know where we are and the folk that don't matter . . . well, least said soonest mended. Are you goin' to come wi' us?'

Molly stared at her. 'How can you be a farmer *and* a traveller?' she asked cautiously. 'Mrs Mathias, it just don't make sense.'

Mrs Mathias's grim little smile came into play once more. 'Wait and see,' she said mysteriously. 'Just you wait and see, Miss Molly Penelope Hardwick!'

The next day Molly awoke with a blinding headache and a cough so deep and rasping that it sounded as though the big dog was barking. She was still lying on Mrs Mathias's bed, but the fleece beneath her head was damp with sweat, and when she tried to get up she felt so dizzy she collapsed back on to the hay. She called out, but what should have been a shout had again become a croaky whisper and she was about to try to rise from the bed once more when the old woman appeared from the other room. She looked Molly over critically, but when the girl would have risen to her feet – or tried to do so – she pushed her firmly back on to the hay.

'You've been and gone and got yourself a fever, muckin' about in weather like that and you wi'out so much as a proper coat,' she said severely. 'It'd be no wonder if you caught pneumonia, and no one here to nurse you back to health but my good self.'

Molly began to apologise, to say that she was sorry for being such a nuisance, but Mrs Mathias interrupted her. 'I have no doubt you'll pay me back in your own way when you're fit again,' she said. She looked critically round the log cabin. 'When me sons come for the fleeces I'll get them to fetch a basket with invalid grub and a few of my old granny's remedies, for all I've got here is bread and milk and some good bone broth. Fancy a sup?'

Molly shuddered. The previous day she would have welcomed any sort of broth but today for some reason she did not fancy food at all. When Mrs Mathias held the tin mug to her lips she was filled with revulsion and tried to turn her head away, saying fretfully that she was not thirsty and simply wanted to go back to sleep.

'Well, you can't,' Mrs Mathias said decidedly, 'or not until you've drunk this, at any rate. It's made with herbs which I pick every year and dry out in bunches hung up in the sunshine . . .'

'But I don't want to. I'm sure I can't swallow; my throat is red raw,' Molly grumbled. 'Oh, I do feel so ill; why can't you leave me be?'

'I can't leave you be; you're nothin' but a burden while the fever has you,' Mrs Mathias said crossly. 'Stop makin' such a fuss and drink my good broth or I'll call the dog.'

Molly gasped at such a cruel threat and with the gasp a mouthful of broth was sucked in and swallowed. It was bitter, and very hot, but when Molly tried to protest the old woman simply made her take another gulp, and she realised her ordeal would be over a good deal more quickly if she accepted the loathsome potion. And why should she not? She had read many times of herbal remedies which had saved the lives of people seized by strong fevers, and judging by the horrid taste she supposed it really must be doing her good. She tried to take the cup from Mrs Mathias, meaning to drain it as quickly as possible, but before she could do so the old women had tipped the mug so that she must drink the contents or drown, and as she swallowed the last mouthful she turned her eyes up to her hostess's face and tried to look grateful.

'I was going to drink it myself,' she whispered. 'I'm such a trouble to you, and I'm so sorry . . . but don't bring the dog in here, please. Once I'm well I'll do as you say and find some way to repay your kindness.'

Mrs Mathias sniffed, but she did not look displeased. 'About time you come to your senses and reckernised a well-wisher,' she said. 'Feelin' better? Sleepier?'

Molly suddenly realised that the old woman's face was looking blurred and odd, very odd indeed. Not only did Mrs Mathias have two heads instead of the usual one, but the second head looked remarkably like that of the large dog.

Horrified, Molly tried to sit up on her elbow. 'What have you given me?' she asked in a small voice. 'Was it poison?' For a moment Mrs Mathias seemed to swell with rage, but then she began to chuckle. It was an infectious laugh and Molly joined in, very soon finding herself giggling helplessly.

'I'm so silly, Mrs Mathias,' she said, tears of weakness and amusement filling her eyes and trickling down her cheeks. 'If you'd wanted me dead you wouldn't have had to poison me with broth. You could have just left me lying in the wood for your dog to gobble up.'

'Well I'm glad you've come to your senses at last,' Mrs Mathias said, producing a handkerchief and blotting the tears from her own wet cheeks. 'You're not a bad lass and I've no doubt you'll find a way to repay me when you're up and about once more; that's what we both want, ain't it? As for the dog, I'll keep him in the other room, well away from yourself. Now heed what I tell you: that broth is a fine medicine but sleep's the best remedy of all, and when next you wake you'll be well on the road to recoverin' yourself.'

Molly lifted her heavy lids and gave the old woman a tiny smile before she slid into slumber.

*

For a whole week Bumble and Lenny spent every spare moment searching for Molly and grew to know the area very well. Matron, having discovered that it was her pet, Jane, who had taken her watch, bruited it abroad that there had been no theft and inserted a notice in the newspaper asking Molly to return. *No action will be taken*, the notice said rather pompously, *since, although foolish, such a prank can be forgiven, so if Molly Penelope Hardwick will return to the Haisborough Orphanage we shall let bygones be bygones.*

But after the week had passed and there had been no response from Molly, even Bumble's anxiety began to wane. He knew Lenny was right really; had Molly wished to return she could easily have done so. Still, he kept an eye open for a large lorry with a green tarpaulin stretched over a mass of fleeces, and often went down to the docks with some small gift of food for the large black cat, because he felt that the creature had done its best to point out Molly's hiding place and he himself had not pursued it. It had not occurred to him to even so much as glance at the lorry's licence plates, so although haunting the docks whenever he had the time made him feel he was doing *something* to find Molly, it was, he knew, fruitless.

*

Molly awoke from a deep sleep. It was not the first time she had done so since Mrs Mathias had started dosing her with the broth, but this waking was different; her headache had gone completely and for the first time she felt hungry. Bread and milk actually sounded attractive. But she could not remember the past with any clarity, save that she had run away from the home and at some stage had found herself wandering in a great forest or wood. How and where Mrs Mathias and Sinbad had found her she had no idea and decided it would be useless to ask, at least until her own mind was clearer.

She heard the burr of voices coming from the other room and opened her mouth to call out that she was awake, but then she stopped short. She had heard her own name and it was pronounced, not in Mrs Mathias's gentle voice, but by a man. She listened hard; it might be eavesdropping, it might be sneaky, but they knew she was there and were scarcely likely to whisper secrets, even if they did believe her to be still sleeping off whatever it was that Mrs Mathias's broth contained. So she sat creakily up on one elbow and listened with all her might.

'How long is you goin' to keep this girl, this Molly, in the lap o' luxury, with you waitin' on her hand and foot?' the man said querulously. 'I should have thought you'd enough on your plate wi'out addin' a sick girl to your load. Even if she were fit I reckon she'd be more of a burden than a help. I took a peek at her earlier and I admit she looks better now and could probably help you with the housework when she's back on her feet – cookin' and that – but I think she knows too much. How d'you know she won't blab?'

Mrs Mathias chuckled. 'When she first come she answered any question I asked, so o' course I got it all out of her. She's an orphan, dumped in a Liverpool orphanage when she were three or so, and she's a runaway. The woman in charge branded her a thief and threatened her with the Garda, so she upped and ran. Silly thing to do, 'cos I'd swear she never took nothin' that weren't hers, but she was scared, see—'

The man cut across Mrs Mathias's gentle tones and this time there was amusement in his voice. 'A little thief, eh? Well she's come to the right place. And no parents, you said? No aunts or uncles, no cousins, nor grans or grandpas. Well, that's all to the good . . . if you want her to stay, that is. I s'pose you could say she'd be company, if you're sure of her. But we don't want no spies in the camp.'

Molly was so surprised at the turn the conversation had taken that she jumped and knocked over the tin mug, spilling the remains of Mrs Mathias's broth on to the clean wooden floor. It did not make much noise but the man must have had exceptional hearing for he spoke at once, his voice sharp.

'What were that? You said . . .'

Molly knew she must act quickly or forfeit the trust which Mrs Mathias had placed in her. She flung out one arm from its thin blanket covering, and when Mrs Mathias came to her bedside she kept her eyes closed, trying to look as though she had turned over in her sleep and knocked the mug on the floor as she did so. The older woman put her hand to Molly's forehead, then ran it across her cheek.

'Time you had another sup of me broth,' she said gently. 'Or would you rather have bread and milk?'

Molly pretended not to hear, and presently the old woman went away, but it was not until Molly heard the male voice talking again, and on other subjects, that she stirred on her hay bed and gave a feeble call.

Mrs Mathias appeared at her bedside with a bowl which steamed gently, and Molly smiled up at her. 'Do you know, I actually feel hungry? Is that bread and milk? I'm sure I could eat all of it, and probably something more solid too. I must be getting better if the thought of food doesn't make me feel ill.'

Mrs Mathias smiled back. 'There's a grand rabbit stew simmerin' on the fire,' she announced. 'Just you eat up this bread and milk and by evenin' time you'll be ready to try it.'

'Can I get up now, as I feel so much stronger?' Molly said as soon as she had eaten the last spoonful of bread and milk. 'I expect I'll be a bit wobbly at first, because I've been in bed for days and days, haven't I? Only now I feel so much better I think some gentle exercise would help me get back to normal in no time. You've been so good, Mrs Mathias, but I s'pose I really must be on my way. Only I can't really remember where I was goin' when you found me. There was somethin' about a gold watch, and a job . . . oh dear, I'm afraid I'm still dreadfully confused.'

Mrs Mathias twinkled at her and Molly reflected once more how much easier it was to be grateful to her rescuer when she was smiling.

'Sit up first, get up later,' the old woman advised. 'Heard the expression mustn't run before you can walk? Well, that's very true. You've been bedfast longer than you realise, but you're gettin' better every hour. If you sit up now and get up this evenin' I don't reckon you'll need my broth to help you sleep, and by tomorrer mornin' – or the next day at the latest – you'll be fit as a flea.'

When the old woman had left her, Molly smiled to herself. So there *had* been something in the broth, something which had made her sleepy, even if it had not actually sent her to sleep. Mrs Mathias was right; with the return of her appetite the desperate desire for rest had left her. Already her thoughts were clearer as the fog which had hidden the past from her began to thin.

So that night, when Mrs Mathias had retired to the makeshift bed she had set up for herself in the far corner of the room, Molly lay and thought about the home, her friend Lenny, good little Ellen and big, well-meaning Bumble. When she had been accused of stealing Matron's gold watch she had known they would believe in her. Then there was Miss Hornby; Molly was certain that she, who had trusted Molly with her own beloved books, would stoutly defend her. But by running away Molly might have made it difficult for her supporters. She looked round the cabin, dark but for the glow from the fire. Whilst the weather was so bitter, Mrs Mathias had informed her, she kept the fire in day and night, even to the extent of getting up in the early hours to add fresh logs to those smouldering in the grate.

'Whilst you're poorly you need to be kept warm,' she had said on one occasion. 'But you're getting stronger with every day that passes.' She had chuckled. 'Soon it'll be your job to make up the fire at two in the morning; chilly work but important.'

Now, thinking back, Molly realised that Mrs Mathias had shown no enthusiasm about the idea of her guest's leaving the shelter of her roof, and she remembered the conversation she should not have heard. Mrs Mathias had looked after Molly no doubt from the kindness of her heart, but now she had every intention of asking the girl to remain with her. And why should she not? So far as the old woman knew her unexpected guest was alone in the world, as lonely in fact as Mrs Mathias herself. When Molly had said she would repay her for her generosity she had merely meant she would help around the house until she was fully fit again. Then she really must return to the orphanage, for how else could she clear her name? She did not suppose for one moment that Mrs Mathias wanted her as a permanent companion, but merely as someone to chat to until she left the log cabin and the forest behind her and moved on. Thinking it over, Molly realised she could be nothing more than a house guest even had she wanted to stay, for she was afraid of the dog and even more afraid of the wild creatures – rabbits, badgers, foxes, weasels – which she knew from her reading inhabited the wild woods. She would be of little help to the old woman outdoors if she was perpetually looking behind her and expecting trouble.

In the opposite bed Mrs Mathias gave a groan, turned on to her back and began to snore loudly. Molly giggled. She decided that as they ate their breakfast porridge next morning she would explain to Mrs Mathias that she must go home eventually to face the music, but would stay for a short while at least to help in any way she could. Satisfied, she closed her eyes, but at that moment Mrs Mathias gave another loud groan and began to mutter. Molly grinned to herself; she was not the only one who talked in her sleep. Stealthily she sat up on her hay bed and leaned towards her companion, listening hard. Mrs Mathias mumbled some more and then began to speak more clearly.

'Set a thief to catch a thief,' she announced, and giggled. 'She wants that job in the factory for money, so if I offers her a job here why shouldn't she take it and stay wi' me? If it weren't for Sinbad she'd not hesitate. Drat the girl! I need Sinbad; he's the best. Why can't she see that?'

There was another short pause whilst the old woman made a chumbling sound with her mouth, and Molly, looking at her face, got quite a shock. On the box she used as a bedside table reposed a glass of water in which lay a set of false teeth.

Despite herself, Molly smiled. So that was why Mrs Mathias sounded different from the way she sounded during the day, but before she could stop to consider the hazards of ageing the old woman was off again.

'Ah, but I forgot me boyo in me calculations. One glance out of them lovely blue eyes and there'll be no more talk of leavin'. The girl what can resist me laddo ain't been born yet, so we're safe enough. Besides, me little helper is no fool; she won't run away from good food and a roof over her head. What's a factory job compared with being in the country?' She sighed deeply and began to mumble again, this time about her youth, when her husband had been alive and her children young. She sounded so wistful that Molly felt like the spy the man had thought her. Guiltily she pulled her blanket up over her head, and before Mrs Mathias's words had ceased she was fast asleep.

Next day she got up before her hostess and slipped into the next room to start preparing breakfast. As she worked, she went over everything she had heard in the last twenty-four hours and found only some of it made sense. The strange man had seemed at first not to approve of her at all, but then he had apparently changed his mind and talked of her staying with the old woman for as long as she wanted the company. As for Mrs Mathias herself, on reflection Molly could not make head nor tail of her ramblings. All she was sure of was that Sinbad was necessary to the old woman, for he would undoubtedly fly to his mistress's defence, teeth bared, should she need protection. Molly knew that the big dog roamed outside the cabin, both at night and during the day, and warned his mistress of the approach of any strangers. She assumed he had a kennel into which he retreated when he felt the need to sleep or when the weather was bad, but the rest of the time he padded softly around the clearing, discouraging visitors.

She worked away busily, spooning tea into the pot whilst keeping an eye on her porridge, simmering on the old-fashioned black woodburning stove. Presently, Mrs Mathias joined her, nodding approvingly as Molly ladled porridge on to two tin plates and sprinkled each helping with coarse brown sugar. Then she poured the tea, added a dash of milk from the can keeping cool on the windowsill and settled herself at the table.

'Grand to have me breakfast made for me,' Mrs Mathias said happily. 'You and me gerralong just fine, and we'll be even better when the lorries begin to come through.'

'Through?' Molly said, rather surprised. She could not see how any lorry, or van, or other vehicle could possibly wend its way amongst the trees to end up in the clearing. She said as much, which made Mrs Mathias chuckle again.

'That's where you and me come in,' she said contentedly. 'We's meet the lorry by the track and unload the stock and bring it to the cabin, where it'll stay until me laddos have found a buyer.'

'Oh, I see,' Molly said rather helplessly, for she did not see at all, and judging from the glance the old woman shot her Mrs Mathias was well aware of it.

'Never mind, queen,' she said. 'You'll understand all right once we get a-goin' again. Ever heard that poem by that feller Kipling?'

Her grin broadened so much that Molly felt that another inch or so would see the top of her head fall off, but then she put such thoughts aside and remembered with real nostalgia all the poems she had learned by heart to please Miss Hornby.

'Which one? He wrote an awful lot,' she said guardedly.

But Mrs Mathias shook her head. 'Never mind, never mind,' she said genially. 'You'll find out in your own good time, I make no doubt.'

As Molly grew stronger Mrs Mathias began to explain the differences between the great city of Liverpool and the countryside in which it seemed a family like the Mathiases went about their daily business. At first Molly secretly thought these lessons were a waste of time since she had no intention of staying here once she felt she had paid off her debt to the old woman. It also worried her a little that most of the people who came to the log cabin came at night; why should this be so? And she had still not met her companion's sons, for such she assumed 'me laddos' to be. And then, after two or three weeks – she found she was losing track of time – she finally put two and two together. When the boxes of cigarettes were neatly stacked at the back of the log cabin before undertaking their onward journey she stared accusingly at the old woman.

'*So watch the wall, my darling, when the Gentlemen go by,*' she quoted. 'That's out of the poem by Kipling, "A Smuggler's Song". You're smugglers, aren't you, or even something worse. Oh, Mrs Mathias, don't say you're something worse!'

Mrs Mathias cackled, sounding so like the wicked witch in the fairy tale that Molly winced. Why wasn't life simple, she mused crossly. One minute Mrs Mathias sounded, and indeed behaved, like everyone's favourite granny and the next minute like a . . . well, like a wicked witch in a fairy tale. If only she always cackled or always chuckled, life would be so much simpler. But now Mrs Mathias was speaking.

'Ever heard of "dockers' perks"? You must have heard of dockers! Them fellers works damned hard for small wages. They risks their lives to bring in goods from foreign countries, and because the bosses don't shell out enough for a docker to save for a rainy day the fellers help themselves now and then . . . a few boxes of cigarettes here, a big bunch of bananas there . . . see what I mean? Sometimes they can sell the stuff in the dockside pubs, but now we've got ourselves organised me and me laddos sell wharrever the dockies can't move theirselves, so we does it for them. Satisfied?'

This conversation took place as the two women were sitting over the stove, each nursing a tin mug of tea, for the weather had not improved; in fact if anything it had worsened. The thick curtain had not been pulled across one of the windows, and outside Molly could see snow whirling in the spiteful wind, which occasionally knocked the contents of a branch down on to the forest floor. She began to speak, but Mrs Mathias cut across her.

'I allus tell folks we're like that chap what ruled Sherwood Forest, many a year ago,' she said. 'Robin Hood, weren't that his name? He took from the rich and give to the poor, and that's what me and my lads is doin'. Call it smugglin' if you wish, but the way I see it we're savin' the lives of folk who might die of hunger if it weren't for us. Do you agree?'

Molly was torn. She had always admired Robin Hood and was secretly rather struck by Mrs Mathias's explanation, but she knew that now the truth was out at last she must make up her mind when to return to Princes Row. Surely if she stayed just a couple more weeks she would have repaid her debt to the old woman? And once back at the home she would explain her absence by some as yet undecided means and hope that she could prove she had never so much as entered Matron's quarters. Of course it would have been better had she returned sooner, but if she was still disbelieved she could always take off again. She did not mean to contact the staff, not even Miss Hornby, until she had spoken to her friends and taken their advice.

So when Mrs Mathias barked out 'Well?' she gave her a reluctant smile.

'It's all right, Mrs Mathias. If you like to consider yourselves modern-day Robin Hoods that's fine by me, but I s'pose you know there are folk who would call it by another name. Still, that's none of my business. And seeing that you've explained what you do I think it only fair to explain to you why I ran away from the home – unless I did already? My mind is still a bit fuzzy, and I can't remember how much I told you when you first brought me here.'

'Tell on,' Mrs Mathias said. 'Let's say I know nothing, save what you're going to tell me now.'

'Right,' Molly said, and then noticed the twinkle in her companion's eyes. I gave away more than I thought when I was ill, she guessed. But never mind. I'll willingly tell my story again if it means Mrs Mathias and I have both told the whole truth. 'Well, it was like this . . .'

She finished her story with a flourish, explaining that, had she not tucked herself away amongst the fleeces, she would have returned to the home the next day and consulted with her friends how best to prove her innocence.

Mrs Mathias looked smug. 'So that was how you came to be wanderin' in the forest, luv,' she said. She chuckled, her rosy face once more split by a huge grin. 'There's them as might not believe you, but I ain't one of 'em. So long as you think of me as a sort of modern Robin Hood, I'm content to believe your story.'

At this point Molly was tempted to say that Mrs Mathias's own story was every bit as hard to swallow as hers, and to point out that she still had every intention of returning to the home to clear the whole matter up, but as she opened her mouth she remembered Mrs Mathias's many kindnesses, and closed it again. No point in upsetting the boat just yet.

At that moment the door of the cabin burst open and a figure entered the room, saying as he began to divest himself of coats, waterproofs, scarves and leather gauntlets: 'Mammy, 'tis the sort of weather not even a dog should be out; Sinbad is right in the back of his kennel, but I dare say he'd sooner be indoors. Shall I fetch him?'

Mrs Mathias had got to her feet as soon as the intruder – clearly one of her sons – had entered the cabin. 'I'll put the kettle on . . .' she was beginning when Molly, seeing the young man turning back towards the door, gave a gasp of horror which stopped him in his tracks. He swung round to face her.

'Sure and wasn't I forgettin'?' he said in a rich Irish brogue. 'Dis is the little colleen what don't like dogs.' He held out a broad tanned hand. 'Sure and aren't you the prettiest t'ing ever to grace me mammy's cabin? But I must introduce myself. I'm Cian Mathias, what you might call the youngest, for Declan's older'n me, and you'll be – oh, the devil take it, you've some long fancy name, but Mammy calls you Molly. Sure and haven't you wended your way into her heart, so I'll t'ink of you as me pretty little sister. Oh, I could kill for a cup of tay, so I could.' He plunged a hand into his pocket and produced a bottle which he waved enticingly towards the two women. ''Tis brandy; a tot of this in a cup o' tay sets a man – or a woman for that matter – up for whatever lies ahead.' He picked up the clothing which he had flung to the floor and draped it across a ladder-backed chair near the stove. 'That'll dry off nicely,' he announced. He smiled blindingly at Molly and she saw that he had the brightest blue eyes, a handsome, devil-may-care face and a red bandanna worn as pirates wear them around his black and curly hair.

Molly thought she had never seen anyone so handsome and charming in her whole life. When he smiled it was as though the cabin was suddenly bathed in sunlight, despite the fact that it was after ten o'clock at night. But he had asked her something; she must not let him see her admiration.

'Oh! I'm – I'm Molly Penelope Hardwick,' she said rather breathlessly. 'And you'll be . . . Cian, did you say? And – and if you promise not to let Sinbad come near me I s'pose you can let him into the warm.'

The young man promptly crossed the cabin, flung open the door and called the dog's name. Sinbad trotted into the room, gave a quick shake to rid himself of the few flakes which had landed on his ruff on the way and went and sat by the stove where Mrs Mathias was preparing to brew the tea. He cast a glance at Molly which could have been one of reproach.

Once more the young man spoke to the dog, telling him to lie down and then stay where he was; then he turned to Molly.

'I'll be here on and off while the weather stays cruel so I'll have time on me hands to prove to you our Sinbad's a broth of a dog, and not one to hurt a pal, I promise you.'

Despite her admiration of his master, the thought of getting to know Sinbad better did not appeal to Molly at all. With a shudder, she remembered their previous encounter. A couple of days before, the fire in the stove had burned low and

Mrs Mathias had suggested that Molly might step outside and collect the odd branch which the weight of snow had brought down. Molly had been willing, even eager, and had tugged round her the borrowed cloak which Mrs Mathias had told her she might use. It had a hood and was made of some rough but warm material, and since the snow had temporarily stopped Molly found that she was glad of an excuse to get some exercise. She had looked closely around her before setting off, but it seemed that Sinbad was away on some business of his own, so she had not felt constrained by his presence. Indeed, she had found herself looking forward to a bit of a wander through the forest. She had set off quite merrily, having carefully checked again that Sinbad was not in sight, but no sooner had she stepped outside the clearing than she had a feeling that she was being watched. She stopped in her tracks, looking cautiously around her. No one. No large dog, no Mrs Mathias, not even a rabbit. Imagination, she had told herself crossly, and began to move once more.

Immediately, the big dog had appeared before her on the little path she had chosen. He did not bark or threaten, did not in fact move unless she did, but it was soon obvious that for some reason best known to himself he thought she ought to return to the clearing, and when she tried a tentative step forward his upper lip curled and he showed her an excellent set of teeth. Wolf's teeth, Molly thought.

Gulping with fear she had hastily retraced her steps, but when she told Mrs Mathias that Sinbad had followed her the old woman had laughed indulgently.

'He were accompanying you to make sure you didn't come to harm,' she had explained. 'You'd be a deal safer with Sinbad to keep an eye on you than you would be without him.'

Molly had said nothing more, but there and then she had decided that, when the time came to leave, she would ask the old woman to shut him in the cabin; otherwise, no doubt, he would consider it his duty to drive her back into what he plainly considered his territory.

But now Cian was looking down at her, one dark brow raised. 'Well? Will you let me teach you to know forest life – and Sinbad – better?' He grinned wickedly. 'I'm a grand teacher so I am, and you'll be a grand pupil.'

Molly felt a blush warming her cheeks. It was tempting to say she would love to be his pupil, but was it fair? Though her inward image of Lenny had grown somewhat faint of late, she knew she owed it to him to let him know where she was. And only a few minutes before she had decided that she should get back to the home as soon as she could and sort things out. She was fit now.

But now . . . Molly's heart gave a couple of uneven thumps . . . she desperately wanted to take up Cian's suggestion. After all, what did the city offer her when you came down to it? A bed in number four dormitory, meagre food, a place on the bench in the munitions factory – if the job was even still open – and that was about it. On the other hand there were her friends: funny little Ellen, on Molly's side no matter what, and Lenny who would have laughed scornfully at the idea that she was dishonest.

And now there was Cian, the handsomest young man she had ever dreamed of meeting, and he had referred to her as his pretty little sister! Made her feel like a member of a real family – something she had always longed for but never known. If she agreed to stay in the forest for a few more weeks, or maybe even months, then judging from what Cian had said she would be spending a great deal of time with him. Wasn't that worth a good deal more than trekking back through the forest, back to Princes Row and the Haisborough Orphanage, and the possibility of facing punishment for a crime she didn't commit?

Cian was still looking down at her quizzically and Molly broke into hasty speech. 'It's awful good of you, Cian, but I really should go back to Liverpool . . .'

Mrs Mathias, putting three mugs of strong tea down on the table, interrupted. 'Are you thinkin' of leavin' me?' she said pathetically. ''Tis awful lonely, I've been stuck out in the middle of the forest wi' no companion save for the dog.' She pushed one of the mugs towards her son and the other towards Molly. 'Why not write a letter to one of your pals, explainin' where you are and how you're lookin' after a poor old woman, cut off from civilisation in the heart of the great forest? Tell 'em you're safe and well, tell 'em you're happy wi' good friends, and say you're needed here.' She settled herself once more in the creaky old basket chair and held out her mug for Cian to pour into it a judicious amount of the brandy. When Cian would have given Molly some, however, she shook a chiding head. 'None of that, Cian,' she said rather sharply. 'Molly's too young for strong drink; the tea will warm her enough.' She turned to Molly. 'I've no paper by me but next time he comes Cian will bring you a sheet or so and an envelope, and you can write your letter.'

'Well?' Cian said encouragingly. 'Is you goin' to accept me kind offer? Soon spring will be here and the last thing on your mind will be a return to the city. There's work on the farms for a strong young woman, paid work. But you contact your pals if it'll make you feel better, and when they reply you can put the whole matter out of your head.'

'Right,' Molly said happily. Once she was able to send a letter to Lenny she was sure he would write back. The only thing that puzzled her a little was that she had several times asked Mrs Mathias to give her paper and pencil so that she could write to him explaining the situation, and had always been put off, the old lady each time quoting one cause or another which stopped her from providing writing materials.

It was soon obvious to Molly that Cian was a good deal more reliable than his mother, for when he did return to the cabin almost a week later he brought with him a sheet of blue lined paper and a rather scruffy envelope – had he rescued it from a rubbish tip? Molly found herself wondering unkindly – with the original address crossed out but enough space left for her to write in the home's.

'Thanks ever so much, Cian; it'll be a weight off my mind once the letter's gone off,' Molly said joyfully. 'I'll have to give Lenny an address, of course, though I can't think what it can be.' She giggled. 'Would "log cabin in the forest" find us, do you think? Only I can't imagine a postman pushing his way through all those trees.' She giggled again. 'And then there's Sinbad . . .'

Cian wrinkled his beautiful nose. 'What's the hurry?' he asked. 'This here Lenny Smith, or Brown, or Clarke – can't remember what name you called him – is a part of your past.' He grinned wickedly at her, raising a black brow. 'He's probably forgot all about you by now; the mammy was tellin' me she found you in February and March is almost over. Still, if you want to write to him anyway, who am I to stop you?' He handed the blue page to her as he spoke and Molly sighed, but took it.

She did not wish to antagonise Cian by saying that Lenny would not have forgotten her, indeed would come to her aid if she told him she was in trouble. Not that I am in trouble, she reminded herself quickly, smiling into Cian's beautiful face. I've got good friends here who will see me right, and I am, I know, useful to them. It isn't just that I'm getting to know the tracks and can guide the drivers to and from the cabin; if it wasn't for me I don't think 'the mammy', as Cian calls her, would stay in the forest. Several times she's had a moan to me, saying she would like a share of the action, whatever that may mean. But I gather that somewhere well away from here they have some sort of shop or trading post where they exchange these 'dockers' perks' for hard cash. Again I suppose I'm guessing, but it seems to me that they want to buy property here, a good solid farm perhaps. If that is so perhaps they could find me work on the farm; well, I'm sure they could. Paid work what's more, because of course I don't get paid for what I do here. And why should I? If it hadn't been for Mrs Mathias I'd have died back in February, like a babe in the wood, falling asleep under the snow and being found when the thaw came, dead as a herring.

But at this point Mrs Mathias announced that supper was ready, and Molly shoved the sheet of paper and the envelope into her pocket and decided that her letter could wait. The important thing now was supper but as soon as it was eaten and cleared away she would have the leisure to write to Lenny.

Later, sitting by the stove and chewing the end of the rather blunt pencil which Mrs Mathias had found for her, Molly realised she had set herself an almost impossible task. She had intended to tell her story right from the moment when she had woken up in the back of the lorry, but soon realised that this was impossible: she could not give the Mathias family away by explaining what they were doing in the middle of the forest. In the end the letter consisted of half a dozen lines written with a blunt pencil saying nothing other than that she was well, amongst friends, and would come back to the orphanage as soon as she was able, in order to clear her name.

Cian had been hovering over her while she wrote, and she had felt obliged to let him read the epistle before tucking it into the envelope and addressing it. Cian had read it without comment and she suddenly realised she had not given Lenny a return address. Laughing, she pointed out the lack to Cian, who raised both brows this time.

'Why should you want to give him an address, when you know full well we don't want folk interfering with us?' he said. 'If you want to go back to . . .' he glanced at the front of the envelope, 'to this Princes Row, then you'd not be coming back to us, would you? You'd settle into your old life and never think of the Mathiases again.'

'Oh, Cian, as if I could ever forget you, or your mammy!' Molly said, dismayed. 'I only want Lenny to have my address so he can write and tell me if I'm still believed to have taken the gold watch. I just hate the thought of folk believing I'd steal; can't you understand that?'

Cian sniffed. 'What does it matter what people think? Sure and if it was your friends that'd be different, but you say they know you're no thief. Tell you what, though, I'd planned to take time off from me work to introduce you to the countryside, country ways and such. But if you're goin' to go back to that there orphanage I'll not waste me time.'

At the mere thought of a treat like Cian's company being withheld Molly felt the blood drain from her cheeks. She had not been certain that Cian had actually meant what he said about teaching her, and she could not wait to assure him that she would not disclose to Lenny or anyone else the Mathiases' whereabouts.

'Cian! How ungrateful you must think me,' she said quickly. 'Of course it's not necessary to give Lenny your address. So long as he knows I'm safe and happy.'

She was gazing anxiously into Cian's face as she spoke. He had been frowning heavily but at her words he began to smile once more.

'Well, so long as you're sure,' he said, and even his voice sounded pleased. 'Then your lessons shall begin at dawn when I next come back. I know Mammy managed to get hold of some clothing for you so you'll want to put on a pair of trousers – skirts snag on every bramble – and the little brown jerkin 'cos it's cool in the forest before the sun comes up. Then the two of us will go adventurin' until you're as wise to the ways of the country as I am meself.' He clicked his fingers and held out an imperative hand. 'Give me the letter; I'll see it is posted. Are you sure, now, that you don't want to give this pal of yours an address?'

'Not if you really mean to teach me everything I should know about country ways,' Molly said quickly, but behind her back she was crossing her fingers. She realised that much though she liked Cian, there might come a day when she needed to make sure the slate was clean, and that would mean a return to the orphanage. For now, though, she saw Cian off with a light heart, for he had promised to be away for no longer than a couple of weeks this time, and then her lessons would definitely begin.

Cian was as good as his word; better, in fact. He walked into the cabin only a week after he had left it and beamed at her.

'Sit down and listen whiles I tell you what I did,' he demanded. 'Didn't I t'ink me little pal Molly Penelope Hardwick wasn't the sort to take anythin' which weren't her own? So I went to the orphanage and skulked around it for the best part of a day. Some girl told me where to leave the letter, and I asked her about the matron's gold watch . . . and you can relax, pretty Miss Hardwick. She telled me there had been no hue and cry after me little pal, so you can stop worryin'. The culprit was some girl called . . .'

'Jane! I bet it was Jane!' Molly said happily. 'Was it?' And on Cian's nod: 'I might have guessed; well, I did. She wanted the job in the munitions factory which had been offered to me and of course she was Matron's favourite, always in and out of Matron's quarters. I s'pose she planted it in my things and someone told Matron they'd seen her do it. Was that it?'

'More or less,' Cian assured her. 'Anyway, you're in the clear!'

Molly flung herself at Cian, throwing her arms about his neck and kissing his cheek. 'Oh, thank you, Cian. You're a better friend even than Lenny.'

'Now I hope there'll be no more talk about wantin' to go back to the home, 'cos you've no

146

need to clear your name any more.' He grinned. 'We'll start your education as soon as possible.'

*

Bumble missed Lenny. He had not joined up himself but meant to do so as soon as war was declared, though whether he would be allowed to leave the factory job which he had held since he left the home was questionable. He had mentioned the matter to his manager, who had shrugged.

'I shouldn't say so, because munitions is essential work, but I dare say we could turn a blind eye,' the manager had said. 'After all, if you join one of the forces you'd be fighting for your country, and with so many girls itching to take on a well-paid job there'd be no shortage of replacements.'

One day Bumble met Ellen as they were both queuing for gas mask fittings in their lunch hour. Ellen was still at the home but Bumble had a room share in a terraced house on Upper Milk Street, so they only saw each other occasionally. Bumble told Ellen, laughingly, that soon she would be the only one of Molly's friends remaining within reach. 'I warn you, Ellen, as soon as war is declared I'll be off myself. I can't see any recruiting officer turning me down as being underage because I've always looked at least two years older than I really am. Only I do wish Molly would get in touch. I didn't know her all that well before she ran away, but I've spent so much time thinking about her since then that I sort of feel she was my pal every bit as much as Lenny's.'

'Do you think she might have written to Lenny?' Ellen asked. 'He was closer to her than either you or me; as close as he was to Dick. I never met the feller but from what Molly told me Lenny and Dick were like brothers. So if she were going to get in touch, I s'pose it would have been with Lenny.'

Bumble agreed but he could not stop himself: wherever he went – and he was going further and further afield – he kept his eyes open, hoping to see Molly's small figure waitressing in a café, wandering amongst the market stalls, or queuing at a tram stop. But when I get into the Royal Air Force I might be sent anywhere, he told himself. I guess I'll keep asking, and I'll remind Lenny that we still don't know where she is next time I write. Molly is his pal after all; he must worry about her.'

In point of fact, Lenny had long ago stopped worrying about Molly. She was quite capable, he thought, of looking after herself. If she had needed him in one capacity or another she would have either written or come back to the home. Oh, not boldly perhaps, marching in during daylight hours, but at night, when everyone was asleep, waking her friend Ellen to explain why she had not returned before. The fact that she had not done so was, in Lenny's eyes, proof that she was managing very nicely for herself, thank you. And Lenny's new life in the air force was too fascinating to put to one side whilst he searched for a girl who had not given him a second thought. After all, they had been bezzies; if she had wanted to contact anyone it should have been him. Lenny had been taken on in a motor pool, learning all about engines, and had great hopes of being a really good mechanic once his training was finished. In fact, he hoped to be the best, good enough to be promoted to sergeant, and then . . . well, sergeant pilots were not unheard of, and if he could catch the eye of an officer . . .

At present he was at a camp outside Blackpool, and 'keeping company' with a pretty little Waaf who worked in the cookhouse. He had written to Bumble a couple of times but had not mentioned ACW Ramworth, knowing instinctively that his old friend would probably not approve. He seldom mentioned Molly in his letters to Bumble either, but he did think of her from time to time and wished her well, though as the weeks turned into months he found he could scarcely recall her face. But this also was something he preferred not to mention to Bumble, though he did discuss it with Sally Ramworth. Halfway through his explanation, however, she gave a chortle of amusement and slapped him on the back.

'You really are a twerp, Lenny,' she had said derisively. 'You don't need to feel guilty because you stopped looking for the girl, because it's plain as the nose on your face that this Bumble is in love with your runaway bezzie, and for all I know she may be in love with him. So stop fretting and let them work out their own salvation.'

Lenny had stared at her in disbelief. 'That's nonsense,' he said at last. 'Bumble and Molly . . . no, you can't possibly be right. Molly's sharp as a needle and Bumble's slow as a snail. I don't believe Bumble has a clue about girls – he's certainly never had a girlfriend – and I don't think Molly even likes him particularly. But perhaps you're right; you know more about women than I possibly could. Only – only if you're right, why hasn't Molly contacted him? And I don't think she has because he writes to me quite regularly and he'd have said.'

Lily heaved a sigh and reached up to give his cheek a quick peck. 'Stop worrying,' she commanded. 'It'll all come out in the wash and I'm sure your Molly will surface again one of these days and explain why she's not been in touch. If you're right and she's not interested in Bumble then maybe she's found herself another chap and doesn't want to upset the apple cart by telling you what she's been up to since she ran off. You are sure she didn't take the watch, I s'pose?'

Lenny felt the first stirring of indignation. He had told his companion all about the watch and how it had been a spiteful prank, or dismissed

150

as such by Matron, so now he stared at Lily and when he spoke it was with more than a touch of resentment.

'I *told* you Molly didn't have anything to do with the watch. Now do you want to see the film on at the Odeon or do you not?'

Chapter Six

Rather to Molly's surprise Mrs Mathias was not at all pleased to hear that her little helper, as she called Molly, was about to be whisked away from her so that her favourite son – for Cian was definitely her favourite – might introduce her to the countryside.

'I'm the one that found her and took her in; I saved her life, one way and another, so it should be meself who says what's to become of her,' Mrs Mathias had said, on being informed of Cian's plan. 'She's skeered of the wildlife in the forest, which ain't no bad thing . . .'

Cian tutted. 'She's give me her word she won't go runnin' back to that home of hers if I teach her what's what,' he explained. 'Judging by what I've heard these rumours of war are likely to come true, and if so the more she knows the more she'll be able to help you. Remember, Mammy, me and Declan were British born and that means we might get called up. A war will mean we'll have to go back to how we were before . . . before we started helpin' the dockers out, and if Molly's still with us, which she will be, we can't have her frightened at a footfall, because we might be needed elsewhere.'

Mrs Mathias stiffened and Molly smiled to herself, for her friend looked like a little bantam cock when confronted with a rebellion amongst its flock. But Cian continued with his explanation. 'Don't you see, Mammy? A war will change everything. You may say it won't be our war but I'll tell you to your head, I'd rather be ruled by the British than by the Nazis. If they took over . . . but it don't bear thinkin' of. So for once will you let me know best? I know you've always said you're the brains behind our successes, and it's true, but if you were to stop Molly learnin' what's what, you're not the wise woman I once thought you.'

This conversation had been taking place in the log cabin with Molly a silent but interested listener, and now she smiled hopefully at the other woman.

'Don't worry, Mrs M, I won't desert you. If you and Cian both want me on the same day for some reason, your wishes will come first, I promise you. And now I'd best be off, because you said you wanted me to fetch a basket of carrots and onions so's you can make a blind scouse for tomorrer.' She glanced from face to face and saw that Cian was smiling, though his mother still looked grim. 'I don't understand why you should object, Mrs M, because Cian will only be taking me away from you on the odd occasion, from what he's told me, and usually at dawn or sunset.'

Cian laughed and Mrs Mathias suddenly gave a cackle of amusement. 'We'll see how it goes,' she said. 'Off wi' you, my girl; you've a fair old walk to reach that old cottage, so don't linger.'

'I won't . . . linger, I mean,' Molly said. 'Sinbad will come with me, and though I'm glad he keeps his distance I must say I feel safer knowing that he's close at hand. I'll see you both later.' She left the cabin, shutting the door carefully behind her, and popped into the makeshift woodshed Cian and his brother had constructed between Sinbad's kennel and the cabin to find a basket for the vegetables. Just as she spotted one and bent to pick it up she stopped short as Cian's voice came clearly to her ears.

'Look, Mammy, think on,' he said. 'If you remember, Declan wanted to get rid of the girl; send her back to wherever she came from. He said she would know too much, but you pointed out that she was no risk to any of us, because she was a runaway orphan with no one to care what became of her. You said – and I agreed with you – that the kid might be useful, especially if we were kind to her so she wouldn't want to leave us. Well, that's the truth, ain't it? I've got her word that she won't return to the orphanage and that means she sees us as the nearest thing she has to a family. And what's even more to the point is that she's a bright young thing and trustable. If I have to go off to war . . . and I'm sure there's going to be a war, though I don't know when . . . I'd be leaving you alone, or I would if it wasn't for Molly, 'cos Declan would get called up wit' me.'

Mrs Mathias laughed scornfully. 'You won't get called up,' she said. 'You're safe enough here.'

'Well, we'll see, but in any case you won't be alone, Mammy, because Molly's a good kid. She wouldn't go off and leave you, and between the pair of you – and the old fellers what are too old to join up – you'll be able to bring that farm we've got our eye on into full production again. Now do you understand why I don't mean to see young Molly go away? While I keep my side of the bargain she'll keep hers. So let's pledge each other with a nice cup of tay.'

Molly waited, but it seemed that the conversation was over so she picked up the basket and slipped out of the woodshed, setting off at a fast pace across the clearing, her mind in a turmoil. Try though she might she could not make sense of what she had overheard. Why on earth would being an orphan make her more welcome to the Mathias family than if she had lots of relatives? And why should Mrs Mathias object to her being taught all about the country which surrounded them? Talk of war she dismissed as something which might be relevant one day or might not be relevant at all. In the meantime she thought it only sensible to learn as much as Cian could teach her.

Walking briskly along the track Molly soon saw light ahead and knew she would presently emerge from amongst the trees on to the neglected farmland that surrounded the ruined cottage where the camp was. Mrs Mathias had explained that it was useless to expect anything much to grow within the confines of the forest, for the trees sucked all the goodness out of the soil and any plants which had worked hard to produce flowers and fruit would soon give up the unequal struggle. However, if you planted the seed perhaps as much as ten feet from the tree roots, kept your rows of vegetables weeded and harvested them before the caterpillars and blackfly got a hold, then you could be sure of a reasonable crop.

There was a rusty old fork inside what had once been the cottage kitchen, and Molly fetched it and began to dig with great care. When the basket was full of carrots and onions she told Sinbad that it was time to return to the cabin. She had grown used to his company and was no longer afraid of him, believing that providing she did not make an unexpected or aggressive move he would regard her as someone to be protected. On the other hand, he would attack anyone, human or animal, who he felt might threaten his family. Molly had seen him drive off what Cian told her was a five-pointer stag which had strayed far from its home in the high pastures beyond the forest. He had growled menacingly, crouched on the ground until his chest was almost touching the earth, and crept forward until finally, when the stag seemed mesmerised by his presence, he had leapt forward, barking, and the animal had fled, crashing between the trees and no doubt vowing to steer clear of the cabin in future.

'Good boy,' she said experimentally now, and was pleased when he grinned and wagged his tail. Once, she had seen the display of that magnificent row of white teeth as a warning; now she knew him better and recognised the difference between a friendly smile and a threatening leer. 'Good boy,' she said again. 'Home now, and I'm sure you'll get a share of the scouse your mistress is going to make. Is that fair?'

Sinbad fell into step beside her, six feet to her left, and seemed to nod, which made Molly laugh. 'Good boy,' she said for the third time, and remembered how afraid she had been when, more than two months earlier, she had first come across him. Now she thought of him as a friend and looked forward to the day when Cian would tell her the magic words which changed him from guardian to aggressor.

But just at the moment she had more important things on her mind, starting with the exchange she had overheard between Cian and his mother. Frowning, she puzzled over it. She had met Declan, the elder of Mrs Mathias's sons, on only a couple of occasions, and had not liked him any more than he had liked her. Indeed, it had sometimes seemed to Molly that he automatically disliked anyone who was not a Mathias by birth, so it was natural that if anyone distrusted her it should be him.

Walking slowly along the forest track, for the basket of vegetables was heavy, Molly went over the conversation again in her mind. So Declan had wanted to send her back to the home, had he? And Cian and Mrs Mathias had disagreed. So although he might never like her he had had to accept her, because his mother had made it clear that she thought Molly necessary to her comfort. Cian, too, did not want her to leave and go back to the orphanage: he realised that after so many weeks of her company Mrs Mathias relied upon Molly not only for help around the log cabin but also for the sheer comfort of having another person always within call. *That* was the reason he had extracted a promise from her not to return to the Haisborough Orphanage. And it also explained the fact that Declan thought she knew too much. Well, so she did. There were those who would not approve of the dockers' perks, she supposed, because, look at it how you would, the dockers were stealing from whoever owned the goods which passed through the family's hands. By now, Molly had realised that the booty was distributed over a wide area of the country and must have brought the Mathiases a tidy sum.

Molly frowned. The previous day she had guided a truck to a certain point in the forest and had then helped to distribute amongst other things some tinned corned beef which the lorry had contained. She had been given two tins to take back to Mrs Mathias. For the first time it occurred to her to wonder how a docker could possibly have filched as many as a dozen tins of the stuff, but then remembered that it was not one docker but all of them who considered themselves underpaid. Some day she would ask Mrs Mathias about it, but not yet. First she must make sure that Cian had meant it when he promised to teach her the ways of the countryside. It was now nearing the end of April, the trees were in leaf, the birds were building their nests and feeding their young and everywhere new life was emerging. As she entered the log cabin she was already talking.

'Cian, it's a lovely day; why don't we start our adventure now?' She turned to Mrs Mathias. 'I've dug up enough vegetables to last us two or three days; there'll be plenty of time to prepare them for the pot when I get back.'

Cian grinned at her. 'We'll start at dawn tomorrow,' he said easily. 'Sure and don't I want you to get a good impression of the forest itself? I want

159

you to know the names and calls of every bird, the shape of their nests, the colour of their eggs and the songs which they use to attract a mate.'

He told her that dawn was the best time to see the rabbit families which emerged cautiously from their burrows to eat the sweet spring grass and to frolic with their young. It was then that the fox would bring out her cubs, then that the birds began the frantic business of feeding their fledglings, then that the badger emerged from his sett, and the moor beyond the forest buzzed with bees and butterflies as they came to the feast of heather honey which awaited them.

So it was understandable that Molly was so excited she thought she'd never be able to sleep. Cian dossed down in the kitchen and laughed at her exuberance.

'Sure and wasn't I about to say I'd wake you?' he said teasingly. 'But as it is, if you're too restless to sleep you can wake me. I'd suggest a nice cup of tay if you can make it quietly so's we don't wake the mammy.'

But next morning, when Molly went quietly into the kitchen, it was to find that Mrs Mathias had slipped out of their room before her and was already busy at the stove. She handed Molly a tin mug of tea with a rather wintry smile.

'Cian's gone down to the stream to wash the sleep out of his eyes,' she said in a low voice. 'Drink your tea, and by the time it's gone me laddo will be back and you can go down and wash yourself, if you've a mind.'

Still slightly blurred after her sleepless night, the last thing on Molly's mind was a wash in the ice-cold brook which babbled away on the other side of the clearing, but with Mrs Mathias's eye on her she drank the tea down quickly and announced she was ready for the fray.

Cian appeared in the doorway in time to hear her words and raised an eyebrow, a grin lurking. 'You're still half asleep,' he said, catching hold of her by the neck and pulling her outside. 'This'll wake you better than any old cup of tay – and keep you awake, furthermore.' And before she could object she found herself being pushed none too gently to her knees and ducked in the brook.

The water was ice cold and Molly was thoroughly soaked before Cian would let her go. Laughing, she rushed into the log cabin for a towel and rubbed herself dry until her skin glowed, then looked around her. Grey dawn was creeping up beyond the forest trees and Sinbad, who had emerged from his kennel with hopefully pricked ears and wagging tail, seemed to read Cian's expression and realise that his company was not wanted. He heaved a sigh so human that Molly looked twice at him as he retreated into the depths of his kennel, though Molly noticed he kept an eye on them as they crossed the clearing and dived into the wood.

Molly had thought that Cian would probably take her out once or twice and consider his promise kept, but she wronged him. As spring deepened into summer she grew wise in the ways of those who lived off the land. Within a couple of weeks she could pick out the thickening in the hedge which indicated a nest, as well as the frantic piping of the birds to which such a nest belonged. She learned to leave a couple of eggs in each nest she took from, for then the birds seemed not to know they had been robbed. And then one day Cian produced a gun with a long barrel.

'You know I shoot for the pot, and you must learn to do the same,' he said. 'It's no use being squeamish and saying you can't, because you may have to do just that. When war comes and shortages grip, the only meat you and the mammy may see will be what you have killed yourself. In the last war every cottager kept a pig and a few hens, otherwise they would have been hard-pressed to feed their families. I reckon you've guessed by now that I'm relying on you to take care of the mammy, so it's no use you telling me you couldn't shoot a fluffy little bunny. The mammy and myself have welcomed you to our home, and you're part of our family now.'

Molly hated the thought but admitted the practicality of it and consented to fire at a target of Cian's choosing. He chalked a cross on a bit of paper and nailed it to a tree and very soon, sooner than he expected, Molly was hitting the target every time, whipping the shotgun up to her shoulder and receiving his praise with a cautious smile.

The first time she actually fired at and killed a large buck rabbit was a red-letter day. Pleasing Cian had become important to her and he was extremely pleased with the shot which had felled the rabbit, a grandfather of a creature, who, he assured his pupil, had probably enjoyed a long and productive life and would have known nothing of the shot which had killed him.

'A wood pigeon will be next,' he said, laughing at Molly's dismay, for she was often woken by the soft purring coo of the pigeons as they nested in one of the large trees which surrounded the clearing. When Molly told Mrs Mathias that a pigeon was to be her next target, however, the older woman laughed rather grimly.

''Tis the trickiest of all shots and I doubt you'll get a pigeon for many a long month,' she said derisively. 'Any fool can hit a rabbit – even a hare's not impossible – but a pigeon's a different matter, so it is.'

Molly sniffed. 'Cian says I can do it; he says it's the hardest shot, all right, but he has faith in his teaching, so I'm to try for a pigeon the very next time we go out.'

*

Summer had come to an end, however, before Molly had bagged her pigeon. She was actually preparing for what she thought of as a hunting expedition when Cian pushed open the door of the log cabin and came across the room, a broad smile on his face. His arms were full of parcels which he dumped on the kitchen table before turning to address his mother and Molly, beaming at them as though he had a pleasant surprise in store.

'Want to know what this is?' he asked, unwrapping brown paper from around a small square object. 'This, lovely ladies, is what they call a wireless set. It works off a battery; that's what the second parcel is, only it's called a transformer, and it will keep you in touch with the war.' He beamed at his mother. 'And I've got more good news. We managed to purchase that farm – the O'Hare place – and at a good price too! I shall take you over there this afternoon for a tour of inspection.' He turned to Molly. 'It was in production last year and the owners had no thought of sellin' until the husband died, sudden like. With no sons to keep the place goin' his wife decided to move in with her sister what lives in Connemara.' He smiled at Molly. 'You'll love working on the farm.'

'Hang on a minute!' she said urgently. 'I admit you taught me a lot these past few months but it was mainly about the forest and the creatures who live in the wild countryside. I know a bit about harvesting but nothing about looking after beasts.'

Cian laid a hand on her shoulder. 'The old farmhands will teach you everything you need to know about how to tend the stock. Does that satisfy you?'

Molly nodded. She had thought her life had changed for the better ever since being rescued by the Mathiases, but she had never dreamed that she would end up living in a farmhouse, with pigs, sheep and horses to look after. It had been months since she had written to Lenny, and he still hadn't replied. Well, that was his loss. She was living a life that dreams were made of, and if Lenny couldn't be bothered to write to his old pal she would not let it worry her. She nodded her agreement to Cian.

He patted her shoulder. 'Good girl,' he said approvingly before indicating the wireless. 'This is how you turn it on . . .'

The wireless was not difficult to work and both Mrs Mathias and Molly soon conquered it, but it was not until quite late in the afternoon that Cian returned in a horse-drawn trap to take them to their new abode.

'Is it far from here, this nice new farm of yours?' Molly asked. 'Come to that, is it far from the Princes Park area? Or near the docks? All this time I've never even thought about it, but if we're going to have a war – and you wouldn't have brought the wireless unless you thought we were – I ought to know where I am!'

She tried to make it sound jokey but did not altogether succeed, for Cian gave her a narrow-eyed look before relaxing as she beamed at him.

'Does it matter? From what you've told me it wouldn't mean anything to you, since orphans don't get about much beyond the place where they're likely to live and work for the rest of their lives. If I said, for instance, that we're heading for Connemara, or Tralee, you'd be none the wiser.' He added as she helped the old lady into the trap and climbed in after her, 'Isn't that so?'

If Cian had expected a laughing negative he was to be disappointed, for Molly, round-eyed, answered at once. 'But – but they're both in Ireland. I did geography in school, you know.'

'Oh!' Cian said. It was several more moments before he added to the monosyllable, and then he did so slowly. ''Twas just an example I gave you, but you've hit the nail on the head. We're in southern Ireland, of course. I don't t'ink any of us realised you'd thought the forest was near Liverpool.'

'What a girl you are,' Mrs Mathias said comfortably. 'It never occurred to me that you thought we were in England, let alone within striking distance of Liverpool.'

This information gave Molly so much food for thought that she sat silent for a while, brooding over their words. Ireland! Why on earth had she never suspected it before? She remembered the queue of lorries drawn up on the dock, and wondered why it had never occurred to her that lorries went aboard the Irish ferries to return to Ireland. Every single person she had spoken to except Mrs Mathias had had a strong Irish brogue, sometimes so strong that she could scarcely understand the words. And she remembered once or twice hearing somebody referring to 'over the water', but she had always assumed they were referring to the nearby river or even one of the great lakes which she and Cian had fished once or twice. Cian cast her a questioning glance over his shoulder, slapping the reins playfully on the little mare's neck, but making it plain he was waiting for an answer, which Molly hastily gave.

'So when I climbed aboard that lorry full of fleeces on the docks it was waiting to board the ferry,' she said, trying to keep her tone neutral. 'Not that it makes much difference where the farm is, or where I am, for that matter. Only from what you've already told me I shall be responsible for buying in food for your mammy and myself if war comes, so I shall have to know the way to the nearest town.'

Cian was nodding. 'That's right,' he confirmed. 'And don't forget Sinbad, and the rest of the stock we'll buy. We've a deal of land down to wheat and barley at present, some cut already and some awaiting the scythe . . . but I don't know why I'm running on like this when in another five minutes you can see for yourself.'

'One last question,' Molly said quickly. 'Where did you get this trap? And the pony of course? It's a very smart conveyance, very smart indeed.'

Cian swelled his chest and looked smug. 'Bought it fair and square and paid a pretty penny for it too,' he assured her. 'Rich landowner wanted something larger. Like it, do you? Then you'd best let me teach you to drive it, because although Bella' – he indicated the pony with a flick of his whip – 'is a fine little stepper she needs a firm hand on the rein, or you'll find yourself standing still whilst she eats the grass off the verge. Ah, here we are. What d'you think?'

Molly was so busy trying to get it into her head that ever since waking up aboard the fleece lorry she had been in Ireland that she did not have words to spare to exclaim over the farm. However, she looked carefully around her as they drove into the yard. Someone had recently cleaned it, for there was not so much as a straw lying on the big flat paving stones, and the trees which edged it on one side had not yet begun to shed their leaves. Molly was able to recognise lime, beech and sweet chestnut, and saw with approval that the outbuildings were in good shape. As she studied them a bent old man came hobbling out of what she guessed were the stables, doffing a large cap and welcoming the newcomers in a cracked and wheezy voice to O'Hare Farm.

Cian jumped down and the old man hobbled to Bella's head. The pony nuzzled his shirt front, clearly expecting a reward for good behaviour, and was not disappointed. 'Good girl,' Cian said with proprietorial pride as he watched her crunching down with every sign of satisfaction the carrot which the old man had produced. Molly hid a smile. Already he was beginning to try to sound like landed gentry, she thought with amusement. She remembered how his mother had likened her family to Robin Hood and how pleased he had been with the comparison when she told him. But there were no such things as dockers or perks in Robin Hood's day, and no matter how you looked at it Robin was just a plain old-fashioned thief, which meant the sheriff of Nottingham was on the side of the angels. But it's only a fairy story, Molly told herself, like the babes in the wood, and Snow White . . . and I know Cian would never see anyone go hungry whilst he had food. He *is* rather like Robin Hood, because I'm sure he gives as much as he can to the poor; why else would he continue with the dockers' perks business?

She scrambled out of the trap and helped Mrs Mathias to alight, and the two women made their way into the house where Cian was beckoning. They entered a large kitchen with a stone-flagged floor, and Molly saw a low stone sink with a pump over it. She smiled. This was an improvement on the log cabin, for the pump meant running water in the house, a pleasant change for one who had been carrying full buckets into their dwelling for many months. What was more, the windows had glass in them, and shutters which could be closed and locked at night so that no wandering thief could gain access to the premises. Cian insisted that both women should join him in a tour of the outbuildings. They did not go into the tied cottages, which were still occupied, Cian assuring them that they were simple two-room dwellings kept in good order by the inhabitants. When they returned to the house and entered the kitchen, Mrs Mathias trotted across the flagged floor and threw open a door to the right of the woodburning stove, revealing a large empty pantry.

'It may be empty now but soon it will be full of jams and preserves, for the orchard is fair laden, far more than we can eat, so you and me, miss, have a busy time ahead of us.' She chuckled. 'When you came to the cabin you were a skinny little urchin without a peck of meat on your bones, and no more strength than a kitten. God alone knows what they fed you at that orphanage, but it weren't much. Once you started eatin' Mathias food, though, you began to put on muscle. I reckon if you went back to that orphanage tomorrer they'd not reckernise you.' As she spoke she slammed the pantry door shut.

Molly sighed, then crossed the kitchen and gave Mrs Mathias a hug. She might not approve of dockers' perks but, albeit unknowingly, she had undoubtedly benefited from them. Now that she knew more about what had been going on she also understood Declan's desire, when they first met, to be rid of her before, either on purpose or inadvertently, she gave their game away to the authorities.

If I'd shown disapproval or too much curiosity Declan would have got rid of me anyway, one way or another, she thought ruefully.

Two weeks later the move to the new farm was complete, even to the extent of Cian's arriving with a sow and her bonaveens – piglets – who were to take up residence in the large pigsty adjacent to the house. In the stables were two elderly carthorses, Bess and Ben, bought at the sale of yet another failing farm, and the beginnings of a flock of good sheep grazed on the pastures. To Molly's pleasure Cian had paid the asking price for the sheep, though he boasted that they were worth at least double that.

He entered the room as Molly was scrubbing potatoes at the sink and she turned and smiled at him before popping the last one into the saucepan and carrying it over to the stove. 'Here you are, Mrs Mathias,' she said cheerfully. 'No blind scouse for us tonight; I saw a piece of pork in the meat safe on the slate slab in the pantry. Is that for supper?'

'That's right,' Mrs Mathias said after a short pause. She turned to her son. 'Shall I get me little helper to make an apple pie? I know you're fond of such things.'

Cian grinned at her. 'Aye.' He turned to Molly. 'Declan will be comin' home later and one or two of the fellers. Cook enough for half a dozen.'

Molly nodded. She had noticed that Cian no longer bothered to charm her but treated her like a sister, often giving her a brotherly hug or helping her with some small task. She had never received so much as a penny from him for the work she did in the cabin but supposed he thought feeding and housing her was sufficient; she felt it was likely that in his eyes her main value lay in taking care of 'the mammy'. Her thoughts turned to her old life at Haisborough and she remembered the strict discipline, the tiny meals and the general misery of life in the home. For a moment she felt quite guilty, for Ellen had been a good friend, as had Lenny. She thought it unlikely that they would be sitting down to a fine dinner of roast pork that evening, or chattering with the ease of a family member, as she was herself. Then she shook her head. By now both Ellen and Lenny would be working, as she was. They were old enough to look after themselves; it was pointless to feel guilty just because she was happy and they might not be. Resolutely she began to make the pastry for the apple pie.

*

'Well, hello stranger!' Bumble exclaimed. 'I haven't seen you for weeks and weeks. Not in the forces yet, then?'

Ellen and Bumble, emerging from different factories at the end of their shifts, beamed at each other. Because of the vagaries of the shift system they either met every day or not at all for weeks, and usually they were too tired to do more than say hello, but on this occasion Bumble had news to impart and caught hold of Ellen's arm when she would have turned away.

'Hang on a minute!' he said urgently. 'Didn't you say you were applying to join the Land Army? Did you change your mind and decide to stick to munitions?'

Ellen sighed and looked up at Bumble's face. 'Come and sit down and I'll tell you what's happening in my life and you can tell me what's happening in yours,' she commanded. She waited while he hoisted his large frame on to the wall beside her and then continued: 'I've applied to join the WAAF but there's a long waiting list. What about you?'

'I've joined the air force and I'm just waiting for my papers to arrive,' Bumble said. 'I s'pose it's silly to ask if you've had any news of Molly? Lenny keeps his eyes open, or did, but now he's in Scotland somewhere so he can't do much, though I'm sure he's willing.'

Ellen sniffed. 'Did you know I went to Lincolnshire to see him just before he was sent to Scotland? We met in Lincoln at a great big pub called the Saracen's Head. Lenny was there with the prettiest little Waaf you can imagine, all blue eyes and bubbly blonde curls. To be fair to Lenny, he made no bones about it. Her name's Sally and you've only got to look at her, at her expression I mean, to see she thinks a lot of our Lenny. So if you're thinking he's waiting for Molly, you're wrong. She was his good friend, same as she was mine, and there it ended.' With a small sigh, she got to her feet. 'Want to walk down to the docks?' she enquired. 'I like to get a bit of exercise after work and the docks are always interesting, especially now.'

Bumble stood up too. 'Sure thing. A walk will do me good,' he said amiably. 'And it doesn't surprise me that Lenny has a girlfriend; he's a very nice bloke. Now tell me about the home. It seems a lifetime since I lived there.'

Chatting amicably, the two made their way through the streets until they reached the Pier Head. There were several lorries lined up waiting to board a ferry and Bumble turned to Ellen.

'I know it's months since Molly disappeared, yet I'm still looking for her. As soon as I realised she must have been in a lorry I reckon I also realised she could be anywhere in England, anywhere at all. Only why should that stop her from getting in touch, letting us know she was all right?'

Ellen pointed at the line of lorries. 'If she was in one of those, chances are she would have been carried off to Ireland, 'cos that's where most of the ferries from here are bound.'

Bumble slapped his forehead with the back of his hand. 'Of course! If she was in Ireland she wouldn't have seen Matron's piece in the *Echo*, and she would have to earn the money for a ticket before she could return, so she'll have found a job near the docks somewhere. That's where she'll be.' Bumble grabbed Ellen and did a little dance. 'We've cracked it, or rather you have. I'll see my boss tomorrow and get leave to go over to Ireland. I'll take my savings and before you know it Molly will be with us once more.'

*

As Mr Chamberlain finished speaking Cian, who had been seated at the head of the table in the farmhouse kitchen, pushed his chair back and got to his feet.

175

'I knew it, I knew it,' he crowed, grinning round at the assembled company.

His brother Declan was grinning as well, but most of the other faces – the old farmhands and the two lorry drivers who had helped to shift the latest dockers' perks – looked as serious as Molly, and one of them gave voice to his feelings; it was, Molly thought, the man who had driven the lorryload of fleeces whilst unbeknown to him or his co-driver Molly had lain a few feet behind him.

''Tis all very well for you since you can stay safe down here, Eire being a neutral country,' the man said slowly. 'But I'm from the north, and I seen what them Nazis did to Madrid with their bombing raids and I don't fancy being drawn in, which I shall be when the conscription reaches my age group.'

Cian's grin widened and he stuck his thumbs behind the lapels of his jacket. 'They can call me up if they like, call as loud as they may, but I won't be goin' anywhere,' he said boastfully.

One of the farmhands spoke up. 'But why should they come after you, unless you volunteer,' he said timidly. 'You're as Irish as the rest of us.'

'Well, I guess Dec and I could volunteer, though it ain't likely,' Cian said. He jerked an accusing thumb at his mother. ''Tis all the mammy's fault so it is. Our da went to Liverpool on business and fell for her hook, line and sinker. They moved into a nice house on Mozart Street in Bootle and it were there that Dec and I were born. Our da brought the mammy and us kids back to Eire, but she'd registered our births in Liverpool, so I reckon there's them as counts us as English, even though we's Irish through and through.'

There were murmurs from the farmhands but it was Molly who spoke.

'Well, if you mean that – about staying in Eire, I mean – then you won't mind if I go back to help with the war effort in any way I can,' she said, trying to keep her voice steady. She smiled at Cian, unable to read his expression. 'Ah, go on, Cian! You know very well you only want me here to look after Mrs Mathias and the farm and you can do that a great deal better than I could.'

But Cian was shaking his head, the look she could not quite interpret still on his face. 'You listen to me,' he said in a gentle tone. 'Britain is going to be a dangerous place to live – they're already evacuating children out of the big cities – and there's you wantin' to move back! If the Luftwaffe start bombin' the ports Liverpool will be one of their main targets, and didn't you say the orphanage was near the docks? If that's so I won't have you puttin' yourself in danger like that.' He turned quickly to flash a smile at his mother. 'You'll stay here and look after the mammy.'

'Oh, Cian, you could get a nice Irish colleen to look after her . . .' Molly began, but already Cian was shaking his head and looking back at her as though he had anticipated her reaction.

'I'm not havin' a stranger come into the house. The fewer people who know about us Mathiases the better. So I'd like you to give me your word that you'll not desert my poor old mammy.'

'All right, Cian,' she said in a tired voice. 'I'll stay here as long as she needs me. I can't say I'd much relish being in Liverpool if the bombing raids really do start; in fact I'd probably be quite willing to take your advice.' She smiled across at the old lady. 'We're good pals, ain't we, Mrs M? And this farmhouse is a deal more comfortable than the Haisborough home, so I reckon I'll see the war out in relative comfort.'

Mrs Mathias had been sitting next to Cian and staring very hard at Molly, who was standing by the back door, but now she seemed to relax.

'You're norra bad kid; I trusts you to do what's best for us both,' she said. 'And now let's get a meal on the table before these fellers start complainin' that they've not ate for a month.'

'Yes, of course.' Molly went over to the stove and prodded the potatoes with a fork, pronounced them cooked to perfection and would have staggered over to the sink to drain the pan except that Cian took it from her and performed the task, advising her to begin instead to dish out the stew, whose fragrance had been filling the kitchen for some time now. Molly, thanking him, thought what an odd mixture he was. She knew he was cross with her for even suggesting that she might leave them, yet he had hurried over to help her rather than see her struggle with the heavy pan. Sometimes I think he truly loves me and wants us to be married when I'm old enough, she thought. At other times I think he sees me as naught but a sister, a part of the family, to be protected.

For the next few weeks Molly worked hard in the house and garden. She took lessons in farming from the two old hands who had remained behind when their sons had volunteered for the British forces, and she cooked, cleaned and marketed for the Mathiases. This was no sinecure, for Cian was spending money on restocking their newly acquired acres, and cows have to be milked, pigs must be cleaned and fed and even chickens are extra work, she reminded herself as she searched for their eggs. But even when she was working every hour that God sent there was a little niggle in the back of her mind, a little voice telling her that she had missed the significance of something Cian had said. She went over and over the conversation after Mr Chamberlain's speech, Cian's reasons for not wanting her to leave, and suddenly, one dark morning when she was bringing the cows in for milking, she realised what had worried her. In her mind she replayed Cian's words.

'If the Luftwaffe start bombin' the ports Liverpool will be one of their main targets, and didn't you say the orphanage was near the docks? If that's so I won't have you puttin' yourself in danger like that.'

Molly had been about to sit down and start milking when the realisation struck her. If he had indeed, as he had told her, taken her letter personally to the home then he would not have had to ask her where it was situated. And now that she thought about it she realised she had no proof that the letter had ever been delivered. Thinking it over, she remembered how he had turned away quickly – too quickly – after he had spoken, obviously realising that he had given the game away, and hoping that she had not noticed.

But that was weeks ago, and now farming was the main thing on Molly's mind. The wheat and barley had been cut and Bess and Ben, though elderly and slow, were quite capable of pulling the plough, so the stubble had been ploughed into the good earth and the seed for the new crop scattered. If it hadn't been for the war, Molly found herself thinking, she would have been completely content. The weather was cold but clear, the new cows grazed happily on the pastures and Molly found she could cope very well with the work demanded of her, for the old men were delighted to teach her what they called 'the tricks of the trade' and helped her in every way they could. They were particularly impressed by the large tin plates piled with food which she gave them at midday, often remarking that their wives, though good cooks, could not equal the meals they ate up at the farmhouse.

Molly smiled at the compliment; it made the hard work worth while.

*

Bumble woke up the morning after Ellen's revelation concerning her old pal's whereabouts determined to see his foreman and ask for time off. He rolled out of bed and went straight to the window. The room that he shared with three others was on the first floor of the small terraced house and despite his determination not to oversleep he had clearly done so, for he could hear sounds of breakfast being prepared by his fellow lodgers in the communal kitchen below.

Bumble swore softly beneath his breath and tugged back the blackout curtains. The sight which met his eyes made him groan even harder.

Snow! Judging by the depth of it, it must have started soon after he came up to bed, and even as he watched a few flakes floated gently past his window. The sky overhead looked dark with more to come.

That's torn it, Bumble thought, dismayed. If she's in Ireland it looks as though she'll be stuck there until the spring. I guess she must be happy and settled, so it's about time I took a leaf out of Lenny's book and simply stopped worrying and let things take their course.

He went over to the washstand, broke the ice in the ewer and shrinkingly washed his hands and face. His shift did not start until the evening so the whole day stretched in front of him. He decided he would go to the factory to help clear the snow and then see a flick. After that he fancied blowing some of his wages on a fish supper in the cinema café, and what with one thing and another he would forget all about Molly. She was independent and capable; whichever side of the Irish Sea she was on, she was there from choice. He had wasted too much time worrying about her; now he would concentrate on his forthcoming service in the RAF and get himself a nice little Waaf, as Lenny had. After all, Molly was Lenny's problem, not his. Yes, he would do that. Once his papers arrived he could begin his training within a matter of weeks. Bumble dressed quickly, then clattered down the stairs and burst into the kitchen.

Jim Nethercott waved a spoon at him. 'Seen the snow? I reckon we're in for a spell of really bad weather,' he said. 'Want some porridge? I made it, so there's no lumps.'

*

For many months after Mr Chamberlain's declaration Molly worked as hard as she possibly could to help bring the O'Hare farm back into full production. As the war raged on the family met every evening to listen to the wireless, and it no longer worried Molly that she was not in uniform for Cian had assured her that all the food she was helping to produce was going straight across the Irish Sea to the British government.

'What could one wee girl on her own do to help the war effort, save fire-watching or some such?' he had asked her. 'But that same wee girl – you, me darlin' – can play a part in providing food for a perishin' regiment. You're doin' a marvellous job helpin' me and Declan so don't go feelin' you've no part in this war.' He had grinned at her. 'Oh, I know you doubted us at times, and you were right to do so. Dockers' perks, I mean.' His grin had broadened. 'But that's all at an end; now we're all in it together.'

So Molly worked on, certain she was doing the right thing. Cian wanted the war to be won by the British, and so did she. So when June came and they heard about the evacuation of the forces from Dunkirk she worked even harder than usual, knowing she was helping to feed men who must be in desperate need of a good meal, and later, when the Battle of Britain raged in the sky, she continued to harvest the good crops, knowing that this was as important as any other job in wartime.

Things might have continued in this happy way had it not been for the sudden eruption into their lives of Cian's cousin Esme. Apparently her home on the Scottie Road had been bombed and she had applied to her Irish cousins to take her in.

Molly and Mrs Mathias had settled down to listen to the wireless when Cian had entered the room, producing a letter as he did so and reading its contents aloud to his astonished audience.

I may not know a lot about farming but I'm a hard worker, she had written. *I dare say you could do with a hand, for your old mammy won't want to stir herself more'n she must. I hear you've some young gal gives a hand. Well, no need for her wages once I'm settled in. Just you tell me what next to do and it'll be done in a trice, for I'm no idler I promise you. Your affec cousin, Esme Brannigan.*

'Sounds good,' Molly said at once. 'Only . . . you can't save a wage which you don't pay!'

She had meant it as a joke, but Cian took her seriously. 'What need would you have of a wage?' he asked defensively. 'You've only to say the word and either the mammy or meself will buy anything you need. You've never complained about it before. You're a member of the family, so it never occurred to me that you might want the feel of cash in your hot little hand.'

Molly felt a hot flush rise up her neck and invade her cheeks. He had made it sound as though being paid a wage would put her on a level with the three old farm workers, way below the Mathiases themselves.

'I *don't* want a wage!' she said indignantly. 'I want everything to go on just as before. Only I guess, with the extra pair of hands, we'll be able to produce even more food than we do already.'

Cian was beginning to reply when the back door opened and Declan entered the room, slamming the door behind him and going straight to a plate of shortbread which had been placed in the middle of the kitchen table where anyone might help themselves. He grinned at his brother, grabbed some shortbread and jerked a thumb at the letter.

'Have you told them?' he asked through his mouthful. 'Esme used to work at the pickle factory; she'll soon have you hoppin' around like cats on a hot tin roof.' He gave Molly what he no doubt thought was a friendly smile, but was really a rather unpleasant leer. 'You think you work hard now; wait till our Esme gets goin'.'

Molly shrugged and helped herself to a piece of shortbread. 'If she's a hard worker, she's welcome,' she said coolly. 'Even if she only gives an eye to your mam, Declan, she'll be a welcome addition. In fact . . . Ah.' She leaned across and twiddled the wireless knobs. 'News time!'

*

Esme Brannigan arrived and within a matter of days Molly knew the older woman was going to be no help whatsoever on the farm. She was short and squat with thin greying hair pulled into a knob at the nape of her neck, small, spiteful brown eyes, a blob of a nose and a tight little mouth. Molly told herself appearances meant nothing; the woman could scarcely help her unprepossessing looks, but she very soon realised that the newcomer had not the slightest intention of working either in the fields or around the house. Almost as soon as she had settled in she insisted on changing bedchambers with Molly, saying contemptuously that a hired hand should have one of the box rooms so that she herself might have more space, a soft eiderdown and a carpeted floor. At the time, Molly had shrugged.

'I don't care which room I have; in fact I prefer the smaller room,' she had said coldly, and untruthfully. 'It'll be warmer when the really bad weather comes.'

After that, things simply went from bad to worse. Esme was not a good cook, but if it was a choice between cleaning out the cow byre and pottering in the kitchen she insisted that she should do the latter. Her bread was inedible, because she was too impatient to wait whilst the dough proved; her pastry was lumpy and indigestible; and her cakes didn't rise since she never bothered to check the heat of the stove before inserting them. Thus it was usually Mrs Mathias or Molly who did the cooking whilst Esme sat by the fire looking smug and accepting compliments on baked goods which someone else had made.

Molly waited hopefully for Cian to realise that Esme was lazy and idle as well as inefficient, but it soon appeared that he simply did not believe what Molly told him when she found him alone.

'Ah well, mebbe she's no cook,' he admitted at last. 'But she looks after the mammy to the manner born. Mammy says she's never been taken care of so good. And she's a grand marketer, so she is.' He grinned affectionately at Molly. 'She gets more for our money than you ever did, my dear. She's a good bargainer!'

Molly opened her mouth to reply, then tightened her lips. She had seen Esme Brannigan's ploys, seen her nick a couple of pork chops and slide them into her big marketing bag along with other goods she had purloined. One day she'll get caught out and Cian will see she's just a nasty old cheat, Molly told herself. I wonder why Declan always takes her side? I wonder if they realise that if I were to go the farm would be in dead trouble. I've warned Cian but he just said Esme was family and wouldn't cheat them; he didn't seem to care that she might cheat other people.

Molly had very soon discovered that Esme never hesitated to help herself to the housekeeping money. She often took a few bob either from the change she got from the stallholders at the market or from the large tin teapot which the Mathiases used for their loose cash. Either way Esme always had money, whereas Molly herself had never either taken or asked for a wage. It wasn't fair! She had been meaning to write to her old friends in Liverpool ever since she realised that Cian had probably never visited the orphanage, but had simply not got round to it as the work at the farm was so demanding. And when she had asked Esme about the extent of the raids, the other woman had been evasive.

'Why do you want to know?' she had asked suspiciously. 'Thinking of leaving this nice soft billet and going back to all them nasty bombs?' She had sniffed. 'I know your type; bomb dodgers, they call 'em. You'd go into the bombed houses for anything you could sell for a few bob. Well, if you think I'm going to help you, you're wrong. I've noticed you always do what Cian says' – she had sniggered unpleasantly – 'so I can tell you straight out what he'll think if you try to get away. He'll soon put a stop to that, 'cos though you ain't much use you'll do to clean out the cowsheds and such.'

The two women had been in the kitchen, Molly making a beef and onion pie whilst Esme sat in one of the fireside chairs sporadically darning socks.

Molly lined her tin with pastry then looked carefully round her. She never criticised Esme when Mrs Mathias was near, for the old woman liked to think Esme had come to the farm specifically to look after her, but on this occasion Mrs Mathias had tottered out, as she put it, to see if she could find some eggs. Molly felt that for once she could tell Esme what she thought of her.

'You'd be in a poor way without me,' she said bluntly. 'Why, you can't even milk a cow, and you're frightened of the horses. If I were to leave . . .'

Esme gave a snort. 'You can't leave; you've got no money, nor no pals,' she said tauntingly. 'Let's face it, you're no better than a perishing slave! My cousin Cian brought me over here so's I could make sure you didn't run out on them, 'cos although you're just a farmhand you have your uses.'

Molly felt a slow tide of hot blood invade her cheeks and was about to reply indignantly when the back door opened and Mrs Mathias tottered back into the room. She held a small box with half a dozen eggs in it, and looked pleased with herself.

'I found these here eggs wi' the grey pullet nearby, so I reckon it's her what's layin' astray,' she said.

Esme hauled herself out of the basket chair and reached across to grab the rolling pin. 'Made the pastry,' she said briskly. 'Delicious this pie will be, 'cos though I say it as shouldn't I've a light hand with pastry.'

So light she never touches it, Molly thought to herself, although she said nothing, and presently, with the pie in the oven, the two older ladies began to make a list of the things they wanted to buy when they visited the market town the next day.

'We'll have some more of that minced pork . . .' Mrs Mathias was saying, but Molly scarcely heard her. For the first time since Esme Brannigan had arrived at the farm she had been touched on the raw by something the older woman had said. All unknowingly, Esme had spoken no more than the truth. Molly could not leave, because she had no money, and no pals in a position to help her. A while ago, when war had just been declared, she had suggested to Mrs Mathias that she really ought to go back to Liverpool to see what she could do to help. Mrs Mathias had turned straight round and told Declan, who happened to be in the kitchen at the time, that the girl he thought of as his little sister wanted to go gadding off to Liverpool.

'It'll be the uniform she's after,' she had said fretfully. 'Ah, there's no respect from the young these days.' She had turned on Molly, her eyes gleaming with malice. 'And I thought you really was one of the family and wouldn't let us down.'

At the time Molly had not seen that she was being manipulated and had simply accepted, joyfully, the fact that the old woman thought of her as family. In fact she had said so, had crossed the room to give Mrs Mathias a warm hug and had been thrilled when it was as warmly returned.

But that had been a long time ago and she had not then heard Esme's remark or realised its truth. It was true that if she had asked for something it would be given to her, but no amount of little gifts – Cian was always giving her little gifts – could make up for the fact that she did not have so much as a penny piece to call her own. When she had been turned out of her bedroom she had pretended not to mind, but now it occurred to her that neither Mrs Mathias nor her sons had objected. It was all very well to shrug it off, to pretend she didn't care, but if she had been real family surely someone would have pointed out that it was Molly's room and should remain so. But nobody had, not even Cian, whom she still thought very much her friend. She knew he didn't really like Esme but once again the inescapable truth reared its head: Esme was family. Her mother had been Mrs Mathias's older sister, and Molly was beginning to see that, to the Mathiases, what mattered was blood. A blood relative could do or say practically anything and be accepted without question. If Molly herself married Cian she too would become a true member of the family, but that once longed-for day was not only far off, but might never happen. I *am* a slave, and I'm beginning to think I'm a prisoner as well, Molly told herself, for now she thought about it she realised that she never did anything or went anywhere alone. When she went into the market town either Mrs Mathias or one of her sons accompanied her, and every time she said she wanted to write to one of her friends some reason was given to discourage her. Last time she had started a letter to Lenny, Cian had looked over her shoulder and said that when she had finished it he would post it for her.

'Don't give the letter to Declan, he's a head like a sieve so he has, but I'll see that it's delivered.' He had grinned engagingly at her. 'And don't you go tellin' your pal you ain't happy, because that would be a downright lie so it would.' He had put a brotherly arm around her shoulders and dropped a kiss on the top of her head, in the way that only a short time before would have made Molly almost swoon with pleasure. 'Now, how about a walk in the woods? 'Tis ages since we did such a thing.'

She was sure that Cian was trying to distract her, but nevertheless she had written the letter, although when she had finished it Cian had playfully snatched the envelope from her hands, stating that he was about to drive into town and would post it whilst he was there. That had been many weeks ago, and now she realised she had no proof, save for Cian's word, that the letter had ever been dispatched.

That evening, getting ready for bed, she decided she would write again. Lenny, of course, must have left the home months before, but she was sure there would be someone there who could forward her letter on to him. This time she would not give it to anyone else, not even Cian, but would hand it in at the post office when she collected Mrs Mathias's pension.

Having made up her mind, she wrote a long and passionate letter, explaining the situation and begging for Lenny's help. She had no envelope, but folded the pages carefully and pushed them into the pocket of her coat. She would buy an envelope from the postmistress, and if anyone queried what she was doing she would say she was writing to an old chum but had run out of stationery.

Next day she was up betimes, and found that for once the luck had favoured her. Since the advent of the hated cousin Esme, the trip into town was taken by all three of them, which would make it difficult for Molly to be certain of visiting the post office unaccompanied. But when she went up to Mrs Mathias's room, it was to find the old lady groaning in pain from a bad attack of arthritis brought on – Molly looked through the window – by the cold and steadily pouring rain.

'No, no, I aren't leavin' my bed this day, not for nobody,' Mrs Mathias said fretfully as Molly picked up her dress and carried it over to the bed. 'I know there's a deal of marketin' to be done but you're young and strong and no doubt Cian or Declan will spare an hour or so to accompany you. I'll keep Esme here to bring up my meals and see to my comfort.'

Molly opened her mouth to say she would stay behind herself, then remembered her letter and shut it again. To the best of her knowledge the Mathias boys were off somewhere and would trust someone else to do the marketing. And whilst it continued to rain she could not imagine cousin Esme suggesting that poor Mrs Mathias might abandon her bed, so it actually looked as though Molly might get into town neither watched nor accompanied for once. So it was in a mood of some exhilaration that she entered the kitchen and began her tasks.

Declan had taken the trap on some business of his own, so Molly had to walk the five miles. When she reached the post office she was aware of a wonderful sense of lightness and freedom as she pulled the letter out of her pocket and thrust it into the envelope she had just purchased, licked the stamp and handed the missive to the postmistress before getting out Mrs Mathias's pension book, signing on the dotted line and tucking away the money, some of which she would use to buy items from her shopping list. When she saw the letter plop into the box the sense of relief was joined by another feeling. Why should she not make her way down to the docks right now and get aboard a ship which would take her to England? But the thought of virtually stealing Mrs Mathias's pension made her uncomfortable, and anyhow the prospect of finding her way to an unknown port in the hope that her money would be sufficient for a voyage to England was fraught with difficulty. No, her letter had given Lenny her address and the details of her situation. With him by her side the idea of her escape was no longer frightening but welcome. The whole point of the letter had been an appeal for Lenny's help; she was sure he would find a way to rescue her. All she had to do now was to wait patiently until Lenny arrived in Ireland and could tell her what to do.

She completed the marketing and set off to walk the five miles which lay between her and the old O'Hare place. The bags were heavy and the rain was constant, but Molly's heart was light. If it had not been for cousin Esme, she would probably never have got round to the realisation that she was a virtual slave, but now she suspected that even Cian was not her true friend. In fact, the sooner she got away from the Mathiases the better. And when, halfway back to the farm, she heard her name called and saw him coming up behind her, although she was grateful for his help with the heavy bags she knew that he had followed her into town in order to make sure that she did not run off, and was no longer fooled when he reproached her for not waiting for him but setting out alone.

Chapter Seven

When no response came to her letter, Molly almost gave up any hope of escape. Yet the more she heard about the war being waged on the other side of the Irish Sea the more she wished to play her part, and, eventually, to be reunited with her old friends. Gradually, hope returned.

As she lay in bed she contemplated her means of escape. She would pin her bedroom shutters back and get out that way, she supposed, but it was a good drop to the farmyard below and she did not wish to find herself with a broken leg. All in all, she decided not to make a bid for freedom until she had heard from Lenny. For one thing, she had no money with which to pay for a ticket from Ireland to Liverpool, and no idea how much such a crossing would cost. She wondered whether it might be possible to work her passage in some capacity or another, but knew in her heart this was wishful thinking. Furthermore, although she knew ferries sailed to Liverpool from Dublin, she had only the haziest idea where the old O'Hare place lay in relation to that port, and still less how she could possibly make her way there alone. No, the sensible thing to do was to wait until Lenny either replied to her letter or came to Ireland in person.

Molly sighed and sat up on her elbow, staring towards the lighter square in the wall which was the window. And suddenly a most unwelcome thought assailed her. Suppose Lenny came, as she had implored him to do, and walked into the waiting jaws of Sinbad? It was all very well telling herself that Lenny liked dogs; that did not mean that all dogs liked Lenny. Had she mentioned Sinbad in her letter to her old friend? She had explained just about everything, but she could not now recall whether she had specifically mentioned the dog.

Sighing, Molly lay down again and forced her mind to concentrate on the letter. Then she gave a sigh of relief. She *had* mentioned Sinbad; she had said the dog was loose at nights. Now she would have to leave it to Lenny to find a way round the problem.

Molly cuddled her head into the pillow, and, very soon, slept.

*

When Bumble saw the letter on the bulletin board he recognised Lenny's handwriting at once. The only thing that surprised him, in fact, was the weight of it, because Lenny's letters were usually more like notes, often merely giving his present address and a few scrawled lines concerning his promotion and training to become a Spitfire pilot. Bumble weighed the letter thoughtfully in his hand, then decided to read it in the comparative comfort of the NAAFI, over a cup of Camp coffee. No point in going back to his hut. He had made his bed and set out his kit, and now all he was waiting for was the officer who would do the inspection. The NAAFI was usually crowded but his friend Tim had saved him a place and a cup of coffee, so Bumble sank into the seat beside him and slit open the envelope. To his surprise, he extracted four or five sheets of paper, closely written in a hand which he did not recognise but knew was not Lenny's. With them came another piece of paper, which looked as though it had been torn from the back of a diary, explaining, in Lenny's writing this time, that the letter had tracked him all the way from Haisborough Orphanage, correctly forwarded from station to station by conscientious clerks, but that he didn't have time to do anything about it and would Bumble help him out? *Thanks – you're a mate. Must rush – only a few more days and I'll be a fully fledged Spitfire pilot! Your old pal, Lenny.* Meanwhile, Tim had leaned forward to peer inquisitively at the airmail pages.

'Someone's got a lot to say for themselves,' he remarked curiously. 'I saw the letter on the bulletin board but I knew you were coming along behind me so I didn't take it off. Is it from your friend Lenny?' He reached out and turned over the last sheet to reveal the sender's name. 'Well I'm dammed; after all this time! I wonder how long this letter's been in the post? It could be absolutely ages; I remember a fellow telling me a letter from his wife saying she'd had a baby followed him all round the world, and the kid was over a year old before he got the news. It's from Molly.'

Bumble jumped. He had not quite stopped hoping for a letter from Molly, yet when it came he had not recognised the writing. Hastily, he gathered up the airmail sheets and flapped a hand at Tim. 'Shurrup,' he commanded, and began to read.

'Is it confidential?' Tim asked presently. 'It looks like someone's life story; Molly's, I presume. Are you going to let me have a read?'

'Might as well, since two heads are better than one,' Bumble said as he finished the first page and handed it to his friend. 'It's a weird story, but apparently Molly's wanted to come home for months only she's been kept . . . well, a virtual prisoner in an Irish farmhouse just outside the village of Caubean, wherever that may be. She's writing to Lenny asking him to help her, 'cos of course she has no way of knowing he's on a fighter station somewhere in the wilds of Lincolnshire and can't do much from there. And *that*, my dear friend, is why he sent her letter on to me, because at least I'm nearer.'

'You are indeed,' Tim said. 'And you'll be even closer when you take up your posting. I don't know how good your geography is, but like the rest of us you're going to Rhosneigr in Anglesey, aren't you? They'll need mechanics once they're operational and they want help with building runways and so on . . . What are you staring at?'

'Tim Donahue! If I'd not forgotten that you're Irish yourself,' Bumble said in an awed voice. 'You don't by any chance know where Caubean is, do you? According to Molly's letter it's not very large . . .'

Tim gave a snort of amusement. 'Not very large! It's what you would call a hamlet, I s'pose. A farm, a couple of tied cottages, maybe a blacksmith and a shop which sells a few basic necessities. I've an aunt lives quite near, so I know the country round there fairly well. Does she tell you the name of the people who've been holding her prisoner? The O'Hares are the only farming family I know of in that area, but I can't imagine the old feller or his wife holding anyone against their will.' Tim cocked a dark eyebrow at Bumble. 'So, does she give her captors a name? I've only read the first page, remember.'

'She says she's at the O'Hare farm, but the family are called the Mathiases. It seems they were good to her at the start, but since some cousin or other came to stay all that's changed. Now she just wants to come home.'

'And of course if they're holding her captive they won't be paying her, so even if she escaped she'd have no money to buy a passage back to England,' Tim said thoughtfully. 'No wonder she's desperate. But what can you do about it, old feller? The letter's dated months ago – for all you know she may have escaped long since.'

Bumble shook his head. 'No, she'll still be in that farmhouse, I'm sure of it.' He spread the letter out on the table and began to read through it again, then stopped and smiled at his friend. 'She says here she won't make any move until I give her the go-ahead – or until Lenny does, she means. She obviously knows about the problems with letters. I just wish we could get word to her that help is at hand, but apparently she doesn't want us to contact her directly for fear of the Mathiases finding out.'

Tim nodded, then reached out a hand. 'Can I read the rest of it? If I'm going to help you I shall need all the information I can get.'

Bumble handed over the letter willingly enough and watched as his friend began to peruse the pages. 'Her writing's awful difficult,' he warned him. 'She's used that thin airmail paper and an indelible pencil which seems to have leaked purple all over the place. She talks of some chap called Sinbad; I don't know where he fits into the story.'

Tim grunted. 'Shut up a minute,' he commanded. 'She's told you, or Lenny rather, all the important bits. It's a shame that we can't get a message to her explaining that we can't get leave until we finish our training in a couple of weeks. From what other fellers have said I gather we then get a week or so off before we take up our postings.' He looked up from his perusal of the letter and grinned at his friend. 'She suggests we make the attempt after dark, for obvious reasons. I take it you've enough money to get us across the water by fair means or foul? Eire is a neutral country, but Wales is not. I don't know whether ferries are still running but there'll be fishing boats going about their business.' He sighed reminiscently. 'Ever tasted Dublin prawns, old feller?'

'No I haven't, nor do I want to,' Bumble said rather crossly. 'I've been saving up my money for months so I've quite enough to get us all across the water. And once we're there it'll just be a matter of finding this O'Hare farm, snatching young Molly and returning to Wales. Is that right?'

Tim nodded. 'Where will Molly go once she gets back to Britain?'

Bumble shrugged. 'Since she wants to help in the war effort – I think that's what she says on the last page, anyway – I s'pose she'll join one of the services. Probably the Land Army, since she can't be more than fifteen or sixteen.'

Tim finished reading the last page of the letter and handed the dirty crumpled sheets back to his friend. 'We've got a couple of weeks to plan our rescue,' he remarked. 'That should be long enough.'

Bumble took the letter and shoved it into his pocket. 'I can't tell you how much better I feel now I know there are two of us,' he admitted. 'If there's ever anything I can do for you, Tim, just let me know. And as for rescuing Molly, I'm sure we'll be successful now that we know exactly where she is.'

*

Molly waited. She was in no hurry, for though she had not been able to receive a reply to her letter she was by now absolutely certain that help would soon be at hand. She kept telling herself that it might be some considerable time before Lenny even received the letter and then he might find it difficult to interpret her writing, but she was sure he would understand her desperate message and come to her. After all, she had repeated the name of the farm and the village of Caubean at least three times. He only had to find someone who knew Ireland and they would be able to pinpoint where she was.

In the meantime she behaved exactly as though all was well, even obeying Esme's commands, though it went against the grain to do so. News of the May Blitz which Liverpool had suffered merely made her more determined to join her fellow countrymen in their fight against the Nazis. As summer eased into autumn, the jobs on the farm changed. She and a good few helpers from the village began to pick and pack the apples from the old orchard, label them and send them off for shipment across the Irish Sea, though of course they made sure to keep a fair number in the apple loft.

She felt instinctively that Lenny had received and understood her rather wild and untidy letter. She was sure that by now he must be in the air force and so he would have to apply for leave, but she waited with calm confidence for the moonless night when Lenny would come to her.

She wondered what arrangements, he would have made to get them back to the coast, but even that did not really worry her. With the posting of the letter it seemed as though she had handed all responsibility to Lenny. He was a man now, but still her first boyfriend, and she was completely certain that he was capable of stealing her from under Esme's nose. It was a pity she could not let him know when the Mathias brothers would be around, but she would just have to hope he would set some sort of watch on the farm and act accordingly.

So each night, when Molly climbed into her bed, she lay for a happy half-hour musing over her forthcoming escape. She knew Lenny had always been popular with other young men and guessed he would not come to her rescue alone, but the others were of little account; so far as Molly was concerned it was Lenny who would lead the expedition and carry her off, if not to safety, at least to the land of her birth. In her mind's eye she saw Lenny as he had been when they had last met and then Lenny as she imagined him now: nearly six foot of muscle and determination, topped by curly black hair and a lean and dangerous face. Oh, yes, Lenny was ideally suited both for a hero and for a rescuer. She told herself that she had loved him almost from the first moment they had met and thought she loved him still, though for some while Cian had taken his place in her affections. Naturally the feeling would be reciprocated once they were together again.

Satisfied, and secure in her dream, Molly slept.

*

'We want a night when the moon's either not there at all or frail as an eyelash. The almanac is on my bedside table – can you check through it, old feller?' Tim said.

Bumble nodded. 'Can you think of somewhere to lie up while we're watchin' the farm? You said the country round there is well wooded and hilly. An old lambing hut would be ideal – one that would give us a good view of the farmhouse.'

'Once we're sure who's in the house we can act accordingly. But daylight's no good, it's got to be at night.'

'Every farmer worth his salt has a gun; I don't fancy being peppered, nor seeing Molly killed before my eyes. If only we could get a message to her; she could steal the ammo without being noticed. So we've got to get away before the feller's even thought about his gun.'

'Quietly, man! Our plan was to watch the farm-house for two days, not to bring someone up here to see who's making so much noise. I wish there was a way of contacting Molly when no one else was around, but I don't think there is. We can't let her know we've arrived until the moment we do the snatch. Tomorrow night there's no moon, but s'pose she doesn't realise we've found her and goes merrily off to sleep?'

'Then she can bloody well merrily wake up,' Tim said rather grimly. 'If only we could get a message through to her. But I s'pose it's impossible without breaking our cover.'

Molly knew they were near; something was differ-ent, though she could not have said what. Sinbad was anxious, prowling the farmhouse and staring up at the shepherd's hut on the heather-covered hill at the back of the farm. But it seemed as though the Mathiases did not notice the dog's preoccupa-tion, and Molly's behaviour had not changed one iota from the way she always behaved. She worked with the beasts in the mornings, milking the cows, feeding the pigs and collecting the eggs. In the afternoons she helped the old woman to cook, bake and preserve, enjoying the simple tasks and admiring the shining glass jars full of plums, apricots from the big old tree spreadeagled across one wall, and strawberries from the bed under the netting which the blackbirds visited in June. She tried not to do so, but found herself constantly glancing out of the window. Sinbad continued to stare at the hut, twisting his neck to look at Molly and whine as he did so. Molly turned away hastily, smiling to herself. If Esme had been here . . . but she was not. She was upstairs knitting herself a thick jumper in preparation for a cold winter and resented anyone interrupting what she considered her work.

So Molly continued with her normal jobs, increasingly certain that help was at hand. She longed to take a chance and wander up to the shepherd's hut, but though she was no longer frightened of Sinbad she realised that if Lenny was already in the hut her appearance there could only do harm. In the normal course of events she had never once visited the place and it would look very suspicious if she did so now. When Mrs Mathias called her in for supper she did not even glance up at the hut as she made her way across the farmyard, and was glad she had not done so when, later in the evening,

Declan came into the kitchen, giving a tremendous yawn.

'What's for supper, our mammy? And don't suggest ham sarnies 'cos I never want to see ham again.'

His mother chuckled but shook her head reprovingly. 'As if I'd give you such things after a long day's work,' she said. 'There's a grand steak and kidney pie keepin' warm in the oven with a pile of mashed tatties and a jug of good gravy. Are you up for it?'

Declan slumped into a chair, rubbed his eyes and gave another enormous yawn. 'I'm half dead wit' fatigue, but I can still eat,' he said. He waited while his mother extracted the pie from the oven and cut him a generous slice, plonking the plate down on the kitchen table and adding a bowl of mashed potatoes and a jug of the aforementioned gravy. Then Declan's weariness seemed to leave him, and Molly was about to make her excuses and go off to bed when he turned and addressed her. 'Comin' back from putting the ponies into the long meadow I met the feller what drives the sheep down from the hills when the weather gets bad,' he said conversationally. 'He told me he's noticed strangers about. Heard any rumours to that effect?'

He was staring at her as he spoke and though Molly's heart plummeted she did her best to return his look with one as frank. 'Not unless you mean the postmistress's niece, what's come to give her a hand while her daughter has her baby,' she said glibly. 'Is that who you mean?'

Declan shrugged. 'I dunno as I mean anythin'; probably it were just gossip,' he said. 'There's a deal of comin' and goin' between us and the Welsh.' He broke off a piece of pie crust and gave it to Sinbad, who took it with all his usual delicacy and crunched it down. Declan rubbed him affectionately behind the ears. 'You notice anything odd while I were away, old fellow? I reckon if a stranger came near this place you'd be the first to give tongue.'

Molly giggled. 'He wouldn't just give tongue, he'd give tooth,' she said with an assumption of gaiety. 'I've never heard Sinbad give warning of strangers, but then you might say strangers simply never come here. If someone did, would Sinbad really fly for them? I'm doubtful, but if you tell me otherwise . . .'

Declan, busy eating, shrugged once more. 'Haven't we told you a dozen times Sinbad's a grand lookout? He's gentle as a lamb to folk he knows, but if he thought someone was a threat to any one of us – even you, Molly – then he'd tear 'em limb from limb. Before we took him he were a guard dog in a big liquor store and folk soon realised he were no pushover.'

Molly giggled again. 'Well, we don't keep any liquor here, apart from the applejack which the mammy tells me you can't make until the weather turns really cold. And now I'm goin' to get some sleep, because I have to be up early tomorrow to start the milking, since cousin Esme still hasn't learned the trick of it.'

Molly made her way up to bed aware of not only the prickly excitement which had been with her all day but also a frisson of fear. The conversation with Declan had been unsettling, and the fact that Sinbad had returned to the yard, although it was a cold and blustery night, made her wonder whether Declan was suspicious. She was pretty sure that Lenny and any friends he had managed to recruit were in that hut and would probably make the attempt to rescue her this very night.

She did not mean to undress, for she imagined that the journey she might presently set out on would make warm clothing essential. So she got into her bed fully clothed and waited, with what patience she could, for Lenny's next move.

She heard Mrs Mathias thump up the stairs and repair to her own room, followed closely by cousin Esme, who would no doubt help the old woman undress and get into bed. Below her, in the kitchen, she heard Cian arrive, take his share of the meat pie, and after about ten minutes of muffled talk with his brother let himself out again and leave the farm. She heard Declan pacing the floor, as though waiting for someone, but when the old grandfather clock in the hall struck midnight it seemed he had given up, for she heard his heavy tread on the stairs and guessed he was going to bed.

She wondered if he had chained Sinbad to his kennel, which he occasionally did to stop the dog following Cian wherever he went, but when she slipped out of bed and peered through her shutters she saw Sinbad strolling around the yard as usual, sniffing and occasionally lifting a leg.

She remained at the window for a few minutes, peering through the crack in the shutters, but it was too cold to linger and she climbed hastily back into bed, heaving the blankets up over her shoulders with a shiver. If tonight was to be her best chance of escape, and all the signs seemed to point to it, she would have to find some way of remaining awake, for as the warmth of the bed enfolded her it became more and more difficult to imagine leaving her cosy nest.

Listening hard she heard the noise of an engine, low and purring, but only for an instant. It faded into silence just as a tiny sound from the yard below alerted her to the fact that someone was creeping quietly across the cobbles. She concluded that, since Sinbad did not bark, it must be Cian, though why he should return to the farmhouse at such a late hour – it was past a quarter to one – she could not imagine. But suppose it was not Cian, but Lenny? Hastily, she slid out of bed, thrust her feet into her boots and began to put on the jacket which was lying on the chair at the foot of her bed, and even as she donned the garment the idea came to her. Rather than run the risk of one of the Mathiases becoming suspicious and checking her room as she was halfway through the window she would use the old trick of trapping a chair-back under the door handle, which could keep an intruder out almost indefinitely.

She carried the chair across, tipped it on its back legs and wedged the back beneath the door handle, and returned to the window. Peering out she saw a tall figure, dark against the cobbles. He was looking up at the farmhouse expectantly and Molly hastily opened the shutters, noting with satisfaction that there was no revealing squeak, either from the shutters or from herself.

Excitedly, she swung her legs over the sill and squiggled out of the window, hanging on to the sill until she felt someone grasp her ankles and guide her to the ground. Then a voice whispered: 'I've got you. Just relax. Two more minutes and we'll be away.'

'Oh, yes!' Molly whispered. 'Where's Sinbad?'

Her rescuer chuckled. 'Some guard dog!' he murmured. 'He treated us like long-lost friends, particularly after I'd fed him some chunks of meat.' He stood Molly down, then grabbed her hand as a rumpus broke out within the farmhouse. 'Can you run like the wind?' he asked urgently. 'We don't want trouble if we can possibly avoid it. I suspected we might disturb the enemy, but when the dog didn't bark I thought we'd got away with it.' A large firm hand grasped Molly's much smaller one, and in seconds it seemed they were in the lane, and running towards a dim figure standing next to a vehicle.

'Get in,' the man ordered breathlessly, and Molly thought how Lenny had changed. He was a lot taller and broader and his voice had lost its slight Liverpool twang, but Molly told herself he was still the Lenny she loved, and as she scrambled into the car he gave her a kiss and rumpled her hair.

'Lenny! I *knew* you'd come,' Molly said, her voice soft. 'When I heard the engine earlier I knew it must be you. Don't bother with the family – just get me back to Liverpool and let them carry on with whatever they're doing. *Please*, Lenny. They can be dangerous.'

Her companion laughed. 'I'm not Lenny,' he said. 'It's me, Bumble.'

Molly frowned, puzzled, then her brow cleared. 'Lenny's friend Bumble!' she exclaimed. 'I remember now. Lenny said you were his pal so when I wanted to pass a message to him I searched you out in the playground.' She felt her cheeks warm. 'Only you didn't want to get involved; I seem to remember you told me to take my own messages and walked away from me.'

It was Bumble's turn to redden. 'That was a long time ago and I was a bit of an idiot,' he said apologetically. 'But I'm making up for it now. The thing is, Lenny got your letter, but he's stationed a long way away so he forwarded it to me in case I could help. When we got somewhere where it's safe to show a light . . .' He was interrupted by the sound of pursuit coming from the farmyard.

Quickly he climbed into the front passenger seat and Molly, watching the farmyard disappear over her shoulder as the car moved forward, sank back with a sigh of relief. She was free! She felt relief wash over her and then, to her astonishment, she felt a pang not only of pain but also of regret. The wind which tousled her hair was a reminder of happier times when she had roamed with Cian through woods and moorland thinking herself as good a family member as any other, learning all about country ways and rejoicing, then, at what had seemed like freedom. Looking back, she had always seen Cian as her friend. Declan she knew neither liked nor trusted her, yet he had never actively tried to be rid of her. In fact, he had listened almost indulgently to her enthusiastic descriptions of her forays with Cian, and suddenly the contrast with her old life in Liverpool came sharply to her mind. Despite all her dreams of this moment, now that it was here Molly almost wished it had not come. Had it not been for Esme, she realised, she would never have made up her mind to leave the country life behind her and work in a factory. She gave herself a mental shake. Esme was there to stay and the Mathiases were part of her past and must be forgotten. Even Cian. But how could she forget watching fox cubs playing outside their earth, or a badger coming back from a hunting expedition on a misty morning before the sun was up, and the squeals of excitement from her cubs as she entered the sett?

Other images, more mundane but no less loved, flashed across her mind: being taught by Mrs Mathias to joint and prepare rabbit meat for a stew, or sitting with her at the kitchen table, each taking a turn to shake the bottle of cream until it became butter. And she remembered how she and Mrs Mathias had listened to Churchill's speeches, the sonorous words rolling out and firing her patriotic fervour more than anything else could. *'Never in the field of human conflict was so much owed by so many to so few,'* Churchill had said, and Molly had been only partly comforted when Mrs Mathias had assured her that the grain they had grown would be milled and made into bread, and the loaves would be sent to help to feed the very airmen who had waged the Battle of Britain in the English skies.

She convinced me, more or less, that though we were living very comfortably in a neutral country we were still doing our bit towards helping Britain, Molly reminded herself. It's not given to everyone to help to fight a war; Mrs Mathias said so long as we didn't encourage the Germans to believe we were on their side, so long as our grain would be shipped to where the British needed it most, then that was just about all anyone could do for the war effort when one was living in a neutral country like Eire.

Molly sighed and snuggled down in the worn upholstery of the little car, and presently the driver drew to a halt. Molly saw his teeth gleam in the dim light and ventured a question.

'Why have we stopped? Have you run out of petrol?'

Both young men had struggled out of the car and now began to fold back the canvas hood. The driver turned to grin at her as he got back in.

'Wind resistance,' he said briefly. 'The rain's stopped and the wind is abating; we'll make more speed with the hood folded away, and the sooner we're out of the country the better.'

Molly nodded her comprehension. It was strange that neither of her rescuers was Lenny, but if he was in the air force, as she supposed, perhaps he had not been able to get away. The kiss was a bit of a mystery, but she had no time to worry her head over what must have been a gesture made in the excitement of the moment. Molly leaned back in her seat and began to enjoy the ride. It was, after all, the ride to freedom, to the life she had waited so long to lead, and this was just the beginning of the adventure. There was still the journey to the coast to be completed before they crossed the Irish Sea. Hesitantly, she leaned forward and tapped the broad shoulder in front of her.

'Bumble, do you think the Mathiases will follow us and snatch me back when we get to the coast?' she queried, and was ashamed of the tremble in her voice. 'I thought once or twice that the elder brother, Declan, felt I should have been allowed to die when I was lost in the forest. He says I know too much.'

Bumble turned to peer at her over his shoulder. She could not see his face in the dim light but his teeth gleamed white in the darkness.

'Little idiot,' he said kindly. 'Now you're with us nothing bad can happen. Before you know it you'll be back in Liverpool deciding what you want to do with your new freedom. No doubt the Mathiases have their own business to attend to, but that needn't concern you. Once you're out of their lives they'll forget all about you. The weather's rough tonight, but the forecast for tomorrow is good. My pal here knows a safe house where we can lie up until conditions are right for crossing. Are you still scared, or do you feel you can trust me, even if I'm not Lenny Smith?'

'Of course I do, trust you I mean,' Molly said indignantly. 'But what I don't know is whether I've been cleared of stealing Matron's watch. I'm sure you heard about all that. I only hope the theft got pinned on the right person. Because, you see, I don't have a mum or dad I can run to, only the orphanage. I s'pose I could get a bed in a YWCA but I don't want to do that if the charge of theft is still hanging over me.'

Bumble laughed. 'Queen, you must have been cleared of that theft before you even reached Ireland, though of course you didn't know it. Apparently the watch hung on a short length of chain with a bar which slid into a buttonhole. Remember Jane? One of the staff knew she was a troublemaker and looked in her drawer, and there was the bar and chain. So you see, you needn't have run away at all; in fact it was the worst possible thing you could've done. It branded you guilty, though not for very long.'

Molly gave a huge gusty sigh of relief. 'I knew it must have been Jane – she was Matron's pet, always in and out of her room, and she was jealous when I got offered a job in one of the factories on Love Lane. I was going to share a room with my friend Ellen, but that was ages ago, long before the war started. I s'pose by now Ellen's joined the forces, like Lenny, and probably has a host of new friends and never thinks of me.'

'Well, you're wrong there,' Bumble said positively. 'It was your friend Ellen who first made us think about Ireland, but I shan't tell you what she's up to because I'm sure she'd rather do so herself. But there's something I should have asked you before; do the Mathiases own a car?'

Molly giggled at the very thought. 'No, only a lorry, and that's always breaking down. So if you're worrying that a sleek Rolls-Royce will presently appear in the rear-view mirror you can relax. If they pursue us it'll be on the carthorses, and I've never seen them even break into a trot.' She glanced at the driver. 'I know who you are, Bumble, but who's your pal?'

Bumble grinned. 'My pal here, the one who got us the loan of the car and the safe house, is Tim – Tim Donahue.' Once more he turned in his seat to smile at her. 'It seems so odd that you didn't recognise me, but I s'pose that's because when we knew each other before you had eyes for no one but Lenny.' He chuckled again. 'And that's strange in itself, because though Lenny is a grand chap he's no Clark Gable.'

Molly stiffened. 'What makes you think I'm looking for someone with a film star's good looks?'

she enquired. 'Character is much more important than – than curly hair or perfect features. I liked Lenny because he was good fun and up for anything which got us out of the home for a while.'

Bumble hesitated. 'If you were to meet Lenny again you might find your idol had feet of clay,' he said at last. 'I mean, he made no effort to get leave and come over to Ireland to rescue you, did he?'

Molly bristled. 'I'm sure he tried, because we've been bezzies ever since we first met,' she said defensively. 'Just you wait till he hears I'm home! He'll be round at Haisborough before you can say knife, wanting to know all about the Mathiases so he can bring them to account.'

In the dim light, Bumble gave her a long hard look. Like Ellen, he did not think his old friend considered Molly as anything but a pal, but he was far too kind-hearted – and far too good a friend – to tell her that Lenny's affections were probably engaged elsewhere. Instead he leaned back in his seat and took a long hard look at himself. Had he been a complete fool to begin to hope that Molly might come to regard him, Bumble, as more than 'Lenny's pal'? Lenny had moved on. That was clear from his infrequent letters, from what Ellen had said, and from the fact that he had not even considered rescuing Molly himself but had passed the responsibility for her escape into Bumble's hands; for Bumble knew enough about the RAF to think that Lenny could have got leave as soon as he had completed his training if he had explained the situation to his squadron leader.

And had Molly been grateful to her rescuer? He realised with a sinking heart that she had not. Her first remark – 'Lenny! I *knew* you'd come' – still rankled. Oh, she might thank him once they reached Liverpool, but then she would thank Tim as well, and Tim was almost a stranger. I've got to stop thinking about a girl who isn't interested in me, Bumble told himself. Perhaps if she'd never got brought to Ireland our relationship might have blossomed, but facts are facts. I do believe, after that incident in the playground, she would rather have almost anyone than me. And it's not as if I don't know other girls who are fancy free. Little Ellen, for instance. Now there's a nice kid who isn't taken in by Lenny's charm.

He exchanged a quick glance with Tim and then said gently, 'Well, remember it's a long way from Lincolnshire, where Lenny's based, to Liverpool. And he's always busy – all through the evacuation of Dunkirk he was on call twenty-four hours a day. Then there was the Battle of Britain, when he was constantly working on the kites. And now he's flying them himself, so no matter how willing, he has to abide by the rules, like the rest of us. Tim and I were about to complete our basic training when your letter arrived, so as soon as we got our leave we came over to fetch you home, but we're bound by the same rules as Lenny and will have to say goodbye once we've got you settled in with your friends. In fact, we've already had our postings to an airfield in North Wales, so you won't see much of any of us after that.'

'Oh!' Molly said rather blankly. She realised that she had been expecting either Lenny or his friend to support her through any ordeals which might lie ahead. But she told herself briskly that she was no longer a child but a young woman, for she knew that her time with the Mathiases had caused her to grow up a good deal more quickly than she would have done at the home. She was, in fact, a different person from the girl who had crawled into the lorry and hidden amongst the fleeces. The Molly she was now could be a real help to her country, whereas the Molly she was then had been more of a burden.

She was thinking as much when the car turned off the road into a narrow lane, at the end of which stood a solid little farmhouse not dissimilar to the O'Hares'. Tim drew the car to a halt with a scream of brakes and Bumble helped Molly to alight.

'This place belongs to Tim's aunt, and she's assured us we will be welcome to stay here until we can arrange a crossing,' Bumble explained as he knocked gently on the front door. 'As I told you, the forecast is for the wind to drop, so it doesn't look as though we'll be here long. Our hostess's name is Anne Marie Donahue.' He cocked his head to one side at the sound of approaching footsteps from within the house. 'And here she comes now.'

*

Declan had suspected all day that something was up, though he could not have said what. The feeling of unease was so strong that having climbed into bed when the clock struck midnight he found himself climbing out again less than an hour later. If anything was wrong, he thought vindictively, it would be something connected with that wretched girl Molly. Had it not been for the fact that his brother liked her he would have tried much harder to persuade their mother to get rid of her, though even he did acknowledge she was a hard worker. Without her, there was no doubt that the farm would not flourish the way it did. Nevertheless, when he peered through his bedroom window and saw nothing stirring in the quiet farmyard he went next to Molly's room, turned the handle with great caution and pushed gently.

The moment he realised the door was blocked he knew his suspicions had been right. He roused the household, shouting loudly that there were burglars, and thundered down the flight of stairs to reach the kitchen where he snatched his coat off the hook, flung open the back door and shouted for Sinbad. Now that he had got his night vision he was able to make out dark figures in the lane and gave a yell of triumph. If Molly was with them he could easily catch her up and bring her back, which would please Cian. He heard an engine start and was about to go over to the patch of shadow which he assumed was their old lorry when it occurred to him, first, that cranking the engine into life would take a good few minutes and next that he actually had no desire whatsoever to impede Molly's escape. Why should he? He neither liked nor approved of the girl but he did not believe she would ever tell tales to the Garda, because such tales might get her beloved Cian into trouble. Yet if he did not pursue her his brother might be upset . . . and at this point he real-ised that what he had taken to be their old vehicle was no such thing; in fact it was just a patch of deep shadow cast by the roof of one of the outbuildings.

The intruders – friends of Molly's, he assumed – had actually taken the trouble to close the farm gate, so now Declan opened it and slid into the lane. There was no sign of the vehicle he had heard and the night was quiet. Pressed against his knee, Sinbad whined softly then looked up into his face and gave a peremptory bark; just one, almost as though he was informing Declan that something was not quite right. Declan looked up the lane in the direction he knew the vehicle must have taken, and saw no sign of it. He grinned to himself; he felt downright pleased. He had never liked Molly and now she was gone and no one could blame him; he had tried to get her back, hadn't he? He had run into the yard intending to start cranking the old lorry so that he could go in pursuit, but the lorry had not been there. Wending his way back to the house, Declan frowned. Where *was* the lorry? So far as he could recall Cian had not mentioned taking it, so how was he, Declan, to know that it wasn't there? For the first time it occurred to him to wonder whether his brother was implicated in some way in Molly's departure, then he dismissed this thought as he reached the kitchen door and flung it open. To his surprise the room was not empty, but even as he opened his mouth to tell the occupant that the disturbance was over and the only thing missing, so far as he could see, was that chit of a girl to whom Cian had taken a liking, cousin Esme shouldered rudely past him and erupted into the yard.

'Burglars, bandits, cattle thieves! That bloody Molly Hardwick must have told them to come to us to get their dirty work afoot.' She rounded angrily on Sinbad. 'Call yourself a guard dog?' she shrieked, then turned her wrath on Declan. 'Go after them, don't just stand in the doorway like a bloody block of wood!' she shouted into his face. 'Get her back! In a few hours them cows will want bringing in from the pasture and milking. I'm not a perishin' farm worker and the old fellers only do evenin's.' She gave him a hard push, and since he was not expecting it he found himself sprawling on the cobbles. Sinbad licked his cheek, but Declan pushed the dog away.

'Get off you great softy,' he ordered. 'Molly can't drive, so I reckon there was at least one man come to fetch her and you did nothin'.' He scrambled to his feet, his lips twitching. This situation was becoming farcical, and angry though he had been he could not help a grin escaping. Esme was still shouting as he propelled her back into the kitchen, so he put a large hand across her mouth. 'Shut up and listen to me,' he commanded. 'You're no fonder of Molly than I am, so why the fuss? She won't go tellin' the authorities about us 'cos though she may hate my guts she swoons over Cian, same as all the girls do. Besides, the Luftwaffe are bombing the hell out of Britain so the chances are she won't live long enough to make trouble for anyone.' He looked around the kitchen, at the fire still glowing in the Aga, the table laid for breakfast, and through the open pantry door the gleam of lamplight on the bottles of preserves.

'I tell you, Esme, there's scarce a house standing anywhere near the Liverpool docks, so don't you envy Molly her freedom, 'cos it may come at a pretty high price. Why, isn't that the reason ye're here yourself? Now let's get some sleep before the alarm clock goes off to let us know it's breakfast time.'

He was about to turn away, but Esme caught at his sleeve. 'I ain't never milked a cow in me life, and I don't mean to start makin' breakfast either,' she said waspishly. 'I don't like Molly any more than you do, but I don't mean to take over the running of this place. Well, to be honest I couldn't.' She grinned spitefully. 'So you'd best start thinkin' who's goin' to do the work young Molly did, else you'll be in real trouble.'

A querulous voice came from the stairway, down which Mrs Mathias was hobbling. 'What's going on?' she demanded. 'It's the middle of the night. I tried to wake Molly to find out what was happening but her door's got stuck in some way and won't open.' She glanced round the room. 'Where is the girl? When it's breakfast time I'll want some help wi' the porridge . . .'

'Well, you won't get it,' Esme said bluntly. 'The girl's run off, so you'll have to manage the porridge yourself.'

Mrs Mathias looked round the room, eyes widening. 'Gone?' she echoed. 'Gone with Cian, do you mean?'

'Oh, for God's sake,' Declan interrupted. 'Esme will help you today but in future we'll have a girl from the village in, though we'll have to pay her, I suppose.'

'But surely she'll be coming back?' Mrs Mathias said, sounding as confused as she looked. 'I don't like change, and Molly knows my little ways.' She turned on Declan. 'Fetch her back!' she ordered peremptorily. 'Tell Cian he's a bad boy to steal me little helper.'

Declan sighed, took his mother over to a fireside chair and settled her in it. 'It wasn't Cian who took her,' he began. 'Listen carefully, Mammy, to what I'm goin' to tell you . . .'

Chapter Eight

1942

Molly sat on the end of her bed, staring crossly at its metal frame. Not that it was her bed any more; probably the new owner would be along any minute, in time for kit inspection at any rate. And by then Molly would be on her way, because the train which would carry her most of the way to Lincolnshire and RAF Credington was due to leave the station in a quarter of an hour. In fact, she was only still here because she and Ellen were being posted to the same airfield and Ellen was still bidding her friends goodbye and promising to write, a task which Molly had carried out as soon as she finished her breakfast.

Molly glanced at her wristwatch, sighed and stood up. The trouble with the air force, she thought morosely, picking up her bulging kitbag and staggering as she hung it on her shoulder, was its passion for moving people around. She and her fellow Waafs thought it was a bad policy, because just as you got used to one set of people there was your name on the bulletin board with a new posting beneath it, and you had to start getting to know your fellow workers all over again.

Molly picked up Ellen's kitbag – it was a good deal lighter than her own – and went out of the hut. She crossed the parade ground, thinking rather sentimentally that this would be the first drill she had missed since arriving in Southampton to man the ops table. She had loved the work and been good at it, but now it appeared that she was needed elsewhere. Fighter stations had been grand but now the war had changed and it was bomber stations which were crying out for personnel. She had been told that she and Ellen were to re-muster, not as plotters but as radio telephone operators, and the Wing officer, explaining their new duties, had said they had been chosen for the work because both had clear, unaccented voices.

'You will be talking the aircraft down,' she had explained, 'and it's essential that the pilot can hear every word. Regional accents are all very well, but when clarity is essential . . .'

Molly and Ellen had nodded their comprehension and told each other that at least the new job would not be as tense and nerve-racking as the old one. In fact, had it not been for being taken away from an area of which they had grown fond, and people who had become friends, they might have welcomed the move. They would be starting from scratch, of course, knowing nothing about RT operating or, for that matter, Lincolnshire, but both were convinced that the RAF would not have moved them had they not believed them capable of the work in question.

Halfway across the parade ground Molly saw a small figure coming towards her and smiled to herself. Ellen was always late starting, but somehow she also always managed to get where she should be by the skin of her teeth. Molly often complained that half her service life seemed to consist of waiting for Ellen, and Ellen always promised to do better, to ignore friends who held her up, and not to gossip. But what was the use? Ellen might arrive breathless and apologetic at the door of the hut where a lecture was taking place, but she never missed anything important and was, moreover, a great favourite with those in charge.

I wonder why, Molly asked herself as Ellen arrived by her side, took her kitbag with a word of thanks, knocked her cap off and, in bending to retrieve it, dropped the kitbag.

'Oh, Molly, thanks; I'm so sorry I'm late,' Ellen said, her voice full of remorse. 'It was that corporal, the Scottish one, Jamie something or other. He brought me a bag of humbugs, heaven knows how he acquired them, but of course I couldn't just take them and run, because he must have used his sweet ration to get them.' She beamed up at Molly, and giggled. 'He wanted a kiss for every humbug, which would have taken me at least fifteen minutes, so I told him he'd have to be content with one kiss for the whole bag. We had a laugh, and I didn't realise how time was going on. Oh, lor, and you were waiting in the hut. Honest, Molly, I meant to come straight over after breakfast, but somehow . . .'

'Somehow a horrible little corporal with a bag of humbugs matters more to you than catching this bloody train,' Molly said vehemently. She straightened her friend's cap, checked her own was on at just the right angle, and set off in the direction of the railway station, whilst Ellen padded along behind.

'I know I'm a bit late, but I don't see any reason to run,' Ellen said plaintively. 'Do slow down a bit, Molly; trains are always late, so why should this one be any different?'

'Sod's law,' Molly said, speeding up a bit. 'If we'd got plenty of time the perishin' train would be late, but because we haven't it'll be on time, see if it isn't. Oh, crumbs, I see steam in the distance; do get a move on, Ellen. Whatever else we may know, we can be certain that the train will be full, which means we'll be standing until we reach London. Got your rail warrant? Good. It'll get us to the nearest train station to Credington, and after that there should be a gharry waiting to take us the rest of the way.'

Molly was right about the train, which was crowded, but they were in luck. As it pulled into the station a dozen or so aircraftmen piled out and one of them, seeing Ellen trying to board, lifted her bodily and pushed her into his vacated seat, whereupon Ellen thumped her kitbag on to the seat next to her to save it for her friend. Presently they were seated side by side, feeling downright smug as the carriage filled up with other servicemen and women. Ellen produced the precious humbugs and as the train drew out of the station proffered the bag to her friend. Molly, grinning, took one of the sweets and lodged it comfortably in one cheek, then pulled the packed lunch she had been given by the cookhouse from her kitbag and examined its contents, thinking it would probably tell her more about their journey than had been vouchsafed by the aircraftman who had signed her travel warrant. Two Spam sandwiches and one of jam, two digestive biscuits, and half an apple, already turning brown. Molly nudged her neighbour.

'The Spam sandwiches and the apple are lunch, the jam sandwich and the digestive biscuits are tea,' she announced. 'That means the journey's a long one, which I guessed, because I was quite good at geography at school.' She sank back in her seat and pulled a copy of the *Southampton Gazette* out of her kitbag and settled back for a boring few hours.

But as soon as she began to relax, her mind went back to the interview with Matron which had taken place as soon as she had arrived back in Liverpool. It had not been an easy conversation because Matron, stiff and starchy as always, had refused to accept any blame for the misunderstanding over the watch.

'It was a foolish prank,' she announced. 'A girl who was in my confidence and often earned extra pocket money cleaning my rooms was the culprit. I realise of course that you did not know this, but even so, running away made everyone draw the wrong conclusions. You have just explained to me that you were taken to Ireland without your knowledge and consent and worked there for more than two years. However, that is all behind you, and now you say you would like to join one of the services. Your friend Ellen's working in one of the factories and waiting to hear from the WAAF. I expect you would like to join her, so if you need a letter of recommendation . . .'

Molly had meant to work in one of the factories to begin with in order to build up some savings, for she wanted to pay Bumble back for the money he had expended on her behalf, but when she went for the interview she was advised that making munitions was what they called a reserved occupation. If she really meant to join the WAAF she should apply at once and the supervisor would do her best to see that her request was granted. It was a time when girls were desperately needed down south so both Molly and Ellen were accepted, trained, and sent to Southampton as plotters to man the ops tables. It was hard though fascinating work, though they guessed that they would soon re-muster and be posted to a bomber station, most of which were in the north of the country. And our guess was right, Molly told herself now, as the train chugged on, and it may be my chance to meet Lenny again. I don't know precisely where he is at the moment but I'm sure we'll bump into each other soon. Letters are all very well, but it would be so nice to see him in person. Bumble told me he was in Framingham, which is only a few miles from Credington, so maybe, just maybe, we'll be able to renew our old friendship, if he hasn't been re-mustered. Here, however, her thoughts were interrupted.

'You've been asleep!' Ellen's accusing voice said in her ear. 'How can you possibly go to sleep when the train's so full and the seats so uncomfortable? What's more, this damned cigarette smoke is stinging my eyes; the air is positively blue with it.' She sighed. 'I've often wondered what it's like to smoke, but the only time I tried I didn't like the taste, and anyway, I've got better things to spend my money on than fags.'

Molly chuckled. 'What, for instance?' she asked. 'Everything's in demand. Why, even those humbugs cost somebody something at some stage or other.'

Ellen giggled. 'Kissing don't count,' she said. 'Oh, you mean Jamie had to pay for them, and of course that wouldn't have been in kisses!' Her voice grew dreamy. 'Fighter stations are all very well, but it only takes one bod to fly a Spit. I believe bombers have seven or eight in the crew, which will be nice when the NAAFI holds a dance. We'll be able to take our pick of fellers.'

'Oh, you! You're man mad,' Molly said scornfully. 'I saw you staring round the carriage when we first got in, to see if you liked the look of anybody. Well, even if you did I doubt very much he'll be going to the same place as us.'

Ellen grinned. 'I'll find myself a feller, don't you worry,' she said breezily. 'If there's one thing I'm good at, it's finding myself a feller. Oh, I'm never serious, any more than they are, but it is nice to have someone to dance with and talk to.'

The man sitting next to Molly was a soldier with a corporal's stripes on his arm. Molly had thought him absorbed in a book; certainly he had never raised his eyes from the printed page, but now he leaned across Molly and addressed Ellen directly.

'Where are you off to, young lady?' he asked.

Ellen opened her mouth to answer but Molly nudged her in the ribs. 'Walls have ears,' she murmured. 'Do shurrup, Ellen, or you'll get us and everyone else into trouble.'

'Shan't,' Ellen said, giving the corporal her most ravishing smile. 'We're going to somewhere in the north. Where are *you* going, come to that?'

'Ack-ack battery,' the soldier said briefly. 'When we get to Waterloo we'll all have to change trains and do the rest of our journeys on different lines. I'm going north too, which means King's Cross, so if you're a bit thrown by the London crowds, just follow me.'

He then returned to his book and Molly studied her little friend and wondered what magic it was which made total strangers confide in Ellen, and most men vie for her attention. Whilst Ellen applied herself to a copy of *Woman* magazine she had a really good stare at her friend. What *was* it that Ellen had got and she herself had not? Ellen had a small pale face, large honey-brown eyes, a straight little nose and dark hair with a hint of red, which was, Molly assumed, the reason for the band of freckles which ran across the bridge of her nose and cheeks. She had a neat figure – neat but not showy – and her slim legs were clad in regulation lisle stockings. Her hair was cut, as was Molly's own, in the prevailing fashion, which meant it was allowed to grow just past shoulder length and then rolled round a ribbon and pinned into place. Not glamorous, perhaps, but exceedingly practical. Like Molly, she wore no make-up, because what little they possessed they saved for special occasions, and today two Waafs taking up a posting on a new station was in no way remarkable. It happened all the time, Molly told herself, and got lost in a daydream in which the door to the corridor shot open and Lenny appeared, beckoning her to follow him. It was a good dream; she went with Lenny, of course, and found he had managed, by some miracle, to bag an empty compartment. He pulled her in after him, slammed the door shut, hung up a cardboard *Do not disturb* notice and proceeded to kiss her in a most satisfactory way. In fact, when the train drew into Waterloo and everyone began to pick up kitbags and gas mask cases, Ellen had to shake her quite hard and remind her that this was where they left the train.

Molly, coming out of her dreams with a start, found herself for once trailing behind Ellen instead of the other way round. The station was full of uniforms, mostly the RAF blue, though there were a few soldiers in khaki and even one or two sailors. The latter were almost certainly on leave, coming off their ships and rushing home, perhaps whilst their vessels were in for repair. Everyone seemed to be carrying kitbags and there was a fair amount of good-natured pushing, shoving and questioning of porters, but presently Molly and Ellen, close on the heels of the friendly corporal who had advised them to follow him, emerged from the underground railway at King's Cross and found themselves climbing aboard the train which would take them to their eventual destination.

And it was entirely thanks to that corporal, Molly thought, that she and Ellen were amongst the first to board, and therefore were able to find seats next to one another, for it was not long before the carriage filled up and late-coming members of the services were forced to squat or stand in the corridor where the cigarette smoke was already blueing the air.

Molly looked round the compartment. The string racks overhead were filled with kitbags and clothing such as greatcoats that were too big to be packed. Also above the passengers' heads were two pictures: one was a beach scene with a bathing beauty, swimsuited, watching a child build a sandcastle, the other was of a heather-covered moor with mountains in the background and a tumbling stream. For a moment the beauty of the second picture tugged at Molly's heartstrings. How she missed the O'Hare farm, or rather the countryside which surrounded it! Ancient trees, the stream which widened out into a large pool where Cian fished for sweet brown trout, and the moors, purple with heather and golden gorse at this time of year; they would all be there, it was only she who was missing. But then the guard walked past the window waving a green flag and the train began to move, and with the movement Molly saw, reflected in the glass of the picture opposite her, her own face. Light brown hair could just be seen beneath her peaked cap. Thick, light brown lashes framed hazel-coloured eyes above a small, firm mouth and a determined chin, both of which, Molly thought ruefully, revealed the fact that she could be both bossy and opinionated, though heaven knew one had little opportunity to display either charactcristic when one was a mere cipher in the mighty machine that was the Royal Air Force.

She was in the corner seat, and turned with a sigh to watch the suburbs moving past as the train picked up speed. I've got an ordinary face, neither pretty nor plain, clever or stupid, she told herself. It must be wonderful to be really pretty; if I could get hold of some mascara to blacken my lashes it would help. But even as the thought crossed her mind she found herself smiling. How ridiculous! She was fighting a war, not searching for a soulmate, so it didn't really matter if she was twelve foot tall or as fat as Two Ton Tessie from Tennessee. She was an orphan, but she had had a good schooling, even if she hadn't thought so at the time. She had taken on one of the most important jobs a Waaf could do when she was confirmed as a plotter, and now she was about to be trained as a radio operative. She had no idea whether she would pass muster or end up in the cookhouse, scrubbing floors and peeling potatoes, but whatever she did and wherever she was sent she meant to do her best and to conquer any difficulties which she met on the way.

At this somewhat inauspicious moment she caught the eye of a leading aircraftman sitting opposite and responded to his cheerful grin with one of her own. Clearly encouraged by this the young man leaned forward, clasped hands between his knees and his warm brown eyes were full of laughter.

'I saw you and your friend on the platform at Southampton,' he said. He lowered his voice. 'I reckon we're bound for the same destination, but it wouldn't do to say so.' His grin became a trifle rueful. 'Here we are in a train jammed with service personnel not daring to discuss what interests us most in case that feller over there – or even your little friend – might convey the information to some underground spy. Crazy, isn't it?'

Molly smiled. 'Lots of things about the air force seem pretty crazy,' she agreed. 'But there's a certain amount of common sense in most of the dos and don'ts. When I first joined I thought daily drill was completely bonkers, but it isn't, you know. It keeps us all fit, particularly those in sedentary jobs. In fact, I'm fitter than I was before I joined, when I did a stint as a farm worker. And my friend here worked in a munitions factory. She didn't actually sit down on the job – she had to stand by her bench – but she didn't move around very much.' She chuckled. 'But the air force soon dealt with that. Poor Ellen moaned like anything at doing a half-hour drill before breakfast, but now she admits, albeit unwillingly, that it's done her more good than harm.'

The young man agreed. 'And just watching you Waafs drilling quickened *our* heartbeats, so it must have been doing us as much good as it did you,' he said with a twinkle.

As the train began to pick up speed he hooked his gas mask case down from the rack and opened it to reveal two packets wrapped in greaseproof paper and a wrinkled apple.

'Bet you've got the same, which proves at least our point of departure was identical,' he said breezily. 'But isn't it time we introduced ourselves? I'm LAC Adam Hargreaves, and you are . . . ?'

'LACW Hardwick,' Molly said promptly. 'And my friend is LACW Ferris.' They shook hands and then she pointed to the contents of his gas mask case. 'Two Spam and one jam, a couple of biscuits, and that awful little apple; am I right?'

'Spot on,' the young man said. He sighed. 'It's going to be a long journey.'

LAC Hargreaves was right. By the time they reached their destination they were hungry, thirsty and fed up. The train had stopped and started many times; troops had got off and others had got on, and at one point their compartment had been invaded by foreign troops chattering away to each other in a language Molly and Ellen did not even recognise, though Adam Hargreaves thought it was Polish. Eventually, however, the train stopped in a very final sort of way, and, far from being secretive, a corporal with a cheery red face and a loud voice bade everyone for Credington airfield to climb aboard the second gharry in the line of vehicles drawn up outside the station. Molly, with her long legs, climbed up into the gharry with no assistance from anyone, but Ellen would have struggled had she not been hoisted aboard by a husky airman who had nearly come to blows with another man over who should have the privilege of lifting light little Ellen from the roadway into the waiting vehicle. Once this would have annoyed Molly, but after a discussion with LAC Hargreaves in the corridor outside their train compartment as they queued for the lavatory, she felt she now knew why Ellen always got preferential treatment from young men.

'She looks such a child, and a child in need of protection what's more,' Molly's new acquaintance had told her. 'She has a fragile air, as though life has been hard for her, whereas you look capable of defending not only yourself but any number of other people as well. If you ask me you'll be in for officer training before you can say knife. Would you like that?'

Molly did not even have to think; her reply was instinctive and quick. 'No I would not,' she had said firmly. 'They offered me the chance of promotion at Southampton and I turned it down. I've discovered one thing about myself: I enjoy the company of other girls and might occasionally take charge when there's no one else around to do it, but after almost a month of officer training I went to my Wingco and asked to be put back in the ranks. It wasn't that the other girls weren't friendly, and some of them were very nice, but you see I was brought up in an orphanage, so when they talked about their home lives I could only listen. It made me feel very self-conscious knowing I was not "one of them", if you see what I mean, and when I explained to the Wingco she was most understanding. She said to give it some time and then I should try for promotion again. She said I had the right attitude for it, or would have in a couple of years, but she could see I was happy with things as they were for now and she was happy with me.'

The young man had grinned. 'Clever of me to have guessed you were officer material,' he said. 'But you were quite right, being an officer would have set you apart. I take it your friend wasn't given the same opportunity?'

Molly had chuckled as the line shuffled slowly forward. 'Well, no,' she admitted. 'Ellen herself knows she will never be a leader. She wasn't very happy when I went off for training but she was ecstatic when I came back. She's a good friend is Ellen, but as she said at the time she does know her limitations. When we first met she had a Scouse accent you could cut with a knife and I suppose I may have talked a bit Liverpudlian as well. But I got rid of my accent whilst I was in Ireland – don't ask me about that; it's too long a story even for this interminable train journey – and Ellen is an astonishingly clever mimic. Believe me, if she was sent to the wilds of Scotland she'd be talking broad Scots within a week.' She had grinned at the young man as the queue shuffled forward once more. 'So you see, we're a couple of impostors really, both of us pretending to have come from normal home backgrounds and both of us shedding accents that could give us away.'

The young man had laughed. 'I dare say half the men and women on this train are pretending to be something other than they are; have you heard how a sergeant speaks to his officer as refined as you please, and then turns and bawls some poor fellow out in pure Brummie or Mancunian or Cockney?' He smiled as Molly began to shake her head. 'No, of course you haven't, but believe me it's the stone cold sober truth. We're all in this war together and though we may not be spies, we all have our little secrets.'

So, in the gharry, squashed up against a fat sergeant on one side and little Ellen on the other, Molly was happy with her lot. As the transport passed the guardhouse and entered the airfield she cleared her throat and spoke up.

'Anyone know what'll happen to us now we're here?'

As she spoke the gharry came to a shuddering halt and the driver turned and addressed them. 'Yes, lass.' He jerked a thumb at the large building outside which he had stopped his vehicle. 'This is the Waafery. You report to the guardroom in there and they'll send you to the cookhouse for a meal. After that you'll report to the bedding store where you'll be issued with blankets and sheets. Then it's up to you. You can go to the NAAFI or just find someone more experienced who'll fill you in on what's expected of you over the next few days. Hop down, girls. Even if you're in no hurry, I'm a very busy man.'

The men had left the gharry some five minutes previously at the transport's first stop, so Molly scrambled out of the vehicle first and helped Ellen down to the ground. She realised she was almost asleep and shook herself briskly, then led the way to the guardroom in the Waafery. From there the girls were marched to the cookhouse, where the smell of the food reminded them that they had not eaten properly since breakfast. They were given dried eggs – scrambled – on toast.

'I say, the tea's got some colour in it; we've landed on our feet!' someone up the table said joyfully.

Molly, biting into her scrambled eggs, laughed. 'I guess you're right,' she said to the unknown speaker. 'I must say the food makes it a good start.'

As soon as they had finished their meal the girls were marched back across the parade ground and into their huts. They were brick built, though the roofs were of corrugated iron – hot in summer and cold in winter – but Molly and Ellen were too exhausted to complain. The corporal who had brought them to their hut told them to use the bedding which had been given to them, pointed out the ablutions building which was a good hundred yards from where they stood, reminded them that when reveille sounded it would mean that breakfast was about to be served, and indicated that they were now free not only to make up their beds but also to climb into them. She then marched to her own bed, which was curtained off to show she was in charge and therefore a superior being.

It was a chilly night and the thought of the cold water which would be all the ablutions would provide at this time was not appealing. But when Ellen would have wriggled, unwashed, beneath her blankets Molly grabbed her and her washing things and propelled her out of the hut.

'If you start getting lazy it'll become a habit,' she said severely. 'Remember what they told us at the training centre? Girls who have to be forced out of bed don't perform well either in their work or on the parade ground. I know you're tired and I know you're cold but a brisk wash will make you feel much better. No, don't shake your head and blink at me, it's the truth, and even if you haven't got any toothpaste you've got a toothbrush. I hate the feel of teeth with bits of food around them, don't you?'

Ellen heaved a dramatic sigh. 'Ye-es, I suppose I do,' she acknowledged. She stared reproachfully at her friend. 'I *always* wash and that before I get into bed, and usually first thing in the morning as well. But we've had an awful day, with people pushing us around and shouting orders, so why can't we get straight into bed just this once? And the ablutions are miles away. When it's raining or snowing we'll be wet as water rats by the time we get there and shan't have to wash at all.'

'Don't be silly,' Molly said. She looked at her small friend and couldn't help smiling. Ellen reminded her of a sleepy owl, all big reproachful eyes and rumpled feathery hair. But the cold air

249

outside their hut was waking her up and Molly no longer had to physically pull her along. When they reached the ablutions they were pleasantly surprised to find that the water, though by no means hot, was warm enough to make a wash, if not pleasant, at least perfectly bearable. The girl at the basin next to Molly's produced a toothbrush and some paste and brushed vigorously, and when she had finished she turned to her neighbour.

'What job will you be doing here?' she asked curiously. 'I don't know why, but I had the impression that we'd bed down with others in the same trade. Apparently, though, that isn't so. I'm a mechanic, or at least a unit trainee – they're going to teach me and one or two of my mates to service the aircraft.' She grinned widely. 'Just what I wanted! And you . . . ?'

She was a tall dark-haired girl with a wide and friendly grin and Molly took to her at once. 'I'm a u/t radio telephone operator,' she said readily. 'And so is my pal here, Ellen Ferris.'

The tall dark girl shot out a hand, shook Molly's vigorously and then Ellen's a little more gently. 'I'm Penny Burnett,' she said. 'And you?'

'I'm Molly Hardwick, but oddly enough my middle name is Penelope,' Molly said. 'What do you think of the grub here?' As she spoke she was gathering up her washing kit and saw Ellen following suit. Penny shuffled her things into a wash bag and accompanied them back to their hut, where a sleepy voice reminded them that *last one in turns the lights off*. Molly smothered a huge yawn with one hand and climbed thankfully between the blankets. Ellen, being the last to enter the hut, switched off the dim little electric bulb, climbed into her own bed and shudderingly climbed out again to fetch her great-coat from its hook on the wall and spread it over her issue blankets for extra warmth.

'Night, Penny, night, Molly,' she mumbled. 'Last one up tomorrer morning's a sissy.'

'Night, Ellen,' Molly said drowsily. 'I'm looking forward to tomorrow. I hope someone in this hut knows where the RT operators work because no one's seen fit to tell us so far and we'll look real fools if we turn up in the wrong place.'

Next morning, when reveille sounded, Molly was first out of her bed and cruelly dug the still sleeping Ellen in the ribs.

'Come on, girl,' she urged. 'I expect it's the same here as on other airfields: drill first, whilst we're still drugged with sleep, then breakfast, then, hopefully, find where we're supposed to be and what we're supposed to do. I'm sure there must be a proper procedure for newcomers, only we haven't been told it yet.'

Soon enough, they discovered their mistake. Penny, who had been at the airfield a fortnight, went off with several friends, giving them a cheery wave and shouting 'Good luck!' as she left them. Contrary to their expectations, the four girls who had been told to report to the authorities as u/t RT operators seemed to be unwanted. They tried to join the girls doing drill on the parade ground but the sergeant in charge snapped at them, saying that he had never heard of any of them and advising them to find out where they were meant to be as soon as possible. The other two girls, Hetty and Maggie, also bewildered by their sudden anonymity, were soon grumbling even harder than Molly and Ellen. Eventually they were told that they would be working in the watch office, and once things were sorted out each girl would work in four- or eight-hour shifts, depending on the number of operators present. Apparently someone was on duty all of the twenty-four hours, and everyone had a day off between each twelve-hour day. If there were not enough RT operators they had every third day off after an eight-hour night duty. This continued day in and night out, except when someone got leave and their shift had to be covered.

This information was passed to them somewhat laconically by a sergeant who suddenly appeared before them, rubbing his eyes and announcing that he'd just finished a night shift and was longing for his pit. Having explained to them what their duties would be he turned to leave them, but Ellen stopped him, a small hand on the arm of his battledress.

'Yes, but where the devil is the watch office?' she enquired urgently. 'Oh, sarge, we mean to do our best and behave just as we ought, but we've only just come off the plotting tables down south and have no idea what an RT operator has to do. We asked the corporal in charge of our hut and she just shrugged and said we'd better make some enquiries, which we're trying to do. But no one but you seems to know what we're talking about.'

The sergeant grinned, and removed his 'fore and aft' to reveal spiky grey hair above a lined and weary face. He jerked a thumb in the direction of a flight of concrete steps leading up to what looked like a series of boxes.

'Watch office is the top box,' he informed them. 'It's known as the RT cabin, and though it's small and sometimes rather too full of bods you'll soon get used to it.'

'Who else works there?' Molly asked eagerly, for she could see two cabins, one above the other.

The sergeant smiled. 'There are Waafs in the met office, which is below our rooftop eyrie,' he said. 'Nice girls, all of 'em, and hard-working. We don't see a lot of them, though, because like us they work shifts and our shifts don't usually coincide. If I wasn't so bloody tired I'd come up with you and introduce you to Alex and Fred who're on watch at present, but if I don't get to bed soon I think I'll probably drop dead. Just you go up, open the door quietly, go in and explain to the blokes that you're a new intake, come to learn all about RT operating. All right? Understood?'

The girls nodded enthusiastically; at last someone seemed to be taking them seriously. As they climbed the concrete stairs, Hetty jerked at Molly's elbow. 'I was a telephonist before being re-mustered, and so was Maggie. What were you?'

'Ellen and I were plotters,' Molly said briefly, but did not enlarge on the statement, since at that point she opened the door in front of her after the briefest of knocks and the four of them crowded into the watch room.

The watch room was as small and, with three men inside, as crowded as the sergeant had intimated. The work station consisted of a broad bench along the back wall which held two identical radio sets, TR9s they were told later, though the information meant nothing to Molly and Ellen or, it soon transpired, to the other two either. Between them was a microphone like an upright telephone and the airman on duty was wearing earphones. They could not hear what was coming through the head-set but they saw the wearer move a lever on one of the TR9s and heard him speak into the microphone while writing rapidly in an open log book on the bench beside him.

Molly nudged Ellen and bent from her superior height to whisper in her friend's ear. 'I think he's talking to the pilots, or the wireless ops I s'pose, actually on the plane. That's what we shall be doing – a *real* job. This is why they wanted girls with no accents.' She turned to smile at Maggie and Hetty and raised her voice slightly. 'And telephonists, of course. You two must have a head start over Ellen and me. You're used to using microphones and things, I expect.'

Hetty agreed that this was so, and presently a man they thought must be the control officer raised his brows at them and asked them rather coolly what they were doing in the watch office.

Molly smiled at him. 'We're not sure ourselves,' she admitted. 'We've been trailing round the airfield ever since breakfast, trying to find out what we should be doing. We're u/t RT operators, though, we know that much, and a friendly sergeant pointed us in this direction. Are you trying to tell us we're in the wrong place yet again?'

'I'm the senior control officer and no one told me our new shift workers were going to be Waafs,' the man said rather ruefully. 'However, it makes good sense. They're trying to replace fighting men with girls in any job they can, and obviously the powers that be have selected you for this one. I'll give you a quick tour of the watch office now, and since we have two airmen on leave at present two of you can start learning the job tomorrow.' He jerked a thumb at Molly and then at Ellen. 'You'll be on first watch tomorrow morning, which is from eight o'clock until twelve, and then again from four o'clock to midnight. The sky is very overcast, with low cloud and rain threatening, which should mean that our chaps won't take off and hopefully the Luftwaffe won't either. It will give you a chance to get to know the work while the watch office is fairly quiet. Names?'

Molly and Ellen gave him their names and then Molly dared to ask a question. 'Please, sir, when do we eat?'

The officer sighed as though the answer should have been obvious, but the man who had been talking into the microphone when they first entered the watch office laughed.

'You go to the cookhouse, of course, in your breaks,' he explained. 'Sometimes your breaks don't coincide with mealtimes and the cooks get a bit shirty, but they'll feed you if you stick to your guns. Tell you what, I'm on duty tomorrow, so we can face the fury of the cooks together. They'll tell you that four o'clock is too early for supper and midnight too late, but there's always someone with a kind heart who'll make you up a few sandwiches or a slice of so-called fruitcake, not that there's much fruit in it. Does that help?'

'Yes, and thanks very much,' Molly said gratefully. She turned back to the senior officer. 'That's Ellen and me settled, but what about the other two?'

The watch officer strolled to the bulletin board on the wall and consulted it. 'They'll come on the following day and do the same shifts but with different RT operators to teach them the ropes. All clear?' He raised a hand as though to salute but he had shed his cap so turned the salute into a half-hearted little wave before leaving the office, followed at a respectful distance by Hetty and Maggie.

The man before the microphone beckoned to Molly. He was a tall, lean young man with a great deal of untidy dark hair and a very engaging grin. She decided she liked the look of him.

'You won't see much of him, particularly once you gain the necessary experience to do the work. You may think it sounds simple, but it's no such thing. I'll train you, and Fred there will be responsible for training your oppo. Training for the watch office takes a while. You'll be attending various courses without me but when you're actually in the watch office we shall be together until you pass muster. How are you on Morse code? Do you find it easy to think in what is virtually a different language? Oh, and by the way, I didn't catch your name. We don't stand on ceremony up here, we're too busy. I'm Alex, and you are . . . ?'

'I'm Molly,' Molly said, 'and I haven't a clue about Morse code except for SOS being pip pip pip dash dash dash pip pip pip.'

Her instructor laughed. 'Then you know more than I did when I started the job,' he said cheerfully. 'But if I learned everything I needed to know in six months you'll probably do it in three. We'll start tomorrow morning when you do your first shift.' He glanced across to where Ellen was in earnest conversation with the other operator then turned back to Molly, eyebrows raised. 'How *old* is she? She looks about twelve. Is she up to the job, do you think? Only there's an awful lot of technical stuff which has to be memorised, starting with the phonetic alphabet and the simple set replies and instructions. Then there's signalling Morse code by Aldis lamps, to say nothing of the really difficult stuff which includes the technical training; you'll go to a classroom to be taught about electronic theory and Ohm's law, primary and secondary cells and how to look after accumulators. Then there's magnetism, and valve theory, and simple circuits including capacity inductance, resistance and couplings. Wave forms – aerials and their care. You'll be shown how to use the TR9s and the DLs. You will also be taught how to solder, wearing protective goggles of course. Whilst you're under training you'll be taking exams at regular intervals and will only move on to the next trial when you've passed the previous one satisfactorily. It sounds frightening, I know, but it's mainly logic and learning.'

He grinned at Molly and she guessed her face must be a mask of horror. 'Don't worry; if Fred and I could reach our present exalted position, then you two, with us to help you, will end up saying it's a piece of cake. If you take my advice you'll get a good fat exercise book and write everything down.' Once again he laughed at his companion's expression. 'Don't look so terrified. Every lad who joins the air force, no matter how dim, has to learn his trade, and some of them, when they first enter the service, have to be taught how to tie their own bootlaces. You and the little 'un will take to it like ducks to water. But of course there will be times when you truly don't understand, and that's where Fred and I come in. We're simple souls, but if there's one thing we can do it's to clarify what the instructors tell you, so when in doubt you come to me and the little 'un can go to Fred. And don't think we'll get impatient with you, because until you can remove the u/t from your shoulder flash we're right beside you, and if you pass out as fully trained it's a feather in *our* caps.' He hailed the operative who had been instructing Ellen. 'Have you scared that young lady with talk of electronics and other such mysteries? If so you'd better unscare her immediately.'

259

Fred shook his head. 'No, no, despite her size she don't scare easy. In fact I'd put money on her being a quick learner. How about yours? What's her name? Mine's Ellen.'

'Mine's Molly, and like yours I'd put money on her being a quick learner,' Alex said. 'Tell you what, we'll have a contest, see which one of 'em picks up the language first.' He grinned at Molly, produced a crumpled piece of paper from somewhere on his person and handed it to her. 'You're on from eight o'clock to midnight tomorrow, but of course you'll be free all afternoon. Learn these . . .' he tapped the sheet of paper with one finger, 'and we'll see how you get on.' He smiled at her. 'Don't worry, I've never lost a trainee yet. In fact, I shall behave like a mother hen with one chick and guide you through all the procedures you have to learn.' He jerked a thumb at Fred. 'In fact we'll both do our very best to get you conversant with everything you ought to know.'

Molly blinked. 'It's awfully good of you,' she said rather shyly.

Alex patted Molly's shoulder and gestured at the microphone, the log book, and the rest of the paraphernalia on the long bench. 'What did I say?' he demanded. 'I said don't worry, and that's exactly what I meant. I'm your instructor, remember, and if you fall behind it will be my job to do the worrying, but I'm sure you won't – fall behind, I mean.'

Molly smiled up at him. 'I'll do my very best not to let you down,' she promised. 'I already know the phonetic alphabet, but all the rest is a complete mystery.'

Her instructor grinned. 'Not for long it won't be,' he said reassuringly. 'I can see you're a bright young thing; you'll soon catch on.'

Chapter Nine

Both Molly and Ellen had been doubtful if they could ever master the intricacies of radio operating, but their tutors, if you could call them that, were patient and thorough, and it was not long before both girls had mastered the more straightforward parts of their job. At first they were too busy and too worried to want to socialise with the men with whom they spoke on an almost daily basis – mainly the crews of the kites they talked up and then talked down again – but gradually they began to put faces to voices. Alex, who had been friendly from the start, began to suggest that Molly might join him and his friends when they went into Lincoln on the gharry, and though Molly told herself that she was keeping herself for Lenny she soon began to realise that her memory of him was beginning to fade. There were so many other young men eager to introduce her to the charms of the cathedral city.

When Molly had first arrived in Lincolnshire and realised that Framingham, where Lenny was based, was within easy distance both of Credington and of Lincoln city itself she had been elated, sure that this would mean she would begin to see something of her old pal. She wrote him long and interesting letters – at least they were interesting to her – careful what she revealed about her job because of the censor, but managing to convey the excitement she felt when she saw that the big planes took off safely, and were brought down safely on their return. She wrote to Bumble too, rather guiltily aware that she had not shown him sufficient gratitude when he had rescued her from the Mathiases, and his replies were so prompt and entertaining that she soon lost her initial reserve and settled into a regular, if infrequent, correspondence with him.

But it was always Lenny who was first in her thoughts, and she was much distressed when in reply to her comment that she spent a good deal of her free time with her instructor Alex he said that he hoped they would be happy together, since it was clear that they must be in love. Molly was flabbergasted by his casual assumption that if she went round with a chap it must mean she loved him. She wrote back indignantly, assuring him he had got hold of the wrong end of the stick, and then had to wait several weeks for Lenny's half-hearted apology. When eventually she phoned his Mess, though polite and friendly enough, he made it perfectly plain that he was much too busy to meet his old friend, since pilots like himself, who provided a fighter escort on bombing raids, worked most nights and needed to get what rest they could during daylight hours.

Molly had wept over this when she got back to the house she and Ellen now shared with Hetty and Maggie, but not for long; the very fact that she had somewhere private to flee to was cheering in itself.

Molly had taken an instant liking to Maggie, who was a stronger character than quiet little Hetty, with whom Ellen got on well. Maggie was tall and slim with light brown hair and hazel eyes. Like Molly herself she was a quick learner and soon grasped all the essentials of the job in the watch office. She was also sociable, making friends easily and never missing an opportunity to go to a dance or get aboard the gharry heading for Lincoln, where she would watch a film, go sightseeing, or simply eat a fish and chip supper at Mrs Doyle's café near the Stone Bow.

Furthermore, she was not averse to breaking any rules which did not suit her. For instance, Waafs were supposed to wear uniform at all times, but Maggie could see no point in this, and though she wore her uniform to dances and parties held on the airfield she kept a sequin-covered dance dress with a full skirt for private parties and laughed Molly to scorn when her friend told her she would be caught one day.

'Shan't,' she said positively. 'I'd agree with you if I wore it on the station, but I don't.'

Hetty looked frightened. She was a mousy little thing with a pale triangular face, a straight little nose and blue eyes.

'Don't go getting caught breaking the rules, Maggie,' she pleaded. 'I don't know what I'd do if I didn't have you to advise me. *Please* be careful and don't get caught.'

The four of them had got the house because now that they were on permanent shifts they could not afford to be disturbed during their sleep time, and getting a full night's rest in a hut occupied by twenty other women was virtually impossible. What was more, when they were on night duty it seemed unfair that they should be hauled out of bed for kit inspections or domestic chores. Alex and Fred had urged them to explain and complain, and though the Royal Air Force had taken its time – the girls had had a whole month when they were scarcely able to close their eyes for the comings and goings in their hut – Molly's secret doubts that these tactics would work were finally proved wrong.

'The air force does have a heart,' she had exclaimed joyfully, reading the letter addressed to her which she had found on the bulletin board. 'They've given us a requisitioned house, quite near the end of the runway, and said we could move into it as soon as we like. There's a kitchen, but I think we're still expected to get our meals at the cookhouse, and – oh joy! – there's running water from a pump in the sink, or so it says here.' She had been in the NAAFI reading the letter aloud to Ellen, Hetty and Maggie, only to discover that they all had similar epistles.

It was not a large house, nor were the rooms particularly spacious, but to share even a small bedroom with only one other was a luxury they had barely allowed themselves to dream of. Downstairs there was a parlour where the girls sat to write letters and revise for exams, of which there were many, and the kitchen doubled as ablutions and was the only room in the house which had a fire.

It was an extremely cold winter, and despite the fire the four girls were often very chilly. When they peered out of one of the back windows which overlooked a copse of trees they could see icicles hanging from the branches and snowflakes drifting down. One morning, a few days after Christmas, it began to snow in earnest and very soon the call went out for everyone to put on working gear and go out to help clear the runway. Molly and Ellen groaned, and exchanged speaking glances. They had just come off shift and had been looking forward to getting some shut-eye, but both girls realised the importance of keeping the runway free of snow. They were on the way to their billet and immediately speeded up, hoping that there was enough life left in the fire to have a warm before they had to come outside again. They would have burst into the kitchen except that the door opened before they could so much as touch it, and Maggie emerged. She looked startled but held the door open so that the two girls might enter, and then turned back to join them.

Molly raised her brows enquiringly. The house had a back door into a small yard, though it was seldom used, and she thought she had heard a sound coming from that direction.

'What was that? I thought I heard the other door close,' she said.

Maggie nodded. 'You did. It was the feller they call Apple, delivering a bucket of coal to keep our fire going.' She grinned at her friend. 'And don't ask me where he got it from because I guess he nicked it. Satisfied?'

'Definitely,' Molly said at once. Shift workers needed their fire to be kept in at all times, and she had often raided another billet's coal supply simply in order to stop their own fire from going out. Now she went over to the coat rack and took down her heaviest winter gear, seeing with approval that the fire was still burning merrily.

'Did you hear the message over the tannoy?' Maggie enquired. 'All hands are wanted for snow clearance, but since you two have only just come off shift I'm sure the powers that be didn't mean you.

Hetty and I were told not to worry about our shift because only two aircraft took off and they're both home safe. Joe is on Darky and Fred's managing everything else . . .'

Unnoticed by her pals, Molly gave a little shudder. Everyone in the watch office took it in turns to man the Darky station, which was the call sign for emergencies only. Molly had only had one Darky call since becoming an RTO and hoped sincerely she would never have another. She thought the thin boyish voice coming over the ether, trying to hide its owner's fear as he realised he had no idea where he was, would live for ever in her memory. The pilot, probably still in his teens, told her his port engine was on fire and asked desperately for directions, giving his position, height and other details . . . and then she heard the crash, followed by the sudden quiet . . .

But that had happened weeks ago and today, from what Maggie had said, all their aircraft had come home to roost, so it was time to switch off the past and get on with the present. Maggie was still talking about Fred: '. . . his arthritic shoulder is very bad and the MO positively forbade him to try to help clear the runway, so he's stuck in the watch office until the work is done and someone can relieve him, so if you two want to catch up on your sleep there's no reason why you shouldn't.'

'My conscience wouldn't let me sleep whilst everyone else was working,' Molly said regretfully.

'Ellen's the same, aren't you, Ellen? But with so many people shovelling away we'll probably be in bed in half an hour.'

Whilst Maggie had been talking both girls had been putting on every garment they possessed. Molly, sporting her thickest jumper and scarf as well as her greatcoat and boots, could not help smiling at the odd picture Ellen presented. The flying boots were miles too big and the scarf went round her throat three times, but there was no doubt that her pal would be warmer than most. The boots had come courtesy of a corporal in the clothing store who had taken one look at Ellen's face, blue and pinched with cold, and produced the boots, the scarf and the thick woolly mittens from under the counter, handing them to Ellen with a wink.

'Don't tell no one where they come from,' he ordered. 'They'll keep you snug in the coldest weather and they ain't wanted no more by the feller what owned them.' He had grinned widely, found a stockinet cap and rammed it down over Ellen's dusky curls. 'There you are, snug as a bug in a rug,' he had said. He had winked again. 'Can't see a fellow Scouser turned into a bleedin' icicle. Off with you now, queen, and next time there's a dance in the sergeants' Mess you can save me the last waltz.'

Ellen, who had only come to the store to be company for Molly, whose lisle stockings were badly laddered, had giggled. 'You're a pal, corp,' she had said sincerely. She gazed admiringly down at the boots on her small feet. 'For these boots you can have every perishin' waltz, whack.'

The corporal had chuckled, then addressed Molly. 'If I'd had another pair of boots you could have had 'em,' he had said, and Molly, listening to the well-known accent, thanked him politely, picked up her new stockings and led Ellen out of the hut.

'You jammy blighter,' she had said enviously as they made their way back to their billet. 'Is that why you put on a Scouse accent the minute we got inside?'

Ellen nodded vigorously. 'Course it was,' she said, sounding surprised. 'Why else would I want to talk like a scouser? If you'd had the sense you were born with you'd have done the same. I'm not saying he'd have given you flying boots, 'cos they're worth their weight in gold, but you'd have got two pairs of stockings and probably the mittens you were hoping for as well.'

It was Molly's turn to chuckle. 'If the poor beggar had anything left after he'd handed you all his spare stock,' she had said rather ruefully. 'I don't know what it is you've got, but next time there's a dance in the sergeants' Mess I'll be interested to see if you can dance in flying boots at least four sizes too large.'

Ellen had laughed and pushed open the door of their new billet. 'You think it's cold now, but wait until the *real* winter comes,' she had commented. 'If you ask me nicely I might see if I can blag some boots for you, and if they turn out to be too small for you we could do a swap!'

Now Molly picked up a log from the log box and thrust it into the heart of the fire just as Ellen opened the kitchen door. Molly grimaced as the biting wind whirled through the aperture. 'I wish we could hibernate like hedgehogs and dormice and things and wake up to find spring had arrived. But with a bit of luck we'll come back to a warm kitchen when the runway is clear.'

Once outside they took the shovels which were handed to them and began to work alongside some other Waafs, one of whom proved to be Hetty, already looking like a snowman. Nevertheless, she greeted Molly and Ellen cheerfully, and gave Maggie a friendly wave. The sergeant, cheery and red-faced, came over and clapped Molly on the back, so hard that she nearly ended up flat on her face.

'Good girl!' he said approvingly. 'If we can just keep the runway clear so our Lancs can get airborne, knowing that they've got decent landing facilities when they come home, then we'll have done the air force proud. And when it's cleared there'll be char and a hot meal for all the workers;

Cook promised bacon butties at the very least, so keep on shovelling, girl, and earn your reward.'

Molly looked up and wiped sweat from her forehead, for though the cold was bitter the work kept one in a fine glow.

'That's good to hear, sarge,' she said gratefully. And then, as the man began to move off, she added, 'Can you tell us what's happening about the dance in the sergeants' Mess at Framingham? Me and my pals were going to give the lads there the thrill of a lifetime by turning up on the first available gharry. Only judging by that great drift over there' – she pointed a finger at a beautifully curved drift already as high as her head – 'even the toughest gharries aren't going to get through this lot.'

The sergeant pulled a rueful face and shrugged his muffler higher. 'You won't be going anywhere tonight, aircraftwoman,' he said. 'This weather is here to stay, if I'm any judge. Where do you come from?'

'Liverpool, but what's that got to do with the weather?' Molly said.

The sergeant laughed. 'Liverpool's a port, ain't it? Which means of course that it's on the coast. Maybe you get snow now and then, but there's salt in the air so it doesn't hang around for very long. When you've seen a Lincolnshire winter you'll know why I say it's not going to be gone tomorrer. I'm from Sleaford and I've known snow to linger for weeks. So you can say goodbye to that there dance and a few more besides, because the lanes will fill up with snow like a cup filled with milk and until the thaw comes you'll have to make do with whatever the station here has to offer.'

Ellen, who had been listening to the conversation with interest, piped up at this point. 'It's all right for me, sergeant,' she said, 'but my friend here has a feller at Framingham she's not seen for absolutely ages. She's been pinning all her hopes on that dance, and I dare say if we can't get to them then they can't get to us, is that right?'

The sergeant nodded. 'That's it.' He stared closely into Ellen's small pale face. 'You're one of the RT ops, ain't you? Why do you want to go gettin' yourself a feller at Framingham when Credington is full of blokes simply longin' for a nice little Waaf?'

'I told you, it's not me that has a feller over there, it's my mate here. She's known him since they were kids, so mebbe I should have said he was her pal instead of her feller. They were both . . .'

'It doesn't matter, Ellen,' Molly said. 'I just thought it would be fun to see Lenny again, but I dare say there'll be lots of other opportunities. It can't snow for ever, after all.'

When the runway was clear Molly, Ellen and Hetty joined the rush of personnel towards the cookhouse and the promised bacon butties, and Molly was just swallowing the last morsel of hers when Maggie, who had lingered to exchange greetings with a friend, pulled a chair up to the table and sat down.

'Phew! I had a job to persuade Cooky that I'd not already been served with my sandwich,' she announced rather indistinctly through a generous mouthful. 'He said, "Trying to get another one, eh? Well, you can forget that. I give you yours not ten minutes ago, *and* I added ketchup when you asked for it. Second helpings ain't on offer."'

Ellen's eyebrows shot up. 'I don't see . . .' she began, but Hetty interrupted.

'I do, and he's not the first one to think Maggie was Molly. They're the same height, the same build and very similar in colouring, so what with that and the uniform you can't blame the poor feller. How did you persuade him in the end?'

'He wanted proof, he said, before he'd part with another bacon buttie, so I pointed to this table and there you were,' Maggie said thickly. She swallowed, and grinned widely. 'You'll scarcely believe it, but he actually apologised. I felt quite insulted, but if this continues to happen I think I'll bleach my hair. I've always wanted to be a proper blonde; I believe the fellers would appreciate it.'

Molly snorted into her tin mug of tea, choking on her mouthful and spraying the drink all over her empty plate.

274

'You wouldn't! If you go blonde you'll be havin' to touch up the roots every two or three weeks. Besides, if you do it – go blonde I mean – I'll jolly well go blonde as well. I refuse to have every feller in Bomber Command chasin' after you and leavin' me sittin' on the shelf.'

Ellen giggled. 'Why don't all four of us go blonde?' she enquired. 'A change is as good as a rest, they say.' She glanced laughingly at her friends. 'But first let's get back to our billet and see if the fire's still lit. It's always pretty warm in the cookhouse, but we've got a fair walk back so we might as well get going at once.'

When they arrived at the house they found the fire still in and the kitchen welcomingly warm. Molly and Ellen shed their wet coats, hats and scarves and kicked off their boots, then headed for the stairs, but on the way up Molly said rather plaintively: 'I do hope Maggie was only joking when she said she'd like to go blonde. Anyhow, if she does I shan't follow suit. Lenny would hate it, I'm sure, and even Alex, though he's only a friend, said the other day that my hair was the colour of honey which must mean, I suppose, that he likes it. No, I'll stick to what I've got.'

*

'You joined the air force to see the world, and what did you see? You saw GB . . .'

275

Bumble had been bawling out the song whilst working on a Spitfire which had got quite badly shot up in a recent raid over Germany, and was feeling rather pleased with himself. He had started out in the air force as a motor mechanic but he had speedily risen to the point where he was ground crew, servicing first Hampdens and then fighters and thoroughly enjoying both the work and the feeling that he was performing an important task in keeping the craft in the air – a task at which he excelled. In fact he and his fellows felt themselves to be every bit as important as air crew. Recently, however, now that the Hampdens were flying no more, the rumour had been circulated that his crew might train on the engines of the new Mark II Lancaster bombers with their Bristol Hercules engines. But now Bumble, singing to himself as he replaced a bent and broken part, had just been given some rather startling news. Straightening up, he turned to the man who had delivered it and raised his eyebrows.

'Lossiemouth? Isn't that somewhere in Scotland? Why the devil do they want us to train up there – or is it just another course? Either way, it'll be a while before we'll be back here. But it'll be a hell of a train journey; you know what trains are like in wartime!'

John Gilbert was a tall red-haired man with a tiny blond moustache of which he was exceedingly proud. He and Bumble had joined the motor pool at the same time and progressed together to ground crew, and now they were bezzies, never parted for long if they could help it. Bumble felt that as long as he was with Gil he would not be sorry to follow his kite to any part of the world the Royal Air Force decreed, though he would have preferred somewhere warm. He said as much now, and Gil responded with a cheerful grin and a nod.

'It'll be a while, as you say,' he observed. 'And if there's one thing the air force is beginning to understand it's that air crew and ground crew don't like being parted. After all, one gets to know the little idiosyncrasies of the aircraft one services; *Bellissima* is an open book to us but she won't be to any other ground crew. We'll miss the old girl and her crew, isn't that right?'

In response to the question a muffled reply of 'Won't we just' came from under the Spitfire's engine hood where Dickie Bird, another member of the ground crew, was working. Bumble and Gil laughed and Gil cupped his hand around his ear.

'I hear the voice of the engine speaking, telling us to stick together and we can't go wrong,' he said. He pulled an oily rag out of his pocket and rubbed it over his already oily hands. 'Come on, fellers, we've got to clean up before we go to the cookhouse. We will continue this discussion over tea and a wad.'

*

277

The tables in the NAAFI were small and the papers spread out in front of Molly were extensive, but as Alex shuffled them into a neat pile, folded them and crammed them into a brown envelope, he was smiling. Then he sat down again, leaned his chin on his hands and regarded Molly approvingly.

'See my new filing system?' he said. 'I've decided that every time something has been thoroughly learned by you, young Molly, I shall file it in a brown envelope which means, more or less, that it is one more thing you won't have to worry about. But if you do need to consult it again you'll remember my filing system, and even if I'm not there you will be able to find the information you need in seconds.' He handed the envelope to Molly, who looked at its bulging sides with respect.

'Do I really know so much?' she marvelled. 'Oh, Alex, you're a perishing prince. We're way ahead of Ellen in the learning stakes and it's all thanks to you.'

Alex grinned again. 'Why not reward me with a trip in to Lincoln on the gharry?' he said persuasively. 'All work and no play makes Jack a dull boy. We could hire a boat at Brayford Pool and go for a trip. Can you row? Would you like to learn? If so, I'll teach you.'

Molly sighed but shook her head. 'I'd love to have a river trip, but I'm afraid it's out of the question today. Pam Oliver in the radar office says there's make-up to be had at the branch of Boots in the city. I've promised Ellen that I'll go with her, and afterwards we'll go for tea at the café on Silver Street. But I do appreciate everything you're doing for me, Alex, so next time we're free . . .'

'Where have I heard that before?' Alex said gloomily. 'Every time I've asked you to see a flick or have a meal you've always found some excuse. Is it because this Lenny – if that's the chap's name – has a prior claim?'

Molly felt the blood rush to her cheeks. Alex was so nice, so kind, so generous in fact, yet it was true that she still felt Lenny had first call on her. 'I promise on my word of honour that next time we're both free we'll go on this river trip you've talked so much about,' she said. 'And I'm sorry about the make-up trip, but I can't let Ellen down.'

'Never mind. I'll hold you to that,' Alex said, but Molly thought he did mind, and wished she could have cancelled the shopping trip, but it was impossible. Anyway, she didn't think she ought to give Alex ideas, so she smiled regretfully when he touched her cheek and reiterated her promise to go out with him soon.

*

Lenny stared at the girl sitting opposite him in the small café in Lincoln city centre. 'But Sal, I've explained over and over. It's a posting all right, but since it's for training on bombers I'll be coming back down south as soon as I've passed; at least I hope I will. So why d'you want to break up with me? After all, the time will soon pass and at the end of it I'll be in Bomber Command. Of course, fighters are still needed, but to be honest with you, my love, a Spitfire pilot has a pretty bloody lonely life. These new Lancasters have a crew of seven and all seven will have to know everything there is to know about their kite. Are you telling me you're not prepared to wait, or is the truth that you've met someone else? If so I'd rather be told.'

The girl sitting on the opposite side of the table ran a hand through her tousled blonde curls. 'Do you remember when I took you to Tunbridge Wells, to the house on the Pantiles where I was brought up, and introduced you to my parents, and my brother Frank? I thought at the time that it was odd you'd never suggested that I might meet your folks – that you'd never taken me home when we had leave together . . . and then I met this girl, Jane something, and when I mentioned you she sort of sneered and said I must have a taste for low company, because she knew you when you were growing up and she'd always suspected that you were hand in glove with a girl who was little better than a thief. I took no notice of that, of course – she didn't strike me as a very nice girl – but . . . Lenny, why did you never tell me you were brought up in an orphanage?'

'Are you dumping me because I'm an orphan?' Lenny said incredulously. 'I can't believe you would let a little thing like that ruin our relationship. Why, we were talking of getting married when the war was over! Why should my being brought up in an orphanage make such a difference, Sal?'

The girl shrugged helplessly. 'I don't really know, it's difficult to put into words. You see, I come from a large family – oh, not just parents and brothers and sisters, but cousins and uncles and aunts – so marrying someone without anyone at all just seems . . . oh, wrong somehow. It's like marrying half a person. So when you said you were off to train on Lancasters it made me think. I'm very fond of you, Lenny, but I don't think I want to marry someone with no background. And you've told me so many different stories about your life before the air force that I'm totally confused; going out with you on a permanent basis is like going out with ten different men . . .' She put a hand across the table and covered one of his, squeezing his fingers. 'Can you try to understand? After months apart I may realise that marrying you is the right thing for me, but frankly, I don't think so. That's why I decided to tell you how I felt, so that you would understand if I ended our relationship.'

Lenny stared at her, at her rumpled curls, her big blue eyes and her soft, kissable mouth, and made a discovery. Sal was pretty and glamorous but if she could cast him aside just because he had no family he had been much mistaken in his reading of her character. I fell for the mirror image of Betty Grable and never looked beyond the blonde curls and cuddly figure, he told himself. Lily was fun, but Sally was my first real girlfriend, and I was so delighted to have a popsie all the other men envied me for that I never stopped to wonder what she really thought. And the amazing thing is that I've fooled myself into believing that the feeling I had for her was real love and the feeling she had for me was the same.

Lenny grinned. He would have expected to feel rage, or at least annoyance, but he felt neither. The despicable Jane, whatever her motive, had done him a good turn. Oh, Sal was still the prettiest and most desirable girl he had ever met, but if his being an orphan put him out of the running so far as marriage with her was concerned, then Jane's malicious intervention had done him a favour even if she had intended quite the opposite. Much better to discover Sal's feelings now than after they were married. So he smiled gently at his companion, then picked up the teapot and swirled it round before beckoning the waitress to bring more hot water. 'You're a good girl, Sal,' he said. 'You've told me the truth, which is more than some people would have done. I'm sorry that our plans have come to naught, but maybe it's for the best. I've never had a family, which I suppose is why I can't really understand your reaction to discovering that I'm an orphan, but I'm sure someone in this great big world will judge me for what I am, not for an accident of birth. And although I would never have accused you of two-timing me, you aren't the only one who listens to the odd spot of gossip. Before you met me you were going out with a feller from your home town – Pete something or other – and someone told me that you'd taken up with him again. Is that right?'

Sal heaved a sigh. 'I've always had a soft spot for Pete,' she acknowledged. 'It sounds dreadful to say if I can't have you I'll settle for Pete, but I s'pose that's what a lot of people, including my parents, will think.'

Lenny smiled. 'And I'm a Spitfire pilot who is about to train to fly Lancasters,' he said gently. 'Whereas your Pete is a rating aboard HMS *Ulysses* going back and forth to the United States on convoy duty. A very brave man, but not quite as glamorous as you would like, perhaps.' He watched with interest as a bright flush burned in his companion's cheeks, and she gave a shamefaced little nod.

'Pete will never be a hero, but I've known him since I was in kindergarten. Oh, forgive me, Lenny, but going around with Pete is like slipping on an old warm overcoat on a cold day, whereas going out with you was exciting and somehow dangerous but not at all comfortable.' She gave an embarrassed little laugh. 'I was waiting all the time for you to try something on, whereas I knew Pete never would. He respects me, and he respects our joint past as well.'

'Well, thank you for telling me,' Lenny said sincerely. 'I think you've saved us both from making a dreadful mistake.' He picked up his teacup and drained it. 'Perhaps today has been a lesson for the pair of us, but there's still another couple of hours of daylight left. Shall we walk down to Brayford Pool and hire a boat for a trip down the river? Then I must get back to my airfield; I leave there tomorrow and have to finish my packing.'

For the next few weeks Lenny was too busy becoming proficient at piloting a Lancaster to do more than tell himself over and over that he had had a lucky escape. Suppose he and Sally had continued with their affair, neither realising that what they thought was love had really only been infatuation? He did not think in his heart that it would ever have come to marriage, but he might have wasted too much of his precious time trying to please a girl who was constantly looking over his shoulder, wondering when Mr Right would come along – with dozens of relatives in his train.

He told no one that he and Sally were no longer to be regarded as a couple, but longed nonetheless to be able to confide in someone without losing face. So when a familiar voice hailed him as he was making his way, in full flying kit, towards the debriefing hut he stopped in delight when he recognised the once familiar shout.

'Lenny! Hey, Lenny! It is you, under all that gear, isn't it? Don't say you're going to pretend you'd forgotten your old pal!'

Lenny started towards the large, waving figure, letting his crew get ahead of him.

'Bumble!' he exclaimed, grinning at the other man. 'What the devil are you doing here?'

'Ground crew. Sent up from Hereford to learn the new engines,' Bumble said happily. 'You?'

'I'm flying the damned things,' Lenny said at once with more than a trace of pride in his voice. 'We're pretty well finished with the course, though – we're off first thing tomorrow, so we'll be back in Lincolnshire before dinner. Scrimpton this time, I've heard, though of course we haven't been told officially.'

Bumble struck his forehead with the back of his hand. 'Of all the weird things, this must be one of the weirdest,' he said. 'We're off to Lincolnshire as well, me and the rest of the crew, when we've finished the course – and passed out with flying colours, naturally! Who'd have believed it? I've never been to Lincolnshire. What's it like?'

'It's grand,' Lenny said without hesitation. 'I expect you know there're a great many airfields in that part of the country. And of course they all give dances to attract what women there are and gharries go off into the city practically every night. In fact, now I come to think of it, there're a couple of friends of ours there too. D'you remember Molly and her little friend Ellen? I've not met up with them yet, but when I get back I mean to do so. They're at Credington.'

'Of course I remember Molly,' Bumble said indignantly. He looked reproachfully at his old friend. '*You* were the one who sent me her letter asking you to rescue her from that strange set-up in Ireland, if you remember, because you were too busy.'

Lenny felt his cheeks grow warm and thought vengefully that it was just like Bumble to remember the one thing he, Lenny, most wanted to forget. But Bumble was still staring at him reproachfully so he had to think fast.

'You must have realised I was too far away to do much, even if I hadn't been in the middle of my training. I passed Molly's letter on to you because I knew you were a safe pair of hands and would act as my deputy. And there was another reason. I'd gone and got myself engaged to the prettiest little Waaf you ever did see, blonde and blue-eyed, with the tiniest waist you can imagine. In fact there was only one thing wrong with her, and that was jealousy. I've been longing to get in touch with

Molly' – he crossed his fingers behind his back – 'but Sally went berserk if I so much as passed the time of day with another woman. If it hadn't been for that I'd have found a way to see Molly as soon as she wrote to tell me that she was stationed at Credington. Anyway, a few days ago Sal's jealousy got more than I could take and we split up. I've not written to Molly yet, but now that Sal and I have parted I mean to get in touch.'

Bumble gave him a hard stare and it occurred to Lenny that his friend was rather more intelligent than he had supposed. In the old days, the name Bumble had said it all: easy-going, everyone's friend, a feller who never looked behind one's actions to discover whether he'd been told the truth. But this Bumble was different; more cynical and less trusting. Lenny was about to expand on his story when he saw his mate waving frantically from the debriefing hut, so he gave his friend a big smile and a promise to get together again as soon as Bumble's ground crew reached Lincolnshire.

Chapter Ten

As if to make up for the severe winter, the summer of 1943 was fine and warm, and when the girls were not on duty they took advantage of their time off to explore the countryside and become familiar with its many beauties. Once or twice they borrowed bicycles, but often they were able to cadge a lift from someone with a car which enabled them to get very much further than catching local buses or walking did.

After the humiliation of her first telephone conversation with Lenny, Molly had been too hurt – and too busy – to make a second attempt for some months, but with the warmer weather her optimism returned and she rang his Mess again, intending to suggest that they might meet at the café on Silver Street which she had just discovered did a delectable high tea of cakes and sandwiches for the princely sum of three shillings. She even planned to offer to pay, but as soon as she heard Lenny's familiar voice coming from the receiver all her resolve to maintain a cool approach disappeared.

'Lenny?' she squeaked. 'Oh, it's so nice to hear your voice! I suppose you aren't free tomorrow? Only I know how busy you are and how difficult it is to get away for a few hours, but I thought – I thought—'

Lenny's voice cut across hers, sounding, she thought, both warm and friendly. 'Molly! It's grand to hear your voice too. I'm busy tomorrow, but I'm free on Wednesday. Want to meet up? There's always a gharry going into the city, but if you can wangle a whole day away I've recently joined a group of chaps – there are six of us – who've bought an old car. My ground crew fell on it like starving wolves and did all sorts to the engine, and though the bodywork isn't up to much she goes like a bomb. If I picked you up early we could go to the Waggon and Horses at Caythorpe for an early lunch. Do you know it?'

Molly shook her head. 'No, I only know Lincoln because that's where the gharry drops us,' she explained. 'Waafs don't run to motors.' She hesitated. 'Is it very expensive? Only my pay isn't exactly astronomical so I know more about cafés than restaurants. Will it break the bank?'

Lenny's laugh echoed down the line, sounding reassuringly like the Lenny she had once known and much less like the stranger who had spoken so coldly the last time they had spoken on the telephone.

'When I ask a young lady for a day out I'm the one who picks up the bill. Besides, apart from the expense of the car I'm like you, and don't have to send an allowance home to my parents, for obvious reasons. But you haven't answered my question; will you come out with me for a day or won't you?'

His voice had sharpened on the last few words and Molly felt once more a churning in her inside. But this time she did not intend to let her uneasiness show.

'Last time I rang you, Lenny, you snubbed me something rotten,' she said with as much coldness as she could muster. 'If you really want me to come out with you, of course I'd be delighted. It would be like old times – no, much better than old times. But if you're just asking me from a sense of duty . . .'

Lenny laughed. 'Look, I haven't got time to explain now, but we can talk when we meet. I'll pick you up in Credington village at ten o'clock on Wednesday morning, all right?'

'All right,' Molly echoed. 'See you then, Lenny.'

Molly put the receiver back on its hook and the girl next in the queue picked it up. They were in the NAAFI and Ellen was looking at her hopefully, a smile beginning to break out on her small face.

'He's asked you out, and he's done it nicely this time,' Ellen said jubilantly when Molly joined her at the small table she had bagged while Molly made her call. 'I'm so glad, Molly. For myself I can't see that Lenny's a particularly good catch, but you obviously think differently. I never knew him very well but I do know that he hasn't treated you particularly nicely. In fact last time I thought he behaved bloody badly. However, I take it you've forgiven him? If so, just make sure he doesn't see it as a sign of weakness and start trying to bully you again. I don't see why you can't pair up with Alex; he's a sweetie. Everyone likes him, but it's you he pays the most attention to.'

'I know what you mean, but I think I've been a little in love with Lenny ever since that cricket ball I told you about whumped all the air out of me,' Molly said apologetically. 'And as for letting him bully me, if the air force has done one thing, it's been to make me stand up for myself. When I was at the O'Hare farm I had a pretty low opinion of myself, but being an RT op is different.' She grinned at her friend. 'I don't wish to boast but I know we're terribly important to the men who fly the kites, and they're the ones who matter. So I shan't be letting anyone push me around, particularly once I've pased my final exams and can take the u/t off my shoulder flash.'

The girls got simultaneously to their feet and Ellen gave her friend's hand a convulsive squeeze.

'You're definitely off on Wednesday, then?' she asked. 'If so, I shall give in to the entreaties of young Mr Padstow and go to the flicks with him. I know he'll try a kiss and a cuddle in the dark, but what's wrong with that? We like each other and a kiss and a cuddle with someone you like can lead to better things . . . well, perhaps not better, but different things. So if you come back engaged to the oh so wonderful Lenny, you may find that he's been pipped at the post by Mr Paul Padstow, and I shall be gazing at a ring on my finger placed there by him.'

They left the NAAFI and headed for their billet, and Molly gave a derisive snort. 'Some chance! Oh, I don't deny that practically every fellow on the station has a soft spot for you, but I can't see you accepting one when you've a choice of so many. Oh, the bliss of two whole days off! I don't know about you, but I'm going to make the best use of it I can think of and have an early night for once.'

The night before her date with Lenny Molly dreamed that she and Maggie made up a four-some with Lenny and some other bloke whose name she did not catch. What she did catch was that Lenny immediately abandoned her, and paid court to Maggie in the most blatant way.

Molly soon realised why when they reached a charming, old-fashioned pub and Maggie took off her cap to reveal a head covered with bubbly golden curls. One look at Lenny's face made it plain to Molly at least that her old friend was smitten, more by the golden curls than by anything else. As she dreamed, tears trickled down her face at Lenny's behaviour, and as soon as she could she asked him why he had abandoned her for her friend.

Lenny had grinned widely, pushing his cap to the back of his head and scratching his dark curly mop. 'I can't resist blondes,' he said frankly. 'Why don't you bleach your hair the same as your pal Maggie has done? If you do that I'll be perfectly willing to have you for my girlfriend.'

Even in her dream Molly recognised the insult, and before she could stop herself she had dived across the short distance which separated them and slapped Lenny's face with all her strength.

'You're detestable and I hate you,' she screamed at the top of her voice. 'You say you were too far away to rescue me when the Mathiases kidnapped me, but that was just an excuse. Take me home, Lenny Smith, or I'll scream the place down.'

Lenny looked at her, his eyes cold as the snow which she now realised was falling outside the pub. She looked challengingly back, and saw that his smile had turned spiteful.

'Catch a bus,' he said nastily, 'and if you don't want to do that you can bloody well walk.'

In the dream, Molly rubbed her eyes, sniffed, and faced her one-time friend. 'Catch a bus yourself,' she said rudely, and ran out of the pub. The car which had brought them there stood outside and with a whoop of triumph Molly kicked it as hard as she could and was delighted to see it crumble into dust beneath her foot. She turned to face Lenny, who was looking startled to say the least. 'And if there's no bus you can walk,' she said breathlessly. 'And don't worry about me, because this is the end between us.'

She turned away from Lenny, just too late to avoid seeing him link arms with Maggie and return to the pub, and she was about to hurl further abuse after them when she felt a hand on her shoulder and heard Ellen's voice in her ear.

'Wake up, queen, wake up,' Ellen said urgently. 'I dunno what you was dreamin' about, but it must have been somethin' real horrid.' She picked up the alarm clock and gazed at its face. 'No point in getting up, it's not yet five o'clock.' She smoothed a small hand across Molly's brow. 'If you're frightened to go back to sleep you can get in with me, though it's so warm you'd probably rather not.' Even in the dim light coming through the window Molly could see her friend's smile. 'A dream's a dream, and nothing more. I expect you got over-excited, having arranged to see your old pal after so long. Was it that?'

Molly sat up on one elbow. She was still shaking but beginning to feel calmer. 'I dreamed Lenny took up with Maggie and sent me off with a flea in my ear,' she said ruefully. 'It was horrid, but as you say, only a dream. And now let's both of us get back to sleep before the alarm goes off.'

'You can't wear civvies of course but you can wear your very best number ones and some make-up,' Ellen said. 'I know our trip to Boots was unsuccessful, but my contribution to your wonderful day will be a smear of my pre-war lipstick, and Maggie has said she'll give you some of that sooty stuff to darken your lashes and eyebrows. Heaven knows what she puts in it, but several of the girls swear by it. Only you mustn't cry if his majesty takes you to see a sad film, because it runs. And you mustn't rub your eyes, for the same reason.'

'Thanks very much but you can forget all your aids to beauty, even the lipstick,' Molly said, though with a touch of regret. 'I've known Lenny since we were quite little kids and he won't be impressed by even the most professional make-up. In fact he'd probably laugh me to scorn and I can do without that. But if Maggie will lend me her iron I'll press my best blues and I'll polish those horrible walking shoes until I can see my face in them. Lenny is picking me up in a car that half a dozen of them have clubbed together to buy. Don't enquire where they get the petrol from, because I didn't ask and he didn't tell.'

The two girls were in their bedroom getting dressed for the day ahead which, thanks to Paul Padstow, looked like being a good one for them both. Ellen had laughed when young Mr Padstow had apologised for the fact that an aircraftman's pay meant his invitation was a bit 'either or'; in this case, either the cinema or supper in the picture house café.

'Well, I told him I'm not proud,' Ellen had told Molly later. 'They used to say at the home that I had the happy knack of enjoying everything we did, and I'm sure it applies just as much to the RAF; more, in fact. So you go swanning off in your automobile and Paul and I will catch the gharry into Lincoln, and I bet I'll have just as good a time as you do.'

Breakfast in the canteen varied very little from day to day, porridge, tea and toast being the staples Cook turned out, but Molly was so lit up by excitement that even had the porridge been burned she would not have noticed. Ellen saw her look around as soon as they entered the cookhouse, and nudged her sharply in the ribs. 'You're not expecting to see your chap in the Credington cookhouse, are you?' she asked incredulously. 'Who are you looking for?'

'Honestly, Ellen, you must think I'm as mad as you are yourself,' Molly said indignantly. 'I was hoping to see Alex. He knows today is special for me, so I want his seal of approval.'

At that moment Alex approached their table, a bowl of porridge in one hand and a plate of leathery-looking toast in the other. He dumped both plates on the table and raised an eyebrow at Molly. 'I thought you said next time you were free you'd go on a river trip with me?' he said reproachfully.

'Oh, Alex, I'm so sorry,' Molly said, feeling the heat rush to her cheeks. She knew Alex liked her and she also knew that she liked him, but Lenny was an old friend, and this meeting had been planned, by Molly at any rate, ever since she arrived at Credington.

'Don't worry about it, but why you are going to such lengths – best blues indeed – to impress some feller who hasn't bothered with you for years I do not understand,' Alex said, sliding into the chair opposite hers. 'Here am I, wanting to take you out and spend my hard-earned money to give you a grand time, and you pass me over for some little squirt from another station! Well, I can't stop you making a fool of yourself, but at least you can promise me you'll tell me every detail of your wonderful date. I'd reciprocate in kind, only I'm doing a double shift and shall probably be too tired tonight to remember my own name, let alone what I've been doing all day.'

He began to eat his porridge, grinning at Molly over the top of his spoon. 'So don't forget, I shall be with you in spirit if not in the flesh, and that means you can tell this Lenny of yours that there'll be no funny business. *Comprenez?*'

'Oh, Alex, are you really having to do a double shift because Ellen and I are off for the whole day?' Molly asked, dismayed. 'If I'd known . . .'

Alex's best friend and oppo Fred pulled a chair round so that he could join them. 'Don't you listen to a word he says, young Molly,' he said. 'He is *not* doing a double shift, he just wants to spoil your day. But who is this Lenny, anyway? From the way you were talking about him I thought he must be a brother, or have I got it wrong?'

Molly smiled but shook her head. 'We were brought up together in a children's home,' she explained. 'But as for being like brother and sister, you couldn't be more wrong. I s'pose you could say we were best pals . . .'

'Best pals don't usually go all starry-eyed over each other,' Alex observed. 'It's time you grew up, Molly. The feeling you have for this Lenny is hero worship; I bet he was a devil of a guy on the football field, or head of the class at mathematics or – or . . .'

'He wasn't; it isn't,' Molly said wildly. 'He's a good cricketer, but that's a pretty boring sort of game. I like Lenny because . . . oh, I can't explain and I don't intend to try. Shut up, Alex, or I shan't tell you anything at all.'

She finished her porridge, drank the last of the tea in her tin mug and scraped back her chair. 'I'm off.' She grinned at Alex. 'Go and practise your cricket and maybe some lucky Waaf will fall into your loving arms, or maybe she won't. And I don't see why I should tell you about my day, because this will be a first date and nice girls don't tell tales.'

In her secret heart Molly was afraid that something might happen to prevent Lenny from keeping his promise, but in the event they arrived simultaneously on the small village green. Naturally enough with both being in uniform there was no difficulty over recognition but as Molly sank into the passenger seat of the old Bullnose Morris and turned to smile at the driver she received a shock.

'Lenny?' she said uncertainly. 'It is you, isn't it, Lenny?'

Lenny turned to look at her. He stared hard for a moment, then grinned. 'Molly?' he said in a parody of her own tone. 'It is you, isn't it, Molly?'

Molly ducked her head. She knew he was laughing at her and was not sure that she liked it. After all, a good few years had passed since they had last met and they had both changed. Last time he had seen her she had not, for instance, been wearing a peaked WAAF cap. Nevertheless, she had not expected to find him quite so altered, and she supposed that he, too, had anticipated fewer differences from the girl he had once known so well.

Rather to Molly's surprise Lenny had left the engine running, and when she remarked on this, in an effort to ease the slight tension she felt, he leaned over and gripped her hand for a moment.

'Don't worry,' he said. 'The car's old but reasonably reliable. We call her Bunny because when she's in an awkward mood she bounces along like a rabbit, but she'll get us to the Waggon and Horses all right. I've booked the table for twelve thirty, which gives us plenty of time.'

'I'm not worrying,' Molly said rather coolly, as her companion did various things and the car began to move slowly forward. 'I suppose if you can fly a Lancaster then you must be able to drive a mere car.' She sniffed. 'Is the engine supposed to make that racket, or have you inadvertently trapped a cat under the bonnet?'

Lenny laughed, but Molly thought he was not amused and she supposed, rather guiltily, that the car was a proud possession and he would object to anything which could be regarded as criticism. As they trundled slowly up the road she turned to him and saw that he was scowling.

'Sorry, Lenny. I'm sure the car – Bunny, I mean – is a real goer,' she said. It was unfortunate that even as the words left her lips the car jerked, bounced and stopped and the engine died.

'Damn, damn, damn!' Lenny said viciously. He turned to Molly. 'Go on, have a good laugh! It isn't that I'm a bad driver – oh damn it. I should have let the ground crew loose on her before I offered to take you to somewhere a bit off the beaten track. The snag will be if she lets me down once we get to hilly country.' The scowl turned to a rueful expression. 'I told the fellers I was taking you to the Waggon for a meal and then up to a quiet little spot we found weeks back, where we could have a serious talk. I hope to God we make it to the Waggon in time, otherwise some other oik will be eating our dinners. What a start for our meeting!'

'It doesn't matter,' Molly said coolly. 'The meal doesn't matter, I mean. But Lenny, we've simply got to talk. You must admit you haven't treated me like a friend but more as though I were an enemy, and I wouldn't be human if I didn't want to know why.'

Lenny swore and jumped out of the car. 'I'll get her going with the starting handle and we'll throw ourselves on Mrs Bullard's mercy,' he said. 'Just you sit tight, cross your fingers and pray. Mrs Bullard is the landlady of the Waggon and by way of being an old friend, so she'll save the table for as long as she can, but if we're simply too late I'll get her to make some sandwiches and we'll eat them in the car, washing them down with a glass of beer. I know it isn't the romantic meal I'd planned, to make up to you for the way I've behaved, but I'm afraid it's the best I can do.'

By the time they got to the Waggon and Horses, however, it was half past one. Bunny had stalled three times en route, and Lenny was in no very pleasant humour. He got out of the car, telling Molly that she had best stay where she was whilst he went in and made his peace with Mrs Bullard. He disappeared into the pub, leaving Molly feeling embarrassed and let down, though Mrs Bullard proved to be both friendly and understanding when Lenny finally beckoned his passenger inside. She was fat and fifty with grey hair, bright blue eyes and a friendly smile.

'Don't you worry, my love. I'll pack you up a decent lunch and a flask of coffee which you can take to the top of the hill and enjoy whilst you look out over one of the loveliest views in Great Britain. 'Twon't take me but ten minutes, so you go and sit in the snug and you can have a tot of my cherry wine whilst you wait.'

Ensconced at a table with glasses of the promised beverage before them, Lenny grinned at Molly. 'Good thing it isn't raining,' he said cheerfully. 'I've only been up to look at the view once before, and then you couldn't see much further than your own nose, but today there isn't a cloud in sight so you'll be able to boast that you've been to Fulbeck and seen the famous view.' He smiled at her, and for a moment it was his old fascinating smile, the smile which had made her feel warm inside when they were children.

Molly was about to comment that he looked more cheerful already but before she could do so Mrs Bullard came into the snug with two packets of sandwiches and the promised flask of coffee. Lenny thanked her and headed for the car, but Molly jerked his elbow.

'We don't want to go in the car, not if the hill's as steep as you seem to think,' she said tactfully. 'I'd rather walk, honest to God I would. It'll work up my appetite, because I've just peeped inside the greaseproof paper and I've got two ham and pickle sandwiches and two tomato and corned beef, and there's a sort of pastry thing bursting with currants and sultanas. I think they call them Eccles cakes.'

'And she only charged me ten bob for both of us,' Lenny said triumphantly. 'There's an old wooden bench at the top of this hill where we can sit and rave over the view, or simply eat our sandwiches.' He looked consideringly at Molly. 'Let's see who can get up there first!'

Molly grinned. 'I like a challenge,' she said gaily. 'Ready – steady – go!'

They arrived at the bench simultaneously, both pink in the face and breathless as they struggle out of their jackets. Constraint had vanished, and they collapsed on to the bench together and turned to look at the view. It was worth looking at, too, Molly reflected. Miles and miles of country was spread out below them, with farmhouses and cottages dotted here and there and plenty of trees to give shade in the summer. She turned to Lenny.

'It's beautiful,' she breathed. 'But that race has given me an appetite. You can please yourself, but I mean to eat my sandwiches and have a good long swig of coffee before I do anything else.'

Lenny grinned. 'It's known as putting off the evil hour,' he said cheerfully. 'But since I've no desire to talk on an empty stomach, I'll join you and we can leave the explanations for a bit. They're liable to be tedious anyway. But one thing I will tell you before I sink my fangs into those delicious- looking sandwiches. I got a posting this morning. Like most of the communications from on high it doesn't say anything except that I'm heading for a secret destination; so secret apparently that they don't give me so much as a hint of where I'm going to end up. They're giving me some leave so that I can say cheerio to my mates. So just when we've met up again I'm off to God knows where and may not be back until the war's over.'

Molly had already polished off her first sand-wich, but now she turned dismayed eyes on her companion. 'Oh, Lenny, and I did so hope, with our stations being so close, that we might have got to know one another again. Still, you never just know. You might be away for a short period and then be sent home.' She picked up the second sandwich and ate it thoughtfully, staring out over the vista before her whilst her mind was on other things. They ate the rest of the meal in silence, shared the flask of coffee and then leaned back on the old wooden bench, both feeling a good deal more relaxed than they had felt earlier. After a few minutes, when it seemed as though Molly was not going to say a word, Lenny began to speak.

'You say I haven't been friendly towards you since we got back in touch, but what did you expect, Molly? Before you disappeared to Ireland and I joined the air force we were just a couple of kids who happened to be friends. I'd like to stress that all I felt for you was friendship and I assumed it was the same in reverse. When Dick and Beth left we both wanted a friend at the home so we soon became bezzies; isn't that so?'

Dumbly, Molly nodded her head, then shook it. 'Yes – I mean no,' she said, feeling the heat rise up her neck and suffuse her face. 'Perhaps these things aren't the same for boys as they are for girls, but I – I was really keen on you, Lenny, and thought you were keen on me. Now it seems I'd got it all wrong – you thought I was just a pal, the way Dick had been before his parents took him off to Scotland. But we aren't children any more. Indeed, I expect you've got a proper girlfriend now – have you, Lenny?'

For a moment Lenny was tempted to deny any involvement with the fairer sex, but then he changed his mind. Omissions, lies, or even little white fibs, have a way of being found out, and life was complicated enough without that. So when Molly looked at him enquiringly, he shook his head.

'No, not at the moment. But I met a girl when I first arrived in Framingham and – and to tell you the truth I fell for her pretty heavily. However . . .'

He told the story of his infatuation with Sally simply and honestly, and when Molly asked why they had split up he hesitated only fractionally before coming out with the truth.

'She felt she couldn't marry someone who had no background,' he said ruefully. 'And in a way, she was right. She asked me several times if I was ashamed of her and that was the reason I never took her home, and I s'pose I sensed how important meeting each other's family was to her, so I never told her I didn't have one – just made up some excuse or other each time. But, Molly, you'll never guess who *did* tell her, in the end . . .'

When Molly heard how her old enemy had precipitated Sal's decision to break up with Lenny she was suitably amazed, and the pair of them spent an enjoyable few minutes ripping Jane's character to shreds, devising horrible tortures for her, and finally engineering her complete and utter disgrace. At last, however, Molly fell silent, and after a lengthy pause she lifted regretful eyes to Lenny's face.

'I understand what you're doing,' she said. 'You're letting me down lightly, aren't you? Tell me, what did your Sally look like? Judging from what men seem to go for, I'd put money on her being a bubbly, blue-eyed blonde. Oh well, there's always bleach!'

Lenny gave a reluctant chuckle. 'Will you be terribly hurt if I tell you that fond though I am of you, you really aren't my type? Well, no, I don't mean that exactly. The girl I knew when we were both at Haisborough might not have had blonde curls but in any other respect she was just like Sally: full of beans, game for anything and always cocking a snook at authority.' He grinned ruefully. 'Looking at you now with a picture of the old Molly clear in my mind I can see how completely you've changed. You take life seriously now. Well, in your job you have to do just that. So you see, if we're going to have any sort of relationship we'll have to remember we are two different people from our childhood selves. If you met the old Molly in the street you'd not recognise her, and if you did recognise her you'd probably want to walk straight past. Now tell me I'm wrong.'

Molly wrenched her gaze from his and concentrated once more on the view whilst she thought about his words. Had she changed so completely? Was she really a different girl from the one who had sneaked out whenever possible to meet Lenny Smith? She did not feel any different, but when she thought about being on duty in the watch office she had to concede that Lenny's words rang true. Her work was not only the most important thing in her life but also a passion. Getting the kites off the ground was imperative, and getting them back safely even more so. She realised she would not in any circumstances jeopardise the safety of the airmen who relied on her to see them home, and if that meant giving up any chance of renewing her friendship with Lenny then she would do it unhesitatingly and, furthermore, without regrets.

She turned away from the view just as Lenny did and once more their eyes met. 'Well?' he asked. 'Do you agree? The Molly I see before me isn't the Molly of Haisborough Orphanage. So if you want to renew our relationship . . .'

Molly shook her head. 'No can do,' she said quietly. 'We've both of us misread the situation, which is the nicest way I can think of to put it. You've changed as well, Lenny; there are lines of strain on your face which most certainly weren't there when we were both at Haisborough. You've never asked me what happened when I got taken to Ireland by mistake, and I've not asked you why you changed from Spitfires to bombers. Those two things have had a real impact on our lives, and if we were truly interested in each other we'd want to know about them. So I suggest we swap stories and then decide to be content with friendship. Only – only if it's all the same to you I would like to keep on writing to you so we never lose touch so completely again.'

Lenny nodded. 'I'm not much of a hand at letter-writing,' he warned her, 'but I'll do my best to fill you in; perhaps I could write a sort of diary, only we'll have to have some code words because of the censor. I'm going away, remember, and might end up anywhere. And another thing . . . oh dear, how can I put this?'

It was Molly's turn to chuckle, albeit some what ruefully. 'Bubbly blondes,' she said. 'You want to play fair but you also want to play the field without feeling guilty because of me. Well, that's okay. Now that I know where we stand I shall accept any invitation that comes my way too.'

Lenny reached out a hand and gripped Molly's as it lay on the bench between them. 'It's a deal. I didn't realise you'd turned down invitations because of our old friendship. Gosh, I am impressed!'

Molly opened her mouth to say that there had only been one invitation – from Alex – and closed it again; no point in letting Lenny think she was undesirable. 'It's a deal,' she echoed. 'And now you can tell me why you changed from Spitfires.'

Lenny's story was succinct: he had enjoyed flying Spitfires but the loneliness of the job had prompted him to apply to train to become a bomber pilot, and he assured Molly that he was certain he had made the right decision. He told her about the men he worked with: the ground crew he respected, and the air crew he couldn't imagine flying without. 'You see, the ground crew is allocated to us, but we have some say when it comes to air crew. At first the air force didn't understand the importance of keeping crews together if someone was needed elsewhere, but they've gradually come round to our point of view and now they agree that a strong unit like ours shouldn't be split up. All seven of us know our jobs backwards and we're all good mates – though the others know who's boss, of course!

'Now, what happened to you? Bumble said something about your hiding in a lorry at Liverpool docks, so why don't you start your story from there . . .'

'Right,' Molly said briskly. 'I got aboard the lorry, which was full of fleeces, and stupidly fell asleep. I must have slept through the crossing because when I woke up the lorry was thundering along a shockingly bad road through a forest. I couldn't see anything I recognised, and when the driver suddenly jammed on his brakes I think I must have bashed my head against something because everything went black . . .'

Molly told the story well and Lenny listened with bated breath, but made no comment until she introduced Cian into her tale.

'Were they kind to you, those Mathiases?' he asked. His tone became belligerent. 'That Cian, the one who wanted you kept safe; why didn't he help you to get away, to get back to England? What was the point of keeping you captive?'

Molly shrugged. 'I don't think Cian could have helped me to escape from his mother and brother,' she explained. 'Mrs Mathias wanted me for company, and later for my help around the farm. In a way I was really happy. I'd never worked on a farm before, but I loved it. The countryside was beautiful and I learned how to milk the cows, and how to make butter and so on, and I really think they couldn't have managed without me. Then Cian's cousin Esme was bombed out – she lived in Bootle – and begged the Mathiases to take her in. Right from the start she hated me and did everything she could to blacken my reputation with them. She said I was lazy and selfish and nothing more than a slave. And when she said that I realised that in a way it was true, which is why I wrote to you, Lenny, imploring you to help me.'

Lenny reddened. 'The letter didn't reach me for a long while,' he said feebly. 'And when it did I was miles away, here in Lincolnshire in fact, training to be a Spitfire pilot. But I knew old Bumble was closer to you than I was, because we had written to each other once or twice, so I forwarded your letter to him, expecting him to go to the police. But as you know, he decided it would be best to rescue you himself.' He grinned at his companion. 'And from what he told me, good old Bumble did the trick with only the help of his pal Tim Donahue.' He looked hopefully at Molly. 'Is that clear? I feel ashamed, now, that I passed the buck, but honestly, what else could I do? And old Bumble was nothing if not reliable. I used to think he was a figure of fun but he's not, is he?'

'He's a perishing hero,' Molly said fervently. 'If it hadn't been for him I'd either be still a prisoner or dead as a dodo.'

Lenny's eyebrows shot up. 'Dead as a dodo?' he echoed. 'But from what you've told me you were really useful to the Mathiases, and Cian and his mother liked you.'

312

'Yes, but Declan hated the ground I walked on,' Molly admitted. 'I don't know quite what he suspected I'd done to arrive in the forest the way I did, but he certainly knew I'd twigged that the family and their associates were handling stolen goods. When they first found me – though I think it was their dog Sinbad who actually did that – I heard Declan saying something about "spies in the camp". At that time I was swimming in and out of consciousness, so it was only long afterwards that I realised Declan was my enemy, though I'm darned if I know why.'

'Oh, Molly, honestly,' Lenny said. 'One word from you and their whole operation could have been blown apart. Selling stolen goods is illegal.'

'Yes of course, but though it goes against the grain I'd never have told,' Molly explained. 'Whether willingly or not, they saved my life. If it hadn't been for Sinbad finding me and Mrs Mathias taking me in Declan wouldn't have had to move a muscle; I would have died from exposure.'

She stood up as she spoke and smiled at Lenny. 'Haven't we cleared up a lot of misunderstandings! And are we agreed? Once you have a permanent address we'll start corresponding the way friends do, and never lose touch again.'

Chapter Eleven

The drive home was conducted almost in silence. Molly told herself it was because the car engine was noisy, to say nothing of the wind of their going, but in her heart she knew this was not the real reason. She and Lenny had had to acknowledge that what she had thought of as a close and loving relationship was not how Lenny saw it at all. He had agreed to keep in touch, but had made no effort to even pretend that Molly might take Sally's place as the girl in his life. Any future friendship between them would start off as so many wartime romances did, between pen pals, as though there had been no Haisborough Orphanage, no midnight wanderings, and definitely, Molly thought, no illusions that they shared a loving relationship. It was hard, because she had always taken it for granted that Lenny's feelings matched her own, and realising that they most certainly did not was painful. However, the mature Molly who now sat in the old Bullnose

Morris was far more sensible than the starry-eyed orphan who had thought of Lenny as some sort of Prince Charming. When the car stopped outside the Credington gates and the guard came over to them she did not wait for Lenny to produce his pass but immediately opened the passenger door and then, on impulse, leaned across and gave him a kiss on the cheek.

'Thanks for a wonderful day out and a much needed lesson on relationships,' she said quietly. 'You will telephone as soon as you know your date of departure? And as soon as I've got a permanent address for you – or as permanent as the RAF will allow – then I'll write.' She grinned mischievously at him. 'Not love letters, I promise, just the sort of things I'd write if we really were brother and sister.'

Lenny began to protest, saying that any letter from her would be welcome, but Molly shook her head chidingly.

'Don't be so daft; we've agreed to be just friends,' she said briskly. 'Thanks again for a lovely day.'

Lenny opened his mouth, presumably to argue further, then sighed, wheeled the car round and drove away. Molly did not watch him out of sight but set off briskly for the NAAFI where she guessed she would find Ellen, waiting eagerly for news of her day.

*

As soon as the door opened and Molly appeared Ellen was on her feet, waving, and patting the chair beside her.

'Come and sit down and tell me everything,' she said imperiously. 'Did you have a good time? Where did he take you? Did you have a meal? How was the car ride? I bet it was awkward at first, but no doubt you sorted out all your differences . . .'

Molly interrupted ruthlessly as she slid into the vacant chair, looking around the crowded room, at the girls sipping Camp coffee or drinking ginger beer as they chatted with their friends. 'Yes, thanks, we had a nice day out, though the wretched car broke down three times which meant we missed the meal Lenny'd booked. Look, Ellen, can we go somewhere a bit more private? You'd better know the truth . . .'

Ellen stared. 'Well, yes, if you like, but I thought . . . still, there'll be no one in our billet at this time of day. Will that be private enough for you?'

Molly smiled. 'It'll do,' she admitted. 'But don't think you're going to hear a lurid story of love, because you'd be way out.' She stood up, picked up her cap and headed for the door, with Ellen close on her heels.

Presently the two girls faced one another across the kitchen table. Although it was evening it was still warm and the fire in the stove had gone out.

However, the girls had purchased a small Primus stove so that they could make themselves hot drinks, and Ellen immediately filled the kettle from the pump at the sink, lit the Primus under it and returned to the table.

'Start at the very beginning!' she commanded. 'I want every tiny detail . . . well, the ones that aren't too private to pass on to a best pal. Go on, shoot!'

Molly pulled a face. For a moment she considered telling a big fat lie, then laughed at herself. She could no more lie to Ellen than she could have done to Lenny. Truth, even painful truth, was the only way she knew.

'You'll be disappointed,' she warned. 'The fact is, Ellen, that I'd got hold of the wrong end of the stick. Lenny's had a serious girlfriend called Sally, but when she found out he'd been brought up in a children's home she dropped him. I guess he's still feeling hurt, hurt enough to tell me the complete truth, anyway. He says he's realised his feelings for her were just infatuation, but . . .'

Ellen leaned forward. 'Perhaps losing Sally was more bearable because you were waiting in the wings, so to speak. Did he say anything like that?'

At this point the kettle began to hop, and instead of answering immediately Molly got to her feet, fetched tea, saccharin tablets and dried milk from the little cupboard by the sink, and made their drinks. She pushed one towards Ellen, then sat down once more.

'Well, no,' she said slowly. 'He was absolutely frank. He said he had never thought of me as anything but a friend, almost a sister. Oh, Ellen, he pointed out that we'd not met for years and were now two different people from the ones who had lived at Haisborough Orphanage. If we want a relationship – and I'm not sure that I do now – it will mean starting from scratch.'

'Oh,' Ellen said. 'Oh, Molly, were you very upset? I know Lenny meant an awful lot to you, but now you've put it into words I can see what he means.' After a moment, a grin began to form. 'Heavens, what a difference this will make to *my* life, let alone yours. Alex and Fred are always trying to persuade us to make up a foursome for one thing or another, but you never would because of Lenny. But now you'll have no excuse and we can all begin to live a little.'

For one speechless moment Molly stared across the table at her old friend. Then she smiled and let out her breath in a long whistle.

'I feel as though a great weight has been lifted from my shoulders,' she said joyfully. 'Do you know, until you said that, I thought I was actually losing his friendship, but I haven't, have I? I'd talked myself into believing I was in love with Lenny but in truth it was nothing of the sort; I was just carrying a childhood crush into adulthood, and now I'm free of it. Free to go out with other blokes and enjoy myself without feeling guilty. Oh, Ellen, I never thought Lenny was doing me a good turn, but he was, wasn't he?'

'He certainly was,' Ellen agreed. 'Now, there's a dance in the sergeants' Mess tomorrow evening. I take it you're coming? They're always nagging me about the shortage of women at these dos but they won't be able to nag me any longer if I take one of the best-looking Waafs in the watch office along.'

Molly took a long pull of her tea, then put the mug down and leaned across the table to squeeze her friend's hand. 'One of the four, you mean? If you take into account the fact that Maggie, Hetty, you and I are the only Waafs in the watch office, that compliment isn't entirely undeserved,' she said with a chuckle. 'All right, I'll come. Best blues at the ready, and I've got one pair of silk stockings which I was saving for a special occasion. I reckon discovering the truth about myself and gaining a proper life is a special enough occasion for anyone.'

Ellen agreed, and at the appointed time the following evening the two girls set off for the sergeants' Mess. Alex had been off duty all day, so they had not seen him in the watch office, but now he beamed when he spotted Molly. 'So you've given in to the lure of our old Dansette at last,' he said delightedly 'What's got into you? You look downright happy.'

'I am happy,' Molly said, nodding vigorously. 'Oh, Alex, I've been a complete fool, shutting myself away from all the fun. But I shan't do so any more, I promise. I shall enjoy my time off as much as I enjoy my work, and that's saying a lot.'

Alex grinned. 'Does that mean the river trip is on?'

Molly nodded eagerly. 'As soon as we can!'

'Well, I'd like to think I can guess what's changed your mind, but I won't ask if you don't want me to,' Alex said. 'Can you quickstep? Or is it a foxtrot? I just smooch along with whatever my partner's doing, and it seems to work all right. Now come on, are you willing to tell me what's changed you from a killjoy to the girl who is about to melt into my arms and dance the night away?'

For a moment, Molly considered making up some story or other, but Alex had been a good friend and she decided he deserved the truth. 'It was Lenny, of course,' she said. 'Well, it turned out that he's never thought of me as anything but a pal – and meeting him again made *me* realise that I simply had a schoolgirl crush on him. And as soon as I realised that everything fell into place. I used to write him long newsy letters and he'd reply with a two-liner, and the first time I rang his Mess he was downright dismissive. Oh, Alex, I've been the most complete idiot, but I shan't make the same mistake again.' The music came to an end and couples began to drift off the floor. 'Are you going to get me a drink? I know it's only orange squash, but . . . good heavens!'

Molly stopped stock still, staring at the back of someone who, with his arm round a girl's waist, was also making his way off the floor. 'Who's that?'

Alex swivelled round to stare at the crowd around them. 'Who's which?'

'Him,' Molly said urgently. 'The tall one with his arm round that blonde. D'you know him?'

Alex stared, then shook his head as the couple made for the door. 'Not a clue – not that I can tell from the back, of course. But I can guess they've gone to have a kiss and a cuddle, when all you want is a glass of orange squash,' he said mournfully. 'Do you know him? I say, shall we follow them out and have a kiss and cuddle of our own?'

Molly laughed, and made for the makeshift bar. 'It's all right. I was probably mistaken,' she said.

For the rest of the evening, although she danced with several men, it was mainly with Alex that she trod the light fantastic. She kept an eye on the doorway, watching for the tall figure she had spotted earlier, but it was the sight of someone else entirely that made her stop dead in the middle of an energetic foxtrot and then lead Alex off the dance floor towards him.

'Hello Lenny,' she said awkwardly. 'I'm glad you don't feel you need to avoid me; friends bump into each other all the time, so why should we be different?'

Lenny gave a rather strained smile. 'My thoughts exactly,' he said. 'Are you going to introduce me to your friend?'

'Oh, sorry. This is Alex, who's teaching me everything I need to know to become a fully qualified RT operator – I've told you about him.' She turned to Alex. 'Alex, this is Lenny Smith. He flies Lancasters.'

Lenny looked Alex critically up and down, and to her surprise Molly thought she saw a gleam of jealousy in his eyes. The two men shook hands politely, but neither seemed to want to be the first to speak, so Molly touched Lenny's sleeve.

'I saw a feller I thought I recognised just now; he's not one of ours, so he might have come from Scrimpton with you,' she said. 'He was dancing with a blonde and I only caught a glimpse of him before he headed for the door. If we see him again perhaps you could tell me who he is.'

Lenny laughed. 'Could be anyone. Where is he?'

'He went outside.'

'Well, I expect his name will come back to you sooner or later.' He turned to Alex. 'I don't know whether you'd be interested, but my crew and I are being posted shortly and we're looking to sell our old Morris before we go. Molly may have mentioned that Bunny played up yesterday, but the ground crew did something to her engine this morning and now she goes like a bomb again.'

'I'll ask around,' Alex said politely. 'Give me a couple of days and I'll let you know. What's the figure?'

'Same as we paid,' Lenny said promptly, and named the price.

Alex grinned. 'I think most of the blokes could manage that,' he said. 'I'll be in touch. Don't go letting anyone else buy it. I'm sure the watch office alone will probably take all the shares.' He gave Molly's hand a squeeze. 'Goodnight, sweetie. See you in the morning.'

Molly and Ellen made their way to their billet almost too tired to discuss their evening, but by the time they had washed and changed into pyjamas they were beginning to come to life again. Ellen went to the window to draw back the blackout curtains and let in some fresh air. She stood for a moment gazing down at the moonlit scene before her, and suddenly she put her finger to her lips, breathing 'Shush' as she did so.

Molly, who had already got into bed, said nothing, and after a moment's silence she heard what Ellen meant. Below them the door opened and closed very softly, and then someone trod almost silently up the stairs and went quietly into the other bedroom. Molly stared at her friend.

'Is that Maggie coming back after the dance?' she asked, keeping her voice low. 'But I saw her leaving the Mess ages ago, with one of the chaps. What on earth did they find to talk about until now?'

Ellen cast her eyes at the ceiling. 'Oh, Molly, don't be such a twerp. Whatever they were doing I don't believe it involved very much talking. Our lovely Maggie is getting quite a reputation, and if you ask me it's deserved.'

Molly's forehead wrinkled. 'What sort of reputation?' she asked, thoroughly bewildered. 'She's never mentioned a boyfriend.'

Ellen, climbing at last into her own bed, chuckled. 'I think our Maggie enjoys playing the field, or so Hetty has led me to believe,' she said. 'Honestly, Molly, where have you been? Maggie will go out with anyone who promises to give her a good time. Does that tell you nothing?'

Molly sighed deeply and snuggled her head into the pillow. 'Is she what they used to call a "good-time girl"?' she asked sleepily. 'What's the harm in that? I suppose she's searching for the right man, which if we're honest is what we're all doing. Now I'm going to sleep, so you can jolly well shut up. You may be used to late nights, but I'm not. See you in the morning.'

*

It was a glorious day, and when Alex called for her Molly knew she was looking her best. Inside, however, sadness lurked, waiting to pounce. The story of the faithless Sally had strengthened her resolve to try to find a mate who would understand her history. In fact, before the knock came on the door she had been sitting hunched up in one of the creaky old chairs, and had even shed a few tears. What is to become of me? she asked herself. I know it's silly to feel that I could only marry someone with a similar background to my own, but that's how it is.

It was at this point that Alex arrived and when she opened the door he was beaming from ear to ear.

'Hurry up, girl. The gharry's waiting, and I've planned a really good day for us.'

Molly blew her nose, shoved the handkerchief into her gas mask case and smiled at him. 'Did you get a packed lunch from the canteen? I'm afraid I forgot.'

Alex held the door open for her, shaking his head. 'What sort of fellow do you think I am?' he said plaintively. 'When I take my favourite RT operator on a river trip I arrange to feed her somewhere nice, and not with cookhouse sandwiches.'

When the gharry had dumped them quite near the Brayford Pool, Molly walked over to examine the boats and presently found herself ensconced in the bows of a new-looking rowing boat with Alex handling the sculls as though he were born to it.

'Let me know when you want to take over,' he said as they skimmed across the surface of the quiet river. 'You did say you wanted to learn to row, didn't you?'

Molly hesitated. It was so pleasant sitting here with the hot sun burning down on her that the thought of exchanging places with Alex held little attraction. But on the other hand, Alex was looking at her with bright, questioning eyes, and rowing was an accomplishment not many girls possessed. 'Yes please,' she said firmly. 'But I'll watch you for a bit longer first.'

'Great,' Alex said. 'We'll leave your lesson until after lunch.' He looked over the side and pointed downward, momentarily ceasing to row. 'See the fish? I think they're trout, and there are lots of other things to see once we get a bit further on our voyage.'

Molly began to enjoy herself, and by the time they returned to Brayford Pool after her rowing lesson, which had involved much splashing and the turning of several complete circles, she was laughing and chattering, appreciating Alex's warm friendship, and the fact that he had taken so much trouble to give her a wonderful day out.

Going home in the gharry, squeezed up between the other passengers, Alex took her hand and began to play with her fingers. He was looking down.

'You did enjoy today, didn't you?' he enquired softly. 'If this glorious weather holds for a week or two we could go out again – perhaps catch a train and visit my old home. You'll like it, I'm sure.'

Molly felt a pang of guilt. Alex was her best pal, better even than Ellen or Maggie, but she was not yet ready to move their relationship beyond its present friendly footing. She turned to look up into his face.

'You've given me a fantastic day, Alex,' she said gently. 'You are easily my favourite colleague and best friend. Let's keep it that way for now, shall we?'

Alex shrugged, then gave her hand a squeeze. 'All right, honeybunch. You're the boss.'

Alex breezed into his billet and found Fred sitting at the table writing busily. He looked up as Alex entered the room.

'Have a good day?' he asked. 'It's been pretty quiet in the watch office, so you weren't missed. Spoke to my first Liberator – they're quite some kites, aren't they? Or should I say ships, since they're Yankee planes?'

Alex responded suitably, but his mind was on Molly. He had found an old glass jar in the bottom of the boat, presumably used if one needed to bale out, so they had drawn into the bank and he had dipped the jar into the water, and when he lifted it out again it was full of things which had enchanted his companion. Tiny fish, a tadpole which had half turned into a frog, the larva of a caddis fly, a water boatman, were commonplace to Alex, but extraordinarily novel to Molly. He smiled reminiscently, and found that Fred was looking at him, eyebrows raised.

'Make any headway? It's easy to see you're more than fond of the girl. Have you tried saying so?'

'It was a wonderful day, but not a particularly romantic one,' Alex said regretfully. 'Someone with a shoulder to lean on is what she wants at the moment, and that is going to be me. After that . . . who knows?'

Molly, Ellen, Maggie and Hetty were in the watch office when the Wing officer poked her head around the door and waved a sheaf of papers in their direction.

'I got the results this morning and came as soon as I could,' she said cheerfully. 'All four of you passed your final exams and can now remove the u/t badge from your uniforms. Congratulations, girls. I'm thrilled for all of you.'

Alex, at the microphone, recorded his conversation in the log book and then came over and gave Molly a congratulatory kiss.

'Clever girl,' he said approvingly. 'I knew you'd do it, because with a teacher like me you couldn't possibly fail.' He turned to Ellen. 'Wait till Fred hears . . . and the other fellows, of course.'

Maggie beamed. 'What shall we do to celebrate?' she asked. 'Let's go into Lincoln and have a slap-up meal. Goodness, we've been working towards this moment for a long while, so it's about time the RAF showed their appreciation. Who's game to take the old jalopy into town? We could see a flick and then go to Mrs Doyle's for fish and chips.'

'I'm on shift,' Alex said regretfully. 'Can't get away until after midnight, and I don't imagine Mrs Doyle would welcome a customer at that hour. What's more, I think the sarge has already taken Bunny to Sleaford. It's his kid's tenth birthday – double figures – and they're having a bit of a party to celebrate.'

Presently the four girls left the watch office, having made up their minds that they would catch the gharry into Lincoln. 'It's annoying that we'll have to pay for our own cinema tickets and supper,' Maggie said ruminatively as they entered their billet. 'But you can't expect the fellers to be as thrilled as we are over passing our exams, and anyway you know what the blokes are like; they'll want to see a thriller or a cowboy film, whereas I for one would rather see a comedy, or a romance. I think *The Butler's Dilemma* is showing at the Central. What d'you say to that for a girls' night out?'

'Fine by me,' Ellen said at once. 'It'll be nice to concentrate on the film and not have to be polite to whoever bought you a ticket.' She turned to Molly. 'What d'you say, Molly? We'll have a gay old time, the four of us.'

Ellen offered to make tea whilst the other three had a quick wash and brush up, and then the four of them made their way out to where the gharry waited. Quite often the gharries were driven by Waafs but on this occasion the driver was a burly sergeant in his fifties, and he greeted them with great good humour.

'What are you celebratin'?' he said as he helped them board by the tail of the lorry. 'And where's your fellers? Don't say this is a hen party!'

'Yes it is,' Molly assured him, sliding along the tin seat to give the other girls room, for the space was already half full. She indicated her shoulder. 'See that, sarge? We heard today that we've passed our finals, and we thought a celebration was called for. A hen party, just as you said.'

As soon as the gharry reached Lincoln the girls set off for the cinema but here Molly was in for a disappointment. One look at the posters outside the cinema told them that they had been misinformed. The film showing was not *The Butler's Dilemma*, but a romance which Molly had already seen. She gave a moan of disappointment; she and Alex had visited the cinema only a week previously, and she had no wish to see the film for a second time.

'But you said you enjoyed it,' Ellen pointed out when she explained. 'Oh, be a sport, Molly; it'll be just as good the second time round, I'm sure.'

'That's as may be,' Molly said, 'but once is enough, thanks very much. Tell you what, I'll walk down to the High Street and see what's showing there. And then we'll all meet up at Mrs Doyle's at, say, nine o'clock. All right by everyone? See you later, then.'

She did not wait to see her friends disappear into the foyer but set off at once. When she reached the Odeon she glanced briefly at the posters and decided she would rather keep her money than waste it on a cowboy film, but it was a fine evening and it had been some while since she had visited the city. I'll walk up to the cathedral and have a nice quiet wander around it, she told herself. Last time we came Ellen chattered like a magpie and I missed half the interesting parts, though I did catch a glimpse of the Lincoln Imp. This time I'll have a good look at everything.

She was admiring the magnificent building rather than looking where she was going when she bumped into a tall figure in air force uniform. She began to apologise, then bit the words off short and stood staring up at him for an incredulous moment.

'Cian!' and 'It's you!' came simultaneously from two throats, and Molly's heart began to beat overtime. She looked up into that well-remembered face, the blue eyes looking down into her own, and had to remind herself that she had run away from O'Hare farm without so much as a word of explanation.

'Cian? My God, I never expected to see you again. And you're in uniform! What went wrong? And don't you think I'm fooled any more by your so obvious charm, because it won't wash. You hung on to me because you wanted someone to take care of your mammy.' She grinned mischievously. 'But I got away, didn't I? And you can scarcely kidnap a member of the Women's Auxiliary Air Force!'

Cian had begun to reply when another couple came round the corner of the cathedral, and he seized Molly's arm to lead her away from the building.

'We can't talk here,' he said. 'There's a bench further along, set back against the bushes; we can be private there.'

They found the bench and settled themselves, though Molly had the impression that Cian would have preferred to avoid a conversation. She said as much, and he nodded, shamefaced.

'When you upped and left us, sure and wasn't me heart near broke, darlin' girl? Dec and meself searched all over, but when you disappear you make a good job of it!' He sighed dramatically. 'The only girl who ever mattered to me was gone. I tell you, Molly, I were desperate to find you, but after weeks of searchin' I gave up.'

'And joined the Royal Air Force, I suppose, hoping that by some miracle I'd appear,' Molly said sarcastically. 'Cian, when we met just now you couldn't even remember my name!' She waited for Cian's cheeks to redden but he was far too experienced in the art of deception to let anything show. Instead he looked outraged at the very suggestion.

'And how could I do that, Molly Hardwick? To be sure, I was knocked sideways and mebbe it took me a moment or two, but you can't blame me for that. As for joining the air force, that was no idea of mine, nor of Dec's. When our call-up papers arrived he took himself off to wild country and kept well out of sight, but I went to the recruitin' office to explain I was only a few months old when we left England and was now a citizen of Eire, but they just laughed at me. I was posted to a training camp for the Royal Air Force and soon found it suited me pretty well.'

'What happened to Declan?' Molly enquired. 'Did he manage to avoid conscription altogether?'

'No, they got him in the end.' Cian chuckled. 'First go off they conscripted him into the army, to the pioneer corps. They do all the dirty work – dig latrines, get rid of rubbish, that sort of thing. Now he's on ack-ack batteries somewhere in the south of England, and still up to his old tricks, I gather. Last time I met him he gave me four packets of Woodbines and some Five Boy chocolate bars, which leads me to believe he's still playing the same old game, if on a smaller scale. But he managed to elude the military police for getting on for two years, so I dare say he's settlin' in quite nicely as a black marketeer.'

'Are you involved in the black market as well?' Molly asked suspiciously. 'If so . . .'

Cian looked outraged. 'No, I am not,' he said, with emphasis. 'I've tried to explain to Dec that he's helping the enemy, but he's not one to listen to a younger brother. No, I want to defeat the Nazis, particularly the Luftwaffe. I'm tail gunner in a Lancaster, you see.' He gripped Molly's hand and stared earnestly into her face. 'I swear to God, Molly, I'm in this war to win it. I don't deny I ate the chocolate and smoked the fags, but I told Dec

I didn't want to get involved in his so-called business dealings, and I've not seen him since.'

'Good,' Molly said in heartfelt tones, though even her mouth had watered at the thought of chocolate. 'So you are air crew, Cian! A pal of mine once told me that tail-end Charlie was the most dangerous position a gunner could have, though he never explained why.' She was looking at her companion's face as she spoke and saw, for the first time, the deeply etched lines which ran from his nose to the corners of his mouth. For all his bravado, Cian did not have to be told that his job was a dangerous one, but it was clear to her that he would stick to it. Hastily, she changed the subject, sorry that she had been so tactless.

'How's Mrs Mathias?' she asked instead. 'I was truly sorry to leave her in the lurch, but I wasn't prepared to stay in Eire simply because she didn't like change. No doubt Esme has taken my place to some extent, or have you got yourself another prisoner?'

Cian laughed. 'Some prisoner!' he said mockingly. 'You had the run of the O'Hare place, as much food as you could eat with no thought of rationing, and the company of meself and me lovely brother.'

Molly snorted. 'You must have forgotten that your "lovely brother" wanted to have me put away quietly because he thought I knew too much.

Indeed, if he'd found me when I ran away I've no doubt I'd have been in real trouble.'

Cian looked shocked. 'D'you think I'm the sort of feller to let harm come to me favourite colleen?' he asked, his very tone a caress. 'And as for cousin Esme, I rather fear she was all talk. She never managed to milk a cow or clip a sheep, let alone make any decent grub . . .'

Molly nodded. 'I could have told you that virtually from the moment she arrived,' she informed him. 'It wasn't just that she didn't know how; she was too lazy to learn.'

Cian nodded. 'The mammy's got a lass from the village livin' with her now; Biddy's her name, and she's one of a big family, so the O'Hare place seems like heaven to her. The mammy's in her element, having someone to boss about, and she's taught Biddy all kinds of housewifely tricks so now she can hold her own at all sorts.'

'And Sinbad?' Molly asked rather apprehensively. It had always worried her that the dog might be punished for not attacking her rescuers on the night of her escape, but apparently this had not been so.

Cian laughed. 'He's our mascot; I should say, the squadron's mascot,' he said. 'He has a kennel outside my billet with a good strong chain so he can't wander, but we seldom use the chain and he's always with either myself or another member of the crew. Satisfied?'

'Well, yes,' Molly admitted. 'I was always afraid he'd get into trouble for not preventing me from getting away, because I'd already begun to suspect he was a real softy. When I used to think he was baring his teeth before attacking he was actually smiling, wasn't he, or doing what dogs do when they greet you?' She glanced at her wristwatch. 'Goodness, look at the time! I'm meeting three of my pals at Mrs Doyle's; want to come along?'

Even as the words passed her lips she regretted them. To walk into the fish and chip café with the best-looking man any of them was likely to meet would be asking for the sort of questions she did not want to have to answer. Passing him off as someone she had known for years might work very well for Maggie and Hetty but it would not do for Ellen. As soon as Ellen heard his Irish brogue – and his name – she would realise she was in the presence of the man who had imprisoned her friend in his Irish home, and whether she would be able to stop herself from exclaiming was a moot point. But Cian was pulling a doubtful face.

'I dunno; are they fellers or girls? I don't want to horn in on your evening out . . .'

'They're girls. We were celebrating the fact that we've all passed our exams and are now fully fledged RT operators.' She tapped her brevet shoulder flash significantly. 'It used to be u/t but now it's just RT, so Ellen, Hetty, Maggie and I are having a bit of a celebration. And that reminds me, where are you based? I'm at Credington, and you can't be far away, so how come I've never set eyes on you until today?'

Cian smiled. 'And I'm not easy to miss,' he said truthfully. 'And I'm at Credington too, since yesterday – I've been in Scrimpton for the past few months. It looks as though we'll be seeing a lot of each other in future, so if you don't mind I'll give the fish and chips a miss.' He got leisurely to his feet and then held out his hands to help her to rise. 'I want to see this Lincoln Imp of yours; have you got time to show me?'

Molly was still reeling from the knowledge that Cian was now based at Credington – indeed, that it had been him she had seen at the dance in the Sergeants' Mess – and said quickly, 'I don't think I have – I'm awfully sorry. But we're bound to bump into each other in the cookhouse or the NAAFI, so we'll have plenty of opportunities to talk.'

'Right you are,' Cian said easily. 'See you around.' He turned away, heading back towards the cathedral where he would presumably search for the Lincoln Imp, and after taking a moment to collect her scattered wits, Molly set off down the path which would lead her to Silver Street.

She reached the café just as the girls had finished ordering their meal and were taking their places at a table towards the back of the room. They greeted her enthusiastically, told her they had thoroughly enjoyed the film, and asked how she had got on.

Molly smiled. 'There was a Western on at the Odeon, which I didn't fancy seeing, so I went up to the cathedral instead and guess what? I met an old pal, someone I've not seen for years, and we spent the best part of two hours catching up on each other's news.' She smiled as the fat and friendly proprietor approached their table. 'Can I have the same as the girls please, Mrs D? And if you've any ginger beer I'll have a glass of that instead of tea, because it's a warm night.'

As they waited for the food to arrive, Maggie looked curiously at Molly.

'Who was this friend?' she asked. 'You didn't say whether it was a man or a woman, but I'd put money on its being a man, because you're all lit up and excited. Didn't you ask him to join us for supper?' She laughed. 'Provided he paid for his own food he would have been welcome.'

Molly shook her head. 'No, I expect he'd already eaten. I did tell him we were eating here and suggested he might come along, but he didn't take up my invitation. Gosh, look at those chips. Even the sight of them sets my taste buds dancing.'

The girls ate their supper and then had to run down the hill to where the gharry stood, though the driver assured them he would have waited.

'Can't have lovely ladies like yourselves walking all the way out to Credington from here,' he said jovially. 'In you hop, ladies! How was the fillum?'

'Excellent,' Maggie said, and Molly was just wondering how Cian had got from Credington to Lincoln when she saw a second gharry pulling out. Silently, she sighed with relief. It might be putting off the evil hour, but she had no wish to introduce Cian to her friends in a gharry full of their fellow airmen and women. For one thing, she decided, as the heavy vehicle rumbled along the quiet country lanes, she would have to take Ellen into her confidence first. Before she told anyone else she must explain to Ellen who her old friend was.

In their billet once more no one was much inclined for conversation, for it had been a long and tiring day, but once Molly and Ellen were alone in their room, with the blackout blinds up and the window open to let in the evening breeze, Molly spoke.

'You know I said I'd met an old friend, Ellen, someone the rest of you didn't know? Well, that wasn't quite true. You've heard me talk about him, and you'll remember the name, because it's such an unusual one . . . it was Cian.'

Ellen had been brushing out her hair and plaiting it into its night-time braid, but now she turned wide, astonished eyes on her friend.

'Oh my God, not *the* Cian? The one who kept you prisoner in Ireland? Oh, Molly, don't say he's come after you? If so, you must tell Wingco at once, and have him arrested.'

Ellen listened to Molly's tale with widening eyes, and as soon as her friend had finished her story she gave her usual forthright opinion.

'If he's a tail-end Charlie then he's on the side of the angels,' she said decidedly. 'If you come across him when I'm with you, you must introduce us. Didn't you say he was the best-lookin' feller you'd ever met? Better keep him out of Maggie's clutches; she eats handsome men alive.'

'Oh, Maggie's not so bad,' Molly said tolerantly. 'It's not her fault that she attracts men who think the payment for a cinema show is more than a "thank you". I know you think she goes too far, but that's only guesswork, isn't it? And look, Ellen, I really don't want all that stuff about Ireland to become common knowledge. And though Cian may have wanted to prevent my escaping, I'm sure he was only worried about my safety, so his part in the affair must never be mentioned. *Comprenez?*'

'I suppose you're right,' Ellen said, having given the matter some thought. 'But what about his brother? I remember you said that he really disliked you and wanted to kill you, but if that's so, why didn't Cian help you to escape himself?

Perhaps Declan never really wanted to hurt you, but was just worried in case you went to the police.'

Molly climbed into bed, kicked off the blanket, and scowled thoughtfully.

'Do you know, that never occurred to me,' she said slowly. 'Sometimes I've wondered how I managed to get away with so little fuss, and only old Bumble and his mate to help me. I suppose that could be the answer: Declan just wanted to be rid of me, and when I ran away he was pleased that he finally was! But anyway, when I introduce you to Cian, which I'm bound to have to do sooner or later, you'll know enough to act naturally.'

The opportunity came sooner perhaps than Molly had expected. The four girls had decided to go to a dance being held at Framingham Station, but thanks to the shift system Hetty and Maggie got there well before their friends. When Molly and Ellen arrived the first thing Molly saw, as she drew the blackout curtain across the entrance behind them, was Cian, dancing very smoochily with . . . gracious! With Maggie!

Ellen, following her gaze, needed only a second before she looked round and grinned at her friend. 'I've never met your Cian, but I'd put money on the fact that he's the fellow our Maggie's cuddlin' up to,' she said. 'I remember you saying you'd never set eyes on anyone so beautiful, and maybe it's my over-vivid imagination but I can't believe there's anyone better-looking than Maggie's partner. Gosh, Molly, no wonder you let him talk you into believing he was an honest citizen. I can tell you one thing though; neither you nor myself stands a cat's chance in hell of getting his attention, not now pussycat Maggie has got her claws into him.'

Molly smiled. 'She's welcome to him,' she said. 'Looks aren't everything. Yes, Cian is pretty gorgeous, but compared to someone like Lenny, for instance, he's downright dull. There's no dangerous magic about Cian.'

As she spoke the music came to an end and there was a rush for the little tables and the fruit squash and ginger snaps which were all the refreshments on offer.

Molly and Ellen grabbed four chairs and presently Maggie and Cian joined them. The dance had been a quickstep and both were pink-cheeked, though only Maggie was starry-eyed. She sank into one of the chairs, and, when Cian offered to fetch everyone drinks, only waited until he was out of hearing before exclaiming: 'Phew! I gather you know him already, Molly? Well don't think you can walk away with him, because from now on he's mine.'

Ellen giggled. 'If you knew what we knew, you wouldn't be so keen,' she said provocatively. 'What do *you* know about him, Maggie?'

'He's a tail-end Charlie in a Lancaster bomber; his name's Cian, and all his crew seem to get on well with him. Isn't that enough?' Maggie said, sounding a trifle defensive.

Ellen giggled again. 'He might have three wives and six kids for all you know,' she said.

Maggie shook her head. 'I don't believe he has kids . . . he doesn't have that worried look.' She turned to Molly. 'He said he was an old friend from way back; *is* he married? If so I s'pose I have to behave myself; it wouldn't do to become a marriage breaker.'

Molly thought of the old O'Hare place; the cows she had milked and the sheep she had helped to shear, the hens whose eggs she had collected, and smiled. Never, in all the time she had known Cian, had she thought he was the marrying kind. He had his own interests, and she thought that by and large, they did not include women. Oh, there was nothing feminine about him, but at this stage in his life he was more interested in building up his business and keeping the mammy safe.

When she did not answer at once, Maggie leaned across and poked her in the ribs. 'You didn't answer me; I asked you if he was married.'

Molly brought her mind back to the present. 'Not so far as I know,' she said cautiously. 'In civilian life he's a farmer and looks after his old mother,

344

who is running his farm whilst he fights the war. Does that satisfy you?'

'Yes, for the moment . . .' Maggie was beginning when Cian returned to the table carrying a tray with several glasses of lemon and orange squash upon it. He set it down tenderly on the small table and gestured to the drinks with a lordly hand.

'Help yourselves, ladies,' he said. 'Sorry it's not champagne, but as you may have heard people mention, there is a war on!'

Chapter Twelve

September 1944

Lenny was writing, but because of the extreme secrecy both of the work he was doing and of where he was, letters were pretty stiff affairs. Now, sitting before a small card table, and trying to think of something he could tell Molly which would not immediately be snipped out by the censor, he let his mind roam over the past few months.

Operation Overlord had been a success, though his own part in it had been fairly small. With thousands of troops crossing the Channel and landing on the Normandy beaches, all Lenny's squadron had been able to do had been to provide as much cover air as possible. The British and Americans had thrown everything into the fight and attempts had been made, Lenny knew, to destroy the factories which made the doodlebugs – the flying bombs – and the V2 rockets which were making Londoners' lives a misery, but even so, as the troops neared Paris, the fighting had grown fiercer and there must have been times, Lenny reflected, when the outcome had been in doubt. But all that was over, or near as dammit. All they had to do now was liberate every country still suffering under Nazi rule and search out the perpetrators who had started this war, so that they could be brought to book. But it won't really be over until the war in the Far East is won and the Japanese have surrendered, Lenny mused. But of course he could not say so in his letter, so he turned his thoughts back to this small airfield in the wilds of Scotland.

He had been pleased and surprised when, a few days after his arrival, he had looked at the queue waiting in the cookhouse and recognised his old friend from Haisborough Orphanage.

'Bumble!' he had exclaimed. 'What the devil are you doing here?'

Bumble grinned and made room for him in the queue, handing him a tin plate as he did so. 'Servicing aeroplanes, of course,' he said. 'The powers that be decided in their wisdom that I had had experience on so many different engines that I might be useful on this particular station. The work's grand, varied and interesting . . .' he eyed Lenny closely, 'and from what I recall your experience must be pretty wide too. You've flown heavy bombers, Spitfires and Hurricanes. I recall you even had a spell on Swordfish.'

Lenny nodded. 'There aren't many planes I've not flown over the past few years,' he admitted. 'And if I had to choose someone I could trust to look after the engines of the kites I fly, it'd be you. I seem to remember you getting some sort of award for something – am I right?'

He saw a faint flush mantle his friend's cheeks and grinned. Bumble had always been modest and clearly he had not changed, for, as Lenny recalled it, his friend had gone into a blazing plane to rescue an injured crew member. Lenny could not remember the exact details, but he knew the man had told everyone Bumble had saved his life.

'When did you arrive?' he asked, just as they reached the head of the queue. 'You can't have been here long or we'd have met before. The station's only small, and everyone knows everyone else.'

'Came in this evening,' Bumble said. He looked hopefully at his plate, then grimaced. 'Oh, God, it's stew; I might have guessed. The RAF might just as well be Haisborough Orphanage so far as food goes.'

'You're wrong there,' Lenny said, holding out his own plate. 'So far as I remember, the stew at the home was just vegetables, and not a lot of them. This stew always has rabbit or pigeon or some other sort of meat. It's pretty good, too. They use potatoes grown by the crofters and all sorts of root vegetables, so don't you complain until you've tried it.'

Bumble grinned. 'One of the chaps in my hut told me the jam roly is good,' he said. 'Apparently there's some old woman who goes out and picks the berries that grow on the mountain – they're called whinberries, I think – and turns 'em into jam, which Cooky uses in the pud. And then there's heather honey . . . you eat better here than in any of the stations down south, or so I've been told.'

That had been weeks ago, and right now – Lenny glanced at his wristwatch – it would be another hour before he could go to the cookhouse and enjoy whatever the kitchen staff had prepared.

Lenny heaved a sigh and picked up his pen. *The food here is awfully good*, he wrote. *We think it's because of the cold, which means we need to have our stomachs lined before going off to do our day's work.*

At this moment the door of the hut opened and Bumble staggered in, lugging a bucket full of what looked like large squares of crumbly gingerbread. He grinned at Lenny, dumped the bucket beside the tortoise stove and opened the lid. Lenny, who had been sitting as near the stove as possible without actually burning himself, made a disgruntled noise and pulled the table and chair further back.

'Peat!' he said disgustedly. 'That stuff gives out more smoke than heat, and the smell gets into everything.'

Bumble stood with a brick of peat in one hand, poised above the stove. 'You can choose to freeze if you don't like the smell of the peat,' he said cheerfully. 'Or you can put up with being pickled and warm. Which is it going to be?' He looked at the sheet of paper in front of his friend and tutted. 'When I went out of here half an hour ago you'd written three lines. You've now written five. Why on earth do you write to the girl if you can't find anything to say?'

Lenny pulled a face. 'Her letters are full of chatter,' he said resentfully. 'It makes me feel – oh, inadequate I suppose – when I can't think of anything to say.'

'I always manage to think of something,' Bumble said complacently, dropping the peat brick into the stove and replacing the lid. 'There's always the views, and beachcombing, and what the other chaps say about their lives at home. No, don't sneer, it's just because you find writing letters a chore. What you have to do is imagine yourself sitting on a soft sofa pulled up to a roaring fire. Molly is sitting beside you, of course, and you are holding her hand and telling her about your day, and before you know it your letter will be written.'

'And the censor will cut it all out; the interesting bits I mean,' Lenny said at once. 'Oh do shut up,

Bumble, and go away. Unless you'd like to write the letter for me, of course.' He bent over the page, then looked up suddenly. 'Mark Humble, do you write to Molly? If so, the poor girl will get any news we've got twice over. *Do* you? Write to Molly?'

He saw a faint flush darken his friend's cheeks. 'And why shouldn't I?' Bumble said defiantly. 'I write to several people, and Molly's one of them. And she writes back. I love her letters, too. Sometimes they're so funny I'm still chuckling over them half an hour after I've finished reading. I told her I was going to save them and turn them into a book.' He laughed. 'I'm sure it would sell like hot cakes.'

Lenny pricked up his ears. 'I wonder why she writes to you as well as to me? I mean, she hardly knew you at the home, though I suppose after you'd galloped up on your white charger and got her back from Ireland she might have felt obliged to thank you for your interference.'

Bumble stared at his friend. 'Can it be that you're jealous?' he asked wonderingly. 'Not that you've anything to be jealous about. Friends can exchange letters as well as lovers – and which category do you fall into, Lenny Smith?'

For a moment the question struck Lenny dumb. Since his affair with Sally he had not really considered looking for another girlfriend; in the back of his mind he supposed he had always assumed that

351

if he wanted to he could always go out with Molly. True, she was not a blonde, not his type, but at least he would not have to start the business of courtship with a girl who already worshipped the ground he trod on. Now Bumble's words had jolted him out of his complacency, and he felt a stab of shame when he realised he had actually told himself that if his feelings for Molly were not sufficiently strong, he could simply move on, find someone more congenial and let Molly take care of herself.

Bumble was still staring at him. Hastily, Lenny cleared his throat.

'Sorry, old fellow; I'm afraid I wasn't really attending. I was trying to remember just what Molly looks like. What did you say again?'

'I asked you if you were jealous,' Bumble said slowly. 'But I take that back. You aren't jealous of me, because you think I'm not in the running so far as girls are concerned. Well, you're wrong. There's a little Wren down in Portsmouth who's pretty as a picture, and she likes me too, so who knows what will happen in the future? I know you think Molly's in love with you, and I know she was, a few years back, but she's grown up a lot since then. By the time the war's over she'll be a completely different person from the one we used to know.'

'Oh, rubbish,' Lenny said easily. 'Molly doesn't change any more than I do. And now clear out of here and let me get on with my letter.'

'Oh? So you mean to add another two lines, do you?' Bumble said sarcastically. 'Right, I'll leave you to it. And don't appeal to me if you run out of news.' He struck his forehead with one hand. 'Damn you, Smith! I nearly forget – I meant to tell you there's a gharry going into town, and a good film showing at the cinema. Want to come?'

Lenny hesitated. He felt annoyed with Bumble, and for a moment considered saying he was busy trying to write his letter and could not spare the time to go gadding. Then he looked up and saw from Bumble's expression that his friend had read his mind and was probably ready with another sarcastic remark if he turned the invitation down. Also, there were girls in the town, one or two of whom were both pretty and provocative. Most of them were happy to go out with a member of the RAF provided it was in a foursome. He and Bumble together might pick up a couple and have a pleasant evening, either at the cinema or at one of the local dance halls. If he backed out, told Bumble to find someone else, he would be losing an opportunity to widen his circle of friends. One of the usherettes in particular was a very fetching little blonde. Lenny smiled to himself. Nothing much could be done whilst the girl was at work, but he could offer to walk her home when the film was over. Bumble could escort her friend, and they could make a proper date for later in the week.

But Bumble had turned to leave, saying over his shoulder 'Staying to sulk in your tent? If so . . .' and Lenny hastily pushed his letter aside and got to his feet.

'Oh aye, I'll come,' he said casually. 'There's this little blonde usherette . . .'

*

Molly did not wake immediately when the alarm went off, but eventually the bell penetrated her dreams and she reached out a sleepy hand to slap the button. The ringing stopped and after another minute. Molly sat up groggily and looked around the darkened room, blowing out her breath in a silent whistle. I have to admire Ellen's ability to sleep through almost anything, she thought; I take it she *is* in her bed? She leaned across to give Ellen a poke, then stopped short, slapping her forehead. Ellen and Hetty had asked for leave together so that they might visit Hetty's parents, for of all the strange coincidences Ellen had met Hetty's brother Peter and fallen heavily in love, and almost as though not to be outdone Hetty had formed a strong attachment for Peter's best friend Jim. The two girls had left the previous day, and would not be back for another twenty-four hours.

Molly went over to the window to pull the blackout blinds across – although everyone knew the war would soon be over showing a light

354

was still an offence – and stood looking out for a moment. An overnight gale had brought down a great many leaves, and she reflected that it would soon be Christmas, a thought which sent a tingle of excitement running up her spine. Lenny had promised that they would spend it together, and though their relationship was still that of friends rather than lovers Molly fancied she could see a more appreciative glow in his eyes every time they met, which was often, for Lenny had been recalled from Scotland and he and Bumble were now both at Scrimpton. Several times she had thought Lenny hovered on the brink of a declaration, but knowing how fragile their relationship still was she had not yet encouraged him to regard her as anything but an old friend.

Shivering, Molly pulled off her pyjamas, splashed cold water into the basin from the tall ewer and began, shrinkingly, to wash. She was just reaching for her towel when she heard Maggie's alarm go off in the bedroom next door. She grinned to herself. Dear Maggie! Several times, because of their shifts, Maggie and Ellen had swapped beds, and Molly had always marvelled at Maggie's ability to rouse from sleep, leap out of bed, wash and dress in five minutes flat, whereas she herself needed at least a quarter of an hour to prepare for the day ahead. As she dressed, she reflected that the lives of all three of her friends had changed in the past few months. Maggie was now desperately in love with Cian, and it was easy to see that her feelings were reciprocated. At one time Maggie had gone out with anyone who asked her and had rapidly been getting the reputation of a good-time girl, and also a bit of a jinx, since several of the men she honoured with her temporary affection were amongst those whose aircraft did not return.

But Maggie and Cian, it seemed to Molly, were ideally suited. They liked the same things, never argued over which film to see, sat together in the NAAFI or the cookhouse and shared a great many jokes. When their friendship had first blossomed Molly had agonised over the knowledge of Cian's past; should she tell or was it something best forgotten? But she knew in her heart that the war had brought enormous changes in almost everyone, and the only information she had let fall, and that reluctantly, was that Cian had a brother who was almost certainly engaged in the black market. Maggie had merely shrugged.

'Oh well, so long as Cian himself isn't,' she had said airily. 'And anyway, once the war is over there won't be any need for a black market.'

So now, hearing water splashing, and then Maggie bursting into song, Molly reached for her shoes and rapped on the wall between the two rooms.

'I bet you're already dressed and ready to go,' she shouted. 'I forgot Ellen and Hetty were on leave, so we'd better get a move on or Alex and Fred will think we're taking advantage.' She stifled a yawn. 'Maggie? Did you hear what I said?' There was a short pause, and just as she reached for her coat the door burst open and Maggie bounced into the room.

'Of course I heard you,' she said, and giggled. 'Don't tell a soul – well, there's nothing to tell really – but Cian spent the night in Hetty's bed! I promise you there was no funny business, but we talked until two or three in the morning and then it was too late and he was too tired to go back to his own billet.' She smiled wickedly at her friend. 'Going to tell on me? Cian went before six o'clock, so I don't suppose anybody in his billet noticed a thing.'

Molly stared at her friend, her eyes rounding in horror. 'Oh, Maggie, how could you? And in our own billet, too! If anyone saw you . . . well, it could cause the most awful scandal.' She hesitated, remembering comments she had heard in the past indicating that a good few people thought Maggie fast. But that had been a while ago and best forgotten. It was not as though she believed for one moment that Cian had misbehaved with Maggie, even though he might have been sorely tempted. So she smiled at her friend and patted her on the cheek. 'All right, I believe you, though thousands wouldn't. Only for my sake, Maggie, *please* don't do it again.'

Maggie laughed but shook her head. 'I suppose you're frightened that someone might think it was you sneaking Lenny into our billet.' She laughed again. 'Little Miss Purity herself, but who might I ask would muddle Cian and Lenny? Only a blind woman, since Cian is a good six inches taller than Lenny and a great deal handsomer.'

'Oh, don't be so daft,' Molly said impatiently. 'Yes, Lenny and I are good friends – *just* good friends – but how could I possibly sneak him into our billet even if I wanted to when he's not even on this airfield?'

The two girls clattered down the stairs and shot across the kitchen, then ran all the way to the control tower where they were greeted with relief by Alex and Fred, both anxious to get back to their billets so that they could catch up on their sleep. Molly collapsed into the chair still warm from Alex's recent occupation and waved a dismissive hand towards the door.

'I know you aren't officially off for another fifteen minutes, but away you go. I'd put money on the fact that you won't be missing much work,' she said.

Alex, about to let himself out of the door, looked at her over his shoulder. 'I'd like to have a good long talk with you before too long, my girl,' he said. 'And you jolly well know it. Every time I get you alone you make some excuse or other to keep things light, but one of these days you're going to have to face facts.' His serious expression gave way to a broad grin. 'And I'm one of those facts. Care to have grub with me in your split shift?'

Molly pulled a face. 'You're a grand chap, Alex, and easily my best friend – present company excepted, of course, Maggie – but while the war's still going on I don't see much point in serious discussions,' she said. 'Go off and have your brekker like a good little RT operator, and I'll see you later.'

Christmas passed with all the usual attempts at jollity, including a festive meal and the exchange of tiny gifts amongst close friends. Ellen's Pete gave her a ring and Jim promised Hetty she should have one too as soon as he could get his hands on something suitable. But as soon as the festivities were over, almost as though the weather knew it, it began to snow, and to snow in earnest, what was more. Clearing the runway became the most important task on the station and though everyone piled on every garment they could lay their hands on they were always cold. The Waafs were told that doing exercises would warm them up, but whilst the snow continued to fall exercising was the last thing on their minds. Parents wrote of horrendous conditions at home, and one farmhand, making his way across a sugar beet field near Ipswich, lay down in the snow and was found by a friend next morning, stiff and dead by the clamp he had been trying to open.

The girls had imagined that life in the watch office, with the war so obviously nearing its end, would become easier, but as though to prove that the RAF had its own agenda it actually became more difficult. Shifts were now a good deal longer than before, with routine training exercises continuing unabated, and the number of raids if anything increasing. When the manoeuvre to be practised was 'circuits and bumps' – coming in to land and then merely touching down before taking off again – the RT operators were constantly on their feet. Not only did they have to log the times of every take-off and landing, but they had to chalk the information up on the ops board each time the command post rang it through.

'With the result that we have one ear to the telephone and the other to the RT all night long,' Molly grumbled as she and Maggie made their way back to their billet after yet another sleepless night. 'Do you know, Maggie, I even dream about work, which I never did before. Even calm, cool-headed Alex says there must be some easier way of doing things, but no one seems to have discovered it yet.'

*

Hetty entered the billet and shook a reproving finger at her friend, who was sitting at the kitchen table, pen poised.

'You were due on shift five minutes ago,' she said. 'Alex is hanging on for you on Darky, but he can't be in two places at once and the bombers should begin coming back at any minute . . .'

Molly squeaked and thrust her writing materials into the sideboard drawer.

'Thanks, Hetty,' she said breathlessly, grabbing her cap and rushing outside, slamming the door behind her. She belted across the parade ground and burst into the RT watch office with an apologetic smile on her face, which faded when she saw Alex speaking into the Darky microphone and flapping a hand at her to ensure silence.

At the same moment one of the other microphones squawked and immediately all thoughts except that she should already have been at her post left her mind. She slid into the vacant seat, clapped the headset into place and gave the station's call sign. What rotten luck, she was thinking, that a Darky call should come just as the squadron was returning from yet another bombing raid on Germany. She glanced across at Alex and saw him nodding with satisfaction and giving her the thumbs-up sign.

'Port engine went but he came down all right, at Scrimpton, it sounded like,' he said, and the relief in his voice was obvious. He stood up, stretched and yawned, then smiled at Molly, jerking a thumb at the Darky mike. 'Going to take over? I'm jiggered. And if you're tired once the squadron's down and home, you can have a nice little zizz. Provided you regain consciousness immediately if there's a Darky call, and how often do we get one of them, let alone two in the same night?'

Maggie leaned back in the other seat and gave an enormous yawn.

'I counted them out and now I've counted them in,' she informed her friend, as Alex said goodnight and slipped out of the control room door. 'The only one not safely home was Alex's Darky, and we know he's all right, so hopefully we're in for a quiet shift.'

Molly was not attending. 'Damn,' she said remorsefully. 'I didn't apologise to Alex for keeping him late. The truth is I was writing a letter to Lenny and forgot the time, but Alex is a good bloke; I'm sure he'll forgive me.'

Maggie was agreeing that Alex was indeed a good bloke when the door opened again to admit Fred – and the noise of an aircraft engine, growing louder as the plane approached. Molly frowned. It sounded . . . wrong. Was this another Darky, lost out there in obscurity? Waiting for her to acknowledge him so that he might attempt to land? Hastily she gave her call sign and instead of being rewarded with a cheery request for clearance she heard nothing but heavy breathing and what sounded a little like a chuckle. She stared across at Fred.

'He's on the Darky frequency but he didn't answer my call sign, or give me his own,' she said uncertainly. 'And now that I'm listening properly I don't think I know the sound of that engine. Mind you, other foreigners have ended up here before now . . .'

'What strength is his call sign?' Maggie asked urgently. 'He's circling just above the runway. It should be strength niner, if he chose to give it . . . my God, someone's just turned the landing lights off! What . . .'

'Get down!' Fred shouted suddenly. 'If they've switched the landing lights off, it means they think ...'

With one accord everyone hit the deck. Which was as well, since tracer bullets ripped across the watch office a second later, accompanied by the fiendish shrieking of engines working at their full capacity.

'Oh, God, I wonder if he's shooting up the huts?' Molly said helplessly into Maggie's ear. 'Do you think there was time for Alex to get to a shelter before the raid started? If you can call one aircraft a raid ...' She faltered to a stop, aware that she was babbling.

'I don't care what you call it so long as its over soon,' Maggie muttered. 'I hope to God Cian is tucked away safely somewhere.'

Pulling herself together, Molly hissed, 'Say a prayer for me, Mags. I'm going to crawl over to the headsets and see if someone can tell us what's going on.'

She began to cross the office on hands and knees as she heard the aircraft's engine begin to fade and finally disappear, but before she reached the bench the door opened to reveal the white and startled faces of the girls from the met office on the floor below. Molly stood up cautiously and began to dust herself down, feeling rather foolish, as though she had been caught in some childish game.

'I think it was one of those dive bomber things – did you hear it?' she said. 'Just like a banshee – not that I've ever heard a banshee, of course . . .' She bit her lip; she was babbling again. Instead, she jerked a thumb at the bullet holes in the walls. 'My God, weren't we lucky? Another six inches lower and he'd have had all three of us. If Fred hadn't shouted at us to hit the deck . . . well, we wouldn't all be standing here for a start.'

The leading met girl nodded solemnly. 'It's the admin offices that took most of the attack, and the runway, of course,' she said. 'Did he follow one of our chaps in, d'you reckon? Or was he on his way to somewhere else and spotted the airfield?'

Glancing at Fred and Maggie, Molly said, 'We had a Lancaster in trouble – it's all right, Alex talked him down to Scrimpton – and this one was probably going to attack it when he intercepted the Darky call. He must have decided to follow the Lanc to its destination and shoot up all the kites which had already returned, but then he spotted our lights. If someone hadn't had the good sense to turn them off he might have done even more damage, because we certainly didn't have time to take evasive action of any description. We just had to sit here and take it until he either ran out of tracer or grew short on fuel. What do we do now?' As Molly stopped speaking the tannoy boomed out.

'All personnel, check for damage,' an authoritarian voice said crisply. 'Check huts, domestic offices, admin and so on. Someone go to the gharries and check them, then report to your places of work and return to your duties.'

Without another word Molly and Maggie set off at a run, both knowing exactly what – or rather who – they were looking for.

'If anything's happened to Alex I shall blame myself for the rest of my life,' Molly said as they crossed the parade ground. Maggie caught her sleeve.

'Don't be so daft! Just keep looking.'

'But if I'd not been late Alex would have been back in his hut . . .'

'Well so far as I can see his billet is in the clear ...'
Maggie was beginning when Molly stopped short
and pointed. Something was lying in a crumpled
heap on the snow only a few feet from the nearest
hut.

Molly's heart gave an enormous bound and sick
dread filled her mind. She became aware that she
was trembling all over and clutched Maggie's arm.
'Alex! He would have come this way.' She ran forward and fell to her knees beside the motionless
figure, aware suddenly that it lay in a pool which
might be water, but she feared was blood. Maggie
dropped to her knees beside her.

'Who is it?' she asked in a hoarse whisper.

'Oh, Maggie, don't let it be Alex. And it's
no use saying it isn't my fault . . . dear God, it
mustn't be Alex!' Feverishly, she fished a small
torch out of her pocket and shone it into the
man's face. For one awful moment she was just
so grateful that it was not Alex that she scarcely
took in the familiar features, but then she drew
in a gasping breath and reached out to take her
friend's trembling hand.

'Oh, Molly, it's Cian,' Maggie breathed. 'Is he . . .
is he . . .'

Molly looked down into Cian's beautiful face
through a blur of tears. Once she had fancied herself deeply in love with him, and even now, despite
his many faults, she could not forget how he had

taught her to love the country and how often he had said that he only wanted her to stay in Eire with the mammy so that she would be safe.

'He's not bleeding,' she said in a tiny whisper. 'They taught us in our first aid lessons that once the heart stops . . . and the tracer got him right across the throat . . . I think . . . I think . . . '

Maggie gave a muffled groan and clutched Cian's hands. 'He can't be dead. He can't be! We were going to get married as soon as the war ended. Oh, Molly, he can't be dead. But his hands . . . they're like ice . . .'

Molly looked down at Cian again and thought she had never seen him look so peaceful, and she knew that Maggie's hopes were of no avail. Gently, she took her friend's hands from Cian's, then put an arm around her shoulders.

'Perhaps he's not dead,' she said in a voice so low that it was almost a whisper. 'We'll call an ambulance and get him to hospital. And we'd better hurry. Where's Sinbad? He was never far from . . .' But even as she spoke they heard Sinbad's howl begin to rise towards the dark and sparkling sky.

*

Lenny was part of Operation Thunderclap, designed to destroy Germany's rail network. Dresden, being a transit centre for the eastern front, had to be a target if they were to hasten the end of the war. And

367

when Lenny saw what had once been a fine city reduced to rubble and flame he had to drag his mind away from the terrible slaughter and remind himself of what the Germans had done to London, with no more regard for the lives of the inhabitants than he must now feel for the victims of Dresden.

He guessed that by dealing Germany such a tremendous blow the authorities both hoped and expected that the Nazis would realise their position was hopeless and surrender to the Western allies, for an even more feared enemy was advancing perilously close to Berlin. Everyone knew that the Russians would show no mercy to the army that had besieged Leningrad, and surely the Germans must wish to surrender to a less despotic conqueror.

As their trusty Lancaster, Bouncing Bessie, delivered the last of her bombs, Lenny's navigator pressed his nose to the window and saw, in the light of the burning city, and of the flares which the Allies had dropped, that he was in amongst over a hundred B17 Flying Fortresses. He whistled beneath his breath.

'It's what you might call a belt and braces attack,' he said into his microphone. 'Dear God, I've never seen anything like it. There can't be a soul down there left alive.' He half turned in his seat to address the bomb aimer. 'All your eggs gone, Middy? Then let's get out of here.' He turned back to Lenny as the plane changed direction. 'No flak? If you ask me they already know they're beat . . .' He glanced again through the Perspex window. 'I'll never forget this night if I live to be a hundred. If we survive, that is.'

Everyone was in the watch office; counting the planes out and counting them back was possible as a rule, but not tonight. There were just too many; they blotted out the stars as they flew overhead, heading for every airfield in the county. Definite information was always hard to come by, but on this occasion the watch officers had been told days in advance of Operation Thunderclap, and judging by the number of kites in the sky they could see for themselves that this was no ordinary raid.

Lenny had promised Molly, rather half-heartedly, that as soon as he'd gone through debriefing he would give her a ring and let her know that he was safe. All leave had been cancelled, of course, but if she knew anything about human nature the telephone wires would be buzzing, everyone hoping that this time the death blow to Germany's hopes of world domination would finally have been delivered.

When at last the girls were dismissed to return to their billet they were secretly longing for their beds, and Molly decided not to wait for Lenny to ring her but to ring his Mess just to make sure that

Bouncing Bessie was still all in one piece. When the aircraftman who answered the telephone said she could speak to the pilot himself if she wanted she knew in her heart she should ring off, knowing that Lenny was on terra firma once more, but the temptation to hear his voice was too strong. And presently a tired voice in her ear confirmed that the raid had been a success, although the devastation had been so terrible that Lenny told her he had no wish to discuss it.

'I've never seen anything like it. And now I'm off to bed, and heaven help anyone who disturbs me before I've had my sleep out.'

Molly returned to her billet and climbed into her own bed. At first she tried to imagine how the citizens of Dresden must be feeling, but it was a pointless exercise. Heaven knew the British had suffered terribly, so she told herself she need have no pity for the citizens of Dresden, who had thought themselves safe and then discovered that that was not the case. No one can go through life handing it out without expecting something in return, she told herself drowsily, turning her head into the pillow. I wonder what exactly did happen? But it'll be in all the papers tomorrow, no doubt.

And on that thought she pulled the blankets up round her ears, for it was an extremely cold night, and fell rapidly asleep.

Chapter Thirteen

A soft March wind had cleared the snow, which had hung around far too long in Molly's opinion, and now they could believe in their hearts as well as their heads that spring was on its way at last. Molly approached their billet after a gruelling shift, wondering which of the boys had bagged the car, and pulled a rueful face to herself. She knew that spring would bring painful thoughts of Cian, for he had loved that season in the countryside and had taught her to love it too. She tried never to think back to that terrible night, remembering how all she had cared about had been that Alex was not involved. He was her best friend, always there, always reliable; even thinking about him gave her a warm glow. He was a much nicer man than Lenny would ever be, she acknowledged. He was good – too good for someone like herself, who had no family, no background. People like Alex didn't end up with someone like her. No, she and Lenny were far better suited to go through life together.

But Cian had been gone now for many weeks, and Molly thought it was time that Maggie began to come to terms with her loss. She had behaved very strangely since Cian's death, not mourning him quietly as Molly had expected but throwing herself into a mad whirl of gaiety. Soon she began to get a reputation, the men smiled secretly to one another when her name was mentioned, and Alex, always thoughtful for others, had told Molly that it was her duty as Maggie's friend to tell her to stop behaving like an idiot.

'Most of the girls on the station have lost a lover at some time during the war but they haven't been fool enough to try to replace him with four or five others at a time,' he had said a few days before. 'I'm not saying she goes all the way or takes on just anyone who asks her, but I am saying that she's getting a reputation for doing exactly that. You're one of her best friends and I often think you are very alike; surely you can make her see that she'll deeply regret what she's doing one of these days. Talk to her, Molly. I'd do it myself, but it would come better from a woman.'

They had been leaving the control office at the time, walking down the concrete steps and bypassing the radar unit, and Alex had caught Molly's arm and given it a squeeze.

'Tell her Cian wouldn't like the way she's acting,' he had urged. 'I know it's a rotten job, but you knew them both and might be able to make her see reason.'

Molly had sighed as they headed towards their billets.

'I only hope it doesn't lose me a friend,' she had said gloomily. 'Don't think I haven't tried hinting, because I have. But she always says she's got to do something when she's off duty or she starts remembering Cian and that hurts too much to contemplate.' She had glanced at her wristwatch. 'It's too late to do anything this afternoon, but maybe one day I'll get her to come into Lincoln with me. We might hire a rowing boat now that the bad weather seems to have gone elsewhere. They tell me Snowdonia and Scotland are still suffering, but they expect it at this time of year.'

So now Molly hung up her coat and cap and smiled across the firelit kitchen at her friend.

'Any plans for this afternoon?' she asked with all the nonchalance she could muster. 'It's a dream of a day for a country walk, or a ride in the old jalopy if you feel like going further afield.'

Maggie's forehead wrinkled. 'Don't you want to see a flick, or get in touch with Scrimpton and see if Lenny's free?' she asked, and Molly was distressed to hear the hope in her voice. To one who knew her well it was obvious that Maggie would have preferred either her own company or that of some male she had her eye on, but Molly pretended not to notice.

'I said it was a nice afternoon for a country walk,' she pointed out. 'I know I mentioned the car, but we can forget about that if it means we have to take some feller along. I'd like it to be just the two of us, because if we were to take Lenny we shouldn't see so much as a blackbird's nest or primrose buds or a hedgehog's hideaway, because he just isn't interested. He'd hustle us past and start talking about trying to down doodlebugs whilst they're over the sea, or bombing the factory where the V2 rockets are made. Men have quite different feelings about war from us, and on a day like today I want to forget the watch office, and everything to do with work. How about you?'

There was a long pause before Maggie spoke. 'We could catch a bus into the country,' she said dreamily. 'Do you know, I think a country walk would be fun, but not if you're going to use it to lecture me. Hetty nagged me the other night, because I fell asleep in the flicks and she said the chap I was with was fast and falling asleep in his company might lead to more than I bargained for.' She giggled. 'And wasn't she right! But the moment his hands started to stray I woke up – who wouldn't? – and punched him on the nose.

He took it very well, all things considered, but he won't try that again.'

She laughed, and Molly laughed with her, thinking hopefully that this encounter might make her own job of begging Maggie to be more careful easier.

'Right,' she said briskly. 'Someone was telling me that one or two of the farms will give you afternoon tea for a few bob. That would be nice, wouldn't it? A real break from war and the rest of it. In fact, if we talk about anything to do with the air force it should be about the victory celebration which Mr Churchill has promised us.' She beamed at her friend. 'And of course about being demobbed. They won't tell anyone about dates or anything yet, but I suppose that will come in due course. So are we agreed? We'll catch the 22a from the village green and buy ourselves afternoon tea at the first farmhouse we see!'

The light was beginning to fade by the time the girls caught the bus back to the airfield. Both had enjoyed the complete break from routine.

'That was a good idea of yours, Molly,' Maggie said as they entered their billet. 'I haven't enjoyed myself so much since my darling Cian left.' She turned a smiling face to Molly, who was removing her cap and coat and hanging them on the peg by the door. 'And though I was sure you were going to give me a talking-to, you managed to bite your tongue and keep the conversation casual.' She flung an arm around Molly's shoulders. 'I thought you were going to tell me to back off the boys and on no account to get in touch with that Declan person but once we got going I think you realised that even though you'd not said it, it had been very much on my mind.'

Molly returned the hug. 'If anyone suggests you've been doing anything you shouldn't I'll tell them that either Hetty or myself was with you all the time,' she said firmly. 'And it's true – except for that one occasion when Hetty was on leave and you let Cian spend the night you've really not had any opportunity for naughty carryings-on.'

Maggie chuckled. 'I remember one of the girls – one of the naughty ones, I should say – saying that her mother would not allow her to take a feller home after eight o'clock in the evening. We had a good laugh together, because if you're going to be a bad girl you can do it as well at two in the afternoon as at midnight. She's left now because she's in the club, so she obviously had a point.'

'Well, maybe she did, but don't go repeating that story to anybody but me, Hetty and Ellen,' Molly commanded. As for Maggie's carryings-on, as she called them, she knew that Alex had been right; they were common knowledge. No one had actually said out loud what a good few of the men were thinking, but that did not mean there were not rumours flying around. However, she felt she had done what she could to persuade Maggie not to give rise to any more gossip, and hoped that Alex would be pleased.

She turned her thoughts to her own affairs. She and Lenny were certainly closer than they had been, but nowhere near as close as, despite herself, she had once again allowed herself to hope they might become. Lenny was always polite, danced with her, invited her out, bought her meals and sat correctly at her side in the cinema holding her hand, but thanks to Bumble, Molly knew that she was not his only girlfriend. There was no getting away from the fact that Lenny liked blondes, and to be fair to him he never denied it; in fact, quite the opposite.

'We said we'd be friends, and that's exactly what we are,' he had told her. He grinned provocatively. 'If you're as fond of me as you say you are, why won't you put some sort of lightener on your hair? I know the fellers will call you a bottle blonde, but what does that matter? I like bottle blondes, and if I saw you with beautiful golden tresses I'd probably propose to you on the spot.'

He was only joking, but Molly did not think it at all funny. She had no intention of bleaching her thick, gleaming fawn-coloured hair, and knew in her heart that had she done so it would have made no difference to either Lenny's feelings for her or to her feelings for Lenny. The simple truth was that he liked girls who were willing to go a good deal further than his old friend, but every time he suggested that she might unbend a little Molly found it quite impossible to oblige him. He never seemed to mind; when they were together he was charming, funny and affectionate, but he never even hinted at any deeper feelings.

Sometimes Molly wondered why she bothered. It was true he had been her first boyfriend, that she had known him ever since she was eight years old, but that was a poor reason for tying oneself to a man for life, and Lenny had made it clear, without actually putting it into words, that she was not his type.

'On this Victory Day, if it ever comes, I shall demand that Lenny either tells me he wants me for his wife or that he does not intend to marry anyone,' she had told Alex one day, when they were both in the watch office, filling in forms so that they might, in the fullness of time, be demobilised, or demobbed as they called it. Alex had laughed.

'I don't see why you have to wait until Victory Day,' he had said. 'Why not simply give up any hope of Lenny and become your own woman once again?'

Alex and Molly had just finished a thoroughly boring shift during which nothing whatsoever had happened and were sitting in the NAAFI drinking coffee and – money was short – sharing a scone. They were talking, as was everyone else, about Mr Churchill's announcement that VE Day – Victory in Europe Day – would be celebrated on the eighth of May. This was great news, but not the news that members of the forces were waiting for; the date of demob day.

Alex fished a small bottle of saccharin tablets out of his pocket and dropped one into his coffee, then raised an eyebrow at Molly, who shook her head.

'I'm trying to give up sweetening tea and coffee,' she explained. 'Then, when rationing stops, I probably won't even like sweetened drinks.'

Alex pushed the bottle back into his pocket and sighed. 'I had hoped that Winnie would remember how eagerly the forces await demob, but I suppose that will be the next important announcement,' he said. 'Somehow, when they announced they'd done all the signing of the documents and so on, I had a sort of mental picture of every soldier, sailor and airman chucking our uniforms into a great big bin and fishing out the silly clothing we were wearing when we joined the forces.' He grinned at Molly across the table. 'Daft, wasn't it? I talked to the CO about it and he said rather apologetically that we would be among the last to go because someone's got to man the watch office and we've been specially trained.

The girls on radar are the same as us, so it'll be a while before we're free citizens once more. After all, it takes ages to become an RT op, and there are still a few aircraft using the runway and needing us to guide them in and out. Civilians couldn't do it with the best will in the world, so we shall be here for a bit yet.' He looked curiously at Molly. 'Mind if I ask a personal question?'

Molly laughed. 'Oh, Alex, surely you don't need to ask? You know everything about me, including, I hope, that I'm fool enough to be in love with a man who doesn't give a hoot for me! Go on, fire ahead, ask your question.'

Alex grinned. 'Most of the people I know will rush home to their families the moment they get their papers. No doubt you've a heap of friends who'll take you in, but that's not quite the same as family, is it? I was just wondering if you'd thought ahead, to a time when you're a civilian again. You see, I'm a fair bit older than you, so both my parents are dead – they were elderly, and both of them died before the war even started – so I shan't be going home. I've made my plans and will be having to share a cousin's bedroom until I find myself a job that pays enough to support me and to pay for a lodging somewhere. As you know, I was born and brought up in Norwich, which isn't exactly teeming with jobs for ex radio ops. In fact, it's an agricultural county, lots of farms and so on.

All along the coast is a big fishing industry – or there was before the war – and inland there are the Broads, wide stretches of water where they made the motor torpedo boats – did you know? So it's quite a diverse place. Before the war I worked in insurance, but that's the last thing I want to do now. And I suppose they won't be building MTBs now that the war's over; it'll probably be pleasure craft. If I could find someone to come in with me I'd love to build boats. There was a yard – Hunter's Yard – which built beautiful yachts. Of course, I've had six years away from anything to do with boatbuilding, but I took a keen interest in it at the time, and I can almost feel that interest coming to light again. If I can get someone to take me on . . .' He stopped speaking, staring at Molly as though he was waiting for her to speak. 'We're all going to be given a lump sum, you know, and there will be people coming round to answer questions. Maybe . . .'

Molly waited, but when he didn't finish the sentence she said, 'You asked me what I mean to do in the peace. Well, I don't want to be cooped up in a factory, or even in an office. I want to work out of doors. I've told you how I loved the countryside and how much I know about farming from the time I spent helping Cian's mum to run the farm in Ireland. I can milk a cow, harness a horse and plough a field; in fact I sometimes think I should have been a land girl. Some of them are being kept on, you know, to help get the farms straight again, because although we'll still need food, the way it's produced may be very different from what happens now. One of the girls from the met room was telling me farmers are going to be able to sell straight to customers and not via the Min of Ag, or whatever it's called. It's my belief that lovely things like orchards, raspberry canes and strawberry plants will be springing up all over the country, and farms will begin to flourish in a way which has not been possible whilst we were fighting the Nazis.'

'Good for you, girl,' Alex said appreciatively. 'And how does this fit in with Lenny, may I ask? As I recall it he never had a job in civvy street, but went straight from school into the RAF.'

Molly stared. It had simply never occurred to her to ask Lenny about his post war plans. She wondered whether to lie, to pretend that Lenny had shared his hopes with her, then decided against it. Alex was far too good a friend not to be told the truth, and anyway he'd probably guessed it. Bumble had worked in a large factory for a brief period, but did not mean to go back to that life. The last Molly heard, he was hoping to get taken on by a garage of some description where he could use the knowledge of engines he had built up whilst in the air force. Ellen and Hetty both intended marriage to become their careers, though Ellen did admit that she might work as a telephonist just whilst she and Pete 'got their act together', as she put it.

But Alex was looking at her, eyebrows slowly rising, so Molly burst into hasty speech. 'I don't know. We've never discussed it . . .'

Alex, seeing her confusion, came to her rescue as he had done so many times. 'Well, he might stay a pilot for several years; they're bound to want them to move people and products from one place to another. I take it he's not going to try farming or country work of any description himself?'

'I don't know,' Molly said miserably. 'I've never asked him.' Suddenly, a giggle escaped her. 'The only thing he really wants to do after the war is persuade me to bleach my hair. Perhaps he'd like to be a hairdresser . . .' She giggled again. 'You can never tell with Lenny; perhaps that's one of the things I like about him.'

Alex compressed his lips, then took a sip of coffee and pulled a face. 'I can't wait for rationing to end,' he said. 'Well, if I were you, my love, I'd make it my business to ask Lenny just what he does mean to do when he gets demobbed.'

'I'll do that; you are so sensible, Alex,' Molly said gratefully. 'I don't know where I'd be without you to advise me.' She chuckled. 'There you are, that's my plan for the peace: to settle somewhere near you, so I can pick up the phone and wail for help every time I get in a pickle.'

Alex laughed. 'Feel free, I'll always be there for you,' he said, and it wasn't until much later that Molly wondered exactly what he had meant by those few words.

VE Day dawned bright and beautiful, the golden sunlight pouring over the countryside as though it knew the importance of the eighth of May. Everyone was excited, and when the four girls set off for breakfast they were not the only ones who could not stop smiling.

'I wonder if there will be bacon, or even a real egg since it's such a special day,' Ellen said as they entered the cookhouse. She choked on a chuckle. 'It'd be awfully nice to start the day with a stomach lined with something more exciting than porridge and bread and jam.'

Maggie, a good four inches taller than Ellen, stood on tiptoe to peer ahead and then gave a squeak. 'Well I'm damned! You've hit the nail on the head. Only it isn't just bacon, it's a *real* breakfast: egg, fried bread, and something which looks a bit like baked beans. Yummy, yummy, yummy!'

There was a buzz of excited conversation as the queue moved slowly towards the serving point, and presently the four girls sat down at their table with their tin plates well filled with the 'real breakfast' which no one had foreseen.

'What a wonderful way to start the day,' Hetty remarked through a mouthful of fried bread. 'Gracious, I'm a poet *and* didn't know it!'

Molly, finishing up her own helping, thought she had never seen the cookhouse so full of happy faces. She knew it wasn't just the food, or the thought of a day off, but the fact that this meant that the war in Europe had definitely come to an end. Of course, fighting was still going on in the Far East and Japan, but surely now, with the might of the American forces arrayed against them, it was only a matter of time before the last theatre of war would be forced to surrender.

So it was with light hearts that they all got aboard the gharries, but Molly, waving her friends off, was the happiest of all, because by dint of bribery and corruption Lenny had managed to get hold of Bunny.

'I'm a city man myself,' he had admitted, helping her into the passenger seat. 'But today, my pretty one, is yours, and I know you prefer the countryside.'

'It's yours too,' Molly protested as Lenny climbed into the driver's seat. 'But on a day like this I should think even city dwellers must long for the country. The wild roses are out and I bet every time the car slows the perfume will be almost overwhelming. How I hope I can get a job in the country when we're demobbed.'

Lenny revved the engine and they drew slowly away, and once they were on the road he turned to Molly and pulled a face. 'There aren't any jobs in the country for women, unless you count land girls,' he said dismissively. 'What you want is a nice, well-paid factory job, then you and I can put our gratuities together and buy a little garage. Only in order to make a decent living it'll have to be a city garage. I was going to ask Bumble to join us but I gather he has new plans of his own. He wants a small café somewhere in the city where he and that little Wren he talks about can sell food, because apparently she's a very good cook.'

He slowed the car and drove off the road to a beauty spot where one could see for miles. He leaned across and pointed. 'Will you look at that view!'

They abandoned the car and strolled on the grassy headland, and for the first time that day – the first time for ages, now she came to think of it – Lenny took her hand. 'Shall we drive down to the coast?' he enquired. 'I know most of the beaches are mined but there's nothing to stop us looking at the sea. Or we can carry on inland; there's a little pub I know where we can get a good lunch . . .'

As they climbed back into the car Molly laughed. 'Not, I trust, the Waggon and Horses? Remember that day when we were too late for the lunch you'd reserved?'

Lenny joined in her laughter. 'Of course I remember. I messed up, didn't I? But now every-thing's changed. The war's over and you and I are planning the peace together.' He reached into the glove compartment and produced a map of the area. 'Name somewhere you'd like to see,' he com-manded, 'and your chariot shall take you there, queen.'

With Molly sitting comfortably on the soft red leather of the passenger seat, the old car took them to many places which Molly had heard of but never visited. Lenny was his charming self, and when her own suggestions proved impossible for some reason he was quick to choose other destinations which he was sure she would enjoy.

'It's your day,' he kept repeating, and yet all the time Molly was aware that something was missing, though she could not have said what. They had elevenses at a funny little café overlooking golden sands and blue sea, then drove back inland to a pub Lenny knew – he seemed to know a lot of pubs – and had an excellent lunch. After that they stopped in a well-wooded area and walked for a while, and still Molly's feeling that something was missing persisted, although Lenny bent over backwards to make this what he called her special day. Once or twice she reminded him that it was his special day as well, but he brushed this aside. But by the time darkness fell and they were heading for their airfields once more she had begun to suspect that the reason for her lovely day was a rather more selfish one than Lenny had admitted. He wanted the garage he had mentioned, wanted it badly, and Bumble had, in a way, let him down by taking it into his head to buy a café with his girlfriend once they were demobbed. So what had Lenny done? He had bethought him of another friend who might not yet have made her plans for the peace, and given her a wonderful day out purely in order to broach the subject of starting a garage with their gratuities. When eventually he stopped outside the Credington gates she waited for him to suggest a partnership, but he did not.

'I'll give you a ring to tell you when I'm next free,' he promised. 'I've got to dash.' And he drove off.

Chapter Fourteen

It was over. After the terrible atom bombs had exploded on Hiroshima and Nagasaki, the Japanese had surrendered, and everyone on the airfields which surrounded the city of Lincoln had got together to plan an enormous party, for they were to have a two-day holiday. VE Day, which had occurred some three months earlier, had been somewhat subdued for some members of the Royal Air Force, but everyone was determined that VJ Day, which heralded the absolute end of the war, would be different. Anyone who was not actually working had a hand in the planning of the event, which was masterminded by the crews at Scrimpton, who were on stand down. The staff of the watch room at Credington, however, were working their shifts as usual, so Lenny formed the habit of visiting the control centre to let Molly – and her colleagues, of course – know how the party preparations were progressing. Because the Prime Minister had not given them much notice, the dance of the century as Lenny called it would be held on the second day of the promised holiday, after most of the celebrations were over, but nevertheless it was an event to which everyone looked forward.

And now the girls were in the larger of the two bedrooms in their billet, getting ready for the party.

Molly was sitting in front of the small mirror which Ellen had acquired from her boyfriend's mother. Despite her determination not to reflect on the dream she had had the night before, she found she could not entirely dismiss it from her mind.

The previous evening, Ellen had informed Molly that she wanted to talk to her. They had been sitting in the kitchen, a large sack of pickling onions between them as well as a number of gleaming glass jars. They had decided to pickle onions and sell them at the market in Lincoln to get themselves a bit of extra money, for the gratuity the RAF paid them would in Ellen's case be swallowed up by her trousseau and in Molly's by the purchase of the garage. For Lenny had taken her to see both the garage and the adjoining cottage and Molly had approved them both.

Molly had looked enquiringly at Ellen. 'What is it?' she had asked suspiciously. 'I've told you as much as I know myself, which is that Lenny and I are going into partnership and judging from the way he smiled at me – oh, Ellen, it was his old smile, the one I remember from the children's home – he's going to pop the question. So what do you want to talk about?'

Ellen topped and tailed an onion, skinned it and popped it into the nearest jar, then dabbed at her streaming eyes. The onions were powerful, and both girls had already shed many tears as they worked.

'Molly, don't take offence, but have you really thought about marriage? About the bad points as well as the good? I know you've known Lenny for a great many years, but you've got your ideas about marriage from the cinema and magazines, not from experience . . .'

Molly had fished out a handkerchief and dabbed rather fruitlessly at her own streaming eyes. 'I don't understand you,' she said slowly. 'You know I was brought up in a children's home and have no experience of family life, if that's what you mean. But Ellen, you're going to marry Pete, and you were brought up in the home too . . . why are you shaking your head?'

'Because I wasn't – brought up in the home, I mean. Remember, I was ten when my father was killed and my mother had to put me in the orphanage. I've seen both the good side of marriage and the bad. My mam and dad loved each other, I'm sure they did, but there were times when they fought like cat and dog, times when money was short and it was a choice between buying food or a few sticks of wood for the fire. Sometimes my mam nursed a black eye, because my dad had lost his temper when he wanted some beer money and she wouldn't shell out. So you see I'm going into marriage with my eyes wide open. For me, the leap in the dark simply won't happen, because I know the good and the bad. But you, Molly, are still at the roses round the door stage. D'you know what I mean?'

Molly had rubbed her painful eyes, then nodded slowly. 'You think I'm looking at marriage through rose-coloured spectacles. Well, maybe I am, but if so, Lenny is as well. Does that make a difference?' She began to peel another onion.

Ellen had screwed up her face as she gave this new thought her attention. 'From what you've said Lenny isn't really thinking about the changes which marriage will make in his life,' she had said slowly. 'Like you, he entered the home when he was very young and probably has about as much idea of family life as you do yourself.' She sighed. 'Well, you can't say I haven't warned you. Marriage is not a bed of roses – for every rose there are half a dozen thorns – but I suppose whatever I say will make no difference. Remember, though, I've heard you complaining that you never know where you are with Lenny, that he blows hot and cold, dancing half the night away with you one day and going off with some little blonde the next, behaviour like that is no foundation for a business partnership, let alone a happy marriage.'

'Hah! That's where your lecture falls down,' Molly had said triumphantly. 'You know nothing about business partnerships – well, no more do I – but you should take that into account when you're discussing me and Lenny because we're going to be business partners as well as man and wife and that's bound to make a difference, isn't it? And anyhow, he hasn't asked me to marry him yet. Perhaps he never will, but if he does I'm going to take the chance. I may never get another.'

Ellen had snorted. 'If you mean you'll never get another proposal of marriage you must be even blinder than I thought,' she said. 'Oh, Molly, your trouble is you're so busy staring at Lenny that you can't see what's right in front of your nose. No, no, I shan't say any more. I shall just watch your descent into marriage with a man who's never even said he loves you, you poor sap.'

In bed that night, Molly thought long and hard about the conversation. Oddly enough, it had not occurred to her until Ellen had mentioned it that in all their years of friendship Lenny had never once said he loved her, and now that she came to think of it she had never said she loved him either. Or not to him at any rate. I've always taken it for granted that loving him would be enough, she thought, but now wretched Ellen has put a doubt in my mind. She sighed, and looked across the room to the small hump in the bed which was her friend. Whatever Ellen may have said, she and Pete would also be diving into the unknown, and Ellen seemed quite satisfied that it was the right thing to do, so why should Molly and Lenny be any different? She was sure that he loved her, even if he had not said the words, and she was sure that she loved him. That was all that mattered.

She turned over restlessly, thinking she would never go to sleep whilst the overpowering smell of onions haunted her, and immediately found herself dreaming. She was in a wood – no, it was the forest in which the Mathiases had found her – and there was the log cabin, and Cian, alive again, and smiling at her. He came towards her and took her hand, and even as she was exclaiming joyfully 'Oh, Cian, you're alive!' the fingers that held hers slackened and, looking up into his face, she saw him shake his head sadly.

'No, alanna, but I've come to rescue the babes in the wood. I don't want the old witch to reach you first, to be sure, so we'd best hide up in the gingerbread cottage until old Sinbad tells us the coast is clear.'

'It's not . . .' Molly bit off the words and stared. It *was* a gingerbread cottage. One that looked just like the log cabin in which she had spent so many months. Cian led her towards the door, pushed it open, and settled her in a chair by the stove.

'Sure and haven't I come to give you a warning?' he asked. 'That feller, the one who didn't come to your rescue, are you going to marry him?'

Molly looked across at him in the firelight's glow and thought he had never looked more beautiful. But looks are not everything, and neither was charm. She said as much and Cian laughed.

'Then why're you goin' to marry that Lenny feller?' he asked derisively. 'All you know about him is the outside. He could be the wicked old witch who's lured you into her den for all you know of him.'

Molly began to protest, to say that Lenny was not in the least like any witch, when the door creaked open and a bent figure appeared. It was wearing a tattered black cloak and it removed a pointed hat from its shaggy head as it entered the kitchen, revealing a large pointed nose and tiny mean little eyes.

'Hello, Molly. They told me I'd find you here,' the newcomer said.

Molly jumped to her feet just as the witch held out a gnarled hand. 'I need your gratuity to put down a deposit on that garage,' the unknown figure said, but the voice sounded familiar. The old woman snapped her fingers impatiently when Molly did not move towards her. 'Come along; it's not as if you didn't know where your money would be going. Hand it over!' The voice had become harsh and demanding, and there was menace in the look the witch gave Molly.

Molly gave a squeak of fright and turned to Cian, but he was fading, growing less real with every moment that passed.

'Cian, help me,' she whispered. 'Oh, Cian, don't go. Ellen was right; I need . . . I need . . .'

But she was waking up, looking desperately around the darkened bedroom while her heart thumped out its message of fear. What a nightmare! But that was all it was, just a silly dream. And it was all Ellen's fault for putting thoughts into her head.

Molly had sat up in her agitation and now she glanced at the alarm clock. Ten to three; she'd best try to get back to sleep again, since she and Ellen meant to take turns in the zinc bath tub in the morning and scrub themselves free the miasma of pickled onions. But suppose she re-entered the dream? Now that she was awake, she could remember very little about it, save that she had been one of the babes in the wood. Was there another? She could not recall, and anyway what did it matter? It was only a dream, after all. Molly lay down again and tried to put the nightmare out of her head. Presently, succeeding at last, she slept dreamlessly until morning.

*

Molly alighted from the old jalopy. All the others had gone off to the victory dance in the gharries, but when she had suggested going with them Lenny had immediately vetoed the idea.

'You're my girl,' he had said, with more possessiveness than he had ever used towards her before. 'I shall pick you up a bit earlier, because I shall have to help set up the bar and so on.' He had put a caressing hand around the nape of her neck and given her shoulder a proprietorial squeeze.

Molly had been delighted with the new arrangement and had extended Lenny's offer of a lift to Ellen and Pete, though this invitation had been refused.

'It'll be more fun with all of us squeezed into the gharry. Besides, we promised Maggie and Patrick that we'd go as a foursome. Maggie seems to have settled down at last, doesn't she? And he's really keen on her too – has she told you that he's taking her back to Ireland as soon as they can get away, to meet his family?' Ellen had beamed at her friend. 'Happy endings all round. I think they'll make a match of it, don't you?'

'Perhaps,' Molly said guardedly. 'He's a nice bloke, and Maggie certainly deserves some luck. But what about Sinbad? He's hardly left her side since Cian died, and anyone can tell they adore each other. She won't abandon him, surely?'

'That's another happy ending,' Ellen assured her. 'Gethyn's family have a farm, and they've already told Maggie that they'll be delighted to welcome Sinbad too.' She chuckled. 'So thanks for your invitation, but we'll go in the gharry. I expect we'll be very correct on our way to the dance, but on the way back I dare say we shall want to have a kiss and a cuddle, and there's definitely not enough room in Bunny for that!'

So now Molly watched Lenny park the car and followed him inside, where she was soon busy amongst the other helpers. Most of the people coming to the dance had brought food along, some of which had been provided by parents, anxious that their sons and daughters should have a night to remember. Molly, following in Lenny's wake, could only gasp with admiration at the piles of food set out on every available surface.

'If everyone eats their share of this lot they'll be too full to dance a step,' she observed. 'But I dare say they'll manage.'

Lenny smoothed the hair off his forehead, and something in the way he did it reminded her of the dream she had had. Startled, she looked very hard at his face. Just for a moment she saw a pointed nose and a rat trap of a mouth, but even as she stepped back Lenny smiled and the nightmare fled. What rubbish, to be frightened by a nightmare, she told herself, and then the band arrived and began tuning up their instruments. Lenny jerked a thumb towards the enormous dance floor and held out a hand to Molly.

'Someone's got to be first on the floor, and you know how they all hang back . . . Oh, look who's here. Evening, Alex. If you've come to ask Molly for the first waltz you're out of luck.' Smiling, he put a proprietorial arm round Molly's waist and led her on to the floor, and very soon other couples swirled into the dance, all clearly anticipating an evening of pleasure.

Molly said as much, her head near Lenny's. But halfway through the proceedings Lenny went and whispered something to the band leader, and the music stopped. This is it, Molly said to herself as Lenny led her towards the bandstand. This is the moment I've waited for since I was eleven years old.

'I have an announcement to make,' Lenny said to the room at large, and turned towards his partner. 'Molly, my old mate, there's only one question on my mind at the moment and only one person who can answer that question.' He swung her round to face the crowd on the dance floor. 'Molly Penelope Hardwick, RT Operator Supreme, will you make me the happiest man on earth and agree to be my wife?'

Molly opened her mouth to give him the answer he wanted, and suddenly knew she could not do it. She tilted her head a little, for he was taller than her, and said the words which she should have said long ago.

'Thanks very much, Lenny, but no, I won't marry you,' she said, and much to her surprise her voice did not even wobble. 'And now can we get on with the dance?'

She was looking into her partner's face as she spoke and to her very real pleasure saw relief in his eyes. And then, whilst the conversation began to buzz around them, Lenny spoke.

'And what about my garage?' he asked. 'If you won't marry me I suppose you won't let me use your gratuity to help me buy it. Why, you nasty little cheat.'

There was a commotion at the front of the dance floor as Alex covered the space between them in two strides, and before Molly could say a word his fist had crashed into Lenny's jaw. Lenny went down, and Molly, looking at Alex, saw a slow smile dawn on his face. Lenny was getting to his feet, swaying and swearing as he did so, and Alex grabbed his jacket and heaved him upright before giving him a push towards the nearest chair.

'That little blonde you've been going about with is waiting for you in the wings,' he said. 'So you can jolly well buzz off and stop making an exhibition of yourself.' He turned to Molly, and the smile lit up his whole face now. 'I know I'm not the man of your dreams, but I've loved you ever since that first day when you walked into the watch office. How about marrying me instead? I'm a steady sort of bloke, not good-looking, nor charming, but I love you, Molly Penelope Hardwick, and I think if you look under all the kerfuffle you may well discover that you love me too.' He took her hand and led her out of the dance hall and into the starry August night.

Molly squeezed his fingers. 'Oh, Alex, if only life were that simple! Ellen pointed out the other night that because I was brought up in a children's home I know nothing about love or marriage, and I'm rather afraid she's right. You are my best friend, no one could be a better one, and I am truly grateful that despite everything you still say you want to marry me. But I'm sure you understand that I can't possibly say yes. I've never thought of you as any-thing except a friend, you see. But we could start going out properly, like other people, and perhaps love will just happen, the way it did with Ellen and Pete. Only it will mean rather a lot of waiting, I'm afraid.'

Alex gave a subdued cheer and lifted her off her feet, and her heart swooped dizzily as their lips met. The kiss went on for rather longer than either of them had anticipated. And when he put her down, he cupped her face in his hands. 'Phew, that was something! You must have had an awful lot of practice.'

'Do you know, that was my very first kiss?' Molly said breathlessly. 'Oh, Alex, I think we're going to be all right.'

In Time for Christmas

Katie Flynn

Addy and Prue Fairweather live with Nell, their widowed mother, in a flat above her shop on the Scotland Road. The sisters, however, are very different. Addy is dark-haired, plain and always in trouble, whereas Prue is flaxen-haired, blue-eyed and as angelic as her looks imply. To make matters worse, Nell makes no secret of her preference for the younger girl, increasing Addy's jealousy and resentment.

On the other side of the coin, Giles Frobisher and his twin sister, Gillian, live in a crumbling mansion near the sea in Devon. The family have lost most of their money in the Depression, so Giles leaves university and joins the Fleet Air Arm. He meets the Fairweather girls briefly on a visit to Liverpool but they lose touch. When they meet again Addy and Prue are no longer children, and Giles realises he is falling in love . . .

arrow books

A Sixpenny Christmas

Katie Flynn

As the worst storm of the century sweeps through the mountains of Snowdonia and across the Mersey, two women, Molly and Ellen, give birth to girls in a Liverpool maternity hospital.

Molly and Rhys Roberts farm sheep in Snowdonia and Ellen is married to a docker, Sam O'Mara, but despite their different backgrounds the two young women become firm friends, though Molly has a secret she can share with no one.

But despite promises Ellen's husband continues to be violent, so she throws him out and years later, when Molly is taken to hospital after an accident, Ellen and her daughter Lana are free to help out. They approach this new life with enthusiasm, unaware that they are being watched, but on the very day of Molly's release from hospital there is another terrible thunderstorm and the hidden watcher makes his move at last . . .

arrow books

To find out more about Katie
and her books visit

www.katieflynn.com

Or you can join our mailing list by
sending in your name and contact
details (address and email) to

Saga books
Random House
20 Vauxhall Bridge Road
London
SW1V 2SA